Before I Forget

Leonard Pitts, Jr.

Before I Forget

Leonard Pitts, Jr.

A BOLDEN BOOK

AGATE

CHICAGO

Printed in the United States.

Library of Congress Cataloging-in-Publication Data

Pitts, Leonard.
  Before I forget / Leonard Pitts Jr.
    p. cm.
  Summary: "A man recently diagnosed with early-onset Alzheimer's disease takes a road trip to visit his ailing, estranged father, along with his troubled teen-aged son"--Provided by publisher.
  ISBN-13: 978-1-932841-43-5 (pbk.)
  ISBN-10: 1-932841-43-1 (pbk.)
  1. Alzheimer's disease--Patients--Fiction. 2. Fathers and sons--Fiction. 3. Psychological fiction. I. Title.

PS3616.I92B44 2009
813'.6--dc22
                                        2008049946

9 8 7 6 5 4 3 2 1

Bolden Books is an imprint of Agate Publishing. Agate books are available in bulk at discount prices. Single copies are available prepaid direct from the publisher.

Agatepublishing.com

For Boochie and Bear

one

He forgot. That was how it started.

He took a wrong turn somewhere—never did find out where—on a route he had driven three times a month for five years. Three times a month from his home in Bowie, up to Shucky's, a restaurant and bar in Fell's Point, a couple miles and a world away from the tourist traps of the Inner Harbor. Three times a month to sit in with the band, noodle some jazz standards, maybe sing some of the old hits if somebody in the crowd called out for them and he was in a good enough mood. (Somebody always called out and he was always in a good enough mood.) Three times a month.

Until that day, when he forgot. Until he took a wrong turn on a route he had driven a hundred times and found himself on a street of boarded-up row houses, night shadows slanting ominously, corner boys glancing menace as the big, black Escalade rolled slow and shiny down the street, looking for Shucky's. Looking for something he recognized. Finding only corner boys who straightened up now from crouched positions, adjusted pants whose crotches rode somewhere below their knees, making ready to come see who this buster was rolling up in here all slow and shit.

He pressed the accelerator. Got out of there.

It is hard to get lost in a Cadillac Escalade. Touch the screen recessed into the gleaming wood of the console and you bring up maps and a computer voice that tells you where to turn. Touch a button and a live human being spots you with a GPS tracker and helps you get wherever it is you're trying to go.

Later, he would wonder why he hadn't done either. Right now, all he felt was annoyance building itself steadily toward anger. Worse, it was unspecified anger, anger without function, focus, or release. It was just...*how could this happen? How could you lose a place you knew?* You felt so stupid. So helpless and frustrated.

He hammered the steering wheel with the flat of his palm. It made no sense.

Yet there it was. Somehow, he had taken a turn or missed an exit and now Baltimore, where he'd been hundreds of times, was an alien city rising above him, glaring down at him, pitiless, unfriendly, unknown. And the numbers on the digital clock kept ticking forward relentlessly. Twenty minutes to the first set. Twenty minutes. He had never missed a gig in his life. Not even in the old days, when he was using. Never. The steering wheel took another hit.

The lights from the gas station on the corner of the next block shone like a beacon. He pulled in gratefully. Heads turned at the sight of the Escalade. The man in the greasy overalls with the cigarette drooping off his lips, the woman in the banged up 14-year-old Toyota filled with children, took note of its passing and agitated as he was, he paused to check himself in the mirror, slip on the Dolce & Gabbana sunglasses, make sure he was looking his best. He knew it was vanity, but he excused that in himself. Vanity was a job hazard in his line of work. You always had to look your best. You never knew when you might be recognized.

He was not recognized. They knew he was somebody—you could see that in the way their eyes trailed after him. But nobody called his name or pointed his way and cried, "Aren't you…didn't you used to be…"

He was mildly disappointed. Then he reminded himself they were probably too young. The '70s were something they had only heard about on the History Channel. He waited his turn behind a wizened old woman buying lottery tickets and a teenage girl chattering on her cell phone, bought a pack of Kools just to be polite, then told the cashier he was lost. "I'm trying to get to…"

The hesitation probably lasted half a second. It felt longer. It felt long. As if some black fog had just rolled in and covered a word spelled out in 200-watt bulbs. He knew the word was there, he could see the glow of it behind the fog, feel the heat from the bulbs. But he couldn't make it out, couldn't say it, couldn't say…

"Shucky's." The word jumped out of him all at once. Made him sound like he had a speech impediment. "I'm trying to get to Shucky's," he repeated.

The cashier, a tall, Indian man, gave him a strange look, then told him in heavily accented English how to get where he was going. Shucky's was 15 minutes away. How in the hell had he managed to get 15 minutes out of the way? The digital clock said it was 13 minutes before the gig. His wheels made noise as he took off.

When he got to Shucky's it was a few minutes after the hour. He could hear his old pianist, Mario Gaines, playing with his quartet as he came through the door. He could not remember ever being more embarrassed.

Mario gave him a look, nodded. There was something sad in the look. Like somebody had died. Mo was smiling, about to make his way up to the bandstand, his mind already working up a one-liner to cover his late arrival, when a hand hooked his elbow. It was the manager, spindly little old white woman named Sophie. He had always liked Sophie. She smoked like a tailpipe and had a croaking voice you could hear all the way out to the alley in the back.

She led him back to her office, a cluttered room the size of a walk-in closet. She motioned to a chair and he sat. "What happened to you?" she said, sitting on the edge of her desk.

He couldn't think of a lie quickly enough, so he told her the truth. Told her he had missed a turn and gotten lost. The big voice turned softer than he'd ever heard. "You've been forgetting a lot of things lately, Mo," she said.

That pissed him off for some reason and he asked what the hell she was talking about.

Her voice was still gentle, so damn gentle, he felt like slapping her. She told him people had been talking. They said he sometimes asked the same question two and three times. They said sometimes he had trouble following a conversation and couldn't remember simple things. They said he was moody.

He told her she was full of shit, so she took his hand, grabbed it the way you would a recalcitrant child, and led him around the restaurant. He had to stand there and listen to them all, the busboys, the cashier, the waiter, their voices soft like hers as they told him she wasn't exaggerating. As they told him he had a problem.

He said they were *all* full of shit. And that's when the gentleness finally went out of Sophie's voice.

"Moses," she said, "you've got to go get yourself tested."

He told her there was no need. She said he should consider himself fired until he did. He told her they could all fuck themselves. He said it loudly and customers looked up. Everyone except Mario, who kept his head down, concentrating on "That's Life."

Mo made sure to slam the door as he left. Fuck them. Fuck them all.

But he began to miss them even as he drove away. He didn't need the money. But he would miss the music. And the companionship. He had always told himself and behaved as if he was doing the place a favor, doing his old piano player a favor, by showing up a few times a month, lending his star power to a waterfront dive. But he knew better and, probably, they did too. They were doing him a favor as well, allowing him one last tenuous link to music, to performance. Hell, to life itself.

He got home without getting lost. Ate leftover takeout and watched a *Law & Order* rerun. Promised himself he wouldn't give it another thought.

It took him three days to make the appointment, three days in which the fear of not knowing wrestled with the fear of knowing. He told himself he was just going so he could get a clean bill of health from the doctor and wave it in Sophie's face and tell her again to fuck herself.

He did not get a clean bill. The doctor sent him to a specialist. The specialist sent him to another specialist. They interviewed him. They did tests.

"I'm going to give you five items I want you to remember and in a few moments, I'm going to ask you to repeat them to me," the second specialist said. "Are you ready?"

And Mo nodded.

"Hammer, nails, pliers, screwdriver, wrench," the specialist said. And then he asked Mo how he thought the Nats might do next year and if the Wizards had a prayer of making the playoffs. After a moment he said, "Can you repeat that list of items?"

Mo said, "Hammer, nails…" Then the black fog rolled in. He stammered, went silent.

The diagnosis was Alzheimer's disease.

Early onset Alzheimer's. That's what the specialist called it when Mo insisted he was too young for a disease only old people got. The doctor explained that, while the more common form of the disease strikes seniors at random, the early onset kind is genetic, passed down generation to generation like some ugly brooch.

"Did one of your parents have it?" the doctor asked. A vast expanse of desk separated him from Mo. "Maybe a grandparent or an uncle or something?" And Mo, who had not spoken to another member of his family except his son and grandson for 30 years, could only shrug and admit that he didn't know.

He was numb with the effort of trying to take it in. Reality had become too real, its colors too bright, its sounds too sharp, its spiked edges and unforgiving curves too clear. Life had turned itself sideways and Mo was scrabbling against a wall that just a second ago had been a floor, looking for a handhold where there was none.

Numb. He felt everything. He couldn't feel anything.

It struck him that this was all too terribly unfair. After all, he had only done this to get Sophie off his back. But he hadn't expected…hadn't thought…. In his darkest imaginings, he had never anticipated anything so damn…unfair. Something inside him, some vicious damn…*thing* he couldn't even see, was wiping his mind like a blackboard. One day, the black fog would roll in and it would stay. He would wake up and he wouldn't know his own songs, wouldn't know his own son, wouldn't know his own self. That wasn't right. He was Moses Johnson. He was The Prophet. He deserved better.

Across that expanse of desk, the doctor was waiting him out.

"How long?" Mo managed to ask.

"It's impossible to say," said the doctor. "Everyone experiences the disease differently."

"But I shouldn't start reading any long books," said Mo.

A tolerant smile. *Take your time*, the smile said. *Make all the weak jokes you need. I can wait.*

Mo was seized with sudden rage, a need to smash what he saw in that smile. He snarled. "Goddamn it! Don't sit there fucking grinning at me like a moron. Talk to me. Tell me what to do."

Crying. Suddenly, his face was awash in tears.

He choked out the words. "You just told me I'm going to lose everything I am, everything I ever did or saw. This thing is going to wipe me away like I was never here. There's got to be something else you can tell me, some way you can help me *deal* with this shit."

The smile on the other side of the desk turned thoughtful. Then the doctor said, "It won't be like you were never here, Mr. Johnson. Your family and friends will remember you. Hell, you sold 30 million records. Thirty million people will remember. Thirty million and then some."

Mo almost laughed. He had forgotten the doctor was a Fan.

Then it hit him, like a truck that comes barreling through the intersection.

"You said this thing is genetic. I have a son and a grandson…"

The doctor got there before him. "They'll both be at increased risk, yes. You should advise them to go for frequent screenings after the age of 30."

It never ceased to amaze Mo. You think you've reached the bottom. Then you find out the bottom has a basement.

He had never given his son much of anything. A name, yes, some living expenses, yes. But the things that mattered—first day of school, catch in the backyard, basketball in the driveway, Dad, can I borrow the car, just the simple weight of his very presence—these things he had never given.

Yet he had left his son this time bomb ticking in his genetic code. The knowledge that one day he, too, might know how it felt to have his life erased. To walk on sand and leave no footprint.

Mo brought his hands to his face and wept inconsolably. He was 49 years old.

two

Five days after Mo learned that he was dying, his son robbed a gas station convenience store at gunpoint.

His name was James Moses Johnson III. His family called him Trey. His boys called him Profit. He was 19 years old, lean, with skin the color of unfinished maple. Trey wore his hair in short dreadlocks and he was handsome, like Mo—high cheekbones, intense green eyes, a noble nose. His father thought he looked like something sculpted.

Trey came through the door that night behind his boys, DC (so called because he was from the District of Columbia) and Fury (so called because he was crazy). He was sweating and itching underneath the black knit ski mask Fury had insisted he wear. He was also trembling violently. His bladder felt full and urgent.

This was Trey's first time. Tonight he would pop his cherry. That was how DC and Fury always put it, laughing when they said it. Like it wasn't nothing more than getting laid for the first time. Pop his cherry. Put like that, it sounded like a rite of passage, something you had to go through to be a man. Something that might even be fun.

It didn't feel fun. Trey thought he might throw up.

DC was yelling at the guy behind the counter, a tall, thin Indian. "Keep them hands where I can see 'em, nigger!" He had a pistol trained on the Indian's brow. DC was big, a pile of flesh so mammoth his arms at rest wouldn't go down. Fury was the opposite, a wiry little man maybe 5'7" and 140 pounds if he was that. But it was all pure meanness.

A woman was bent over a small child, sheltering the girl in the hollow of her own body. For no reason Trey could see, Fury backhanded her with a gun. She fell, crying out, blood leaping from a gash under her eye. The little girl screamed.

Trey couldn't stop looking at her. She was just a little kid.

"The fuck you waitin' for, nigger?"

Fury's voice, suddenly rasping angrily in his ear. Trey realized he was just standing there.

"All right, all right," he said. "It's on, it's on." Nonsense words, but they felt right. He vaulted the counter like they'd practiced. The Indian man retreated a few steps. His dark eyes were baleful. His hands were up.

Trey punched a button on the cash register. It didn't respond. He tried it again. Nothing.

"The fuck's taking so long?" demanded Fury. His voice rose on the last words. There was an edge of crazy panic.

"It won't open!" cried Trey, not far from panic himself.

Fury swung his pistol from the mother and the little girl, trained it on the Indian man. "Open it," he said.

The Indian man didn't move. The defiant eyes were steady.

Fury worked the slide on the pistol. "Nigger, you don't do what I told you, I'ma shoot you in your fuckin' throat."

Trey said, "Ain't no need for that. He'll open it. Right?" A look at the Indian man. Hoping he'd see that Trey was trying to save his life. He didn't know how crazy Fury could be. The Indian man's eyes flickered. He was about to give in.

Then DC yelled, "Y'all niggers better hurry up! We ain't got all night!"

Fury shot the Indian man.

The explosion reverberated. Trey jumped. Tiny droplets of blood splashed the ski mask on his face. He looked and there was a ragged red hole in the Indian man's white polo shirt in the upper quadrant of his chest. The Indian man looked shocked. There was finally fear in his eyes. The woman moaned.

Fury shifted the gun. "Next one goes through your neck," he said.

The man stabbed a finger down on the register and the drawer popped open.

"What you waitin' for, nigger?" Trey realized he was just standing there again. He couldn't help it. It was going so fast. He had to piss so bad.

He scooped the money out of the drawer, stuffed it into the pockets of the windbreaker, and vaulted the counter.

"I got it," he said. "Let's go."

But Fury still had the gun trained on the Indian man. "Ought to shoot your ass anyway," he said. "Makin' me wait." His eyes were livid. His lip curled in something that could have been a snarl, could have been a smile.

Trey said, "Ain't no need for that. We got what we came for. Let's ride."

Fury turned those awful eyes on him. Trey had to force himself not to look away. It wasn't easy. You didn't like being seen by those eyes.

Then, they softened almost imperceptibly. Fury said, "You right. Let's ride. Let's get the fuck out of here."

DC was through the door first. Trey went after him. He turned as he went through. Saw the little girl down there on the floor with her wounded mother, just shrieking her head off. Then Trey saw her eyes and that stopped him. He had expected pain. He saw outrage. He had expected fear. He saw hate. The child, five years old maybe, screeched pure fury at them. At *him*. Trey was shaken. Some distracted part of him wondered why the girl's mother had her out so late in the first place. Child that young, she should have been home in bed.

Then, DC was pulling his arm. "Come on, nigger. We got to move."

Dazedly, Trey nodded and turned to follow. He took a step. Two. The door was closing behind him. Then he heard the pop.

It drew him around again, hard. There, through the window covered with signs for Newport cigarettes and Miller Lite beer, he saw Fury with his gun still up, and the Indian man clutching his throat. His mouth was working. Blood spilled over his hands like floodwaters over a levee. Then the man fell. It was like some faraway nightmare without sound.

"He shot him." Trey heard himself say this, and it was awful, because it made it real.

"Always was crazy," said DC. There was a note of admiration in his voice.

Fury came through the door. "Nigger shouldn't of made me wait," he said, brushing past them both.

He got into the car. Trey felt frozen. He stared. The car started. DC yelled, "You comin' nigger?"

For the shadow of a moment, he didn't know if he was. Didn't know if he could move, if he would ever move again.

The Indian man, blood rushing out of his torn throat. The little girl, damning him with her furious eyes. Didn't know if he would ever move again.

Then he was jumping into the back seat. DC threw it in reverse and they backed out in a cloud of blue smoke and a screech of tires.

"Slow it down, muh'fucka," said Fury. "You tryin' to get us caught?" He yanked DC's ski mask off impatiently, then snatched at his own. Trey took the hint.

As the car slowed, Fury glanced back at him, flashed a smile, his gold tooth winking in the dark. "You ain't no virgin no more, is you, dog?"

He was waiting for a nod, for a laugh. Trey could barely manage to mumble, "Yeah."

Fury's smile went away. After a beat he said, "You got that money?"

Money. For a moment, the word didn't register. Then Trey remembered. He fished the wadded-up bills out of his pocket and handed them across the seat. Fury's smile came back. "Yeah, that's what I'm talkin' 'bout."

Fury spent a few minutes happily sorting and counting. "Nigger ain't even had that much in the till," he announced.

DC glanced over. "How much?"

"Four hunnert an' change."

"That's all?"

"Yeah. It's all good, though. That's four hunnert closer to the goal." He turned to Trey. "Ain't that right, nigger?"

Blood gushing over the Indian man's hands. Probably lying there behind that counter right this moment. Probably drowning on his own fluids. Probably dying slow. Maybe dead already. "Yeah," said Trey.

DC said, "One or two more of these, we be able to cut that CD, man. Bout to get paid up in this bitch." They had a group. Street Gang, it was called.

Little girl screaming hate at him. Right at him.

Trey heard himself say, "You shot that guy."

"Nigger, you still on about that? That nigger had it comin'."

"You ain't had to do it, all I'm saying."

"Yeah?" Fury looked around at Trey. "What if I wanted to do it? What about that?"

Trey couldn't answer. He didn't dare. Satisfied, Fury turned back. "It's a hard world out there," he said to no one in particular.

They didn't speak again for ten minutes. Ten long minutes, traffic lights reflecting in the hood of the car, Fury leaning back in the passenger seat, eyes closed, DC tapping out a beat on the steering wheel. Trey feeling as if he might throw up. He touched his forehead to the window, watched Baltimore passing by. Warm night for February. People out walking wearing little more than windbreakers.

He took the pistol out of his belt. Dropped it on the seat like an alien thing.

It did not feel real to him. None of it. Busting in that market. That little girl crying. That Indian guy going down. It wasn't supposed to be like this. He wondered if that would make any sense, make any difference, to a jury when he tried to explain it. This wasn't how it was supposed to go. They were supposed to go in, get the cash, get out. No muss, no fuss. Nobody was supposed to get hurt. No little girl was supposed to wind up screeching over her stunned and bleeding mother. No Indian man was supposed to clutch at his throat with red, shining hands. It was supposed to be easy. And it would have been, except...

Trey's eyes flicked to the seat directly in front of his, to the tip of Fury's head that was visible over the headrest, lolling back, not a care in the world.

...except this fool just wanted to shoot somebody.

Fury and DC had talked him into it. Wasn't nothing to it, they said. Couple jobs, they said, and they would have more than enough to pay for studio time, manufacture the CDs. After that, Street Gang would make its own money.

And he had listened to them. It had made sense at the time. They were older. They had done this shit before. Fury had even done time at Jessup. And Trey? Trey was a nothing. Trey was a wannabe. Only reason they even hung out with him was because he had a famous father.

How many times had he used his father's name over the years? It had gotten him into clubs. It had gotten him into cliques. It had gotten him into panties. Now, it had gotten him into this.

Trey felt like he was drowning in his own life.

What had they told him? "If you gon' rap about the life, you got to live the life." Fury, smiling in the darkness as they sat on his couch playing Madden and passing the herb around. "Can't be no fake about the shit, homie. Got to be the real deal." Trey had nodded.

And now look.

Now look.

Now, *look*.

Something rose in his gullet. "Let me out here," he said.

He saw a look pass between Fury and DC. DC said, "What?"

"Ain't you heard? I said, pull over. Let me out."

"I thought we was goin' to my place," said Fury. "Why you in such a hurry to get out?"

"They gon' be lookin' for three muh'fuckas in a car," said Trey. "We need to separate. Y'all need to get rid of the car while you at it."

Again, he saw the look pass between Fury and DC and then, almost imperceptibly, DC shrugged as if to say maybe Trey had a point. They pulled over. Trey reached for the door handle. Fury spoke softly, almost nonchalantly, his head still leaning back against the headrest.

"Hey, homie."

"Yeah?"

"You ain't turnin' pussy on us, is you?"

"No."

"Cause you know what happen to pussies, don't you?"

"Yeah."

"They get fucked."

Trey waited. Fury didn't say anything. He got out of the car, grateful for the touch of a cool breeze on his clammy skin. Fury lowered his window. "Later, homie," he said. The car rolled away. The moment it was out of sight, Trey went down on one knee. He puked in the gutter. When he was able to stand again, he looked around, trying to get his bearings. He stood on a deserted sidewalk in front of a used car lot. Home was east. He started walking. He hoped the breeze would clear his head. It didn't.

Down block after block, it didn't. Instead, his thoughts circled like gulls over a trash barge. It wasn't supposed to go that way. They were supposed to be at Fury's crib right now, laughing, getting high, ready to call the studio and tell them to the book the time.

The Indian man grabbing his bloody throat, like trying to wring his own neck. The little girl with hate in her eyes.

He didn't know what he would do.

Home was a powder-blue row house he shared with his mother. He hoped she wasn't up waiting for him, hoped she wouldn't hear him tipping in. He didn't need it now, the questions, the concerned looks, the lectures. He didn't need her calling his father. He just needed…

He paused. Took a deep breath, standing there in the darkness by his mother's steps.

To think. That's what he needed. He needed to think, figure out what to do. It would all look different in the morning. Trey fished his key out of his pocket.

And that's when the spotlight stabbed his eyes, made him blind. He heard cars screeching to a stop from three directions. Nowhere to run if he tried. Trey had his hands raised before they told him to, before they jumped out with weapons drawn, sheltering themselves with their car doors.

Heart thumping. Breathing shallow. This couldn't be happening. This wasn't happening. It wasn't his fault. He hadn't made the little girl cry. He hadn't shot the Indian man. Please, God. Make them understand.

Hard voices were yelling at him. Rough hands pushed him around, made him face the wall. Hands against the wall. Feet back.

"You got anything in your pocket I'ma get stuck by?"

Beefy white cop, salt and pepper hair, snapping on latex gloves, breathing in his face.

Trey shook his head. "No. No."

They searched him. Hands pushing him, prodding him. Invading him. They pulled out coins. A condom. A door key. Somebody said, "He's clean."

They wheeled him back around, pushed him up against the wall. Lights in his eyes. People starting to gather. A crowd looking on. All he saw of them was shadows. Was his mother one of them? He didn't dare to look. He didn't want to know. Cops brought his hands down behind him. He heard the cuffs snap. The metal was unforgiving against the bones of his wrists.

They told him he was under arrest. They read him his rights. It felt like television.

One of the shadows came forward. It resolved itself into a black man, dapper in a suit and tie, black fedora pushed back off his forehead. He smiled at Trey. He was holding something up. At first, Trey couldn't tell what it was. Too much light in his eyes. The black detective said, still smiling, "You dropped something."

Then Trey recognized it. It was his wallet.

three

"You dropped your wallet, asshole."

It lay on the table in front of him. Thrown there contemptuously by the dapper cop, Det. Bradley, who, Trey was distantly pleased to see, didn't look so dapper anymore as he loomed over Trey and renewed the questioning. Tie loosened, hat gone, sleeves rolled high. Bradley's partner was a Det. Stump, an older guy, also black, with the portly, self-satisfied manner of a church deacon. He sat regarding Trey with a bored smirk, one index finger laid aside his temple, occasionally seconding Bradley like a one-man amen corner.

"Asshole," he said.

Trey had no idea how long they had been at it, sitting across from one another in a small, mustard-colored room. Mirrored glass on two walls. Smell of body sweat and old cigarettes deep in the walls. Trey's father smoked. He hated the smell of cigarettes.

He had called his father hours ago. Left a message on his voicemail. "Dad, it's me. They got me under arrest down here behind some bullshit. Central booking. You got to get me a lawyer, man. You got to get me out of here. I ain't do nothing."

He had about convinced himself that was true. He hadn't done anything. He had just been there. Had he even had a gun? Had he even gone inside? Hadn't it all been out of his control? Fury, that's who they needed to have up in here. A couple times, he had almost said that, had felt Fury's name sitting there, oily and hated, on the edge of his tongue. But he had bitten it back each time.

Keep your cool. Bide your time. Don't say nothing. Don't give 'em a damn thing.

Advice his father had given him years before. They were in Dad's media room—that's what he called the room where the big screen was—watching some cop show on television. *Law & Order, Homicide*, something like that. And the cops had tricked some fool who

21

just couldn't stop talking. Told him they had evidence they didn't have and he better come clean now and try to cut a deal. He just started bawling and giving 'em names and dates and everything they needed to send his ass away.

Dad had paused the show and turned to Trey. "You see that?" he said. "You see what they did there? They ever get you hemmed up in one of them rooms, you bet not say a goddamn thing to 'em." He was not using what he called his "Fan voice," the fruity, fake-sounding one that made it sound like he grew up in England or someplace fancy like that and never even heard of South Central L.A., where he was born and raised. This was his real voice, the one he reserved for when they were alone.

"Name, rank, and serial number," he said. "That's it. 'Cause the moment they get you talking, it's over. They holdin' all the cards, you ain't holdin' nothing but your dick. They twist your words, have you locked up behind some bullshit you ain't even done. They do that to black men all day long, Trey, and I won't have that happen to a child of mine. You ever find yourself in trouble, you shut your damn mouth and call me. I'll get you a lawyer. Let him do your talkin' for you."

It was the only advice Trey could ever remember getting from his father.

He stuck to it now, even though he wanted to plead with them, shout to them, tell him he hadn't shot no Indian man in the throat. He wasn't like that. He wouldn't do that. Trey pressed his lips together to keep the words inside. They saw.

Det. Bradley sat down catercorner from him. Tough Cop was gone now. Father Cop had replaced him. There was a concern in Bradley's eyes that was almost tender. Trey noted this with alarm, shifted warily in his seat, facing away from Bradley. He was uncomfortably aware of how much he needed some tenderness just now, needed someone to understand that he hadn't done anything.

"Look, Johnson," the detective said, "I don't think you're a bad kid. You've never been in trouble in your life, have you? You got no record. And right now, you're scared shitless. Well, you should be. You're about to spend 15 years in prison taking it up the ass till you like it. Then one day they'll come and get you. The priest will walk next to you reading the 23rd Psalm."

"'Yea, though I walk through the valley of the shadow of death,'" intoned Stump.

"They're going to strap you to a gurney," said Bradley, "and make your mother watch as they pump chemicals into your veins. You're going to die, boy. And the bad thing is, you're going to die for something you didn't do."

"Didn't even do it," said Stump.

Trey couldn't help himself. He turned, grateful and surprised, to Bradley. The cop smiled. "Oh yeah, you think I don't know that? You don't have the heart for something like this. Witnesses said there were three men. I'm thinking you were the one who went over the counter. Probably that's how you lost the wallet. But you're not the one who killed that guy. But see, here's the thing: you know who did it. And if you don't give him up, well, we have no choice but to put the whole thing on you." A glance at his partner. "Am I telling the truth, Det. Stump?"

"Pure gospel, Det. Bradley."

Bradley said, "Think about it, kid. Do you really want to go to jail, maybe end up executed, to save these guys? You think they'd do it for you? You think they wouldn't give you up in a heartbeat? But no, you don't want to punk out. You don't want to snitch on your boys. Well, think about this, Johnson: what happens to you when we catch them and they put it all on you? When they say, well, it was Johnson who did it all—Johnson shot that man after he gave up all the money."

Trey glared at the detective. He hadn't thought about that.

Bradley saw he'd hit a nerve. "Oh yeah," he said, "you think that won't happen?"

"Happen sure as we sittin' here," said Stump.

"And when they do, what can we do about it? It'll be your word against theirs. One against two. How we prove they're not telling the truth? But see, if you get out in front of this thing now, if you prove your good intentions by turning these other two in *now*, it makes you look good before the judge. You can help yourself, Johnson. I can talk to the DA, we can cut you a deal."

"A deal?" The words escaped before Trey could bite them back. Bradley smiled. "Am I lying, Det. Stump?"

"Still speaking gospel, Det. Bradley."

"You see, I know you didn't intend it to come out this way, Johnson. You figured you and these other two were just going to be in and out of there in a minute or two. You would scoop out the register and nobody would get hurt and it would all be cake and peaches. But what you didn't figure on was that one of your homies was a little nuts and he would snap shots just for the hell of it.

"But that's what happened, Johnson, and now somebody's got to pay for it because this guy"—four crime scene photos landed one by one, bam, bam, bam, bam on the table in front of him—"sure didn't deserve what happened to him. Take a good look, Johnson. His name was Nasrallah Patel. He was 42 years old. Had a wife and two young daughters. Came over here 10 years ago, bought that little convenience store and worked 14 hours a day, trying to make a better life for them. And look what happens to him. Look at the pictures, Johnson."

Despite himself, Trey looked. The pictures were pornographic in their detail, in the unsparing way they chronicled the end of a life. Patel lay on the dirty tile, his head propped against the cigarette case. The hole in his neck was ragged. The blood pooled beneath his head was so red it was almost black. His eyes were open. They looked surprised.

Hands clutching at his neck. Blood flowing obscenely over them.

Bradley was so close that his voice stirred the fine hairs in Trey's ear. "You can play that hard role all you want," he said softly, "but you don't fool me. I've seen the real hard cases, the ones who kill like breathing and never feel a goddamn thing. And I know you're not one of them. You can try to hide it all you want, Johnson, but you look at this man, you feel something. You know it and I know it, too. You know he didn't deserve what happened to him. You know it needs to be made right."

"You damn sure know it," said Det. Stump.

Trey tried to swallow the golf ball in his throat.

"See, the law says it doesn't matter who pulled the trigger. Any-body who participated in the crime is liable for the outcome. But the law also recognizes that there can be extenuating circumstances. That somebody can be basically a good person who just got caught up in something way over his head. And if that somebody wants to do the right thing, wants to help us put the really bad guys away, why, that person can cut a nice deal for himself. He can go on and have himself a life while those other shitheads are filing their appeals and trying to keep from being strapped down to that gurney. But this good person, he has to strike while the iron is hot, he has to get out in front of this thing before the cops bring in the other guys on their own. Because then it's all done. Then he suffers like they do."

Trey licked his lips. Stared straight ahead. Tried to think what he should do. But his head was stone. Thought would not pass through it. Bradley stood up, gave him a disappointed look, spoke softly. "Can't you see I'm trying to help you here, Johnson? Why would you want to stand up for an asshole who could do this to a man for no reason at all? You better get it through your head, boy: right now, I'm the only friend you've got."

A moment passed. Trey sighed. Looked over at Bradley. He said, "Maybe when my lawyer gets here, we can..."

There was a flash of lightning in the same instant something smashed the back of his head, a violent blow that drove him forward. Trey grabbed his head, came up off the seat, twisting behind him. "Ow, man! What the fuck?"

A meaty hand came down on his shoulder, forcing him back into his seat. "Your lawyer?" growled Stump, suddenly up, suddenly furi-ous. "You want to wait for your fucking lawyer? Ain't you heard the man, you dumb little shit? He trying to help you, he trying to look out for you. And you think you can dick us around talking about wait for some goddamn lawyer?"

"Stumpy, that's okay," said Det. Bradley mildly.

"Hell if it is," said Stump, one meaty fist poised. "You give me five minutes, I'll teach this punk some manners. You think this is a game, you fuckin' little faggot?" A finger thick as a kielbasa stabbed down toward the photos on the table. "That man is dead. This ain't no game. And either you or your asshole buddies are going to pay for it. Me, I don't much care which of you gets the needle. My friend here can waste his time trying to talk sense to you, but I don't give a fuck."

"Det. Stump," said Bradley, his voice sharper.

Stump stopped, stared across the table at his partner. There was a moment. Then he said, "I need some air." The door closed hard behind him.

"I'm sorry about that," said Bradley. "His temper gets the best of him sometimes. Plus, this case, I think he's taking a little more personal than usual. It gets to you, you know, you see a man, a good man, gunned down for basically nothing. Are you okay?"

Trey touched the back of his head. Winced from the pain. "I want to report that asshole," he said. "He ain't got no business puttin' hands on me."

"You have the right to do that," said Bradley. "But how about we take care of this first?"

"Take care of what, man? I told you I ain't done nothin'!"

"Come on, Johnson. We both know that's not true."

Trey stared. He didn't know what to believe. Maybe Bradley was telling the truth—about trying to help him, about Stump. He just didn't know. The door swung open. One man holding for another. Both black, both dressed in conservative dark suits.

Det. Bradley straightened up. "Lieutenant," he said, addressing the first man, "this what I think it is?"

The lieutenant nodded. "This here is Axel Cordero, attorney for Mr. Johnson."

Trey felt himself breathe. It seemed like the first time in hours. Dad. He had come through.

Cordero, a trim man with salt and pepper hair and a neat moustache, stepped to Trey's side. Trey said, "That other muh'fucka hit me. Right here in the back of my head."

The attorney ignored him, didn't so much as acknowledge his existence. "This interview is over," he said, addressing the two cops. "I'd be grateful if you provided a place in which I could consult with my client."

"Yeah, well, you know, we live to make you grateful," said Bradley. The look he gave Trey then was, Trey thought, strangely accusatory. "Get up, Johnson," he said. Trey stood. Bradley handcuffed him.

A moment later, they led him out of the mustard-colored room and into the squad room. Cordero put a hand on his shoulder, leaned in close. "Do not say a word," he said.

"Don't worry," said Trey. And then he stopped so short Bradley bumped him from behind.

Fury was there. DC, too. Both of them handcuffed to chairs, both of them with dirt in their hair, mud on their T-shirts. The big man had his head down. He was sweating a river, laboring so hard to breathe Trey wouldn't have been surprised to see him keel over dead. Fury's head was down, too, but at the sound of Trey's approach, he lifted his eyes. They widened a little at the sight of Trey. Then they went baleful and cold.

Why you lookin' at me like that? I didn't say nothin'. I didn't give you up! I didn't give 'em a damn thing! Everything Trey wanted to say, the words, the protest of his blamelessness, leapt eagerly to his tongue. Even though he knew he shouldn't. Even though he knew he shouldn't so much as acknowledge Fury's presence.

But he wanted to, so badly. Might have, but for a rough hand yanking on his arm. Then Bradley was in his ear and his tone carried a triumphant smirk. "Oh yeah," he said, "I forgot to tell you: We picked up some friends of yours."

four

The rain fell heavily, fat drops punching the roof with a steadiness he had long since ceased to hear. Mo drank coffee, smoked cigarettes, and worked on his suicide note by the dome light.

The only sound in the black leather cab of the Escalade was his pen on the pages of the legal pad, scratching out words of explanation to whom it may concern. He had been working on it for several days.

Mo had a sense that he was going about this all wrong, that a suicide note was supposed to be an impulsive truth dashed off in the heated moments just before you killed yourself. But there would be a lot of interest when he was found. The Fans—he always thought of them in capital letters—would want to know why. Mo wanted to leave them more than a few words scribbled in haste. He felt he owed them that much.

That was ego, he knew, but what the hell? Ego was all he had left.

He was parked on a side street across from the Baltimore detention center. It was ugly enough to make your eyes ache, a colorless jumble of turrets ringed by a high wall of uneven stones and topped with concertina wire. In the middle of the wall was a door through which, the policewoman at the desk had told him two hours ago, detainees passed four to six hours after bail had been posted.

"It takes time to process them," she said.

She had advised him to go home and wait. Trey could call for a ride when he was released. The thought was tempting; it was almost two on a Sunday morning and Mo had been up since Friday afternoon.

But he wanted to see his son.

So he had driven up here and posted a cash bond—a million dollars, secured by his home—and now would sit out here all night if necessary, motor running, waiting.

Shadows clustered the narrow street. Every few minutes some man or woman, usually black, always bedraggled, would step through the door and stand beneath the bus shelter. Awhile later, some shabby old beater would rattle around the corner and the person would pile in gratefully before the vehicle took off, trailing a cloud of pale blue smoke.

Mo took a sip of Starbucks as he regarded what he had written on the legal pad.

First, I apologize to everyone I've hurt by doing this. You're probably wondering why I did it. Well, there are many reasons.

He stared at the words for a full minute, pen strokes on yellow paper attempting to encompass a life. And a death. Mo ripped the paper out of the pad, balled it up and deposited it carefully in a leather-lined pouch he kept hanging from the driver's side door. Sighing, he took pen to paper again.

He was still looking for the right words when the flashlight beam swept across his cheek, blinding him even through the tinted glass. Mo lowered the window, shielding his eyes with his hand.

"Evening," said the cop from behind the wheel of the police cruiser. He was black, maybe 40, white hair just beginning to colonize his scalp. The one in the passenger seat was white and young enough that Mo seriously doubted he shaved everyday.

"Evening," said Mo.

"Nice car."

Mo nodded.

"You got business here?"

Mo hated cops for the offhand authority that let them ask questions that were none of their damn business. And he hated them, too, for the way they made him feel. No longer a man of achievement who could afford to drive an Escalade, but just another nigger who'd better explain himself or else.

He inclined his head toward the stone wall across the street. "Waiting," he said.

"You get a call?"

"Not yet," said Mo.

"They can call when they get out. No need for you to sit out here in the cold."

"I know," said Mo.

"This is your first time," said the cop. It wasn't a question.

"First and last," said Mo, irritated by the cop's smugness. He wondered if it showed and if that meant he'd have to go through the whole license and registration rigamarole, standing in the rain while the cop assured himself Mo wasn't an ax murderer in a stolen car.

Something stern flashed in the other man's eyes. "I know you?" he asked.

Mo could have answered truthfully. It probably would have solved everything, he thought. But he just didn't care.

"No," he said. "I don't think so." And then he waited to see what would happen.

"What's your name?" asked the cop.

"James Johnson," said Mo.

Which was factual without being true. Though he had always gone by his middle name, Mo's full name, like that of his son and his father, was James Moses Johnson. Neither of them used their real name much, either. Trey preferred the nickname his father had given him the night of his birth. And the first James M. Johnson had always insisted on being called Jack Johnson, like the fighter.

The cop regarded Mo dubiously. "You look like somebody I used to know," he insisted. But apparently, he didn't want to stand in the rain any more than Mo did. So all he said was, "Well, you have a good evening."

The light went dark and the cruiser pulled away, tires hissing against the wet pavement. Mo put the legal pad aside and leaned back into the heated leather, heart drumming. His left hand dropped to the armrest and he started to thumb the switch to raise the window. Then he changed his mind. The cold air felt good on his face.

This was the upside of dying, he thought. You just didn't give a damn anymore.

Across the street, three young black men with cornrowed hair and T-shirts long as dresses came through the door in the wall, hugging their shoulders and muttering curses because they were under-dressed for the weather. It had been unseasonably warm that after-noon—60 degrees and dry. The temperature had fallen hard after dark, followed by a rain that was expected to go till dawn. The men huddled under the shelter, looking miserable.

He was shocked by the bitterness he felt, just seeing them there. Three more dumb-ass young niggers living useless lives, he thought. Just like his son. Just like Trey.

And then his conscience whispered, *Whose fault is that?*

The question did not need an answer.

He had never wanted a son, had never wanted children at all. But life gives a man little choice about that. You play, you pay. So he had made peace long before with the fact that what he wanted did not matter. He had a son, a son he had loved, but distantly and indifferently. Now that son had committed—*allegedly* committed, he forced his mind to say—armed robbery.

Three days after he'd gotten the call, it was still as if someone had punched a ragged hole in him and filled it with pain. He was numb from aching. And from fear.

His son...he was not an angel, no. But he couldn't have done what they said, could he? Not Trey.

No, not Trey.

And yet, they had him in there with the drunks and dealers and punks and thugs. And they would not give him back, would not let Mo even see him, even hear his voice, until they were done doing whatever it was they did, shuffling whatever papers needing shuf-fling.

Mo, who had never been arrested in his life, wondered what it was like on the other side of that wall. He had an irrational impulse to go storming in, banging on the furniture, screaming like Mel Gib-son in *Ransom*, "Give me back my son!"

Instead, he waited.

Tash, Trey's mother, had been in hysterics when she called and told him. It had taken awhile before he could even decipher what she was saying. When he finally understood, he fell onto a chair.

His boy had tried to rob somebody? With a gun? No way in hell. Not his son.

But if he had…

If he had…

Whose fault…?

Mo shook his head, denying the thought entry. He would not allow himself to even consider the possibility. Not yet. It was a mistake. Cops made mistakes all the time. He hit the button and the tinted window slid into place.

Mo fired a cigarette and took a deep drag. He cracked the window just far enough to lure the smoke. Across the street, two prostitutes came through the door in the wall and stood under the bus shelter. One of them had a cell phone to her ear.

Mo watched them. How does life deliver you to these places, he thought. A bus shelter outside a detention center, after midnight on a cold and rainy morning waiting on a ride. And why is it that so many of the people who wind up in a place like this are black? Hair unkempt, faces slack, clad in orange jumpsuits, telling it to the judge.

Now his son was one of them.

And then Mo reminded himself that he wasn't exactly immune to life's nasty bounces. Once, he had been king of the mountain. Now he was a dying man writing a suicide note while waiting for his only child to be released from jail. He glanced at the latest version of the note, decided he didn't like this one either, and tossed the legal pad on to the passenger's seat. He leaned back, closed his eyes, smoked.

He had already bought the gun. A black Smith & Wesson that sat evilly on his nightstand, waiting. He had updated his will, left funeral instructions, sold his dog. All that remained was the note saying goodbye. Then he would press the weapon to his temple, pull the trigger, and wake up wherever it was you went when life was done.

Mo lowered the window to eject his half-smoked cigarette. When he did, he saw one of the hookers walking toward him, holding a newspaper up to shield herself from the rain.

"Can you give us a ride?" she called when she was still ten paces away.

Mo shook his head. "I'm waiting on somebody," he said.

"It ain't far. You be back in twenty minutes."

"I can't help you," said Mo.

She tried charm. "Come on, baby, don't be like that. It's cold out here. My man ain't answering his cell and these buses don't run worth a damn this time of night. Me and her, we'll make it worth your time."

"I'm sorry," said Mo.

She shook her head, more disgusted than angry, he thought. Like there was nothing new about not getting what she wanted. "You got a cigarette?" she said.

Mo nodded. She came closer to the window, a black girl with hair a shade of red not found in nature. He gave her the Kool and lit it for her. Rain tumbled off her improvised umbrella. She exhaled a gray cloud, took a step back. Then he saw the same look of stern recognition that had crossed the cop's face.

"I know you, don't I?"

"You might," admitted Mo.

"You a cop?"

"No. Singer. At least, I used to be."

The hand with the cigarette came up to her mouth, which had opened wide. "You had that band," she said. "Momentum, right?"

The original billing—he had quickly gone solo and dropped the band concept altogether—had been Moses Johnson and Momentum. When he named the band, he had considered that a witty word play. Now, it felt like another lifetime. His smile was automatic and she would never know he didn't feel it. He slipped on his Fan voice so smoothly he didn't even realize he had done it. "That's me," he said. "But what do you know about my music, darling? You're rather young for that, aren't you?"

"Are you kidding? My mom, she played all that old-school shit. I grew up with Momentum and Maze, Commodores, O'Jays, all that shit. You were the lead singer, right? Had that song, "My Prophecy." You wrote that, right? What was it they used to call you?"

"The Prophet of Love," he said.

For all the pain that ever was
I dream a world that never was
This is my prophecy.

And I believe, I really do believe…

A legendary song sung on stages around the world, cigarette lighters moving back and forth in the darkness, voices rising, his words coming back at him in gentle waves.

So long ago.

The hand with the cigarette darted out, two fingers pointing his way. "That's right," the woman said. "Mama used to shush us up when you was singing on the radio. 'Hush. Don't you hear the Prophet testifying?'"

Mo's hand went to the window switch. "Well," he said, dismissing her, "tell your mom hi for me. Would you do that, darling?"

"Oh, she died a long time ago, mister. I must of been ten."

"I'm sorry to hear that."

"The Prophet of Love," she repeated speculatively. She seemed in no hurry to go. Took a happy drag from the cigarette, which was speckled with rain drops. The newspaper above her head was so sodden it barely maintained its shape.

"Well…" said Mo, trying to move her along.

"What you doing down here anyway?" she asked.

Mo sighed. This was not part of the script, not part of so glad to meet you, and I have all your records and, can I have your autograph? Suddenly, he was exhausted. "Waiting," he said. "They got my son locked up in there." He had slipped out of his Fan voice, the one that called even a prostitute "darling." He didn't notice.

"For real?"

"For real."

"Damn. I would never of thought something like that. Not for somebody like you."

"Me neither," said Mo. He nodded toward the bus shelter. "Go on and get out the rain before you catch something."

She nodded, but then she reached for his hand, which he extended. She shook it once, her thumb caressing the flesh between his thumb and forefinger, an invitation. Mo pulled his hand back, gently. "Go on," he said.

"Prophet of Love," she said, grinning as she backed across the street.

When she was gone, Mo raised the window. He fished out a tiny bottle of Purell hand sanitizer with aloe that he kept in the center console, uncapped it and rubbed some into his palms. When they were dry again and soft and smelled fresh, he replaced the bottle. Then he leaned back into the seat and smoked.

It was a little after six when Mo awoke with a start. He had been nodding. Now he looked around the cab of the idling SUV and felt fear trickling down his back like sweat, because he didn't know where he was. Across the street, a skinny white boy with red hair and acne-scarred cheeks was coming through a door in a stone wall. It was dark and rain water stood in puddles on the shiny street.

A fist knocked impatiently against the passenger window and Mo jerked toward it, realizing for the first time that this was what had awakened him. His son was there.

Mo clicked the button to unlock the door. He whisked the legal pad off the passenger seat as Trey climbed in.

"Hey, Dad," he said.

"Are you all right? Tell me what happened. What is all this about armed robbery?"

The questions seemed to catch Trey by surprise. He stammered, began the sentence three times before he finally managed to say, "It wasn't like that." Mo's heart deflated like a balloon. He had been hoping for a flat and angry denial. Instead he got "It wasn't like that."

"Then what was it like?" he said.

"DC and Fury, they..."

"Who and who?"

Trey sighed. "My homies," he said. "DC, his name Carter Clark. Fury, his name Cedric something. Gamble, I think. Cedric Gamble."

"So, Mr. Gamble and Mr. Clark, what did they do?"

Trey sighed. "I'm tired, Pop. Can we talk about this later?"

"I've been out here since before midnight. Your poor mother is going crazy with fear. No, we can't talk about it later."

This brought another sigh. "We was comin' from rehearsal," Trey said.

"Rehearsal," said Mo. "You got no job, but you got time for 'rehearsal.'"

"We got an audition next week. Guy say he might want to manage us."

"This is this rap group of yours."

"Why you got to say it like that?"

"So go on. You're all in this group."

Trey nodded. "Street Gang."

"Street Gang," said Mo. "Of course."

"Man, why you always got to do that?" demanded Trey. "Why you got to be down on everything I do?"

"'Cause you ain't doing nothing."

"Oh, my group don't count as doing nothing?"

"Yeah. It's just what the world needs. Another rap group talking about bitches and hos."

"You know what? Thanks for bailing me out. I think I'll walk." Trey shoved the door open.

"Get back in the car, Trey," ordered Mo.

He saw the hesitation in his son's eyes. Trey had always been, whatever his faults, an obedient son. Now that instinct was at war with his anger. Mo took him off the hook. "Would you get back in the car, please," he said.

Trey closed the door. Mo put the SUV in gear and wheeled it slowly out of its parking space. The sky in the east was just beginning to turn from black to gray.

"So," said Mo, "you were coming out of rehearsal with these other two. What were their names again?"

"Carter Clark. Cedric Gamble."

"And what happened?"

Trey didn't answer. Mo glanced over. Adrenaline was a spike hammered straight through his chest. "Look," he said, "whatever it is, we can make it right."

"You already heard. We stopped at this store."

"Yeah?"

"And they say we robbed it."

"They say." Mo didn't bother trying to hide his skepticism. His chest ached.

"Look," said Trey, "the lawyer said I wasn't supposed to give you no details, on account of they can make you testify against me. He

said there ain't nothin' in the law—no kind of privilege, he said—
between, like, father and son."

"Trey, tell me nobody got hurt in this thing."

Trey only looked at him.

Mo's mouth was so dry it hurt. "Tell me nobody got killed."

Trey's eyes flickered. He found something out the window to
look at. "I can't talk about it," he said.

"Oh, my God," breathed Mo. He put a hand to his chest. Tears
were on his cheeks. He didn't bother to wipe. "Oh, my God," he said.
"Do you know what you've done? Do you know what you've done?"
It was hard to breathe.

"I ain't done nothing!" Trey rushed to say that. "You hear me,
Pop? I ain't had nothing to do with it."

Mo turned on him, frightened of his own fierce need to believe.

"So these other two—what were their names again?"

"Carter Clark. Cedric Gamble."

"Clark and Gamble, Clark and Gamble," mumbled Mo, trying
to commit the names to memory. "They're the ones who...?"

"I can't talk about it, Pop. Lawyer said it would be bad for the
case."

"I'm your father, Trey."

"I know. But the lawyer said."

Mo waved the words away, impatiently. "So somebody was killed
in this thing? Is that what you're telling me?"

Trey said, "Pop, you really don't want to..."

"Oh, God, is that what you're telling me? Somebody was
killed?"

It took a long moment, Trey wrestling for an easier way to say it.
But easy had nothing to do with this. Easy and dead didn't belong
to the same universe. "Yeah," he said. Mo's head went back into the
headrest hard, his free hand came up over his mouth. Tears continued to fall.

They drove in silence for a few minutes. Around them, the tow-
ers of downtown Baltimore gave way to row houses, tall, narrow
structures squeezed grimly together, like people huddling for warmth
in the cold.

"Why did you do it?" Mo asked finally.

"I didn't do nothing," said Trey.

"*Why*, son?"

Trey took a deep breath. "I can't talk to you about none of that."

Mo said, "I see."

Trey said, "I'm sorry, Pop. Not just 'cause I can't talk to you but, you know…all of it."

Mo ran a hand through his hair. He felt old. "I'm the one who's sorry," he said.

"What do you mean?"

"Just…nothing. I don't mean nothing."

A few minutes passed. Then Mo said, "You want to get something to eat? We could find an all-night place."

"That's all right," said Trey. "When I called Mom, she said she was putting breakfast on. Bacon and eggs and waffles, she said. She told me to say you was welcome to stay. But I wouldn't, I was you."

"Why?"

"Well, she ain't in the best mood. Besides, that guy is going to be there."

"That guy" was Philip Reed. He was a widower with two daughters, a midlevel executive with some big telecommunications company—Mo could never remember which. He and Tash had been dating for three years. And "dating," quaint as it sounded, was the right word. They had not moved in together because Reed was a deacon in some big Baptist church and felt it wouldn't look right. Tash had spent the years alternately fearing and hoping he would ask her to marry him. So far, he had not seemed terribly inclined to do so.

"Mom say he want to talk to me," said Trey.

It made Mo's jaw tighten. Obviously he wasn't capable of getting through to his own son. Obviously, that was the real message here.

He took a moment to master his anger, a moment to remind himself—*confess* to himself—that Tash had her reasons. Good ones at that. "Your mom probably doesn't think I've done the best job with you over the years," he finally said. "Maybe she's got a point."

"But you didn't—"

Mo lifted his hand to stem the protest. "Just listen to the man. Give him a chance. Let him say his piece." Mo hoped the advice didn't sound as empty as it felt. As empty as *he* felt.

The sun was up now, lightening the clouds to a silver gray. Around them, the city was beginning to come to life. A delivery truck with the logo of the *Baltimore Sun* lumbered heavily past them.

Trey said, "He don't want me around his daughters. Did you know that?"

"What do you mean?"

"He told Mom I'm a bad influence."

"Well, aren't you?"

Trey's lips pursed and his jaw tightened like a lug nut. Mo turned away, unwilling to let Trey see the indignation that fired up his chest. Philip Reed had two daughters, Ashanti and Kadijah, ages 10 and 12. He called them his princesses and as far as he was concerned, they were genetically incapable of wrong. Mo let a sigh escape him. "You need to try to get along with the guy, Trey. Your mother's hoping he'll pop the question someday. Don't mess that up for her, okay?"

Trey's eyes flashed. "She'da married you if you asked. I think she still would, tell you the truth. Why didn't you never ask?"

The answer was cocaine, groupies, fear, the delusion of infinite time. "I don't know," said Mo. And that was true, too.

They didn't speak for long moments after that. Then Trey said, "Dad!" in a voice of mild alarm.

"Yeah?"

"You missed the turn."

The streets whizzing past them jumped suddenly back into focus. Mo didn't recognize them.

"Back there," said Trey. "How you miss that?"

"Wasn't paying attention," said Mo.

"They say memory is the second thing to go," said Trey.

"So I've heard," said Mo as he made the U-turn.

The SUV pulled to a stop in front of Tash's place a few minutes later. A powder-blue row house squashed together in the middle of the block with some bedraggled plants in a box sitting on the railing of the tiny porch. She flung the door open while Trey's key was still in the lock, threw her arms around his neck and started crying. In one hand, she held a spatula flecked with bits of egg.

"Mom, I'm okay," Trey whispered. He looked to his father for help and, finding none there, he patted her on the arm and repeated it. "I'm okay, Mom."

Whereupon she drew back and slapped him hard in the face. "What in the hell have you got yourself involved in?" she cried. "What in the hell have you done? Answer me, James Moses Johnson, or as Jesus is my witness, I will whip your natural ass this morning."

Trey touched his face where she had slapped him and he began to stammer. "I'm sorry, Mama, it wasn't my fault. I was just in the wrong place at the wrong time, that's all."

"That's not good enough!" She almost shrieked it. "That's not good enough," she cried again. Then she mashed her face against his chest and wept.

Trey looked another plea toward his father. Mo took Tash by the shoulders and gently pulled her away. "What have you done?" she whispered. "What have you done?"

"We don't know that he's done anything yet," said Mo. "And whatever they think he's done, he can't talk about it, even to us. His lawyer said."

"But we're his parents," said Tash.

"I know. But they can make us testify to anything he says."

"Oh, my God," said Tash.

"We'll get this all settled," said Mo. "You'll see."

Tash nodded, still sniffling. "Lord, Mo, I hope you're right." And then, to her son: "Well, Trey, your breakfast is ready. After we eat, you go take a shower and get dressed. We have just enough time to make it to church."

"Church? Come on, Mama. I been in a lockup. I ain't been to sleep all night."

Her eyes narrowed. "You being in a lockup all night is precisely the reason you need to have your behind in church this morning, Trey. And besides that, you know Philip doesn't like it when you skip church. He likes us to worship as a family."

"We ain't no family."

Mo jumped in before Tash could reply. "Trey," he said, "obey your mother."

Trey glowered at them. He went to wash his hands. When he walked inside, Tash said, "Thank you, Moses. I don't know what we're going to do with that boy. Armed robbery? Lord, have mercy."

"He'll be all right," said Mo.

"You've been telling me the same thing for as long as I can re-member, Moses Johnson. *He'll be all right. He'll grow up.* When does that happen, Mo? When does that kick in? 'Cause right now, I'm scared as I can be for him. That's my only son—*our* only son—and seems like he's going down the wrong path as fast as he can and all you do is tell me not to worry. Well, I *am* worried."

"Look, Tash—"

She held up her palm. "I'm sorry. I didn't mean to dump all that on you."

Mo lifted her chin on the crook of his index finger. Tash was tiny, dark-skinned, still a handsome woman in her forty-eighth year. The billowy Afro of her youth was short and neatly clipped now, but she still had those eyes that seemed to know everything there was worth knowing. Mo said, "He's going to be fine, Tash. I promise you."

The eyes questioned him, but apparently, she decided to let it go. "Are you hungry?" she asked. "You want to come in and eat?"

"Thanks," said Mo, "but I'm more sleepy than hungry. You go on. I'm going home and…"

He stopped when he realized she wasn't looking at him. Instead, she was looking over his shoulder. "There's Philip and the girls."

Mo turned, hoping his disappointment didn't show. He had wanted to be away before Philip Reed arrived, but there he was, climbing out of his minivan. Reed was a slim, angular man well over six feet tall. His blue suit was immaculate, his thin moustache pruned with such precision Mo was secretly convinced a ruler or some other straight edge was involved. Behind him came the girls, frilly in pink dresses. Trey had told him once that he felt sorry for them because all the other kids, lounging on the back pews in jeans and oversized T-shirts, made fun of them, thought they were conceited.

"They ain't like that," Trey had said, genuinely concerned. "It's just him. He won't let 'em dress normal."

Reed was smiling amiably as he bounded onto the porch. Big, fake smile, thought Mo. Reed kissed Tash, pumped Mo's arm. "Morning, Moses," he said. "I guess seeing you here means I don't have to wonder if Moses Jr. got out. How is our boy anyway?"

"Our boy is inside," said Mo. Reed was the only one in the world who called Trey Moses.

"Good," said Philip. "I'm looking forward to having a long talk with that young man." He clapped Mo on the shoulder. "I mean, I'm sure you've already let him have an earful, but I figure hearing the same thing from another direction won't hurt."

"Yeah," said Mo. "I'm sure I need all the help I can get."

Tash shot him a look, then smiled falsely. "Well," she said, "let's not stand out here in the cold. Breakfast is on. I made waffles."

The girls said in unison, "Yummy!"

Philip opened the door. "You going to join us, Moses?"

The decision and the words were simultaneous. "Yeah," said Mo. "Waffles do sound yummy."

He ignored the warning shooting from Tash's eyes. Slapped Philip hard on the back. "Come on," he said, heartily, "let's go get that young man straight."

five

He had met her in high school. Thirtysomething years ago. She had been a standoffish, vaguely exotic new kid in school. Black militant type. He was the popular boy who, because he was cute, because he could sing, could have his pick of all the girls. He chose her.

Mo toyed with the memory as he watched her sit down, then take Philip's hand. He found himself testing his memory often now, pulling images from his mental file to see if they remained clear. Or if the image had begun to obscure behind black fog. The memory of meeting Tash was still sharp enough to cut yourself on.

Tash took Mo's right hand. Ashanti took his left. Mo was confused. Then Philip said, "Let's pray it up." He lowered his head and spoke a blessing over the meal.

"Amen" was barely out of his mouth when Trey sprang on his food as if the plate might otherwise get away.

"Hungry there, Moses?" Philip didn't bother to hide his amusement. Trey didn't bother to answer.

Ashanti piped up then, raising her hand as if she were in school. "Daddy, can we go watch TV in the living room?"

Philip nodded. "I think that would be a good idea," he said. "We have to have a talk in here anyway." He wrinkled his nose in mock distaste and added, "Grownup things."

It was, Mo thought, sickeningly cute, more fake than the Fan voice at its worst. Except it wasn't fake, was it? It was real. It was just how Philip Reed was with his daughters, down to the wink he gave them as they took their plates and climbed down from the table.

Mo found himself wondering why he had ever thought it would be a good idea to be here. It wasn't. Philip Reed outclassed him at every step, showed him his deficiencies as a father without even trying, without even being conscious of it. Just by being attentive and playful with his daughters. Hell, just by being there.

The girls scampered from the room as fast as they could without spilling their plates. Moments later, Mo heard cartoon sounds spilling into the kitchen. He fixed himself a plate, small portions. Ate without tasting as he looked at his son. Trey was halfway through his meal. Where did he put it all? Seemed like yesterday—seemed like an hour ago—he was a one-year-old, tottering around underfoot as his parents argued. Now he was 19. He had committed an armed robbery. And here he sat three days later, his jaws moving like pistons, flecks of egg caught in the wisp of moustache above his lip.

Without knowing he was going to do it, Mo reached across and smacked Trey hard across the back of his head.

Trey's head came up sharply. "Ow! What you do that for?"

"I just want to know what the hell you were thinking."

"I think we'd all like to know," said Tash softly.

"Look," said Trey, fork poised, "my lawyer said he don't think they got no case. He think they bluffin'. So don't worry about it."

"You don't get it, do you, son?" Philip was shaking his head. "It's not about what they can prove or disprove. It's about what you did or didn't do."

"I ain't done nothin'!" cried Trey. His voice was plaintive.

"No, you did something," said Philip. "Why else would they haul you down there?"

"I'm a nigger," said Trey. "They don't need no other excuse."

Philip said, "No, Moses. You're the one making excuses."

"They call me Trey. Can you please remember that?"

"Very well then, 'Trey.'" The way Philip said it sounded as if he were picking up garbage with his thumb and forefingers. It made Mo shift uneasily in his chair. "Will you please tell us what happened?"

"Like I told my dad, my lawyer don't want me to talk about it. He say anything I say, even to my parents, they could be subpoenaed to talk about it. And if I can't talk to them about it, I sure as hell can't talk to you."

"But don't you get it, Moses? The very fact that your lawyer won't let you talk tells us you were out there doing something you had no business doing."

"No, man, you the one don't get it." Trey made talking motions with his hand, spoke slowly, as if to an idiot. "I cannot talk about it."

"But Moses—"

"He said he can't talk about it," said Mo.

Philip said, "Look, Mo, I'm just trying to get at the truth here."

"Yeah, but that's not your place."

"What's that supposed to mean?"

"He has a father," said Mo. "In case you hadn't noticed."

Tash said, "Don't you two start fighting."

"We're not fighting," snapped Mo. Then he heard himself. "We're not fighting," he said, his voice softer.

There was a silence. Mo glanced at his son. *Six pounds, nine ounces.* Trey's birth weight. Mo could remember that. He could *remember.* He almost smiled. Instead, he faced Philip.

"We're going in circles here. He should obey his attorney, period."

"I understand what you're saying, Mo," said Tash. "And you're right. But Philip is right, too, isn't he? The simple fact that his attorney won't let him talk, that tells us something, doesn't it?"

Nobody answered.

"Yeah," she said, "that's what I thought. So in a way, it doesn't matter what the details are. It doesn't matter what they can or can't prove in court. What matters is what this whole thing tells us about who you are, Trey." She touched her chest and added. "In here. And what it tells me is that you're not who I thought you were, son. You're not the man I hoped you'd be." Her eyes were moist.

Mo lowered his head. She had hit it square on. Truth too painful for seeing. And he knew he bore the blame.

Trey's eyes flashed. "Oh, so you disappointed in me because I won't let this guy treat me like some kind of punk?"

Philip said, "I'm not trying to treat you like a punk, Moses. I'm just trying to get the facts."

"You got all the facts I can give you. Why you can't see that?"

"You want to know what I see, son?"

"I ain't your son."

Philip ignored him. "I see somebody headed for trouble as fast as he can get there. I see somebody who was lucky to graduate high school—a year late. I see somebody who's not in college, who doesn't expect to go to college, who doesn't have a job, who doesn't have anything except a four-year-old son he can't take care of."

"I handle mine, man," said Trey.

Again, Philip ignored him. "I see somebody who has no plan and no future unless he gets his act together. What are you going to do with your life, Moses?"

"I told you: My name is Trey. And I already know what I'm gon' do with my life. I'm a rapper."

"You're a rapper." Philip dismissed it with a laugh. For some reason, it grated Mo, even though he felt the same way. Philip was shaking his head. "You and every other uneducated young fool out there wants to be a so-called rapper. You all think the same thing, all think you're going to get rich making that noise you call music. How many do you figure have that dream? Just in this block? A hundred? Maybe more? That's not a plan, Moses. It's a daydream."

"So...*what*? I'm s'posed to want to be like you? A sucker in a suit, sittin' in some office all day like some imitation white man? That ain't me, man. I'd shoot myself if I thought I was gon' end up like you."

A sigh of patient suffering. "Moses, I'm not the enemy here," said Philip. "I want to help you. Your mother wants to help you. Your father, too. But first, you have to want to help yourself."

Trey's smile was cold. "Yeah, you trying to help all right. You trying to help yourself to my mother."

Tash slapped him. Philip lowered his head. Mo looked away, afraid he might smile. The girls appeared in the doorway, mouths forming little ovals of surprise. Their father said, "Go back and watch cartoons," and they did.

Trey shoved his chair back from the table. "I'm going to my room," he said.

"*You* are not going anywhere," said Tash. She was standing now, her finger stabbing at his brow. "You're going to stay right here, and you're going to apologize to this man and you're going to apologize to me and you're going to listen to what he has to say. Do you understand me, James Moses Johnson? Do you hear what I'm telling you?"

It took a moment. A long moment when the only sound in the whole house was the smash of a two-by-four against a cartoon character's head.

Finally, Trey pulled the chair back to him and sat down. "I'm sorry, man," he said without looking at Philip. "I'm sorry, Mama."

Philip began, "Look, Moses—"

Tash silenced him with a look. "Trey," she said, "look at me." The eyes he lifted to her were rimmed in red.

"I'm *worried* about you, son. We are all worried about you. You need to stop pushing us away. You need to let us help you before it's too late. This thing that happened, whatever it was, that's not how you were raised. You know better than that. Now, you need to make some changes in your life. It's not about Philip, it's not about me. It's about you. And it's about my grandson. He's four years old, Trey, just getting to an age where he's beginning to understand certain things. Do you want him to grow up without his father around, like…"

Tash fell silent, as if suddenly aware of having said too much. But Trey finished the thought for her anyway. "Like I did? Is that what you mean?" He regarded his father for a long moment. Then he said, "Well, you right. He wasn't around. He was always off in the studio or giving some concert somewhere. But you know the one thing I can say about him? He trusts me. He believes in me."

Trey stood up from the table. "That's more than I can say about you. Or this guy."

"Trey…"

"Can I go now, Mama? I need to shower and get dressed. Can I be excused?"

He was gone the moment she nodded. Philip covered her hand with his. "Don't," he said, and she realized that she was crying.

Tash bit her lip, not trusting herself to speak. Philip's hand came up and touched her cheek and she leaned in to his caress. The sight of it made Mo turn in his chair. Then he realized Philip was saying something.

"Beg pardon?" he said.

"I said, he thinks the world of you, Moses," said Philip, repeating himself.

"I'm his father," said Mo.

"I'm just saying."

"You're just saying that because I was a lousy father, it's kind of a surprise he thinks so much of me."

"I did not say that," said Philip stiffly.

"You didn't have to." Mo uttered a tired little laugh. He wondered where his life had gone. Then he heard himself say, "It's true, isn't it? It's true."

He wanted to say more, but to his surprise, his throat was full. He felt tears crawling on ant's feet down his cheek. It surprised him.

Alzheimer's causes mood swings. He remembered—*remembered! Give that man a cigar!*—the doctor saying that. Apparently, it was true. Which made him laugh.

Tash was looking at him hard. "Moses," she said, "are you okay?"

"I've got to go," he said. He waved down her concern. "I've got to go."

She followed him to the front door. "Moses, are you all right?"

He smiled. "Just tired," he said. "Ain't slept in two days. I'm going home and rest. Call you tomorrow."

And he was through the door before she could ask him more questions, waving the back of his hand at her without ever turning around.

———————

She had not seen him cry since his mother's death.

They had known each other since they were both little more than kids. And in all that time, she had seen him cry only the once. It was jarring. If Mo could cry, mountains could cry. If Mo could cry, trees and traffic lights could cry. Yet there he was, crying. It made no sense.

Tash was still wrestling with it half an hour later when she stepped from the shower and began to towel herself dry. She had a bad feeling. She tried to ignore it, tried to pray it away. But it was stubborn as a stain. Wouldn't go away. Just sat there in her chest, a heavy lump, waiting.

Her son. Her only child. How could he be out there with a gun robbing people? Hadn't she worked her ass off to make a good life for him? Hadn't she taught him and trained him and loved him with all the strength that was in her? What good was it, what did it matter, if it all came down to a moment like this?

He trusts me. He believes in me.

What the hell did that mean? How could he say that about a man he barely knew? This was the first time since Trey was in diapers that they had even lived in the same state; Mo had moved to Maryland two years ago. To be closer to his son, he said at the time, but Tash wondered if the cost of living in New York City didn't have more to do with it. It had been many years since Mo had a hit. He wasn't touring as much as he used to, either. She had no idea how much he was making, but she was sure it was a lot less than in his heyday.

Before the move, Trey had been lucky to see his father once a year. Even now, with Moses living down in Bowie, just 45 minutes away, they didn't see each other much more than that. So what did it mean that his father "trusted" him? His father didn't even know him. Mo hadn't been there—not for the first day of school, not for parent-teacher conferences, not for birthdays or holidays. She had done all of that, alone.

They had been luckier than most. Mo's checks had always been punctual and generous. But, thought Tash, they didn't make up for his absence. Not even a little bit.

She was in her closet now, flicking through her outfits with sharp motions. It was a good thing she was going to church, she thought. She needed to pray away this anger.

He trusts me. He believes in me.

Yeah, but where was he when your little ass was in the hospital with a fever? Where was he when those boys beat you up after school?

Tash made herself stop, her hand on a cream-colored outfit. She could hear herself breathing, her chest rising and falling heavily. She hoped she wasn't about to cry again.

The pregnancy had been an accident. She and Mo weren't even together then, Tash having finally given up on the idea that he would ever learn to be content with one woman when so many made themselves so readily available on a nightly basis. Somewhere along the way, she had dropped the dashiki and the sullen militancy of her youth. Militancy was fine, she realized, but it didn't pay the rent. And besides, how much of militancy had been a pose, a way to win the attention of her own father, a harsh, rigid man who would never have noticed her otherwise?

But he was years dead and she had been well into her 20s, well into adulthood. Time, she decided, to grow up. So she had earned an associates degree at the local junior college, then enrolled in nursing school, determined to get on with her life and stop chasing Moses Johnson around the world.

Then he had swept into town and given her a call, something about getting together for old times' sake. She had known it was a mistake, but she had allowed herself to listen to him anyway. And next thing she knew, she was throwing up every morning and her ankles were swelling.

She was nervous the night she tracked him down in the studio and told him about it, but Mo took the news better than she thought he would. Stoic, that was the word for it. Not happy, anyone could see that. But he had not moaned and whined either, had not begged her to get rid of it.

All he said was, "You're going to keep it?" and if he was hoping she would answer one way or another, his voice did not betray it. It was midnight and they were alone in the recording booth, the band and the engineers having gone out to eat.

"Yes," she said, surprising herself. She had not known until just that moment.

He had come to her, pressed her shoulders, and softly kissed the middle of her forehead. "Then I guess we're going to be a mommy and daddy," he said. He left town two days later to begin a concert tour and the checks had begun to arrive a week after that, checks not cut by the machine in the accounting office, but written out in Mo's careless scrawl, arriving with postmarks from around the country and the world.

She had gone into labor one night seven months later, as she was dressing to attend a United Negro College Fund benefit where Mo was performing. The delivery was hard. Her doctor gave her the bad news afterward as she lay in her bed recuperating. She would never have any more children.

And Tash had looked over to where James Moses Johnson III lay, a white cap on his head, cotton booties on his fists, mouth moving in his sleep. She had given a wan smile. "Well at least I got this one," she said.

It was after midnight when Mo got there. She was sitting up in bed, the baby settled in the crook of her arm, nursing, the *Tonight Show* playing on the television on the wall. Then the door opened and he peeked around.

"Hey," he said.

"Hey," she said.

A nod. "Is that him?"

Tash smiled. "This is your son," she said.

Mo entered the room. He was wearing a purple sequined tuxedo. His face was flushed and the curls on his head were jelled into immobility. It touched her that he had rushed to her bedside straight from the stage. Still, Mo was hesitant as he came around the bed to meet his son. He looked both eager and terrified. Finally he said, "He looks like you."

"People always say that," Tash replied. "He's too young. He doesn't even look like himself, yet."

"Oh." Mo looked chastened and Tash was sorry she had said it.

He recovered nicely, though, smiling and bringing a bouquet of flowers out from behind his back. "Here. These are for you."

Tash nodded toward a water pitcher on the counter. "They're beautiful," she said. "Tell Chuck I said thanks."

Why am I being such a bitch? she wondered.

Chuck was the road manager who always cleaned up after Mo and tried to make him look like a human being. At the sound of the name, Mo smirked. He dropped the flowers on the night table and said, "Chuck works for me, you know."

She noticed his eyes then. They were shiny and red. "You been using again," she said. Mo's eyes flickered. *Embarrassment,* she thought, surprised. He turned away and became very interested in some story George Burns was telling Johnny Carson. Tash lifted the baby, shrugging her breast back into the hospital gown. "Here," she said, "why don't you hold your son?"

"Oh, that's okay. I don't...I don't need to...I shouldn't..."

Mo was still mumbling protests when Tash put the baby in his arms. After a few moments, she said, "You haven't asked his name."

Mo, who had been regarding his son with some strange mix of pride and apprehension, glanced up at her, blinking. "What *is* his name?" he asked.

"James Moses Johnson III," she said.

"So you went and did it, huh?" They had talked about it. Mo said he didn't care what name she gave the baby, as long as she didn't name it after him. "That's the same as naming it after Jack," he said. Meaning his father.

Now Tash said quietly, "It's a good name."

"No, it's not," he said.

But he didn't press it further. Instead, Mo waggled his fingers in his son's face. The baby was stuporous with breast milk, nearly asleep. "Hello, Moses, the third," said Mo. "Hello, Trey."

Tash watched him for a moment. Then she said, "It was a hard delivery."

He looked up. "Are you all right?"

"Yeah. But the doctor said he's the first and the last. I can't have any more." She felt the tears massing behind her eyes and she slapped at them impatiently. Tash had thought she was done crying.

Mo saw. "Tash," he said, moving toward her, "I'm sorry."

She waved him back. "It's okay."

"I didn't know," he said.

"I told you it's okay." An edge in her voice.

Mo nodded. He looked down at the baby. "Well, you did good, Tash. You did real good."

For a few minutes, they watched Carson in silence. Mo told a funny story about the one time he did the show. She laughed in the right places. The baby began to fret in its sleep and Mo leaned over and transferred it to Tash's arms.

"They're supposed to discharge me day after tomorrow," she said.

"I'm not doing anything that day. Catch up with me and I'll give you a ride."

"Okay," said Tash.

He leaned over the bed, kissed her on the forehead and said it again. "You did good." Tash nodded. She watched as he picked up the flowers and settled them into a vase. Then he waved and moved toward the door, already ready to go. She wasn't surprised. He had always been this way. No time to sit. Places to be. Things to do. Probably some woman waiting in the car.

She couldn't help herself. She called his name when his hand was on the knob. Moses turned expectantly and she heard herself ask, "Are you happy?" Hating herself for even wanting to know.

Mo said, "Beg pardon?"

She nodded toward Trey, sleeping in her arm, nestled against her breast. "About the baby, I mean. Are you happy?"

He put on a smile she could see right through. "Of course, I am, babe. Of course I am." He was through the door before she could ask him anything else.

Trey was walking before Tash saw Moses again.

She never felt especially guilty about having a baby she knew he didn't want or giving him a name she knew he hated. She had often thought maybe she should feel guilt, had wondered what it said about her that she did not, but it really didn't matter, did it? The feeling simply wasn't there. That man had taken so much from her. He *owed* her this.

If that was selfish, she didn't care.

There was a soft knock at the bedroom door. Tash had been applying eye shadow. "Come in, Trey," she said.

The door swung inward and Trey entered, wearing an oversized T-shirt with some scowling rapper on the front. "What do you want?" she asked.

"I wanted to apologize," he said. And then, pointedly: "To *you*. A real apology, I mean. I ain't meant to be disrespectful."

Tash went back to the mirror, dabbing at the color above her eyelid. "For somebody not trying to be disrespectful, you do a good job of it."

"Yeah," he said.

He shoved his hands in his pockets and studied the frayed carpet for a long moment. Finally he said, "You really want to marry this guy? You waiting for him to ask?"

That made Tash look up. "Who told you that?" she said.

When Trey didn't answer, she knew. "Your father needs to mind his own business," she said.

"Mom?"

"Yeah?"

"Did you love him?"

"Your father?" She was stalling.

"Yeah."

Tash closed her eyes, remembering an afternoon spent on Catalina Island, walking hand in hand with Moses, both of them impossibly young, laughing at some joke she could no longer recall. "Yes," she said. "I loved him."

"What about now?"

"Yes," she said. "In some way, I'll always love him."

"Then how you gon' marry this guy?"

"Philip is a good man, Trey. You've never given him a chance. You're too young to understand. I'll always care about your father, but we can't be together. I realized that a long time ago. I think we both did."

"But—"

"Trey, please."

He fell silent then, sat there watching intently as she finished touching color to her face. When she was finished, she pulled on the cream-colored jacket and stood back to admire her handiwork. "You ready to go?" she asked. Trey nodded.

"I called LaShonda," he said. "Asked her if I could pick up DeVante and take him to church with us. You think that guy mind going by there?" DeVante was Trey's little boy. LaShonda was his mother.

"I think he'd mind a lot less if you stopped calling him 'that guy,'" said Tash. Trey only response was to grunt. Tash shook her head. "Grow up, Trey," she said.

Still, when she went downstairs to where Philip was watching cartoons with the girls, she whispered Trey's request in his ear. "He couldn't ask me himself?" said Philip.

"You know how he is," said Tash.

"Yeah, I do: spoiled and immature."

She let it pass. He was right, after all. Philip never gave her an answer, just stood and began herding the girls toward the door. Still, Tash wasn't surprised when the minivan pulled up in front of the public housing complex where LaShonda Watkins lived with her mother. Philip didn't speak. Trey didn't either. He just got out and walked up the path between red brick buildings with card-table-sized patches of dirt flanking the front steps. At the third building, he knocked.

LaShonda's mother Michaela appeared first, dressed for church. She glared at Trey—the woman seemed to take his continued existence as a personal affront—then went to fetch her daughter. Tash and the woman had spoken only a few times, usually to argue bitterly over whose child was most at fault for their grandson's existence. It embarrassed Tash to think about it. She made a mental note to call Michaela. They were adults, both Christian women. They should be able to put aside their disappointment and anger for the sake of the little boy they both adored.

LaShonda came to the door next, wearing a robe. She and Trey exchanged sharp words Tash couldn't hear. And then the little boy appeared. DeVante Tyler Watkins was a bright little fellow, four years old, with close-cropped hair. He was dressed neatly in a sweater and slacks, wearing the coat Tash had given him for Christmas. The boy was shy in the presence of his father, smiling bashfully as he took Trey's hand. There was another unfriendly exchange with LaShonda and then Tash's son and grandson came toward the car.

"He's getting big," said Philip.

"Looks like his grandfather more every day," said Tash. And it was true. Or at least, he looked like Moses once had, the eyes lively and ready for fun, the mouth always in motion. It occurred to her, now that she thought about it, that Mo hadn't really looked that way for a long time. Indeed, there was a deep sadness in him lately that she couldn't quite place.

She lowered the window as her grandson approached and leaned down to accept the kiss he stood on tiptoe to give her. They exchanged their greetings and Trey got the boy settled into his seat. He seemed changed by the presence of his son, seemed lighter somehow. He didn't even bristle when Philip reminded him to buckle the boy in.

She heard DeVante say, "I haven't seen you in a long time, Daddy."

"Aw man, it ain't been that long," Trey said. The door closed and Philip pulled away from the curb. Glancing back, Tash saw LaShonda standing there on the patch of dirt at her front door, folded arms barricading her heart as she watched them go.

six

The sound drew Mo up from the darkness. For a moment he was nowhere, suspended in that place between places, unable even to form the thought to ask himself where he was. Then he heard it again, a thin wheedling. And now Mo was lurching about in his bed, covers tangling about his thighs. His hand flung itself out toward the sound. It landed on something, something cold.

Eyes closed, mind still swimming against sleep, he felt the unknown object. Felt the barrel, felt the trigger guard, felt the grip. When he finally knew what it was his laugh was a short bark, sour as old milk. For all his intentions of suicide, wouldn't it be funny if he accidentally blew his brains out trying to answer the phone?

It wheedled again and Mo lifted his face out of the pillow to search out the clock. Ten thirty in the morning. Who could be calling him at this hour? He was no longer active in the music business, but he still kept musician's hours, up all night, asleep till mid-afternoon. Anyone who knew him knew that. He lifted the receiver.

"Yeah," he said.

"Mr. Johnson?" She was young and her voice was brutal in its perkiness.

"Yeah," he said again.

"This is Dr. Ruelas's office. I was calling to remind you of the support group meeting. Today at noon?"

"I remember," said Moses.

This was a lie, though one so smooth and guiltless that it went right past her.

"Good then," she said. "So I'll tell them to expect you at noon."

Moses made his voice a sunny smile. "I'll be there."

"Great!" she said enthusiastically. She was immune to parody.

Moses hung up the receiver and rolled out of bed. He lit the first cigarette of the day. It tasted like dry grass. He found the remote control and aimed it at the television in the corner. Regis Philbin was interviewing some blonde starlet about a hit movie Mo had never heard of. Or maybe he had known the title once and forgotten. The thought made Mo flip channels a few times more. He stopped when he found Marshall Dillon confronting some bad guy outside the Long Branch saloon.

Mo smoked and watched. Once, but only once, he glanced at the gun on his nightstand and allowed himself a fleeting thought of putting it to his temple right then and there and blowing a hole through his malfunctioning mind. But that would be an act of pique, he knew. Just a way of getting out of an engagement he didn't want to keep. When he finally killed himself, it had to be about more than that.

Still, Mo could not imagine a less appealing prospect than sitting in a room with a group of strangers talking about his impending demise. The doctor had said it would help him to talk it out, enable him to "come to terms" with the fact that he was dying. Like the pain, the fury of being fucked in the ass by life and knowing he could do nothing about it, was something he could just wrap up neatly in a gift box of psychobabble and put to the side, never to worry about again.

If only.

Why should he care about coming to terms with his demise? At the end of the day, his demise was still coming, whether he came to terms with it or not.

Mo glanced around for an ashtray. It was out of reach, so he stubbed out the cigarette on his nightstand, a cherry-stained antique littered now with old cigarette butts and assorted papers. Lately, something in him enjoyed ruining the furniture. He had always been a neat man before, had always taken pride in owning and maintaining beautiful and expensive things. But really, what did it matter? What did anything matter?

Scratching himself, Mo padded into the bathroom and turned on the shower. His bedroom was palatial, the bathroom larger than some apartments. Mo's home was a McMansion sitting on three acres, a two-story brick house with a columned portico, woods in the back, an expansive lawn in the front, six large bedrooms, one converted to a theater, another to a small recording studio where, mostly for his own amusement because no one else seemed interested, he sometimes worked on new material. Marble staircases descended to marble floors.

He lived there alone. His last serious girlfriend had moved out a year ago and he had fired Rosalie, his live-in cook and housekeeper, a week ago, right after he got the diagnosis. Of the two, he missed Rosalie more.

Mo paused to regard his image in the bathroom mirror and decided, as he did every morning, that he was still looking good. True, he had thickened some and his moustache contained nearly as much salt as pepper these days. But he was still tall and powerfully built, still had the same thick shock of curly hair that had once made girls write his name alongside theirs inside valentine hearts, still had the sea-foam colored eyes that, as a woman writer once put it, you could get lost in and never care about finding your way back. He tested out his smile and it was still roguish and blinding. How many times had it gotten him laid? Hell, it would get him laid tonight, if he wanted it. Yes, to all outward appearances, he was still Mo Johnson, still the Prophet, still a star.

Just to look at him, he thought, you'd have considered him the picture of health. You'd have figured this guy was going to live forever. You'd never have thought he was dying of a disease old people get.

It was as he was thinking this that a bank of steam rolled out of the shower and attached itself to the mirror, obscuring the image of the handsome man. He gave God props for the metaphor. Not subtle in the slightest. To lose your memory is not just to lose everything you have. It's to lose everything you *are*. It's to lose your very self. What are you without the things you remember?

Mo showered and patted himself dry. He stepped inside a very large closet where his clothes hung in orderly rows on motorized racks. He pressed a button, watched his wardrobe parade past him, then selected a pair of olive brown slacks with a shirt the color of Merlot. He chose a Cartier watch, tucked the designer sunglasses into his breast pocket, and hung a diamond-encrusted cross from a gold chain just below his sternum. The need to look good in public was his last remaining vanity. Lately, it had come to feel more like an obligation.

You could never tell when someone's eyes might narrow in recognition.

Aren't you…?

Didn't you…?

Do I know you from somewhere?

It was their one chance at meeting you, a chance some had dreamt of for 30 years. You owed it to them to validate their imaginings, to look like a star, no matter what you really felt like inside. That was part of the job. Al Green had taken him aside one day and explained that to him. Or maybe it was Teddy Pendergrass.

When he was finished dressing, Mo trotted down to the kitchen and plucked a breakfast bar from a box on top of the stainless steel refrigerator. He leaned against the sink and unwrapped it, knowing Rosalie would have thrown a fit at the sight. She was a big believer in solid breakfasts.

She'd have been appalled at the kitchen, too. Every plate and fork he owned was piled in the sink, the microwave had generations of gluey crud baked into the glass tray, and a week's worth of takeout containers bulged from the garbage pail and stacked up on the floor. The room reeked of decay. Whatever it was in him that enjoyed ruining the furniture was quickly turning the house ramshackle. The place was a mess, just like its owner.

Mr. Clean Freak has left the building, he thought. It gave him a rueful smile.

The phone rang. He scrutinized the Caller ID, which said the call originated in the 213 area code: Los Angeles. Home. Curious, Mo picked up the receiver.

"Hello?"

"Is this James Johnson?" The voice was familiar. He knew this person, but no name leapt to mind.

Mo hardened his voice. "Who is this?"

"Hello, Mosey."

Only one man had ever called him that. "Cooley?" he said.

At the other end of the connection, Arthur Cooley laughed. It sounded like rocks laughing. Mo did some quick math. Cooley had to be—what?—in his 70s by now? Mo had not heard his voice in almost 30 years. Hearing it now swept him back through memory to places he had not been for decades. Not all of them were places he wanted to go.

"How you doing, Mosey?" said the voice on the other end.

Something about it made Mo wary. "I'm doing fine," he said. "How are you?"

"Okay for an old man," he said. "I can't complain."

A silence followed. Mo didn't rush to fill it.

"You still singing?" asked Cooley, after a moment.

"To my toothbrush every morning."

Cooley laughed more heartily than the joke required. "Well," he said, "with the stuff they call music these days, that's probably just as well. Kids don't know what real talent is."

"How you get this number?" asked Mo.

"Wasn't easy. Finally found somebody who knew Tash. She gave it to me. You and her still together? What about the baby? I imagine he's all grown up now."

"He's 19."

Cooley made the appropriate sounds of amazement. "Whoa. Ain't no baby no more. They grow up fast, don't they?"

"Been a long time, Cooley. What's up?" Mo was tired of pleasantries.

There was another silence. Mo waited this one out as well. Finally, Cooley said, "It's Jack."

Mo had known it would be. "What about him?"

"He's got the cancer, Mosey. Prostate."

"Sorry to hear that," said Mo, not sure if he was or not.

"It's bad, Mosey."

"Maybe not," said Mo. "I hear doctors can cure that pretty good if they catch it early."

Cooley's laugh was harsh. "When you ever known Jack Johnson to run to a doctor 'early,' Mosey? He went when he couldn't control his bladder anymore, started pissing himself like a baby. Told me he'd had blood in his urine for weeks."

"How long ago was this?"

"Six months. The doctor says the cancer has spread since then. It's in his bones. Your father is dying, Mosey."

It had been a long time—a lifetime, almost—since Mo had thought of the first James Moses Johnson as his father. They had not spoken in years, not since that day in a rain-swept cemetery when they had faced one another over Ruth Johnson's fresh grave.

"He killed my mother, Cooley."

"Mosey, you know that's not true."

"Isn't it?" Mo stepped to the window and looked out at the woods that cradled the back of the house. A flock of birds bolted from the trees, a scrawny squirrel darted across the lawn. Mo's hands trembled.

"He's your father, Mosey," said the voice in his ear.

"Jack put you up to this?" asked Mo.

"You know better. Sick as he is, he'd kick my ass if he knew I was calling you."

"Send me the bill for the funeral, Cooley. Send it to my accountant."

"That's not why I'm calling, Mo."

"I know. It's the best I can do."

"I don't believe you, Mosey. He's your father and he's dying. Maybe you should get it straight between the two of you. You don't have much time."

"It is straight," said Mo. "Straight as it's ever going to be."

"Mosey, please. Come see him. He'd never say it—you know how he is—but it would mean so much to him."

"Can't do that, Cooley."

"You mean you won't."

"That too."

"Mosey, I'm begging you. For your own sake. You won't have another chance."

"I've got to go, Cooley. Good to hear from you."

"Think about it, Mosey," said the voice on the other end. "Just promise me you'll do that."

Mo said, "Yeah," and put the phone back in its cradle. He held his hands up in front of him. They were fluttering like leaves in a breeze. Amazing that Jack Johnson could still affect him that way, even now.

Jack Johnson. His father had grown up being called "James" or sometimes, "Jimmy." But as a young man, he had begun to insist that people call him "Jack" after the black boxer whose brashness inflamed white folks to the point of street riots back in the early 1900s.

The real Jack Johnson had been the most frightening man in America back in the era when the motorcar was still a novelty. Bad enough he beat up white men and taunted them about it, but he'd also had the temerity to screw white women at a time when white men were stringing black men up in trees for a whole lot less. Johnson hadn't even had the sense to hide it, had gone about with white women on his arm and jewelry glittering on his fingers and hadn't cared much who saw or what they had to say about it.

"He was a man who plowed his own row," his father had told him once in a rare reflective mood. Mo's father, a plowman's son from the Mississippi Delta, had done everything he could to live up to the name he had chosen for himself.

Now he was dying. Standing alone in his kitchen, Mo shrugged. So what? It happened to everybody, didn't it?

Abruptly, he needed to be out of there. He put on the sunglasses, plucked his brown leather bomber jacket from the coat rack and went out to his truck. He cranked the ignition and the engine grumbled to life, the radio playing an old Kool & the Gang song. He stomped the accelerator and the SUV leapt forward, chewing up a long driveway that took its time getting to the street.

Half an hour later, Mo pulled up in the hospital parking lot. He didn't shut off the ignition, just sat there listening to the radio. The voice coming out of the speakers was his—unbearably earnest, startlingly pure.

I see a world where children live on emptiness

And empty men live on war
And lies go by with alibis
Till nobody knows what the lies were lying for
But for all the pain that ever was
I see a world that never was
And I believe, I surely do believe, one day that world we'll see
This is my prophecy

He could see himself in the studio singing those words. A teen-ager with a Fu Manchu moustache, orange dashiki, headphones clamped down over a Big Apple cap that barely contained his sprawling Afro. Mo remembered every detail of that recording session. It had required 11 takes. Tom Ramsey was on bass, Mario on piano. Johnny Tarr on the drums. It was Johnny's last session before Mo fired him for being an unreliable drunk. There was a bad splice on the lead vocal. You would never catch it unless you knew it was there and were listening closely. Mo had wanted to fix it, but the band was way over budget and the company wouldn't pay for another session.

"My Prophecy" had gone to number one in 1974 when he was 19 years old, and stayed there for six weeks. It catapulted Moses Johnson and Momentum to stardom. He had been "The Prophet of Love" ever since.

"WMFJ," the deejay was saying, "playing a better mix of the timely and the timeless. That's Moses Johnson and Momentum giving a little 'Prophecy' from 1974. Before that, we heard the Jackson 5..." Mo shut off the car.

Minutes later, he walked down a featureless white hall somewhere deep in the hospital. He found the right door and pushed it open on a room where a dozen people, most of them older couples, were sitting on orange plastic chairs. He took a seat in the back.

A young blonde woman was addressing the group. She was all smiling teeth and megawatt eyes. "So," she said, "did anyone else want to talk about how it's been this week?"

There was a moment of hesitation. Then, a man raised his hand. He had ruddy skin and a shock of white hair tucked under a Korean War veteran's cap. "It wasn't a good one," he said, patting the hand of a stick-thin woman perched next to him. "Gladys got it in her mind to take a walk. We searched the neighborhood for hours before we found her in some guy's backyard. Like to scared me to death. I thought we had lost her."

"I got a little mixed up," said the stick woman sharply. "I would have found my way. You always make such a big deal out of every little thing."

The man didn't look at her. "So anyway," he told the blonde, "we're thinking maybe it's time we looked into one of those places you were telling us about."

"Don't say 'we,'" snapped the woman. "'We' didn't come up with that. *You* did. Apparently, what I think doesn't matter anymore."

The old man lowered his eyes, his lips pursed. "Yeah, I guess maybe I did," he said, his voice a pebbly whisper. "But I don't know what else to do, honey."

The blonde woman said, "Well, Mr. Morris, remember what we talked about? Sometimes, wandering is caused by anxiety or restlessness. Exercise can be an effective way to deal with that. Mrs. Morris, what do you think? Would you like maybe to start some kind of exercise program? Maybe you and George could take a walk in the afternoon, make it part of your regular routine."

"What *I* would like," she said, "is to be treated like an adult for a change." She folded her arms across her chest and twisted in her seat until her bony knees were pointing away from her husband. He raised his eyes to the ceiling in a pose of long suffering.

The blonde was still mercilessly chipper. "You absolutely have that right, Gladys," she said. "We apologize if anything we've done gives you the impression we don't understand that. We're just trying to figure out ways to make you more comfortable and help keep you safe. Can you help us think of some?"

It was a ploy so transparent Mo wanted to laugh. It was probably in a book somewhere: validate the subject's feelings, give the subject a chance to contribute to solving the problem. He found it hard to believe anybody would fall for it.

But Gladys shifted in her seat and unpinned her arms. "Well," she said, "I can try. As long as I'm not treated like a child. That's all I object to." A man sitting across the aisle with his own wife shot George a look of commiseration.

"So," said the blonde, "does anybody else want to talk about their week?"

And so it went as the second hand of the wall clock swept slowly around. A husband no longer allowed to drive. A wife who almost set the house on fire. A daughter consigning her mother to hospice care. Bickering. Petty. Resentful. Resigned. Dangling at the end of sanity, two inches above can't take it anymore.

Was this what he had to look forward to? Becoming an argumentative child, dangerous to himself and everyone around? Watching blankly while other people decided his life? Waiting for death without even the comfort of someone to lean on? Mo's life had never seemed so empty. Without meaning to, he stood up.

The blonde said, "Please don't go," interrupting a twinkle-eyed grandmother who had been saying how she couldn't watch television anymore because she couldn't follow the storylines. The woman looked back with malice for the source of the interruption.

"I'm sorry, Mrs. Lottsford," the blonde consoled her. "It's just that I saw the gentleman leaving and I had to get him before he went. You remember how it was the first time you came to group, don't you?"

Mollified, Mrs. Lottsford nodded. "I didn't want to be here," she said softly.

To Moses, the blonde said, "You're Mr. Johnson, aren't you? Your doctor's office said you'd be joining us today." She added, for the benefit of the group, "Mr. Johnson is a singer."

Mo braced himself and prayed at the same time. *Please, no Fans. Not right now.*

But he could see in the eyes that swung toward him that he need not have worried. Most of these people were too old to have bought his music. The blonde was too young. He didn't see adulation in their eyes. Just mild curiosity wanting a glimpse of the latest sap unlucky enough to join their miserable ranks.

"He looks awfully young," Mrs. Lottsford said.

"I have early-onset Alzheimer's," said Mo. "It gets you young." And then, to the blonde woman in the front: "Look, I'm sorry. I didn't mean to interrupt. It's just...I can't be here. I'm not ready for..." His hand swept across the faces all looking up at him.

"I understand," said the woman.

"No, you don't," said Mo, surprising himself with his own vehemence. "I'm sorry, but unless you've got it, you do not understand." He saw people in the group nod.

The blonde said, "What I meant was, being in group the first time can be an overwhelming experience. But if you stick with it, it can also be a helpful experience."

"How? You going to let me talk it out, make me feel better about dying?"

The words hung in the air like a bad smell. People lowered their eyes. Maybe they were embarrassed for him. Mo didn't care.

The woman looked straight at him. "Nothing will ever make you feel better about that," she said. "We try to make the time you have left a little easier. And we try to help you deal with the unfinished business, the things you need to put in order."

"My stuff is in order. I updated my will right after I got the diagnosis."

A tolerant smile. "That's good," she said, "but I'm not just talking about paperwork. I also mean this." She was touching her chest. "The emotional part," she said. "We try to help you put that in order. Do you have family, Mr. Johnson?"

Mo's voice was a whisper. "Not really. A son. We're not close."

"How old?"

"Nineteen."

"Have you told him?"

Mo didn't answer.

"You should talk to him, Mr. Johnson. Besides, you're not going to be able to live by yourself after awhile. You need to make some arrangements. You should tell him what your wishes are."

"Yeah," said Mo. He didn't trust himself to say more.

"Dying sucks, Mr. Johnson." The words surprised him. He looked up and saw the blonde smiling, Mrs. Lottsford nodding. "I may not have Alzheimer's," continued the blonde, "but I understand that much. There's one thing about knowing you're going to die. I mean, if you drop dead of a heart attack, it's sudden, it's unexpected, and you leave unfinished business. But if you know the end is coming, it gives you time to put things in order, time to say the things you need to say, time to fix what's broken in your life. You should use that time."

"Before I forget," said Mo.

Another smile. "Yes, Mr. Johnson. Before you forget."

"I've got to go," said Mo. "I can't be here."

"You'll come back?"

"Sure. Yeah." Mo was edging toward the door.

"And you'll think about what I said?"

"Sure," said Mo.

He opened the door and passed down a hallway he didn't see. Got in his car and drove in silence, drove by instinct, the cars and signs and construction workers not even there. He got home without knowing how he had done it, opened his front door, cool darkness enveloping him like a hug. He was exhausted, every step a chore. It felt like he was slogging through mud, ankle deep.

He wanted nothing so much as just to be…gone.

Mo undressed on the way up the white marble staircase, peeling off his shirt, then his pants, leaving them on the stairs. He dropped the Dolce & Gabbana sunglasses. They shattered without his noticing. He took off the Cartier watch, let it fall. By the time he reached the top of the stairs, Mo was clad only in his briefs, walking toward his bedroom with single-minded purpose.

The smell of rot wafted up the stairs behind him, the odor of unwashed dishes and untended garbage and neglect. He didn't care. Caring required energy he no longer had. Mo's bedroom welcomed him. He walked in gratefully, closed the blinds to shut out the offending light of day. Then he sank to his bed. After a moment, he reached to the nightstand and picked up the pistol. Its weight felt good in his hands. The gun was solid, definite, proof that there were still things he could control.

This is why I don't care about putting things in order. This is why I don't worry about coming to terms. I'm not going to be here long enough for it to matter. The disease thinks it's going to kill me? I'll kill us both.

He put the gun to his temple, his finger on the trigger, and made a sound—a child's imitation of a gunshot. For a moment, Mo didn't move. He sat there, suspended on the precipice of finality, on the line between here and gone.

Then he took the gun away. He contemplated it a full minute. Then, feeling as if he were watching himself in a dream, he opened his mouth and shoved the barrel in. It scraped against the flesh at the roof of his mouth. The bullet would travel straight up through his brain. He wouldn't even hear the explosion.

A voice somewhere inside reminded him that he hadn't finished his suicide note. Had not figured out what he wanted to say.

I don't care.

He was tired. So damned tired. Life sat on him like a mountain. Escape was just a millisecond away. Finality would be a blessing. From far away came the sound of a school bus rumbling down the street, children disembarking into the cold. Mo's finger tightened on the trigger. He looked for courage on the ceiling.

The phone rang.

He closed his eyes. So tired.

The phone rang again, that wheedling electronic tone.

The children squealed. The barrel of the gun was painful against his palate.

Again the phone rang.

Mo drew the weapon from his mouth and sat with it in his lap. He lowered his head and allowed the tears to fall. Twice more the phone rang. Finally, he lifted the receiver. "Hello."

Tash was frantic. "Moses? Did you know about this? Why didn't you tell me?"

"Slow down, Tash. What are you talking about?"

"What am I talking about? I'm talking about Trey."

"What about Trey?" Mo felt as if he were underwater, swimming toward a surface that kept receding.

"Did you know about this?"

"Know about what?"

"Philip…" She sounded like she was out of breath. Sounded like she was crying.

"Yeah? Go on."

"Philip, he has a friend who's a cop. Mo, it's not just armed robbery, bad as that is. Somebody was *killed*."

"I know," said Mo.

"You know?"

"Yeah."

"And you didn't tell me?"

"I thought...I thought Trey would..."

But he hadn't, had he? All the words back and forth at the breakfast table yesterday morning and somehow, that hadn't been said. He had not remembered to say.

"I'm sorry," said Mo. "Trey told me. I thought you knew."

"How would I know, Moses? You didn't tell me. Trey doesn't tell me anything. How would I know? Mo, they're investigating this child for *murder*."

"He'll be all right, Tash."

"How can you know that?"

"He didn't do it. He wouldn't do anything like that."

This time, she screamed it. "How can you *know* that?"

There was a silence. A vast, dead silence. Then he said, "I guess you're right. I guess I don't." Another pause. "Hell of a thing," he said, "to have to say that about your own son."

"I hit him," said Tash. Her voice was small. "When I found out, I hit him with my fists. I called him all sorts of names. God, I was so angry. It hurt so much."

"I know," said Mo.

"I don't know what to do, Moses. I swear, I don't know what to do."

"We'll get it straight," he promised. "I still don't believe my son could do something like that."

"But you can't know for sure, can you?"

"You think this is my fault," said Mo. It wasn't a question.

"Mo, I'm not saying..."

"That's okay." Mo glanced down, mildly surprised to find the gun still in his lap. He transferred it to the nightstand. "Maybe you're right," he said. "Maybe it is. I was never there. Yesterday, he said how I trusted him and I believed in him. And I wanted to say, 'Son, I don't even know you.' How fucked up is that, Tash?"

"I wanted to say the same thing," she said. She gave a little laugh that scraped his heart.

"You're the one who was there," said Mo. "You didn't deserve for him to say that to you."

Another quiet interceded. And then Mo said, "I got a call from Cooley today."

"Arthur Cooley? Yeah, I gave him your number. What's that got to do with—"

"No, *listen* to me. I got a call from Cooley. He told me Jack is dying. Cancer. Cooley wanted me to go out there and, I don't know, stand by the deathbed, let bygones be bygones. And you know something, Tash? When he told me, I didn't feel anything. Not a thing. That's my father. I'm supposed to *feel* something, right? I mean, when your father died, even though y'all didn't get along, you felt something. But me, I felt nothing. That's been on my mind all day. I mean, if somebody came to Trey and told him I was dying, would he feel anything?"

"Trey loves you, Moses. You know that."

He spoke right through the consoling words. "What's wrong with us, Tash? Jack was a fucked-up excuse for a father, I became a fucked-up excuse for a father and now Trey..." He didn't finish. Couldn't.

"Moses..."

"They think he's out there robbing people. *Killing* people. And I can't even get indignant and say, 'My son would never do something like that.' Because I don't know. I don't even know my son."

"It's not too late," said Tash.

The words stabbed him. He almost said, "Yes, it is." Instead, he wept.

Tash said, "Moses, are you all right?"

"No," he said, "I'm not."

"What's the matter, Moses? Tell me what's wrong."

He shook his head, then realized she couldn't see. "Hard times," he mumbled.

"Moses," she said.

"I'm going to see my father, Tash. I think Cooley was right. I think I need to do that."

"Well, if that's what you think you have to do..."

"I'm taking Trey with me."

"What?"

"The court didn't put restrictions on his travel."

"But why?"

"I've got to…" He pawed at the words a moment. "I've got to save my son," he said finally. "I've got to save him while I still can."

She didn't answer right away. Mo sniffed at tears, waited. Then Tash said, "I'll pack his things."

seven

Mo had not been on an airplane in 26 years. His last flight had lurched across storm-filled skies for 15 minutes, then dropped so far, so fast, that Mo had gone weightless, body straining up against the seat belt. He was telling himself to be brave, reminding himself that air travel is perfectly safe, when he saw a flight attendant, strapped into her bulkhead seat, make a furtive sign of the cross. She had caught him looking, smiled abashedly, then grimaced and grabbed her seat as another hard shudder rocked the plane. That was it. Fingers locked on the armrest, Mo had vowed that one way or another, this was the last flight he would ever take. For the rest of his career, he had traveled in a luxury touring bus piloted by a former Greyhound driver.

So he pulled up at Tash's house that morning bearing not a receipt for e-tickets, but rather, a backseat full of snack food and auto club maps. The clouds were just becoming visible, hunkering low against the Baltimore skyline, whispering threats of rain.

Mo was in a better mood than he'd have thought possible. Preparing for the long road trip—canceling mail service, getting the car serviced, plotting his route—had awakened something in him, some long dormant sense of the joy to be found in rushing and doing. The joy to be found in purpose. Then Mo recognized the car he was parked behind—Phil's van—and the smile on his face wilted like salad bar lettuce. What was he doing here?

When Mo went to the porch, he heard voices from inside. The words were not intelligible, but the anger was. Mo stabbed the doorbell. Three seconds later, he stabbed it again.

Tash appeared, dressed in her nurse's whites. "Moses," she said. "Thank goodness."

"What's going on?" he demanded, stepping past a duffel bag sitting ready just inside the door.

"It's Trey and Philip," she said. "They've been going at it. I'm afraid they're going to be fighting if they keep up."

Trey dove into view just then, palms raised, mouth ugly in its contortions. "I done told you, man, get the fuck up off me."

Now came Philip, face flushed, eyes flashing. "Who the *hell* do you think you're talking to, boy? You will not use that gutter language to me. You will respect me, and you will respect your mother's house."

Trey turned slowly. He spoke with deliberate clarity. "Fuck you, man," he said.

Philip grabbed a handful of his collar. Trey's fist went back.

"Hey!" cried Mo.

They turned, seeing him for the first time. Their attention full on him, Mo was suddenly aware that he had no idea what to say next. He had yelled only because yelling seemed a requirement. Philip released Trey's shirt. "Moses, your son is angry that I exposed the truth."

Trey jabbed a finger toward Philip. "'Expose' my ass, muh'fucka. You ain't exposed shit. You ain't my father. You ain't nothing to me. You need to get that through your head."

Amazing, thought Mo, how quickly a good mood can go away. Having had so few recently, he mourned its loss even as he spoke. "Trey," he said, "maybe he ain't your dad, but I am. You need to address this man with some respect. You don't use that kind of language toward him."

The expression of disgust that came into Trey's face was so bitter it took Mo a second to pull his eyes away. When he did, he found Philip facing him with crossed arms and pursed lips. He had to command himself to stay calm. Who did this man think he was to look at him from a posture of judgment?

"And Philip," he said, "I appreciate your concern, but I can handle it from here."

Philip's smile was pinned tightly against his cheeks. "Moses, if what you're saying is, this is your business and would I please butt out and let you deal with your son, believe me, there's nothing I would rather do. But I have my daughters to think of."

"Your daughters? What your daughters got do with this?"

"I have to be concerned with what kind of people they spend time with, Moses...what kind of people have a chance to influence them. And with what young Moses here stands accused of doing, I don't know if he's someone I feel comfortable having them around."

A black and featureless anger rose in Mo then, rose so suddenly that it staggered him. He swallowed, feeling as if he might choke. Then he returned Phil's smile. "Your daughters don't piss ginger ale, Phil. It's time you figured that out."

The pinned-up smile popped open. Phil's laugh was curt. "I beg your pardon?"

"How long you and Tash been seeing each other, Phil?"

"Three years. You know that."

"And in all that time, has my son ever misbehaved toward your girls? Has he ever hurt one of them or acted even the slightest bit out of the way toward them?"

"No, of course not."

"Then I don't appreciate you talking shit about what influence he might have on them. Now, if you'll excuse us, we need to get ourselves together and get on the road."

"You can't dismiss me, Moses. This is not your house. It's hers." Eyes on Tash.

She looked from one to the other, and suddenly Mo regretted asking Philip to leave, because he knew what was coming. He saw the surprise in Philip's face an instant before Tash spoke and realized that he knew, too.

She said, "Honey, we're not going to settle anything this way."

It took a moment for disbelief to work its way into his gaze. Disgust followed closely. Philip Reed regarded Tash as if she was something strange and faintly appalling that had attached itself to his shoe. "I see," he said. And then again, "I see. Well, maybe you've got a point."

Philip moved stiffly to the front door, wounded dignity scraping behind him. He plucked his coat from the rack. Tash said, "Philip..." But he was already through the door.

"I thought that fool would never leave," said Trey.

Mo gave him his son the briefest glance. He saw cocky smugness waiting to be seconded. It made him weary. Mo shook his head,
rested a hand on Tash's shoulder. "Are you okay?" he asked.

The eyes she raised to him were large, brown, and moist. "He's
not a bad man," she said.

"I know."

"I mean it, Moses. He has his ways, but Philip is a good man.
He cares about me."

"You going to be all right?"

She nodded. "I'll talk to him. It'll be okay. You two get going.
You're going to hit all that traffic."

She seemed so small. Before he knew what he was doing, Mo
kissed her cheek. He did it tenderly.

When Mo drew back, Tash touched the spot where he had kissed
her, but otherwise, she didn't react. "Drive carefully," she said. "Give
my best to Cooley."

Mo said he would. He picked up Trey's bag and carried it to the
car, leaving his son a few last moments with his mother. Three minutes later, Trey came ambling down the steps, his gait loose and easy.
He climbed into the car, laughing. "'Your daughters don't piss ginger
ale,'" he said, and then clapped his hands and laughed again. "That's
a good one, Dad. I'm gon' have to remember that one."

Mo started the car and accelerated into traffic. It began to rain.
He felt a hundred years old. Was it just 15 minutes ago he had pulled
up to this door smiling? "A man was killed," he heard himself say.

Trey had been reaching for the seek button on the radio, searching for a hip-hop station. He looked up, eyes blinking. Now Mo
yelled it. "A man was killed! You think Philip shouldn't be concerned?
You think we all shouldn't be concerned?"

"I know he was killed," said Trey. "I was there." His voice was
without inflection. He might as well have been reading the phone
book.

"That's all you've got to say?"

"What else you want me to say?"

"Did you do it?"

"The lawyer said—"

"Fuck the lawyer."

"What you mean?"

"I mean, you're my son. If I have to put my hand on a Bible and perjure myself, that's what I'll do. I'll lie my ass off. But right here in this car, you and me for the next four days, we tell no lies. In here, we trust each other with the truth. Those are the rules. Now, you tell me what happened. I need to know."

It took him a moment. When he spoke, his voice was soft. "Fury and DC, they thought we could take off this store. They told me it would be easy."

"God's sake, why you out there robbing a store, Trey?"

"Money. To cut our demo."

"Money. For a demo. Well, goddamn." Mo blew anger out of him in a hard sigh, his head going slowly from side to side. "All this is about some damn demo? Why didn't you just ask me, Trey? Hell, you could have used the studio at the house."

"Yeah, but…I know you don't like that kind of music. Besides, I wanted to do it on my own."

"That's what this is about? That's why a man is dead? Because you wanted to do it on your own?"

"Wasn't nobody supposed to get hurt!" Trey blurted the words.

Mo watched dispassionately. "Did you shoot him?" he asked at last. His mouth was sand.

Trey gasped. "How you ask me that? You know I couldn't do nothing like that!"

"No, I don't. I thought I did, but I don't. Hell, a week ago, I'd have said you couldn't have been out there robbing people. I would have been wrong. So tell me. I need to hear this: Did you shoot the man?"

The radio was thumping but the car seemed deathly silent. Mo reached across and turned off the music. Trey said, "We was supposed to just go in, snatch the money. But then Fury, he start actin' crazy. He hit this woman. He shot the guy. After the guy gave him the money, he still shot him."

Mo shuddered with relief. After a moment he said, "You tell the police this?"

Trey shook his head. "Took your advice. Ain't told them noth-in'."

"*My* advice?"

"Don't you remember? We was watchin' that cop show that time, they had some fool hemmed up, you told me don't never say nothin' to no police."

Mo didn't remember. "Well," he said, "maybe you should talk to 'em. You can cut a deal. Testify against this guy."

Trey gave him a sharp look. "I ain't no snitch."

"No, you're just a punk who shot an innocent man."

"I ain't shot nobody." Trey was indignant.

"The law doesn't care that your hand wasn't on the trigger," said Mo. "You were involved with the robbery. Makes you just as guilty."

"Why you bein' so hardcore, man?"

"I'm trying to save your life," said Mo.

"I'll be a'ight," said Trey.

"The others, they're still behind bars?"

"Million-dollar cash bond? Oh yeah. They gon' stay behind bars till the trial." Trey turned the radio on again. The speakers pulsed with some menacing hip-hop anthem. Mo turned it down, lit a ciga-rette, lowered the window a sliver and sat back to watch fat raindrops thudding against the windshield. About a half-mile ahead, red and blue emergency flashers sparkled against a nickel colored sky. Mo shook his head, succumbing to frustration that was only partially related to traffic. He took a deep drag off the cigarette.

"Them things gon' kill you," said Trey.

"That's not what's going to do it," said Mo.

He saw the questions collect in his son's eyes, waited to see if Trey would ask. And what would Moses say then? How would he respond here in the car where he had just declared there would be no lies between them? He had no idea. So he waited with cool de-tachment to see what his son would do. But Trey did nothing. Just shrugged and went back to bobbing his head as the man in the song boasted about his stable of whores.

They didn't speak again until the accident scene was long behind them and Mo was driving fast through the outer suburbs. Trey said, "How long you figure it'll take us to get out there?"

"Four days. Maybe five."

"You gon' show me where you grew up?"

"This isn't a sightseeing trip," said Mo. He reached across and changed the radio station. Turned the dial until he heard an old Spinners song lifting from the speakers, ice-cream cool and as familiar to Moses as his own face. He and Tash were dating when this came out. The memory brought a smile. "Now this is called singing," he said.

"I know this song," said Trey. "It's called—hold on—'I'll Be Around.'" When Moses gave him a surprised look, he explained, "Mama play this stuff all the time. Some of it ain't too bad. She even play your stuff. You was all right, back in the day."

"Yeah," said Mo. "Back in the day."

Trey didn't answer. He had his eyes closed and his head back, singing with Bobbie Smith of the Spinners. "Whenever you call me, I'll be there. Whenever you want me, I'll be there..."

Mo said, "So what do they call you?"

Trey's eyes came open. "What you mean?"

"I mean, none of you use real names anymore. 'Fury,' 'DC'... What do they call you? What's your street name?"

Trey's smile broke across his face like an especially proud dawn. "Profit," he said.

Mo was surprised. "You mean, like they used to call me? Prophet of Love?"

"That's where I got the idea," said Trey, "but I spell mine with an 'f.' You know, like making ends. Making money. Profit. That's what I'm all about."

A shiver climbed through Mo. It occurred to him that you could just about sum up the entire difference between his generation and his son's with just that one substitution of letters, that one change of dreamers to schemers. "Profit," he said.

On the radio, Bobbie Smith vowed eternal love. "I'll be skippin' and a jumpin'," he sang. "I'll be there."

Trey closed his eyes. "Old school," he said with a smile.

Dog put his keys and wallet in the basket. The uniformed cop inspected them, then waved him through the metal detector. The device didn't beep, but she ran the wand over him just to be sure, pressing it into the folds of his pants and tees and a hoodie several sizes too large for Dog's narrow frame. He held his arms out to the side—"Christ on the Cross" he always called it—and waited while she did what she had to do. It was nothing he had not gone through before. Dog had learned to be patient and wait for it to be finished.

The name wasn't accidental. Raiford Willis looked like a dog. A Doberman, in fact. He was tall and raw-boned, his thin lips twisted into a perpetual smirk, his nose large and protuberant, his eyes small and mean.

When she was satisfied that Dog was clean, the cop checked his driver's license, handed his property back, gave him a pass, and told him how to get to Unit-H. He already knew the way. How many of his homies had he visited down here? But he kept that to himself. It was easier just to wait until she was done. Then he nodded politely and pushed through the double doors.

Dog walked with a slight swagger, an easy gait that claimed wherever he happened to be as his property. Even here, this place of featureless white brick halls. He kept his eyes up, not bothering to see the occasional mothers carrying Kleenex and girlfriends with children in tow who passed him going the other way.

It took Dog only a few minutes to reach the proper unit and then the proper door. He pulled it open and entered the tiny cubicle, not even as large as his closet at home. There was a stool for him to sit on, so he sat, facing a plastic barrier that was scratched and yellow with age. There was a circular metal grill right in the middle for speaking and hearing. After a few minutes, a uniformed cop admitted his brother into an identical cubicle on the other side. Fury was wearing a surly expression and an orange jumpsuit.

Dog leaned toward the grill. "What up, nigger?" he said. He made his voice loud. He knew from experience that you couldn't hear for shit through that grill.

Fury said, "Took you long enough, nigger."

Dog let it pass. Spending four days in this shithole didn't exactly leave you in the best of moods.

"I feel like I'm going crazy up in here," said Fury.

"You got a million-dollar bond, fool. Ain't nobody got that kind of money. You need to just sit tight."

"Fuck 'sit tight,'" said Fury. "That's easy for you to say. You out there."

"Mama said hi. Said tell you she prayin' for you an' shit. She would have been here herself, but her leg acting up."

Sometimes, Mama's leg swelled up so bad that she couldn't get around, even with her cane. She was a janitor at a local high school and Dog knew she had missed so much work already this year because of her leg that she was scared of getting fired.

Mary Willis was the one parent her sons had in common. Dog's father was a small-time stick-up man Dog had never known, unless you counted that time they had run across each other by chance in a prison mess hall. Neither had known the other was in the same lockup. When the officials realized they had a father and son in the same facility, they transferred Dog out. His father had been killed two months later when someone in the yard stuck a shiv in him because of a love triangle with some punk.

Cedric was seven years younger. His father had died before he was even born. Tried to rob a convenience store. The owner had pretended to be opening the register. Then he had come from behind the counter with a shotgun and cut Fury's dad nearly in half.

When they were boys, Fury had pumped his older brother for anything he could tell him about the man. Before long, Dog had run out of things to say and had started making things up. He had turned his brother's father into some kind of bad-ass superhero, some tragic hero out of a movie who only robbed stores so he could feed his family. Truth was, the nigger had a crack habit. But Fury had lapped it up without question and after awhile, Dog had even believed it a little bit himself.

They also had two younger sisters. The girls' father was a bus driver who had died three years ago of a heart attack. Life ain't easy on a black man, Dog mused.

"How long I'm gon' have to be in here?" pressed Fury.

"Till the trial, I guess. Few months."

"Shit," said Fury.

"Shouldn't of messed up," said Dog.

"Just bad luck," said Fury.

"What about your boys? They doin' okay?"

"DC in here. He a'ight. But Profit, he gone already."

"Gone?"

"Bailed out the other day. Cash, I hear. Didn't even use no bondsman."

Dog was impressed. "A million dollars? How he do that?"

"Ain't you heard? His pops got ends. He used to be some kind of big-time singer back in the day."

"No shit?"

Fury shook his head. Dog said, "You get out of here, you should let Profit's pops listen to some of your shit. Maybe he still got some contacts. He might could hook you up."

"Ain't worried about that right now," said Fury.

"Oh? What you worried about, then?"

"I just hope Profit know enough to keep his mouth shut. If he don't say nothin', we can beat this."

"You think he gon' talk?"

"I don't know. He kind of pussy sometime, tell you the truth. Always tryin' to play that hard role, but he soft."

"What the hell you rollin' with him for, then?"

"He been beggin' me to take him out on a job. He DC's boy. DC think he cool."

"But now you havin' second thoughts."

Fury nodded. "Especially with him being out on the street. Done had the first taste of lockdown in his whole life and I'm sure he don't want to come back. He weak. Them the kind the cops can flip."

Dog was irritated. "How many times I told you, you need to be careful who you roll with?"

"You right, but that ain't the point right now."

"So what is the point?"

Fury looked around, then motioned for Dog to put his ear next to the circular grill. Dog leaned in. "The point," said his brother in a harsh whisper, "is if they push him and he give in, I could be looking at the needle. He might give me up to save his own ass."

"You want me to talk to him?"

"Yeah, that be good."

"You probably ain't got nothin' to worry about."

"Feel better when I hear that from him."

"I'll talk to him, then." Fury still looked worried. Boy had always been the nervous type. Dog was reminded of all the times back in the day when he had gone to school to chill some bully who was making his brother's life miserable. Some things never changed.

"Look," he said, "he won't say nothin'. I'll take care of it." He looked into his brother's eyes and said, "I'm on it, okay?"

Fury leaned back, grinning his relief. "All right," he said. "That's what I'm talkin' 'bout."

eight

Sickness has a smell.

Cooley had never known it before, but he knew it now. Sickness smells warm and rotting. It is the odor of living flesh going bad like meat left out too long. And it doesn't care how much scrubbing you do or how much air freshener you spray. It burrows into your clothes and hair, violates your very dreams, until you smell it everywhere. You'd think you'd get used to it, but you don't.

This morning, as every morning for the past six weeks, Cooley awoke to that smell. He lit a cigarette—the smoke masked the scent—and lay in bed staring at the ceiling, massing strength for the day. Wishing he was home. Not that home was far. Cooley lived across the street, two doors from the corner. He had lived there 49 years, had given his first money order to his current landlord's grandfather.

But for the last six weeks, Cooley had been caring for Jack during the day and sleeping in Mo's old room at night. He hated Mo's room. It was like sleeping in a museum, a shrine to a boy who no longer existed.

Mosey had to be—what?—almost 50 by now? Yet his bedroom was still waiting for a teenager to come slouching in from school. Old 45s and comic books stacked neatly in boxes, old clothes falling to pieces on their hangers, trading cards stacked and bundled on the dresser, poster of Gladys Knight & the Pips smiling down from the wall. Jack had not touched the room in more than 30 years—30 years!—except to sweep the floor and knock down the cobwebs.

How stubborn could one man be? But Jack was determined the room not change. Never change. Even when he finally accepted Cooley's offer to move in, to be with him in these last hours of his life, Jack had warned, in that voice like an angry power saw, not to mess with any of Mo's things. You'd have thought, mused Cooley, that Jack was the one doing *him* the favor. Ungrateful son of a bitch. This thought was not without affection.

The only hint of Cooley in the room was the aluminum ashtray in which he rested his cigarette and, on the floor at the foot of the bed, a valise containing that day's change of clothes. He had not moved many of his own things from across the street, preferring to shuttle back and forth as needed. Even at that, Cooley felt like an interloper.

He was glad Jack didn't know about the call to Mosey or that Mosey had refused to come. It would have killed him to know, taken away whatever fight was left in him. Jack never said it, never even talked about it, but Cooley knew that, even this late in the game, he was still holding out hope his son would come back home. It was as if he thought he could *will* it to happen.

In the next room, Jack coughed. It went on for a long moment. Even through the wall, Cooley could hear the violent rattling in his best friend's chest. When the racking sound finally subsided, he heard Jack moan in his sleep. Cooley sucked deeply on the cigarette. God, he needed a drink.

Sometimes, he thought that was the hardest part of the whole thing. The not drinking. The being stone cold sober so he could check the feeding tubes and change the diaper and clean the sores. It was God's own bitter joke. Just when he needed a drink the most, he couldn't have one. When Jack died, Cooley was going to get blind drunk and stay that way for a week.

With a great grunt of exertion—he was well above 6 feet tall and weighed more than 300 pounds—Cooley hauled himself out of the bed. He threw a robe on over his underwear and went to check on his best friend.

Cooley stood over Jack's bed—it was a hospital bed with railings—and regarded this man he loved better than a brother. Jack had always been a small man—back in Mississippi, people called the two of them Laurel and Hardy—but the cancer had made him smaller still, had caved him in on himself. Looking at his body, you could see where tibia met patella met femur, make an accurate count of his ribs. Jack himself had joked that he would never need another X-ray. Shine a strong flashlight on him and you could see anything you needed to see. He had become a see-through man.

Cooley touched him and announced himself. "Jack? It's me."

You could never tell if he was with you or not, so Cooley liked to talk to him just in case. Just to remind them both that this was still a human being. He never wanted to catch himself treating Jack like a thing, a chore to be done. Cooley pulled latex gloves from a dispenser on the nightstand and snapped them into place.

"Going to check you out, buddy."

In the beginning, he had not been able to make himself do it. The hospice nurse had patiently coached him through it. It was still difficult, but he managed. Cooley pulled back the covers. With gentle hands, he lifted Jack's toothpick shoulders and maneuvered him onto his side. Then Cooley pulled back the waistband of the adult undergarment and looked inside. It was clean and dry. He wasn't surprised. Sometimes—the bad days—Jack couldn't help himself, but for the most part, his stubborn pride didn't allow him to soil that damn diaper. He would make the walk to the bathroom if it killed him, tottering like a one-year-old, his hand weightless in Cooley's.

"Hey, you're clean, buddy," he said, hoping Jack heard him, hoping the news would buoy him.

On the days he couldn't make it, the days he had to submit to the indignity of being cleaned by other hands, Jack sometimes wept. "A man can't wipe his own ass, he ain't a man no more," he had told Cooley once. Cooley had shushed him and gone on cleaning.

Jack wasn't responsive today, so Cooley situated him on his back and pulled the covers back up. "Going to get me some breakfast, buddy," he said. "I'll check in on you in a minute." He wasn't expecting a response, so he was surprised when Jack's hand landed on his. Cooley turned. Jack's eyes were open.

"You want something, buddy?"

Jack swallowed. "Cooley," he said. You had to lean close to hear his voice.

"Yeah?"

"Moses?"

Cooley was paralyzed. Lord, did Jack think his son was standing here? The hospice nurse had warned him to be on the lookout for signs of dementia. Cancer patients sometimes hallucinate, she said. Cooley was still trying to decide how to answer when Jack swallowed again. "Moses," he said, more firmly. "I want you to call Moses."

Stunned, Cooley searched his friend's eyes. Jack nodded. "Call him. Tell him about"—the hand waved limply above a frame so emaciated that it barely dented the sheets—"this. Tell him to come. So I can see him one more time before..." The thought didn't need finishing.

A crushing sadness hammered Arthur Cooley then. Beat him down as surely as big men with blackjacks and brass knuckles. In that moment, there was nothing he would not have done to avoid saying the truth. But he couldn't do that, couldn't lie to his friend, couldn't treat him, especially now, as something less than a man.

"I already called him," said Cooley. "Yesterday."

"You did?" Jack didn't try to hide his excitement. For as long as Cooley had known him, which was the great majority of their lives, Jack had held close to himself any emotion that might make him vulnerable. But with the disease, he seemed to wear his feelings right out on his skin. Maybe he couldn't help himself. Maybe he just didn't care anymore.

Cooley sighed. "Yeah, I called him. Jack, he said he wouldn't come."

You could see in his eyes the words sinking slowly in. After a moment Jack said, "I guess ain't nothing changed, then. Stupid of me to think it would."

"Ain't nothing stupid about wanting to see your boy, Jack."

"Boy?" A rasping laugh. "He damn near 50 years old, Cooley."

"Nothing stupid about wanting to see your *son*," insisted Cooley.

"He stopped being my son the day I killed his mother," said Jack.

"Jack, you didn't—"

Jack stopped him with a cutting look. "Yeah, I did. You know it, I know it, he know it." A pause. "God know it, too," he said.

The coughing started again, an ugly wet sound. Jack plucked a tissue from the box on the crowded nightstand and spat into it. There was blood in the phlegm.

Cooley said, "Do you want me to call him again?"

"Ain't told you to call him the first time. You done that on your own. Why you askin' now?"

Cooley smiled at this flash of the old Jack, but he wasn't fooled by it. He knew how much it had taken for Jack to ask him to make the call, knew it for the painful thing it was: an admission of need, the kind of admission Jack Johnson did not make. And then to hear that his son would not come to see about him? Even now, would not come?

It hurt. Cooley knew this, so he didn't speak. Just stood there, waiting. Jack looked a million years old. The skin on his face was taut. You could make out the contours of his skull. Death was coming up the front walk at a brisk clip, whistling merrily.

"I'm tired, Cooley," said Jack after a moment. "I need to rest a bit. And then I'm gon' get up from here and kick your ass."

Cooley obliged him with a laugh. "Got to bring some to get some," he said. But Jack's eyes were already closed. After a moment, the covers began to rise and fall in a frail and unsteady rhythm.

Cooley watched a moment. Then he drew his robe tight and left the room. He went out the door and stood at the top of the long exterior stairwell that ran down to the street. The morning sky was silver, the sun not yet strong enough to burn away the haze. It was warm but not too hot, palm trees swaying above a busy side street where every house had heavy black bars on the windows and doors.

From somewhere down the block, a radio station was playing a song in Spanish, some man singing a slow, tortured ballad. Forty years ago, you never heard Spanish in this part of town. The radio station would have been KGFJ—"the big K, soulin' in the city" chirped the jingle singers—and the music would have been Temptations or Sam and Dave or maybe Aretha. This had been an all-black neighborhood—Negro, as they said back then. But many of the blacks had left, pushed out by the Mexicans. Lots of people didn't like Mexicans, but some of them were pretty nice people, he'd found.

Cooley cried. His shoulders shook with the force of it.

Stop it. Seventy-five years old, blubbering like a baby.

That only made it worse. But it just wasn't fair. Dying, he could accept. Everything that lived, died. But it wasn't fair of God to shrivel Jack up like that, to let some evil disease eat him piece by piece. It was spiteful, is what it was.

Small as he was, Jack had always shaped events, rather than let them shape him.

They had met as boys the day Jack transferred into Booker T. Washington, the colored high school Cooley ran as his personal kingdom. King Cool, he called himself as he held out his meaty palm, exacting tolls for use of "his" hallway, "his" water fountain, "his" lunchroom. Cooley was bigger than any of them, so he rarely had to ask twice. On the rare occasions some fool stood up to him, that fool wasn't standing for long.

Cooley had knocked Jack down the first time he saw him, walking in a crowded hallway during the change of classes. This wasn't for anything Jack had done, but just to let him know whose school this was. Cooley stood over the new boy, who lay sprawled and surprised on the linoleum. "Don't get up till I say you can," he said.

Jack got up.

It was an act of defiance so unthinkable Cooley had trouble processing it. "Ain't you heard me? This is King Cool talking to you, boy. I said, 'Don't get up.'"

He pushed the smaller boy again, but Jack was braced this time and didn't fall, so Cooley hooked a leg behind his calf and gave another shove. Jack went down to the linoleum again. "Now look," Cooley said, staring down the length of his index finger, "I done told you, don't get—"

Before he could get the warning out, Jack was on his feet. A crowd was gathering, drawn by this rare act of insolence. Cooley could think of only one thing to do. He swung without another word, his massive fist arcing in toward the new boy's face. Except that the new boy was no longer there. To Cooley's surprise, Jack had ducked under the big right arm. As it whooshed harmlessly over his head, he sprang up again on the other side and planted his left fist hard in Cooley's kidney. He hooked Cooley's arm to keep it immobile, and hit him in the same spot twice more.

Cooley forgot himself, eyes shutting in a furious grimace, lips hissing an outraged curse as he reached for the spike of pain in his lower back. When his eyes opened again a second later, he had just enough time to register a curious sight. A schoolbook, *Introduction to Geometry*, was coming toward his face. There was an audible crunch as it struck his nose. Cooley's hands came up to his face to catch the first gush of blood.

"By dose!" he cried. "You broke by dose!"

Jack mocked him, laughing. "By dose," he taunted. "You done broke by dose!"

To Cooley's horror, the other kids picked up on it. Suddenly he was surrounded by them, boys he had locked into lockers, boys whose faces he had shoved into toilets, boys he had hung up on coat racks, all of them holding their noses and chanting the same humiliating thing.

"By dose! You done broke by dose!"

Cooley did the only thing he could. He ran and didn't stop running until he reached the nurse's office. He was suspended for a week. Jack got a day, but that was mainly for show. Everyone knew who had started the fight. Everyone knew who had finally gotten what he deserved.

When Cooley came back, he was wearing a heavy pad of gauze on his wounded nose. If he'd had his way, he would never have returned to Booker T. Cooley spent that day trying to make himself small, trying to be invisible. He saw them looking at him, saw the laughter in eyes that had once beheld him with fear. The day dawdled in its passage.

Cooley was standing at his locker when he saw Jack and another boy approaching. He did everything but climb inside, reaching deep into the recesses of the messy little box, pretending he was too busy searching for a book to even notice them.

It didn't work. As they came abreast of him, the boy—Sheldon, a beanpole who had always paid the hallway toll without a word of complaint—put his hand to his face and said it. "By dose! He done broke by dose!"

Sheldon looked over to Jack then, as if for validation and Cooley knew with a sickening certainty who was the new king of the hallways. But Jack did a strange thing. He shrugged as if none of it were very important anymore. Sheldon's expectant grin melted to sheepish disappointment. He shifted awkwardly in the silence, then walked away. Jack turned to follow him, then paused and leaned toward Cooley.

"You might as well telegraph them punches," he said.

There was no taunt in it. Just a simple tip, a word of advice like you might get from a math teacher. He was gone by the time Cooley remembered to close his mouth.

They became friends after that. Not all at once, but eventually. The way Cooley saw it, he really had no other choice. The guy had kicked his ass and made it look easy. He could never be King Cool again, never again command that kind of fear. He could either sulk about it or he could set about learning to be something else. So he did.

Besides, the new boy intrigued him. Even by the less than lofty standards of Buford, Mississippi, Jack Johnson was poor. It didn't take anyone too long to figure that out. They had the rotation of his wardrobe down after the first week: one pair of jeans, two shirts, and a pair of mud-spattered brogans two sizes too big for him with cardboard stuffed in to cover the places where the sole had worn through.

Yet despite that, Jack soon became one of the most popular guys in school. He could talk to anyone about anything, had a great sense of humor, seemed at home in the middle of a crowd. People liked him without stopping to wonder why.

Jack, Cooley came to believe, was a fellow everybody knew and yet nobody knew. Charm was a light switch he flipped off and on. Cooley had never met anyone as self-possessed, anyone who needed other people so little, even as he seemed to draw them to him without apparent effort. He was a guy who could laugh and talk with the fellows, flirt with the girls, leave everybody smiling, and make you think what you saw on the surface was all there was to him.

But Cooley soon came to realize that Jack kept most of himself for himself. It was in the questions he didn't answer, the silences he

didn't bother to fill. He would talk easily and at length about Satchel
Paige's fastball and how the Japs and the Nazis better hurry up and
end this scrap before he got over there and made them wish they'd
never been born. But ask him where he came from, ask him what his
folks did, ask him what he wanted to do when he got out of school,
ask him who he *was*, and he grew quiet, then resentful. Push him on
it any harder and he got mean, his eyes flashing warning signs just
before he cut you to pieces with some verbal shot as hard and well-
aimed as a jab to the kidneys.

It wasn't until Cooley had known Jack for almost six months
that his friend invited him home. And that was out of embarrassment; Jack had passed so many afternoons at Cooley's playing stick-
ball and listening to radio and joining the family for dinner that it
had become awkward. One day, Cooley's grandmother, Miss Maple,
a surly old woman whose mouth was always wet and black with
snuff, finally asked Jack, "Do you *have* a home, boy? Seem like every
time I look up, you over here."

She had laughed as if to say she was just joking, but she wasn't.
Anybody could see that. Cooley had shot a glance at his mother,
who rolled her eyes. It had taken Jack a moment to answer. Finally
he said, "Yes, ma'am, I got a home."

He said nothing more about it the rest of the afternoon, but
the next day as school was getting out, he tapped Cooley on the
shoulder. "Let's go to my house," he said. Cooley made the mistake
of allowing his surprise to show. "Come on," snapped Jack. "You
wanted to see."

So Cooley followed him home. They wound through the colored neighborhoods that clustered around the school, past the barber
shop, the doctor's office, and the barbecue stand in the little commercial strip that served colored. They crossed the railroad tracks
that carried freight trains rumbling through town without stopping,
passed through downtown, where shop windows were full of manne-
quins modeling men's suits and women's hats and the marquee of the
movie theater announced that *Double Indemnity* was playing twice
a night. They skirted white neighborhoods where people sometimes
set their dogs on you for fun, cut across the service station lot, and
came to the main highway.

Concern began to gnaw at Cooley. It had not occurred to him the walk would be so long. He was going to be very late getting home and he knew that might result in a chewing out, maybe even a licking. It occurred to him to ask how much further they had to go, but a glance at the grim set of Jack's jaw changed his mind. His friend hadn't spoken a word since motioning Cooley to follow and Cooley knew, without knowing how, that it would not be a good idea to say too much.

So he waited until a Hamm's brewery truck had rushed past, then followed Jack across the blacktop. Stray balls of cotton had gathered like snow in the creases of the highway and the truck's passage stirred them up so that they floated about Cooley's head like fireflies. The sky was just beginning its long, slow slide toward evening. They plunged into the barren cotton fields on the far side of the road, Jack leading along a well-worn path through bristly brown stalks that, only a few months before, had bloomed full and white.

And still they walked, tramping through black soil until you couldn't see the buildings of town anymore, until you couldn't even hear the mutter of traffic from the road. Cooley was about to break his silence when he saw it. A cluster of tar paper shacks huddling together in a clearing in the fields. They faced one another across a dirt lane where three barefoot children played. An old woman sat in a chair before one of the shacks, smoking a pipe. It was only when they came abreast of her that Cooley realized she was blind.

She turned in the direction of their footfalls. "That you, Master Jack?" she asked.

"Yes'm."

"Who that with you?"

"This here Cooley. Me an' him go to school together."

She extended a hand so bony it reminded Cooley of a chicken foot. He took it gently, shook it once. The hand was knotted, the skin dry and cool.

"Hello, Master Cooley," she said.

"Pleased to meet you, ma'am," he told her.

"He in there?" asked Jack, looking toward the last shack in the row.

"Yeah."

"Been drinkin'?"

"Yeah, but I think he sleep. Passed out."

Jack turned to Cooley. "My father," he said. "Work like a mule when the cotton high. Drink like a fish when it's all picked."

He started forward. Cooley held back without meaning to and Jack stopped. "What you waitin' for?" he asked. "Come on, you wanted to see."

"I'm sorry," said Cooley, not knowing what he was apologizing for, not moving.

Jack took him by the arm. "Come *on*," he said, and pulled Cooley to the last shack on the row. They stood together in the doorway. Shadows hunched in the corners of the room, the only light entering from two glassless windows. An old roof shingle was nailed to the wall above each for protection from the weather. There was a cot on either side of the room. Running the width of the room between them was a string upon which hung a threadbare sheet, at this moment pushed back to the wall. Lying face down on one cot was a dark man who looked like Jack, except that he had a moustache and thinning hair and his skin was oily with sweat.

"My father," said Jack. "Willie Johnson."

Cooley nodded, looking around. The fireplace was littered with the remains of long-ago fires. A cookpot hung on the wall to one side. The room held a table and three chairs.

"You wanted to see," repeated Jack. "You all wanted to see, so see."

"I didn't mean…" began Cooley.

Jack waved at him as he would a gnat. "Don't really matter what you meant, do it? None of you."

"Your mama, is she—"

"She a maid. Work for some doctor in town. Won't be back for a couple hours."

Without really knowing why, Cooley said, "I got some old shoes you could maybe wear. They beat up a little, but—"

"I don't need your help," said Jack. "Don't want it. You see, what none of you niggers understand is, it don't matter none where you start in life. What matter is where you finish. You hear me?"

"Yeah," said Cooley. "All right."

Jack watched him closely—for signs of condescension, Cooley thought—then nodded. "Come on," he said.

They went back out and stood in the lane. Darkness was creeping in from the east. One of the children was squalling now, sitting alone in the dirt crying his eyes out. "Tyrone, you hush up that noise," said Jack. "Give me a headache."

The little boy fell obediently silent. Cooley said, "I got to get home. My folks be lookin' for me."

"Yeah," said Jack. He didn't move.

Cooley glanced over at him, waiting. Out of nowhere, Jack said, "You think they ever gon' have a colored president?"

The question surprised Cooley. "Of America, you mean?"

Jack nodded. "Yeah. Like when we get old, maybe."

Cooley thought about it no more than two seconds. "No," he said, "not even when we get old. White folks ain't gon' never allow nothin' like that."

"You probably right," said Jack. "But you know what? I'm gon' be somethin' big someday. You remember I said that. Might not be president, but I'm gon' be somethin' big."

Jack looked at him and Cooley had that feeling again, like his response was being carefully weighed. He nodded. "I ain't got a doubt in the world," he said. And he didn't.

"Come on," Jack said. "I'll walk you back out to the road."

Jack quit school two months later, lied about his age and joined the Army. A day after, Cooley did the same. They never saw any Japs. Instead, they wound up in the same company of stevedores and spent the balance of the war unloading American ships in Britain. When they were discharged, Cooley came back to Buford. Jack caught a bus to L.A.

"Who you know in L.A.?" Cooley asked.

"Colored have it better out west," Jack said.

Cooley didn't hear from him for a few years. Then one bright spring day came a letter from Jack asking Cooley to stand beside him at his wedding. Jack wrote that he had met the girl of his dreams—Ruth, a high-toned Creole from Louisiana—and was ready to settle down. Cooley had taken Greyhound out to L.A. for the wedding, liked what he saw, and never went back.

Those first days were good ones. And sometimes Cooley wondered: If he'd known everything that was to come, would he still have stayed? Or would he have run back to Mississippi as fast as Greyhound could carry him?

It was the shattering of glass that drew Cooley back to himself. The Mexican balladeer was still singing his plaintive song, old cars were still lumbering on the street. It took a moment before he realized the sound had come from inside.

Cooley threw open the door and rushed in, breathless with the thought of what he might find. He pulled up short. Jack was leaning against a wall. At his feet, a table was upended. The photograph that had sat on it lay a few feet away. Mosey, wearing his junior high school graduation suit, smiled up through cracked glass. Cooley's relief was ushered aside by his anger.

"Jack! How many damn times I done told you to call me when you need to go to the toilet? You gon' fuck around and hurt yourself, just being stubborn."

Cooley waited for Jack to say, *Kiss my ass.* A good, hard shot like the day they met. But there were no hard shots left in the eyes that Jack Johnson raised to his friend. There was only a sorrow that went down for miles. "Cooley," he said, "I think I'm going to need you to do me a favor. A real big favor."

Cooley's eyes widened. Because he knew what the favor was. Lord help him, he knew. He wanted urgently to say no. *No, Jack, I won't end your misery. No, Jack, I won't take your life.*

But how could he? This was his friend, his best buddy in all the world. This was the man who had saved his life.

Cooley's throat was dry. He barely recognized the sound of his own voice. "Sure, Jack," he said. "Anything you want."

nine

"What you writin'?" asked Trey. He nodded toward the legal pad propped against the steering wheel.

Mo glanced up, surprised. He had been so engrossed in the words flowing from his pen that he had not even heard his son climb into the car. The Escalade sat in the parking lot of an IHOP in southwest Indiana under a cold sun. Mo was pleasantly full after a big breakfast, the gas tank was topped off, and the road awaited. Trey had stopped to use the facilities and Mo had thought to use the time to work on his suicide note.

"Nothing," he said now, turning the legal pad over. Then, seeing the questions rising in Trey's eyes, he said, "Writing a song, that's all."

The face lifted, questions banished. "Really. That's tight. Can I see?"

"Maybe when I finish," said Mo. He slid the pad into the well of the driver's side door. He would have to pack it away in his bags the first chance he got. Foolish of him to let Trey see. Foolish to raise suspicion.

Mo turned the key. The disc in the CD player came in loud enough to drown the engine. A menacing horn, a bass drum hammering home the point, Eddie Levert growling like something pacing a cage. Then the three voices bringing home the chorus. "Put your hands together. Put your hands together, and let us pray."

Mo turned toward the highway, singing with the O'Jays. Late 1973, he thought. Early '74. That would have been just before he signed the contract with Ransom Records. He'd opened for the 'Jays in '74. Levert telling ribald jokes in a hallway backstage. His partner, Walter Williams, cool as jazz in a white suit. "Knock 'em dead, kid," he'd said, pumping Mo's hand just before the MC called Mo's name.

And Mo standing there with his mouth open, brain trying but unable to process the fact that he was hanging out backstage with the O'Jays.

It had happened so fast, success. Had come to him and gone from him like nothing. An eye blink. A lightning flash. Like life itself, he thought.

"You ever miss it?" said Trey.

Mo was startled. Had he spoken out loud? "Miss what?" he asked.

Trey pointed to the stereo. "This," he said. "Old school."

A laugh. "That's what you kids call it," said Mo, accelerating into the fast lane. "Like it's something you keep on a shelf under glass. I'll tell you something: it wasn't old school to us. It was just what we listened to, what was on the radio while we were living life."

Trey persisted. "You ever miss it?"

"It never went away," said Mo. "Not from me."

Trey nodded, looking sage. Then he said, "When did you know you wanted to be a singer?"

"I always was a singer," corrected Mo. "My mom said I'd start kicking in the womb when certain songs came on. Music is all I ever wanted to do."

"I know how you feel," said Trey.

"Oh, really?"

"Yeah. I feel the same way."

"It's not the same," said Mo. "The music isn't the same."

"Yeah, but the feeling is," Trey insisted.

Mo let it ride, concentrated on the fat tires of the SUV chewing up Indiana countryside, pulling Illinois closer. He supposed his son was right. The feeling was probably the same going back as far as you cared to go. To Motown. To Elvis. To Billie and Frank, Satchmo and Duke. To the first beat of the first drum.

Trey said, "You want to hear some of mine?"

"What?" Mo was distracted.

"This joint me and my crew was workin' on. You want to hear?" He was eager like a schoolboy with an A on his homework. And Mo realized, distractedly, that he'd never seen any of Trey's homework. So many things missed.

He nodded toward the CD player. "Put it in."

Trey reached around to the back seat and fished a disc out of his bag. He ejected the O'Jays and replaced it with a disc bearing the logo of an office supply store and the words, "Street Gang" in black marker. After jabbing the forward button a couple of times to locate the right track, Trey sat back, waiting for the music, watching his father for a reaction.

It was the last thing Mo would ever have expected.

Mario Gaines came up playing a piano phrase as familiar to him as his own face, a plaintive bleat of anguish shot through with a wah-wah effect from the guitar. Mo had just turned to his son to ask the question when he heard his own voice, pure and earnest and long ago. "It's my prophecy," he sang. It lingered there half a beat, his voice, his words, flung into a void of expectant silence.

Then a vengeful drum nailed Mo to his seat and he heard the shout-outs from unfamiliar voices.

Drive By Records, all up in this bitch!
Bout to get deep in here, nigger!
Check it!

Another drum shot. And then Trey's voice, pinched and hard.

Son of a man
Can you feel me, son?
Ton of a man
He a real deep one
Prophet sigh, Prophet say
But here come I, a brand new day
Brand new way
Brand new pay.
Can you feel me, son?
Can you feel the one?
You niggers know what I'm talkin' about?

Mo hit the pause button. "What in the hell is this?"

Trey pressed play. "Listen," he said.

Gettin' mine straight off the top
Bens and friends and sparkling rocks
Should'a been a friend to me

Now I run the treasury
Balls of steel and my dick's a Glock
Try me if you will, get your ass on lock
You think you he-men,
But I seen you drinkin' semen
Got no way to defend
Cause I'm the real deal
You niggers just pretend
I got money stacked in piles
Cash flowin' for miles
All you fools jockin' my style
You can't own it
Can't control it
This ain't puppetry
It's my profit, see?

Then Mo's voice: "It's my prophecy."

Trey's voice: "It's my profit, see?"

Mo's voice. "My prophecy."

Trey's voice. "My motherfuckin' profit, see?"

Mo hit eject. Trey looked over in surprise. "You ain't like it?"

Mo reeled. He had to remind to remind himself to watch the road.

"What is—" hand making circles, trying to pull down the right word—"that?"

"It's my theme song," said Trey. "I call it "My Profit, See." You know, like, after your song. Only I changed it up."

"You can't…"

Lord, have mercy.

"You can't do that."

Trey was mystified. "Why I can't?"

"It's my song."

"Yeah, I know that, but—"

"It's my *song*, Trey."

In truth, he had always thought of it as Tash's song. After all, he had only written it to impress her.

"Why don't you write something that *means* something?" she had demanded of him one afternoon from under the brow of that soft Afro. They were walking on the pier in Torrance on a cool Saturday in October. The Pacific Ocean was a grimy blue and gulls were circling above something dead on the sand below.

"What do you mean?" asked Mo. Actually, he didn't care what she meant. He had only asked the question because some response seemed necessary. And because he didn't want her to look too closely and realize she had just stomped his heart.

Mo had been walking his demo tapes out to Hollywood for a month now, haunting lobbies, waiting outside fancy restaurants, putting his music into the hands of anyone who looked like anyone. Now it had paid off. Sort of. Someone from a tiny outfit called Ransom Records had called to say she liked his voice, but did he have any originals? Everything on the tape was Mo singing someone else's song.

In as breezy a voice as he could manage considering that he could barely breathe, he had assured the woman that, yes, he had hundreds of original songs. She said she'd like to hear some of them. He promised to make her a tape.

Then Mo hung up the phone, picked up a notepad, and started writing his very first song.

Three weeks later, he had a dozen tunes, including the one he had played for Tash, a song he was especially proud of. It was a love song, but more than that, it was a song about her and how he had come to feel for her. He called it "Forever, For You."

Tash hardly heard it.

It was a week since the "Saturday Night Massacre," when Richard Nixon fired the attorney general and then the deputy attorney general because neither would fire the special prosecutor who had subpoenaed Watergate-related tape recordings. The country was in an uproar and Tash was in an agony of anger. Before Mo could find words to suggest that what he had played for her *did* mean something, she went off on a tirade about Nixon. This segued without pause into a diatribe on the war in Southeast Asia, the burning of U.S. cities, and white men who went to the moon while black children starved on Earth.

He had heard her do it before. She could rant for 20 minutes without taking a breath. But never had she done it as he was trying to play her a song that expressed his heart. He was hurt. Then hurt became anger.

Write something that means something, she had said.

Fine, then. He would do that.

He had never been a good student. Not because he was dumb, but because he was uninterested. Indifferent. If he could get C's in algebra, geography, social studies, without half trying, he couldn't see any reason to knock himself out striving for As. But English was different. Words had always come easily to him. He heard rhythm in language, cadences that reminded him of music.

So he closeted himself in his room, sculpting language that would encompass everything he felt—more important, everything *Tash* felt—about a world of lies and alibis, incidental cruelties and monstrous hypocrisies that betrayed, with a car dealer's smile, noble ideals that had been etched in parchment two centuries before. He picked out a melody—Mo had never learned to read or write music—on the guitar he had bought with money earned sweeping the stockroom at Wong's Liquor.

It took him two weeks. When he sang it for Tash, she cried.

A year later, Mo recorded that song as a filler track on his second album for Ransom Records, *Moving Forward.* The first single from that album was supposed to have been a dance song called "Look What Your Love Has Done," but instead, the deejays started playing the B-side, that filler tune he had written to impress his girl. "My Prophecy" exploded, launching him from opening act to headliner literally overnight.

It turned out to be a very quick career. Three multiplatinum albums in the mid-'70s, followed by six albums of increasingly pointless disco and techno stretching into the mid-'80s, trying to recapture whatever it was people had loved about him, but never able to do it. The last album was *The Moses Johnson Project* in 1984. When it failed to chart, the record label called him in and told him it was releasing him from his contract. Mo was distraught, but not really surprised. No other offers worth pursuing presented themselves and Mo had retired unceremoniously to the oldies circuit.

He couldn't complain. He'd had the multiplatinum albums; he'd seen the world several times over; and he'd had that one song, the one that made Tash cry, the one that made him "The Prophet." Over the years, it had only become bigger. *Rolling Stone* named it one of the 100 Greatest Rock Songs of All Time; *Billboard* called it "the last great protest song." Thirty years later, people still came up to him, pumping his hand and saying, "Thank you."

Outside of fathering Trey, "My Prophecy" was the one thing Mo had done in life that mattered. It wasn't just a hit song: it was a work of art—all the critics, everyone said so. No matter what else happened to him, he had done this one thing that meant something, written this one song that said something that mattered. And now his own son wanted to turn it into some rap shit about money…

It's my profit, see…

Mo shook his head slowly. Became aware of Trey watching him. Opened his mouth. Closed it.

"What?" said Trey.

"That song means a lot to me," said Mo finally.

"I know that," said Trey.

"No, you don't. Else, you couldn't have done what you did."

"What you mean?"

Moses sighed. "Listen to me, Trey. If a man is lucky, he achieves something in this life he can leave behind. Something that makes him proud. Something people remember him by. That's what "My Prophecy" is. Not just a hit. I had other hits. But "Prophecy" is the song that made people call me an artist. It's the one that made them think I was great. Do you understand?"

He could see from Trey's face that he did not. Mo rested his hands on top of the steering wheel. The road flew by. A fleet of black clouds sat fat and waiting on the horizon. They would be in rain soon.

"You have to understand what the world was like back then," he said. "People were scared. Everything was falling apart. Nothing seemed to make sense anymore. And that song, well…people said it gave them hope."

Mo glanced at his son, searching for comprehension. Trey gave back a scowl. "The song means something," said Mo, mumbling. "And not just to me."

"You saying you ain't want me to use it."

"You made it a song about getting paid."

Trey turned fathomless eyes to his father and repeated himself. "You saying I can't use it."

If only he knew how many people Mo had turned down for the use of that song. People selling sodas, shoes, luxury cars, all waving big checks for the privilege. Sixteen years before, some kid singer had sampled "My Prophecy" without permission.

"Sue him till his eyes bleed," Mo had told his attorney. "Make him stop."

The attorney reminded Mo that his finances had seen better days. Maybe, he said, it would make sense to demand a settlement—money up front and a piece of the action. He happened to know the kid's record company would be open to such an arrangement.

Mo had looked the attorney hard in the eye. "Make him stop," he repeated.

Now he gave his son the same look. "That's right," he said. "I don't want you to use it."

Trey pursed his lips. "I'll think about it," he said.

"Why would you do something like that anyway?" asked Mo, anger firing up in him.

"Like what?"

"Like that," said Mo, stabbing a finger toward the CD console the way you would toward a pile of dog mess on the lawn. "That was a beautiful song about the world and the way it was. And you turn it into that?"

"I made it a song about the world and the way it *is*. It's about profit, see?"

"It's about more than that," said Mo.

Trey chuckled, turning away. "Yeah, right," he told his window.

"It is!" insisted Mo.

Trey turned back. "Man, why you bring me out here anyway? Just to bust my ass, is that it?"

"No," said Mo, "I…" He wanted to say it: I have Alzheimer's. Say it, put it out there, watch the look on the boy's smug face.

But he knew what would come after, and he didn't want that, didn't want his son's pity. Didn't want anybody's pity. And besides, the disease wasn't the only reason. "I never took you anywhere," said Mo. "We never talked. I never taught you anything. I mean, about life. About being a man."

Trey snorted, gave Mo the back of his head. "Too late for that, man," he said. "Way too late."

They drove in silence after that. Mo turned on the radio and found a smooth jazz station. Puff pastry ballads and candied horn solos floated from the speakers. Music to fill spaces with. And the space between James M. Johnson Jr. and James M. Johnson III suddenly yawned like canyons.

Half an hour later, they overtook the cloud on the horizon. It showered them with pebbles of ice, the rattling so loud they would have been forced to yell had words been passing between them. After ten minutes, they were out of the storm, but the sky above still loomed dark and impending.

On sudden thought, Mo turned down the radio and punched up a number on his cell phone. After a couple of rings, a voice on the other end picked up. "Hello?"

"Cooley, it's Mo."

"Mosey?"

"Yeah. How's he doing? He still the same?"

"Yeah, 'bout the same."

"Listen, I changed my mind. I just crossed the border into Illinois. I'm on my way. Should be there in a couple of days."

Cooley's voice trembled. "Mosey, that's...that's..."

Mo was impatient. "Yeah," he said, cutting Cooley off. "Tell Jack, would you? I'll see you in a few days."

He closed the clamshell, saw Trey watching him. "You call your father Jack?"

"Yeah," said Mo.

"Why?"

"Well, we were never like...you know, father and son. Not for real."

"Why you going out there then?"

Mo thought for a moment. Why was he doing this? "Because he's dying," he said finally. "Because it's the right thing to do."

In the front room of the little apartment in South Central, Cooley put down the phone. Then he put down the pistol. Saw Jack watching expectantly, his shirt red with blood freshly vomited. "Mosey's coming," he said. "He say he be here in a few days. All you got to do is hold on, buddy. Just hold on."

Jack's eyes closed as if keeping them open had become an effort too great. His head drooped and for a moment, Cooley thought he had fallen asleep. Then, his friend nodded almost imperceptibly and mouthed words he no longer had voice to say.

Hold on.

ten

Tash had seen enough of winter to last her.

She felt this way every year as the cold season hung on like a bad dream. Skies the color of battleships, snow turning to ice-mud in the corners of the road, the bones of trees reaching for the clouds. Every year, she asked herself what an L.A. girl was doing in a Baltimore winter. Every year, she said this was the last. But here she was again, February in Baltimore.

It wasn't so bad today, cold rain drizzling down, temperatures in the 30s. Not bad at all, but still spring felt like a lie they told you to improve your spirits.

She stood just outside the emergency room, hands snuggling in fur-lined pockets, breath hanging in puffs, wondering if she was making a fool of herself. She had waited here yesterday, too. He hadn't shown up, but then, she hadn't really expected him to. It was still too soon, the wound still too raw.

This was the acid test. This was what determined whether they had a future or whether whatever they had or might have had was dashed to pieces. For two days, her phone had been pointedly silent. She hadn't seen him, spoken to him, even heard of him, since he stormed out. Tash had stared holes in the phone, willing it to beep, but every time it did, every time she pounced on it like a cat upon a mouse, it was only one of her girlfriends or a wrong number, or Trey calling to tell her where he was.

It was never her man.

Assuming he still was her man. These next minutes would determine that. He hadn't picked her up from work yesterday and she had written it off to the fact that he was angry and hurt and needed to make a point. But two days in a row, that wouldn't be making a point. That would be sending a message. That would be, goodbye, it's over, don't let the doorknob hit'cha where the good Lord split'cha.

That would be the end, and she didn't know if she was strong enough for that.

Twice, she had caught herself with the phone in hand, once with five numbers punched in. Twice, she had made herself put it down, lecturing herself from one side of the room to the other.

Have a little respect for yourself, Tash. You didn't do anything. He's the one who stormed out. All you did was make a perfectly reasonable request. How's he going to respect you if you don't know how to respect yourself?

The problem was that she remembered alone all too well. After Mo, she had known all too much of alone.

Not that there had not been offers and opportunities. But she was…

Might as well say it. Might as well admit it, if only to yourself.

…scared.

Giving yourself to a man who could not give himself in return was humiliating. When she had finally realized she could not have a future with Moses Johnson—and how many giggling, jiggling young groupies had had to shove her aside trying to get next to him for that obvious truth to sink in?—she had withdrawn into herself. The sullen militant who wanted to save the world had decided it would be enough just to save herself, just to go to work every day and raise her child. She was alone and she told herself she liked it that way.

Until she met Philip.

Now being alone loomed like night terrors. She could not make peace with it. She did not know how she ever had.

So she waited by the ambulance bay in the cold, hating herself for it, for not at least going inside where it was warm, trusting that he would park the car and come in for her. Hating herself for not wanting to take even the bare chance of missing him. For being so needy.

The pickup time came. And then it went. Five minutes late. Ten minutes. Rain trickling down. And that was it. Dead and done. She couldn't stand out here another day, couldn't even take his call if, perchance, he decided tonight or tomorrow or the next day, to give her a ring. How needy could she be? How little self-respect could she endure?

Then his van pulled into the parking lot. Tash smiled. She hated herself for that, too. But she couldn't make herself stop.

He pulled to a stop in front of her. The door lock jumped up and Tash got in. It was blessedly warm inside. Music was playing on a Christian radio station. "Shackles," by Mary Mary.

"Hi," said Tash.

"Hey," he said. "How you doing?"

"I'm good. You?"

"I've been better."

"I wasn't sure you were coming," said Tash.

"Me neither," he said, pulling away from the ambulance bay.

"Why did you then?" It was out of her mouth before she had a chance to censor it, and she wondered if it was harsh.

"I didn't want to leave it at that," he said.

"Well, I'm glad." Twisting toward the empty back seat. "Where are the girls?"

"With my mother. I felt like we needed some time to talk."

"Fine," she said. "Let's talk."

Tash, stop being such a bitch. Weren't you the one just standing out in the rain wondering what you would do with yourself if the man didn't show?

"Look, I'm sorry. I shouldn't have gotten into it with Moses Jr. My temper got the best of me."

"Yes, it did."

"But you have to admit, your son really knows how to push buttons."

He waited for an answer and when it didn't come, he sighed. "Look, Tash, you have to meet me halfway on this. Your son may have killed a man. I can't be the only one who takes that seriously."

"Don't be silly, Philip. You think I don't take that seriously?" Just talking about it made her stomach cramp.

"And then, when Moses showed up, that just made matters worse."

"That's his son, Philip."

"Yeah, but he doesn't have to treat me like some clown who just wandered in off the street. I've been part of your life three years now. Don't I deserve a little respect?"

"How exactly did he fail to respect you?"

"You heard what he said about the girls. You know, about peeing ginger ale."

Tash wrestled a smile into submission. "Okay, that was uncalled for. But his point was that you idealize them, Phil. You dote on them. It's like you want to raise them in this little plastic bubble where nothing bad will ever get to them. But the world doesn't work that way and you need to understand that."

She touched his arm. "You've done a good job with them, Phil. A wonderful job. But they're not perfect. Nobody's perfect."

"You're saying I was wrong."

"No, I'm saying there was plenty wrong to go around. You're right. Trey shouldn't have disrespected you like that. And I should never have let things get so out of control. Maybe I shouldn't have asked you to leave. Not like that."

"You didn't ask me to leave," said Phil. "You kicked me out. I'm supposed to be your man and you kicked me out."

"You're right. I'm sorry. But you didn't call me for two days. I'd say we're even."

"I wasn't trying to get 'even.' I just…" He gave a frustration sigh, fingers combing back through close-cropped hair. "What are we doing here, Tash?"

"I guess that's what we're trying to figure out," said Tash.

"You know how I feel about you," he said. She wondered if that was true. Philip Reed was not a demonstrative man.

"And the girls," he went on, "they're crazy about you, too. You're a blessing to us. We say that all the time. We call you our gift from God. You have to understand, Tash: It was hard after Marie died. She was sick so long. We prayed so hard for her to get better. For awhile, we thought she would. But every time she tried to take a step forward, the disease pulled her two steps back. She just continued to slide downhill, away from us. You're a nurse," he said. "You know what I mean."

Tash nodded, waited.

"It was a mercy she died," he said. "I mean it. I praised God for it because it meant she was with Him. She was finally done suffering. But for us, our suffering had just begun. Losing her, it was like…losing your arm or your leg, something you depend on every day, just count on it to be there. Then you lose it and it takes you some time to get used to the fact that it's no longer there. You realize you have to find new ways to do things, new ways to get by."

He pulled to a stop at a traffic light, eyes fixed on the road. "I cried for a year after losing her," he said. "A solid year. I tried never to let the girls catch me, tried to be strong for them, but I wasn't strong, Tash. It used to hit me at the darnedest times. Tying my tie in the morning. Watching the baseball game on television. Waiting at the traffic light just like this. 'My wife is gone. I'm never going to see her on this side of life again.' And the tears would just start falling and I'd cry like a lost child."

Now Philip looked at her. "You're what changed that," he said. "And the funny thing is, I wasn't even looking for another woman, wasn't thinking about another woman. Then you walked into the church that day for the first time and suddenly it was all I could think about. Suddenly I was feeling things I had thought I would never feel again. You knocked me off my feet, woman. And when you said you'd have coffee with me—just *coffee*, for goodness sake—I thought I had woken up in heaven."

Tash felt warmed. He had never spoken this way before. And then the realization made her suspicious. "I hear a 'but' coming," she said.

Philip nodded. "But Moses Jr. is a problem," he said.

"Why do you insist on calling him that?"

"What?" The light had changed and Philip was edging the car through the crowded intersection.

"Moses Jr.," she said. "His name is not Moses Jr. His father is Moses Jr. His name is Moses Johnson III. That's why we call him Trey."

"This isn't about what I call him," said Philip.

"Maybe it is, in a way," she said. "Maybe it's about you wanting him to be someone other than he is."

"Just because I forget to use a nickname? That's silly."

"It is *not* silly. And don't tell me you forget. You have a very good memory, Philip Reed. You've never forgotten my birthday or the day we met. You can tell me the stats on every Orioles game going back to 1987. But you can't remember that my son prefers to be called 'Trey?' Come on, Philip."

A glance. "So you think it's something I do on purpose."

"Yes I do," she said. "It's some kind of weird passive-aggressive thing you've got going. He says, 'Call me Trey' and you say okay and then, two seconds later, you're calling him Moses Jr. or little Moses or something else that's not his name."

"Why would I do that on purpose, Tash?"

"You tell me," she said.

He didn't. Half a minute passed and the only sound was the hiss of tires on wet pavement and a gospel choir singing. Finally, Tash said, "Okay, I'll tell you. You don't like my son. You think he's a bad person."

"I think he's 19 years old and he lives off his mama. And even worse, he seems perfectly content to do that. And you seem perfectly content to let him. He should be preparing to get out there in the world, do something, make something out of his life. Instead, he just sits there, Tash, no job, no skills, no real plans or dreams that I can see."

"Well, he does have dreams," corrected Tash. "He wants to be a rapper, remember?"

"A rapper."

"Yeah."

Philip twirled an index finger in the air. "Oh yeah, I forgot."

"It's a phase," she said.

"I'm not so sure," said Philip. "I mean, his father being who he is, your son has to think that maybe he can actually do it. Maybe he can actually be the next Tupac or whoever. And even if, by some miracle, he does do that, then what?"

"What do you mean?"

"That's not exactly something to be proud of. Emulating some foul-mouthed thug who got himself shot to death."

A small shrug. "You're right. But you know what?"

He looked at her. "What?"

"He's still my son."

"I know that."

"He's always going to be my son."

"And Ashanti and Kadijah are my daughters," he said. "I want the best for them."

"And you think that having Trey around, that isn't the best. Especially now, with this going on."

Philip didn't answer. He didn't need to. "Maybe you're right," said Tash. "He'd never hurt your girls. You don't know it, Philip, but Trey is crazy about your daughters. He thinks the world of them."

"Yes, but even so—"

"Even so, you don't like the example he sets. I understand that. But do you understand, Philip, that you can't protect them from everything? There's all sorts of bad things in the world and you can't keep it all from them."

"I can try."

"I tried too, honey. It doesn't work."

He exhaled exasperation. "You're telling me little Moses— 'Trey'—is what I have to look forward to with my girls?"

"I'm telling you that there's only so much that's within your control."

A sharp look. "You really believe that?"

"I do."

"And you don't think things would have been different if his father had been there?"

She did. But she wouldn't give him the satisfaction. "That's like me asking if you thought things would have been different if Marie had lived," she said. She felt him flinch.

"What's that supposed to mean?"

"Forget it. Bad example."

"You're damn right it is," he said.

Tash let it breathe for a moment, Baltimore streets rushing by, Philip's chest rising and falling heavily. Finally, she touched his hand, which was resting on the gear shift. "Are we breaking up here? Is that what's happening?"

He looked over at her and she almost didn't recognize him. The eyes dark and threatening, the mouth set. "I don't know what you want from me," he said. "I don't know what it is you expect."

She thought about it for a moment, then said, "I want you to understand that it's a package deal, Trey and me. He's my son, warts and all. I understand that he's not what he needs to be, but this much will never change: I will always love him. You have to recognize that. You have to accept that if we're going to be together, he's going to be a big part of my life, always."

Philip sighed. He turned his head, slowly, and looked out his window.

Tash regarded his profile for a moment, then said flatly, "So I guess we are breaking up, then."

"I don't want—" He blurted the words, then stopped himself. Tash looked at him expectantly. "I don't want to break up with you," he said, his voice smaller. "And I know that he's your son and he'll always be part of your life. But what about *our* lives? When do we get a chance to build something together, for us? I mean, Tash, you're done raising him. He's 19 years old. He's a *grown man*. Can't he get out and find a place of his own? Or move in with his father?"

"His father." The words came with an automatic smirk. "His father is not stable."

"He seems stable enough. He's been in Maryland for three years. You said he's cut down on the touring. What's not stable? It might be good for him and his son to spend some together, get to know each other. Might help both of them."

"I can't ask Mo to do that."

"I see. But asking me to put up with your son, that's all right."

"That's not what I mean."

"No? Then tell me what you do mean, Tash, because you've got me awful confused."

"I mean…" And she had to stop, because she had no idea what to say.

Philip nodded. "That's what I thought."

"That's not what I mean," she said. And then she made a frustration sound, because she was repeating herself.

"That's okay, Tash."

"No, it's not. You don't understand." She paused for a moment, gathering herself. "Did I ever tell you that I used to be an atheist?"

His shock was so comical she had to smile. "At least, that's what I thought I was," she said. "Big Afro, power to the people, wearing my dashikis. Militant sister too wise to the world to get caught believing in God. That's how I was when I met Moses."

"What are you…?"

She lifted her hand. "Just listen," she said. "I had a hard time with Trey. Delivering him, I mean. I'm in the emergency room, I'm all by myself. Mo's doing a show, I can't reach my mother and this baby is coming too soon and the doctors say he might not make it. We *both* might not make it. I was bleeding so bad, Philip. They couldn't make it stop. And the pain. Lord, felt like a knife tearing me inside out. The doctors are yelling at each other over the table. I could see fear in their eyes and that like to killed me, because if the doctor is scared, what am I supposed to be?"

Tash paused, back in a moment that was never too far away. She reached and turned off the radio. The rain sizzled. She looked over.

"I prayed, Philip," she said. "First time I had done that since I was a little girl kneeling at the bedside with my dad. I said, 'God, I know we haven't talked in a long time. I know I've said some awful things about you. But if you just give me this baby, I promise I'll never ask you for anything else. I'll serve you from this day forward. God, please don't take my child.' That's the last thing I remember. Then they must have put me to sleep.

"I don't know how long I was out. Hours, I guess. When I came to, I didn't know where I was at first, couldn't even remember what had happened. All I knew was that I was alone in a room lying in a bed. Then when I remembered, I kind of jumped, looking around and oh, what did I want to do that for? The pain was unimaginable.

But I didn't care, because there was my son, sleeping in the incubator next to my bed. He was so tiny, Philip. Looked like a little doll. I said it out loud. I said, 'Thank you, God.'"

"God is good," said Philip quietly.

"Yes, He is, but that's not my point. My point is that I went through hell to bring that boy into the world. I love him more than you can imagine. And I will not give up on him, no matter what he's done. Please don't ever ask me to make that choice."

"I see," said Philip. After a moment, he reached to the radio and turned it back up. Deniece Williams sang "His Eye Is on the Sparrow." They didn't speak. Philip guided the car onto Tash's street, parked in front of the blue row house. Neither of them moved. They sat there together, listening to the crystalline voice singing in assurance of God's love.

When the song was finished and a commercial came on, Philip took her hand. "I have to ask you," he said. "Are you sure this is just about your son?"

She looked at him. "What do you mean?"

"Sometimes, I wonder…" A pause. He looked out the window. Gathering himself, she sensed. "Sometimes I wonder if you don't still have feelings for the boy's father."

"Moses?" She laughed and was appalled at how forced it sounded. "No," she said. "Whatever there was between us, that was a long time ago."

"Are you sure?" he asked. "Because sometimes, the way you look at him, the way you took his side the other day…sometimes, I wonder."

"I'm sure," she said.

"Because I can't compete with that guy. I'm not even going to try. He's a rock star and I'm an account executive. I'll never be able to take you on fancy vacations or buy you expensive gifts. You know that."

"I'm sure," she repeated. "But you know, as long as we're on the subject, I can ask you the same question."

"What do you mean?"

"I can't compete with your dead wife, either."

"I've never asked you to."

"Are you sure? Because I feel her in this relationship sometimes. You think you're competing with Mo. At least he's here, somebody living. Try competing with a memory."

"I won't forget her, Tash. I won't ask the girls to forget her, either. For goodness sake, she's their mother."

"Nobody's asking you to forget. Just…could you make some room for me while you're at it?"

"I have," he protested.

"Philip, the first thing you see when you open your front door is that huge portrait of you and her. Why do you think I don't go to your house that often?"

"I see," he said. "So you want me to take the picture down."

"It's not just that," she told him. "It's…how long have we been seeing each other now, Philip?"

"Three years. You know that."

"Exactly. Three years. And when you feel like you want us to be alone together, what do we do? Find a room at a hotel. Can't go to your place because your girls are there. Can't come back here because you're uncomfortable with Trey around. Well, I'll tell you something, Philip: I'm tired of sneaking around like I'm ashamed, like I'm doing something wrong. I want us to be together. Openly. In one house. Preferably as husband and wife. And it doesn't seem like we're getting closer to that. Doesn't seem like we ever will. I mean, what are we doing here, Philip? Where is this going?"

He swallowed. "I didn't know you felt that way," he said.

"I guess there's a lot we don't know about each other," she replied.

"Lot to think about," he said. "Lot to take in."

Tash nodded. "So," she said, "should I look for you to pick me up tomorrow?"

He covered her hand with his. "I'll let you know if that's ever going to change," he said.

"Do I get a kiss?"

The smile was rueful. "You get a kiss," he said.

They leaned across the space separating them, their lips brushing lightly. Tash felt consumed by a sudden sorrow. She wondered if they would ever cross that space again. But she forced herself to smile. "I'll see you tomorrow," she told him. And climbed out of the car.

As always, he watched her go, waited until she had opened the gate and the front door and waved to him that she was safe. Then he waved back and the van pulled away from the curb. Tash opened the mailbox beside her door and retrieved the day's deposit of bills and credit card offers. She was about to step inside when the voice stopped her.

"Scuse me," it said. A man's voice from behind her.

She turned and saw him standing at the bottom of the steps. A tall, raw-boned young man in a long coat was looking up at her. He had a lean, canine face. Something about him made Tash wonder if she could get inside before he could clear the porch.

"Yes?" she said.

"I'm lookin' for Profit."

"Beg your pardon?"

"Your son."

"My son's name is James."

"You call him Trey?"

Tash nodded warily.

"We call him Profit."

"Who is 'we?'"

He smiled. "My name Raiford. My brother, we call him Fury. His real name Cedric. Him and your son was arrested the other day."

"I see. And what did you want?"

"Want to talk to Trey. You know, see how he doin' and like that. Is he in?"

"No, he's not."

"Well, when you spect to see him?"

"He's out of town. He's on a trip with his father."

His face soured. He appeared to consider this for a moment. Didn't speak. Finally Tash said, "Is there anything else?"

"Yeah," he said. "Tell him Dog came by. Dog, that's what they call me. Tell him Fury asked me to check up on him. Ask him to call me. He got the number. You know, they both done caught the same case. They might could help each other."

"Your brother, he's still in jail?"

Dog gave her a nod. "Ain't everybody can raise that kind of bail. Tell Profit he lucky."

His gaze held her. After a moment he nodded—as if giving her permission to go inside unmolested—and walked away. Tash stepped in quickly and closed the heavy black gate. She watched him through the grating as he crossed the street and felt a shiver that had nothing to do with the cold.

———————

The brothers faced one another through the yellowed plastic. Dog put his palm on the barrier and waited for Fury to do the same. But Fury ignored him, leaning toward the grating, his voice an urgent hiss.

"You find Profit? You talk to him?"

Dog drew back, lips puckered as if tasting something bitter. He lowered his hand. "Spoke to his mama," he said. "She say he out of town."

"Bitch prob'ly lyin'."

"She ain't lyin'. Say he gone with his pops."

"Fuck," said Fury in a low voice.

"Man, why you trippin'? I done told you, you need to chill."

"Fuck 'chill,'" spat Fury. "That's easy to say when you outside."

"All I'm sayin' is, you gettin' worked up for nothing. You don't know Profit gon' snitch."

Fury gave him a harsh look. Dog let it pass.

"You got to be strong, man."

"I ain't tryin' to hear that right now, Dog."

"I'm just sayin', is all."

"Yeah? Well say something else. 'Cause you gettin' on my fuckin' nerves."

Dog sighed. His little brother could be a real pain in the balls sometimes. "How DC?" he said. "He doin' okay?"

"Fuck if I know. They moved him last night. He got some warrants in D.C."

"Really?"

"Yeah. Really."

"So you the only one in there, huh?"

"What you think, muh'fucka?" snapped Fury. "Profit on the street. DC in the lock-up in Washington. That would make me the only one in here, wouldn't it? Three minus two is one, ain't it? Damn, you say some stupid shit sometime."

Dog had had enough. "You know what?" he said, coming to his feet. "Fuck it. I ain't come all the way cross town to listen to you whine like a bitch. I'm tryin' to show you love and all you doin' is givin' me a lot of crap."

Fury raised his palms, surrendering. "Look, I'm sorry, okay?" When his brother didn't move, he repeated it. "I'm sorry. Sit down. Please. I'm just going crazy in here is all."

"Man, if you can't deal with this, you bet not never do no hard time."

"Ain't tryin' to do no hard time, man. That's why I want to make sure Profit don't be runnin' off at the mouth."

"Look, baby boy, I got you, all right? I done told you, you ain't got to worry about that. I'll keep an eye on him. If it look like he don't know how to keep his mouth shut, I'll pull the trigger on him my damn self."

Fury looked up. "Really?"

"Shit yeah," said Dog, touched by the surprise in Fury's eyes. "Hell, you my brother, ain't you?"

"Yeah."

He put his palm on the yellowed plastic. This time, Fury pressed his palm against the other side.

eleven

Somewhere in southeast Kansas, Mo allowed the Escalade to rumble to a stop at a rural crossroads and brought the window down. The air was still and brisk. The fields were brown. He was lost.

The nagging fear of it had hardened to dismal certainty over the last hour. He had glanced at the map when he first began to be worried, but that hadn't helped. He could read the map and yet at the same time, it was just words, just lines on a page. It meant nothing. He had kept driving, certain that any moment he would see something that told him where he was, what he was supposed to do. After a while, he had driven past a sign that welcomed him to Kansas.

Mo tried to remember Kansas, tried to remember where it sat in that jumble of states in the great body of the country. Was it on top of Texas? Left of Arkansas? Was it bordered by Colorado? And most important, where was it in relation to where he was trying to go?

Nothing. Black fog had rolled in again, a curtain of smoke with his memory trapped behind it. Mo felt his throat backing up. Beside him, Trey stirred in his sleep. "What's up?" he mumbled. He didn't open his eyes.

"Pit stop," said Mo. "Need to stretch my legs. Go back to sleep."

Trey needed no further encouragement. He shifted on the seat, smacked his lips, dozed. Mo watched him in mute amazement. Snatched the maps off the seat and climbed down from the truck. Sat on the rear bumper looking out over a brown cornfield, unfolded a map and tried to find himself. But the map was still just words and symbols.

He could read it just fine. Pittsburg, Kansas, up there. Baxter Junction down there. Wichita over there. He had the words, but they didn't mean anything. His mind could not put them together into a coherent plan of action that said, continue north for two miles until you come to such and such road, then take that in such and such direction until you reach such and such highway. Whatever the psychic switch was that allowed that to happen, it was down. Maybe for good.

Mo wasn't aware of dropping the map. It simply slipped from his fingers, floated a few feet, then wedged under the rear passenger side tire.

The sudden force of his retching threw Mo off the bumper. He landed on his knees in the grass, breakfast spilling out of him, splashing sour and bitter to the ground. Mo vomited until there was nothing left in him to vomit. Then he vomited some more. When it was finally done, he sat back on the rear bumper, pulled a cigarette pack from his breast pocket and shook one loose. He fished out a lighter and tried to fire the cigarette.

Mo's hand shook. He tried to brace the one with the other, but it was like one drunk trying to steady another. They trembled violently in front of his eyes. Mo ripped the cigarette from his lips and threw it into the brown field. He threw the lighter in behind. His hands came up to his face and he cried.

Part of him saw himself sitting there weeping like a baby on the rear bumper of his car on a seldom-traveled road in the middle of nowhere. Part of him yelled at himself to get up, do something. But that part of himself that was disgusted was also powerless, could only fume in impotence as he sat there crumbling near the end of a wasted life.

"Pop? What's wrong, man?"

Trey was standing there and so, what had been bad became infinitely worse in the space of a heartbeat. Mo knocked tears from his eyes with impatient hands. "Don't feel good," he said. "Something upset my stomach."

"Were you crying?"

"No. Eyes watering, that's all. From throwing up."

And Trey evidently chose to disbelieve the evidence of his own eyes because after a second he said, to his father's great relief, "Oh."

Moses felt it again then, the near overpowering urge to say the words, to tell his son he was dying. But he didn't, because he didn't want to ever see pity in those eyes that now regarded him with mild concern and—he realized it all at once—he didn't want to need anybody, didn't like the idea of having to depend or lean on. Had he always been this way? Always a man who held some part of himself back?

His son had a right to know about the disease. Not least because in ten or twenty years, he might have it himself.

Instead Mo embellished the lie. "My stomach's killing me," he said.

Trey brightened. "You want me to drive?"

It was a running joke between them. Trey was always looking for any excuse to get his hands on the big Cadillac. To lay the driver's seat back until it was almost supine, roll the windows down, crank the sound system until music was a sonic boom more felt than heard, then roll through the neighborhoods nodding at the corner boys and giving girls the eye. "Damn, Pop," he liked to say, "you don't know what I'd do if I had them wheels. I'd show you how to roll."

The boy had had his driver's license for all of two years. On his eighteenth birthday, Mo had bought him a Sentra. Trey had promptly racked up six moving violations before finally totaling the car altogether. Going too fast on winter ice and smacked into a light pole. Mo had pocketed the insurance money and decided, much to Tash's relief, against replacing the car. "Wait till you grow up some," he'd said, "before we see about getting you another car."

Trey had pissed and moaned about it, but Mo had stood firm, for once. And the boy had taken to staring longingly at the black Escalade and saying things like, "You ought to just give me your car. Buy something new for yourself." He was always looking for an excuse to get behind the wheel. The SUV was, Mo had explained to him more than once, too much car for somebody who couldn't even drive a Sentra. But Mo knew what Trey loved about the Escalade.

It looked like money. And wasn't that what it was all about with this generation? Forget about having ideals or believing in a cause or trying to do what was right. And for Lord's sake, forget about trying to change the world. All that mattered was the flash, the surface, the sizzle. The money. When had that happened? What had gone so wrong with them? Why didn't they give a damn about the things that were really important?

"On a cold day in hell," he told Trey, who stood grinning expectantly above him. And the grin faltered because this harsh response was the last thing Trey expected. A little banter, maybe. A little back and forth, sure. All of it leading to a no, of course. But this blunt refusal, this hard foreclosure of any comeback, violated the rules of the game. Denied there had ever been a game in the first place.

Mo saw all of this is in Trey's eyes. He knew he should stop. But he couldn't help himself. "You can't even keep a Sentra on the road," he said. "What makes you think I'd turn over the keys to an Escalade?"

"I was just askin'," muttered Trey defensively.

"Well stop asking," said Mo.

He saw Trey deflate, but it was like something seen from a great distance. Something far off that he was powerless to affect. Or stop. Something about seeing the air go out of his son only made Mo angrier.

"Don't stand there pouting," he said. "You know it's true. Only reason you want to drive the damn car in the first place is so that you can front. Pretend you're something you're not. That's the problem with you, the problem with all you young fools. You ain't nothing but front. Nothing inside." He slapped his chest, hard. "No heart," he said.

"I got heart," said Trey.

"You got shit," said Mo. "Hanging around with those other losers. Pulling armed robberies. Shoot a man after he already gave up the money. Shoot him just because. You didn't know that man. You don't know what his life's about. Maybe he's got children. Maybe he's got a wife. Maybe he's their only means of support. You kids don't give a fuck. Just shoot the man for no good reason. Waste his life over some bullshit. Now you lookin' at going to jail just like your grandfather did. Like maybe shooting people just runs in the family. And you want to drive my car."

"I told you I ain't shot nobody," said Trey.

Mo didn't even glance his way.

"I ain't shot nobody!" Trey shouted it this time, slapping the rear window of the car for emphasis. He waited for Mo to look. Mo didn't. Trey disappeared. A moment later, Mo heard the passenger door open, then slam. The sound was like a gunshot in the stillness. Mo sighed, dropping his head. He felt like a tree, tied into the very soil. He felt like he would never move again.

The anger was misplaced. He was self-aware enough to know that. Not that he wasn't angry at his son. But he was angrier at life, at God, at fate, at whatever you wanted to call it. All he knew was that he didn't deserve what was happening to him, didn't deserve to be sitting here by the side of a Kansas road, dying at the absurd age of 49 years.

And what had he accomplished in those years? Nothing. A song. A great song, yes, but still at the end of the day, just a song. He had Fans, but no friends, a son he barely knew, a father he hated, women, but no woman. He had no life.

So he sat there, lost in corn country, his son sitting up front in the truck, steaming, himself back here on the bumper above a pool of vomit, unable to move. And the minutes dog-piled one another, stacking up until he lost count.

Eventually, an old pickup ambled up the road, chased by a cloud of dust. It was impossible to say what color it once had been. Now it was of no particular shade, except for patches of rust on the hood. The truck drew parallel. Mo stood, kicking dirt and dry grass over the vomit. The driver's side window came down. Two white men in cowboy hats grinned at him, the one behind the wheel a younger copy of the friendly, weather-beaten face closest to Mo.

"You all right there, bud?" asked the older man with a nod toward the Escalade.

"Just lost," said Mo.

"I might have known," said the older man, nodding at the Escalade. "We don't get too many like that in this part of the world. Where you trying to get to?"

Mo had his mouth open to answer when the man pointed a finger at him. "I know you, don't I?" His brow creased with concentration, then he laughed. It was an easy sound. "Oh, my Lord," he said, touching his knuckles against the starched white of the younger man's shirt. "You know who this is?"

The younger man shrugged, shook his head. "I guess you wouldn't. You're so young you think that rap crap is music." He gave an apologetic grin that made Mo feel as if he were being drawn into some conspiracy of age.

"This here is Moses Johnson," said the older man, each word punctuated with a thrust of his index finger toward Mo. "This here is the Prophet."

"I've heard of him," said the younger man.

"He's heard of you," mocked the older man, shaking his head with a rueful grin.

Mo smiled and nodded, hoping the stranger would not prod him for words. He did not know if he could find the Fan Voice inside him. Didn't know if he ever would again.

"This one's 23," said the man, hooking a thumb at the younger man behind the wheel. "His whole life's been video games and Internet. He don't know nothing about how things used to be."

The young man's smile was indulgent. They'd had this discussion before. "Got to live in the present, Pop. Can't expect me to make my life in the past. We've been over this."

"Joe College," said the man. There was exasperation in it, but no ire. Mo got the sense they both enjoyed the argument.

"Man said he was lost, Pop. You want to help him get on his way, or you just want to stand here chewing his ear off?" He didn't wait for an answer, lifting his eyes to Mo. "Where you trying to get to, Mr. Prophet?"

The father buried his head in his hands, but the embarrassment seemed more feigned than real. Mo said, "Los Angeles." Their eyes widened at that. Mo retrieved the map from under the rear wheel of the SUV and brought it to the passenger side door. "Apparently, I missed a turn somewhere."

It turned out he had gone 50 miles out of the way, had traveled north instead of south, wound up in Kansas when he had been looking for Oklahoma. When the father and son were through setting him back on course, the older man looked up. Mo nearly flinched from the concern he saw in his eyes.

"How you get so lost, bud? I mean, I've seen people get turned around before, happens all the time, but this is something else."

Mo hoped his shrug was convincing, his little laugh carefree. "Guess I wasn't paying attention," he said.

"Yeah, well, I know how that it is," the man said dubiously.

It took a few minutes more. The man got out of the truck and posed with Mo while his son snapped a picture with his cell phone. Then there were autographs to sign, an invitation to lunch to politely decline. Finally, Mo stood next to the Escalade and watched as the pick up trundled down the road. He lifted his hand, smiling at the retreating dust cloud.

Then he dropped it like something heavy. A breath, and then Mo opened the driver's side door and climbed in. Trey watched him.

"You was lost?"

"Yeah," said Mo.

"You know where you going now?"

"Yeah," said Mo. He got the Purell out of the console, cleansed his hands from another fan's admiring touch. Then he started the car, staring straight ahead. Put the vehicle in gear. Sat there.

"You didn't shoot the man?" said Mo, still refusing to look at his son.

"I already told you that."

"You didn't shoot him?"

"No, man, I ain't shot him. Been telling you that for days."

Now Mo turned. Saw indignation facing him. "You only robbed him at gunpoint," said Mo. His voice was soft.

Trey swallowed. Indignation drained away slowly. In its place, something hard settled in. "Yeah," he said. "Only that."

Mo stomped the gas pedal. The car leapt forward down the lonely road.

After a moment, he turned on the satellite radio, punched in the code for the R&B oldies station. Booker T. and the MGs did "Green Onions," a sound of lethal cool. Smokey Robinson and the Miracles ground their way through "Ooo Baby Baby." It was a diversionary noise as familiar to Mo' as his own bedroom. It did nothing to fill the silence in the cab. After a moment, he turned the volume down.

"I still can't understand why," he said. "I mean, I know you said you did it because you needed money to make a demo. But what I can't get straight in my head is, how could you think it was okay to go in and take what doesn't belong to you? Take what another man has worked for? Even if you didn't shoot him, even if you never meant for him to get hurt, how could you think it was right to take the money? How could you do something like that?"

Trey hunched his shoulders. "We just wanted it."

Mo didn't bother trying to hide his disgust. "You just wanted it. And that made it okay to take it? If somebody wants something of yours, something of mine, they can just take it? That's all right?"

"No, man. I mean…" Trey stammered. "We ain't thought about it all deep like that, you know? It was just, he had it, we wanted it, know what I mean?"

Mo looked at him a long time. "No," he said finally, "I don't. That's not the way it works, son. There's certain stuff you just don't do because it's wrong. That's what separates people from animals. If you don't understand that, you'll never be a man."

Trey's eyes flashed. "I *am* a man," he said.

Mo shook his head. "No, you're not," he said. "You may look like a man, but you're not."

"Hell I ain't. I don't know what you talkin' about. I'm grown. I handle mine."

"You're 19," said Mo with a sigh. "So as far as the law is concerned, yeah, you're a man. You can do most of the things a man is allowed to do. But see, being a man is not about the law and it's not about a number and it's not about making babies and it's not about grabbing your dick all the time like you're scared somebody's going to take it away from you."

"Man, you talking crazy."

"A man's got to have some…honor," said Mo.

Trey bridled. "I got honor."

Mo flicked his eyes at his son, then returned his gaze to the road, dead cornstalks flying by at 70 miles an hour. "You don't even know what honor is," he said.

"Oh, so now I'm stupid," snapped Trey. "Is that it?" And then, a moment later, after the anger, hurt. "Why you coming down so hard on me?" he asked.

"I'm coming down hard on myself," said Mo. "Quiet as it's kept, I don't think I've been too much of a man myself. If I had been, maybe you'd never have had your ass in that store to begin with."

They did not speak again for a long time. Cornfields gave way to little towns, then back to cornfields and finally, to an interstate. It was late in the afternoon and they had just crossed the Oklahoma state line when Trey's cell phone started yelling at him in the voice of some rapper. "Hey, fool! Pick up the phone!"

Trey answered the phone. He spoke in short questions, which soon became exclamations of disbelief, seeming to grow more animated every second. When he finally flipped the clamshell shut, Mo said, "What was that all about?"

Trey grinned. "That was my lawyer. The DA want to give me a deal. Lawyer say they'll let me go with three to five if I testify against Fury, 'cause he the shooter."

Mo felt his heart thump hard once. "Trey, that's…that's a gift."

Trey shook his head impatiently. "You don't get it," he said. "My lawyer said don't take it."

"What do you mean?"

"He say they tryin' to deal 'cause they got no case. They found my wallet on the floor behind the counter; that's how they was able to find me. But far as they know, I could'a lost the wallet any time. The dead guy could'a even been holdin' it for me."

"But he wasn't," said Mo.

"No," said Trey, "but that ain't the point. That's the only evidence they got. They ain't found no weapon, they ain't got no prints, they ain't got no witness. My lawyer say they bluffin', 'cause they know they gon' have to drop the case. He say if they take me to trial with nothing more than that, the judge would break his foot off in they ass."

He laughed out loud, punched the air twice with right hooks, came back with a left jab. "Yeah!" he crowed. "That's what I'm talkin' 'bout! Yeah, boy! What? *What?*" He glanced over at Mo. "Don't you get it, Pops? I ain't gon' have to do no time. They ain't got nothin' on me."

Mo tried to smile. Wasn't sure if the expression on his face actually got there or not. He watched his son beating up the air, roaring his exuberance and relief, and marveled that he did not share it. Just over a week ago, he had sat outside a detention center on a rainy morning and his greatest fear had been that his son would spend years locked in a place like that. A terrible thing, that fear.

Now they had gotten the word, the reprieve, he had prayed for. His son would not go to jail, would not have his life ruined, would not have to pay for what he had done. He would get away with it. This was good news, wasn't it? Without a doubt, good news.

Mo could not say why, but he feared this just as much. In some ways, maybe more.

twelve

Tash jolted upright in the shadows, suddenly awake without knowing why.

It had not been a good sleep. She had lain there for hours, unable to sink herself into the blissful unaware, making do with fleeting moments of unconsciousness snatched out of a jittery scuttle of thought and worry.

Philip stressing her about Trey, Trey out there getting into heaven knows what trouble. And that man waiting for her at her door, that strange tall man who never said a discourteous word, never made a menacing move, yet somehow made her wonder if she could get inside before...

Before what?

Stop it, girl. You're making yourself crazy.

Her breathing was fast, her night shirt listless and damp against her bosom. She wished she had a cigarette, but she had thrown them out three years ago. Bad enough Trey had badgered her about it for years, but then she had met Philip, and he hated smoking, too. Tash made herself breathe, drew the air in slowly for a seven count, let it expand her, fill her, still her. She held it for another seven.

She was releasing the air over a final seven count when she heard it, a furtive tapping on the front window. This, she realized, was what had awakened her, a tick-tick sound so soft it was as if it didn't want to be heard. She had a doorbell, for goodness sake. Why hadn't whoever was out there used it? Mystified, Tash turned toward the alarm clock on the nightstand and the oversized green numbers she saw swimming in the darkness made her shiver.

2:02. Only bad news and trouble knocked at your door at 2:02 in the morning.

Tash didn't own a gun. Guns scared her. Her father, a career
military man, had kept a cabinet full of them and she had hated that.
But right now she wished she had a gun, a big, heavy, phallic pistol
she could stick in danger's face if need be and make it back off, leave
her door. She thought again of that young man who had come to her
gate—Dog, he called himself—looking for Trey, and another shiver
jagged hard through her body.

The tapping came again. Slightly more insistent now, but still
surreptitious, too. A beg-pardon sound. Tash pushed the covers aside
and swung her legs out of bed. The hardwood floor was punishing
cold. She turned on a light, found her house slippers, pushed her feet
gratefully into the fur lining. For a moment, Tash considered getting
a knife from the kitchen drawer for protection…

Stop it, girl.

…but that seemed silly. So she padded through the house instead, pausing only to flip on a light in the living room and nudge
the thermostat higher, then went to the window at the front door.
She pushed aside the curtain. The porch was dark, but in the light
from a streetlamp, she could see stray flakes of snow tracing curlicues
in the air and LaShonda Watkins standing there in jeans and T-shirt,
body hunched forward as if she had been stomach-punched, hands
pinned in her armpits, breath visible as it leaked from her mouth.
She was crying.

"Oh my God," breathed Tash. And then she was turning on the
porch light, fumbling the locks open, yanking the door inward.

"LaShonda? What's wrong, child?"

"Miss Tash?" Her voice was sorrowful. "Can I come in?"

Tash grabbed her in response, pulling her into the warmth. "Get
in here, girl. What are you doing out here this time of night dressed
like this?" And then a frightening thought closed like a fist around
her heart as she shut the door. "Is something wrong with DeVante?"

LaShonda shook her head vigorously. "DeVante fine. He sleeping at home." And then the tears renewed themselves, her thin arms
shuddering.

Tash rubbed her shoulders. They were icy. "Sit down," she said,
steering the girl toward the couch.

When LaShonda sat, Tash went to the linen closet in the hallway and retrieved a quilt. The girl accepted it gratefully, burrowed deep into its folds, body still trembling violently. Her eyes were red. Twin trails of snot glistened above her upper lip.

She saw Tash looking. "Me and my mama had a fight," she said. "She told me get the fuck—excuse my language, Miss Tash—get the fuck out her house."

Tash was relieved. "Oh. When I saw you out there, I thought DeVante was sick or something."

She didn't bother to hide her annoyance. "DeVante fine, Miss Tash. I'm the one she kicked out in the cold. She love DeVante."

"She loves you, too," said Tash.

LaShonda didn't answer. Didn't even look up. Tash said, "I'll get you some tea."

LaShonda's smile was weak. "Tea be nice," she said.

Tash nodded, retreated to the kitchen, put the water on, got the tea bags out. The mindlessness of the task left her thoughts plenty of room to tumble and spin. She could not begin to guess why the child's mother had put her in the streets on a night—well, morning, really—when the temperature was in the twenties and the puddles had turned to ice. It made Tash angry. Thank God the child had made it to her door. Lord knows what could have happened to her, walking these streets at this hour. Could have been snatched by some crazy man, could have been robbed, could have just frozen to death, out there in nothing but T-shirt and jeans. What the hell was the woman thinking? What was wrong with her?

The kettle shrilled. Tash snapped the stove off and poured two cups, draping the tea bags inside. She put them both on a tray with sugar and a couple wedges of lemon and carried them to the living room, fragrant steam trailing behind her. Then she stopped.

LaShonda had keeled over on her side and pulled the quilt to her chin. She was asleep. Tash regarded her for a moment, then set the tray down on the coffee table. She reached to spread the quilt over the girl but at Tash's first touch, LaShonda's eyes came open.

"Miss Tash?" she said, confused.

"You fell asleep," said Tash.

Now recognition flooded back into her eyes and she sat up. "I'm sorry," she said.

"It's okay," said Tash.

"It's so cold out there," said LaShonda.

"I know," said Tash.

"I'm sorry I woke you up."

"That's all right."

"I didn't know where else to go."

"Have some tea," said Tash, nudging the cup toward her.

The girl didn't even look at it. "We had a fight," she said.

"You and your mother." Tash was blowing softly on her cup.

A nod. "She said I ain't her daughter no more. Called me a bitch. Said I wasn't nothing but a tramp."

Tash stopped blowing. "You're pregnant," she said.

LaShonda didn't answer. She lowered her eyes.

"How far along?" asked Tash.

"Three months," said LaShonda. Voice small.

"Is Trey…"

The eyes came up, indignant. "Me and your son don't go together no more, Miss Tash. No offense, but Trey really ain't the kind of man I need in my life. He ain't that mature, you know."

"*He's* not mature?" Tash almost said more. Sipped her tea and counted ten instead.

LaShonda bristled. "This Water's baby," she said.

Tash knew the name; she went to church with the boy's mother. Water was Walter Paul. He called himself Water because, he said, that was how his rap flowed. He drove an old Impala, was taking business classes in junior college. Tash had seen him two days before, walking down the street with his arm around KaNeshia Bridle. KaNeshia had two children by two men, one of whom was doing 25 years for dealing drugs, the other of whom had simply disappeared. All at once Tash felt tired and too old for this.

"Why didn't you go to Water's house?" she asked.

LaShonda's face clouded. "I tried," she said. "His mama said he wasn't there. When I told her I was carrying Water's baby, she got mad at me. Told me I had to get away from there. I thought she was gon' hit me. Like I say, Miss Tash, I ain't had no place else to go."

She looked nine years old. Tash bit her lip, the sudden fatigue and age sitting heavily upon her. She felt as if it would take more energy than she had just to get to her feet, just to raise a hand to her mouth.

"How old are you, girl?" she heard herself ask.

"Nineteen," said LaShonda. "Next month."

"Nineteen," repeated Tash. "Next month. You're going to have two babies now. Ain't nothing but a baby yourself."

"You sound like my mother," said LaShonda.

"Maybe you should listen to your mother," said Tash.

LaShonda came to her feet. "That's enough," she said. "I ain't come here for this."

Tash surprised herself by yelling. "Girl, sit your silly ass down. It's 27 degrees out there."

LaShonda hesitated a moment. For pride's sake, thought Tash. But they both knew she had no choice. After a moment, LaShonda sat down. She picked up her tea cup and took a sullen sip. "I don't need no lectures, Miss Tash. That's all I'm saying."

"You're going to have this baby?"

A nod. "I don't believe in abortion."

"What are you going to do?"

"What you talking about?"

"What am I...?" Tash was incredulous. "I'm talking about your *life*, child. How are you going to take care of yourself and your baby? Or are you going to lay this one off on your mother too?"

LaShonda shook her head. "I swear, you sound just like her."

"Just trying to get you to think, child."

She shrugged. "Me and Water, we be okay. We love each other."

Tash couldn't help herself. She started laughing. She didn't mean to laugh, hadn't even known laughter was coming. But suddenly she was laughing anyway, her shoulders shaking, her eyes tearing. She tried to make herself stop, but that only made it worse. Caught sight of LaShonda staring at her, eyes filled with insult and disbelief. Tash tried to apologize, but that only brought on another spasm and in the end she had no choice but to ride it until finally the laughter was done with her and she could breathe.

"I'm sorry," she said when she was able to speak.

"I don't see what's so funny," said LaShonda, lips poked out.

Tash dabbed at her eyes. "They always say they love you, child," she said.

"He do love me," insisted LaShonda. She sounded less sure.

"Trey said he loved you too, didn't he? Didn't he tell you he cared about you?"

LaShonda stared at her, didn't answer. It was all the confirmation Tash needed. "By the time DeVante came, you were barely speaking to each other. Isn't that true?"

This brought a nod. Tash's eyes drifted to the mantle where Trey smiled down at her in his white cap and gown. Looking so much like his father. "They always say they love you," she said again.

"You saying they don't *never* love you?"

Tash glanced at her. "I'm saying you better learn to love yourself a little bit first. Stop waiting for a man to approve of you. Stop being so needy."

LaShonda flicked her eyes at the picture on the mantle. "Miss Tash?" she said.

"Yeah?"

"I ain't mean no disrespect, but are you talking about me or you talking about yourself? With Trey's daddy, I mean."

Tash smiled through her regrets. "I'm talking about all of us," she said.

LaShonda appeared to consider this for a moment. "Water love me," she said resolutely.

Tash thought of being tender, considered being considerate. She didn't have the patience. "Really?" she asked. "Is that why I saw him walking down this street two days ago with his hand in KaNeshia Bridle's hip pocket? Because he 'loves' you so much? How much do you want to bet he told her the same thing?"

"You're lying!" Anger flared in her eyes like a match freshly lit.

"No I'm not," said Tash softly. "And what's worse, you know I'm not."

They looked at each other. Then LaShonda began to cry. She didn't weep. It wasn't decorous and quiet. LaShonda wailed bitterly, face contorted and ugly, turning this way and that as if trying to get away from truth that had her surrounded. She stomped like a two-year-old and buried her face in her hands. It took a few minutes. Tash waited her out. Finally the girl looked up, accusation in her eyes. "Why are you doing this?" she demanded.

Tash's gaze didn't waver. "Because you need to hear it," she said. "And because I'm old enough and tired enough to tell you." She motioned with her hand. "Come on, you can sleep in Trey's room tonight. I just changed the bed today."

LaShonda nodded and followed her obediently, defeated now. Tash got the girl settled in Trey's room, then turned out the lights and went back to her own room. She kicked off her slippers and lay back in the bed. She found herself trying to remember if Mo had ever done what she had assured LaShonda all men did. If he had ever told her he loved her. Surely he had, but she couldn't recall. And it occurred to her that maybe she had only wanted him to.

Every few minutes, shadows cast by the headlights of passing cars slid across her bedroom ceiling and down the wall. She watched them until the light from a feeble sun burned them away. The alarm sounded. Tash turned it off, rolled out of bed and got ready for work. When she saw Philip's car pull up, she looked in on LaShonda. Mouth open, arm stretched out, unconscious and unaware. So unaware.

Tash opened the door as Philip was reaching for the doorbell. "Oh," he said, startled. "Aren't we eager."

"I saw your car," she said. She had thought to tell him about LaShonda but decided against it for no reason she could name. She just didn't want his opinion, didn't want to hear him telling her what she should do about the girl. So they kissed good morning and rode mostly in silence except for small talk and music from the Christian station.

"Are you okay?" he asked at one point.

"I'm fine," she said. "Why do you ask?"

"You're awful quiet."

"I'm in a quiet mood, I guess. Didn't sleep well last night."

"Something on your mind?"

"I guess."

"Anything you want to talk about?"

"Not really," she said.

"I see," he said and she knew she had hurt his feelings. Tash put a hand on his knee but didn't say anything.

It was a busy day at work. Lots of slip-and-fall injuries, lots of bickering between the nurses, all topped by a car wreck and a little girl with head injuries so massive the doctors couldn't save her. Tash sat with the child's father, who escaped the accident with only a scratch on his forehead.

"I always make them wear their seatbelts," he said. "I always do. But she took it off and I didn't know. And suddenly, this guy is coming at me, wrong way on the expressway. I tried to get out of the way, but…"

He looked at Tash. "My daughter is dead?" It was the third time in two minutes he had asked.

"I'm sorry," said Tash.

"Oh God," he said. "Oh God, oh God, oh God." He rocked back and forth in the orange plastic chair, holding himself as if otherwise he might fly apart.

It took a year for quitting time to come. The nursing supervisor tried to bully her into working a double, but Tash refused. Her boss would be angry, she knew. She tried to care.

Tash bummed a cigarette from one of the janitors and smoked it as she stood at the emergency entrance waiting for Philip. It tasted like hot dirt and Tash stubbed it out half-smoked. She sucked a breath mint and waited. Philip drove up five minutes later. The girls were with him and the chatter in the car was happily mindless. Tash was grateful she didn't have to pay close attention. She asked Philip to drop her off at LaShonda Watkins's house. Philip, caught laughing at something Ashanti had said, gave a look.

"Something wrong?" he asked.

"I just need to talk to her mother," said Tash.

"You're keeping secrets."

Tash nodded. "I'm sorry," she said. "I'm not trying to be mysterious."

Philip's mouth twisted. "Well, you're doing a darn good job," he said.

"I'll talk to you about it," she promised. "It's just something I need to handle on my own."

"Is it about Trey? Because if it is…"

"It's not about Trey," she said. And then she realized. "You called him Trey."

A shrug. "I guess I did."

She leaned across and kissed his cheek, ignoring the scandalized giggles this produced from the back seat. "You're one of the good ones, Philip Reed," she said.

"If I'd known that's all it took to get some sugar, I'd have called him Trey a long time ago," he said. They were pulling up in front of the projects. "You sure you don't want us to wait on you?" he asked.

"No, I'm probably going to be awhile," she said.

"It's awful cold out there to be walking," he told her.

"I'll be fine, honey," she told him. "I need to talk to this child's mother."

"Okay," he said. "You'll call me when you get home?"

"Yeah." Another kiss, this one lingering on the lips, another siren of giggles rising from the back seat. Tash thumbed a smudge of lipstick off Phil's face, then got out of the car and walked up the path to Michaela Watkins's front door. She rang the bell, heard Philip accelerate into traffic when the door swung open. Michaela was still wearing her work uniform, a tan smock with a nameplate pinned on her bosom that identified her as a housekeeping supervisor for a national hotel chain. She held a half-drained bottle of beer by the neck with two fingers. Her expression curdled when she recognized Tash.

"Oh," she said, "it's you. Was you supposed to be pickin' up DeVante?"

"No," said Tash. "It's not that."

A glance around. "I don't see that son of yours with you."

"No, I'm here about LaShonda," said Tash.

"LaShonda ain't here."

"Yeah, I know. She's at my place. Showed up this morning at two."

Somehow, Michaela Watkins managed to look both guilty and defiant. "She tell you why I kicked her ass out?"

"It's cold out here, Michaela," said Tash. "You mind if I come in for a bit?"

Michaela pursed her lips, then said, "Suit yourself." She turned around and took her beer back inside. Tash caught the storm door before it could close and followed her.

The apartment was tiny, a kitchen with barely enough space to turn around in, a dining area with a table for four that only two people could use at any given time, a living room where a massive couch spilled beyond the edge of the wall and into the hallway. Tash could hear a Disney video playing in the back bedroom DeVante shared with his mother. The place was cluttered, but it was clean.

Michaela sat on the couch. A Denzel Washington movie was playing soundlessly on a 32-inch television that sat too close.

"You mind if I sit down?" asked Tash.

This brought a shrug. "Like I said, suit yourself."

Tash sat, pulling a knit cap off her head, opening her coat. Michaela took a pull on the beer. "So," she said, "you here to tell me what a lousy mother I am for putting her out in the cold?"

"No," said Tash. "Not at all. I just—"

"'Cause you don't know nothing about it, all right? You don't know nothing about me. I don't have to answer to you. I don't have to explain to you why I do a damn thing. You understand me?"

Tash's palms came up. "I'm not here to fight with you, Michaela," she said.

Michaela gave her a hard look. "She okay?" she asked.

"She's fine," said Tash.

The eyes softened almost imperceptibly. Michaela tipped the beer to her lips, took another drink. "You want one?" she said.

Tash considered. She had never been much of a drinker. "Yeah," she said. "I think I'd like one."

Michaela inclined her head toward the kitchen. Tash was closer. "In the fridge. Bring me another one while you're at it."

Tash retrieved the brown bottles from the refrigerator, handed one across to Michaela, twisted the top off her own. It came off with a satisfying hiss, cold trickling up off the amber liquid.

"What are we drinking to?" asked Michaela.

Tash gave it a moment of thought. "Children," she said.

Michaela shook her head. "Not children," she said. "Not the way I'm feeling right now."

Tash nodded toward the television. Denzel Washington was running down some dark corridor, pursued by sweaty men with guns. "To Denzel," she said.

Michaela laughed. "Now him, I'll drink to. His fine ass, I'll drink to any day of the week."

"Ain't that the truth," said Tash and they clinked bottles and watched for a moment as Denzel outflanked his pursuers.

Without looking over, Michaela spoke. "So, you say you ain't come here to cuss me out. Why are you here? You want to beg me to take the little heifer back in?"

"I'm not really sure why I'm here," admitted Tash. "I guess it just seems like we should've sat down and talked a long time ago."

An appraising glance. Another sip.

"We're both grandparents to that little boy," said Tash, looking toward the back bedroom. "We're the only grownups in the picture. Trey and LaShonda…"

Michaela made a sound. "Ain't nothing but children themselves. Make my head hurt, they so stupid."

"Exactly," said Tash. "We should have talked a long time ago, Michaela. But I know you were angry with me because my son got your daughter pregnant. And to tell you the truth, I wasn't too happy with you because your daughter let herself get pregnant. That was silly of us, Michaela. We know how this works. Ain't one more guilty than the other. They both guilty. It takes two to make this mistake."

Michaela snorted. "And now Shonda done made it again," she said. "What that make her? Fool of the year."

Denzel was yelling something at a white man. They watched the scene unfold for a minute. Michaela said, "You tell him, Denzel!"

They laughed. Another moment passed. Then Tash said, "So are you okay, Michaela?"

This brought a look of surprise. Tash turned to meet it. Michaela's eyes shone. "I wanted better for her, you know?"

Tash nodded. "I know," she said. "We always want better."

"I got pregnant young," said Michaela. "Had Shonda and her brothers one right after the other. Daryl—that was my husband—he was a good man. I thought we'd be together forever. Didn't work out that way. Now here I am, broke, alone, struggling to bring up children and she go and do something like this—twice."

"Stuck on stupid," said Tash. "Trey's the same way."

"What's wrong with them, Tash?"

Tash hunched her shoulders. "Hell if I know."

"This isn't where I expected to be. I went to college. Did you know that?"

Tash shook her head.

"Majored in political science, if you can believe that. Then in my second year, along comes Daryl Jr. I figured I'd go back as soon as I had him potty trained. Next thing I know, I'm pregnant again with my son Jerome. College just got further and further away. By the time Shonda came along, I guess I knew I wasn't never going back to get that degree."

"What happened to your husband, you don't mind me asking?"

"I don't mind. Daryl and me divorced when she was a baby. He helps me a little when he can, but he don't have that much himself. He's a mechanic at some shop in Brooklyn. Has a whole other family now. So here I sit, with my two years of college under my belt, scrubbing out toilets and making up beds for some hotel. It's not what I planned, you know? But the thing that made it okay a little was knowing that my daughter wouldn't have to go through the same stuff. And now here this child turns up pregnant. Not once, but twice. Two different boys—I will not say men—two different *boys* and ain't married to neither one of 'em. Ain't got the first clue what she gon' do.

"Why she do something like that? Just tell me why." Tears rimmed her eyes. One fell.

"I don't know," Tash said. "We need to pray on it, I guess."

"I done prayed," said Michaela, knocking the tear from her cheek impatiently. "Done about wore out my knees praying."

"Yeah," said Tash. "Me too."

"I'm tired," said Michaela softly. "Don't know how much more of this I can take, you know?" Tash put a hand on her shoulder.

On the screen, a camera was panning Denzel Washington's face, circling close on a look of iron resolve, a tough moral decision made, a plan laid, action imminent. "Why can't they be more like that brother?" asked Michaela with a little laugh.

Tash smiled. "You know why," she said. "That's movies. That's fantasy. We out here in the real world."

"Ain't that the truth." A contemplative pause. Then Michaela sighed. "I don't know what's going to happen to that girl."

"I tried to talk some sense into her," said Tash.

Another laugh. "Like talking to a cabbage, ain't it?"

Tash nodded. "She think this boy loves her."

A harsh laugh. "Love," said Michaela. "Tina was right, girl. What's love got to do with it?"

"I'll keep trying," promised Tash.

"Suit yourself," said Michaela.

"Don't give up on her," said Tash. Michaela sipped her beer, didn't answer. After a moment, Tash stood up. "Well," she said. "I guess I'd better be getting home. Ain't getting no warmer out there."

Michaela stood. "Listen," she said. "About your son. I'm sorry if I—"

Tash waved it off. "No need," she said. "I'm just sorry it took us so long to sit down and have a talk. Let's not be strangers, Michaela."

They hugged. Tash went to the door and opened it to the cold. Then Michaela said, "If you want to send that silly daughter of mine home, it's okay."

"You sure?"

"Yeah."

"All right," said Tash, nodding.

"I been worried sick about her, you want to know the truth."

"I know."

"But when she told me about it, I just…I couldn't even see straight I was so mad."

"I know," said Tash. Her smile was sad. "We'll get her through this somehow."

Michaela returned the sad smile. "Just us womenfolk, huh?"

Tash shrugged. "What else we got?"

Her eyes held Michaela's a moment longer. Then Tash pulled the knit cap low over her eyes and went out into the cold.

thirteen

Dog watched her go.

From behind the wheel of the old Monte Carlo, squinting through the gray haze that floated from the tip of his cigarette and curled against the ceiling, he observed as Profit's mother tightened the sash on her coat and ducked her head against the malice of the wind. The radio was playing an old Motown song and Dog tapped the steering wheel in time as he watched. Fury hated his taste in music, but Dog didn't care. Rap gave him a headache. Bunch of punks and wannabes, studio gangsters fronting about what hardcore thugs they were when most of them lived on gated estates and sent their children to private schools.

On the radio, David Ruffin was begging the skies to please make rain so nobody would see the tears in his eyes. And his boys the Temptations were stair-stepping up the scale behind him in tight harmony. Dog sang with them, loudly and happily off-key. Now that old-school stuff was real music, he thought, some guy brought down to his knees over a girl.

Real music? Hell, it was real life.

Ronnie said he was an old soul. Probably something to that, Dog thought. He allowed himself a smile in the darkness as he crushed out the cigarette and fanned the smoke. He would have to stop and get some breath mints before he went out to see Ronnie. If she smelled cigarettes on his breath, she would give him grief.

When Profit's mom was a block ahead, Dog pulled his hoodie up over his head and got out of the car. The cold bit down on him and he cursed. It would have been nice to stay in the car where it was warm, but he couldn't take that chance. Few things could be more obvious than a car following one woman on foot, especially on a dark night when the streets were quiet and nobody with any sense was out. Dog didn't even like walking a block behind her. They had the sidewalk to themselves and all she had to do was glance over her shoulder and recognize him and it would all hit the fan.

He had shaken her up a little bit, he knew, coming up on her like that as she was going inside her house. The memory was good for another smile.

Then a wind stiff as a forearm shove slammed into him and he cursed again and tucked his head deeper into the hood. Why Profit's mama hadn't let that boyfriend of hers drive her home, Dog didn't know. When the van had stopped in the projects, he had gotten his hopes up, figuring that maybe here was where she had Profit stashed. But he had walked around looking in windows while the two women sat in the living room watching that Denzel Washington movie. He was pretty sure Profit wasn't there. He would check again tomorrow to be sure, but he didn't expect to find the boy in that lady's place. From what he had heard, she didn't have a whole lot of love for him.

It was just more reason to believe Profit's mom had told him the truth, that her son was out of his town with his pops. But he had to be sure. You didn't get anywhere in this life by taking people's word. So Dog followed Profit's mom, his footfalls soft behind her, keeping to the shadows. He liked following her. There was something intimate about it, about seeing but not being seen. It was like being with somebody who didn't even know you were there.

To his surprise, the thought made him hard and being hard made him think again of Ronnie. It was still early. He looked forward to seeing her when he was done here. They couldn't do anything, he knew that. Sex was out of the question. But sometimes it was enough just to be with her. Dog liked the way he was when he was with her. Like all the bad stuff was put behind him, like she took him to a place where nothing but her could touch him.

Profit's mom looked back.

Caught off guard, caught thinking happy thoughts when he should have been focused on what he was doing, Dog froze. Looked around for a store window to study intently, but there was none. An hour squeezed itself into half a second. He waited for her to scream and run, calculating how long it would take him to reach her and once he did, what he should do to shut her up. Then Profit's mom turned back and kept walking. Dog realized that he was too far back, too close to the shadows. She hadn't seen him. Felt him, maybe, but hadn't seen him.

He breathed, then forced himself to put a foot forward. Time enough later for happy thoughts. Right now, he had to find Profit. Dog had no idea what he would do when he did find that little bitch. Step to him? Take the soft approach and try to figure out where his head was at? Bust a cap in his ass? Which one made sense? Fury was going crazy in lockup, convinced that Profit and DC were both talking their asses off, so Dog knew what his brother would say. *Smoke both their asses. Smoke 'em like a pack of Camels.*

But Dog didn't want to do that without first making sure there was a good reason. He didn't want to kill somebody just because his punk-ass brother was nervous. That wasn't right. Of course, if it turned out either of those boys had been running off at the mouth, Dog would do what needed to be done. Snitches get stitches, as the saying went.

Remembering to stay deep in shadows, Dog followed Profit's mother home. She was a lonely figure on streets mostly emptied out by cold and he almost felt sorry for her. Something about it reminded him of his own mother, shuffling on that leg, the swelling so hideous she seemed on first glance to have no foot at all, just a monstrous calf, the skin stretched shiny black.

There was a grief in her, Dog knew, a grief deep and old. And it dug itself deeper, aged a little more, every time he or his brother went to jail. Every time they showed themselves useless. Every time they made her know she had wasted her time having them.

Used to be, that hadn't bothered him so much. But somewhere along the way, Dog had come to hate making her feel like that. He had not been in trouble in almost two years. He had been taking auto-repair classes at the junior college, applying for jobs. He was thinking that someday, he would even have a shop of his own. And, he had Ronnie. He was getting his life together.

Suddenly, Raiford Willis was furious with his brother, outraged that Fury had put him in this situation. Bad enough the fool had jammed himself up, bad enough he was looking at some serious time, but look where he had put Dog. Out here in the bitter cold, following some other fool's mother down the street. And for what? So he could throw some fear into the other fool? Maybe do him dirt if that was the way it had to be?

And then what would happen? What would become of the life he was trying to build? What would Mary Willis say, if she had to see her oldest son through the plastic window again as she had so many times before? Would she even bother to come? Would he blame her if she did not?

Profit's mother went inside her house. It took a moment to register on Dog, so wrapped was he in anger. He watched the door close, watched the shadow of her shrug out of her coat. Profit wasn't inside. He knew that because he had been in there himself, not two hours before. His heart had jumped painfully in his chest when he came upon some young female he hadn't expected to find. Luckily, she was engrossed in a TV show, didn't see him peeping in from the kitchen. Dog had gotten out of there as fast as he could. But what would have happened if she had seen him? Jumped up and called the cops? What would he have done then?

Damn that Fury.

Dog wheeled around and walked briskly back to the car. It occurred to him that maybe he just didn't have the heart for this stuff anymore. And maybe that wasn't a bad thing. Maybe not a bad thing at all. But what could he do? He was trapped. Fury was a fool, yes. Fury was also his brother. Dog slammed the car door hard. The engine started with a roar, Aretha Franklin came up singing "Respect."

R-E-S-P-E-C-T, find out what it means to me.

He threw the car into gear and pulled out too fast. It took him half an hour, even in light traffic. She lived way on the north side of town. As Dog drove, strip malls and government buildings gave way to mansions surrounded by acres of lawn, vivid green and precision neat, even in the deep of winter. He reached the right subdivision, drove past the guard with a nod, took a left and then another left and finally turned into the driveway of the brick castle where she lived, the old Monte Carlo crawling up the flawless asphalt as conspicuous and ugly as a roach on white tile.

The house loomed over him as he stepped from the car, accent lights looking down from gold sconces, double doors towering high and imperial, windows watching him. It was, he had always felt, a place designed to remind you that you weren't good enough. It did an excellent job. Dog touched the button for the doorbell. He remembered to yank the hood down from his head a moment before the door came open.

The Judge was there. Charles Isaiah Richmond was a lawyer who had made his fortune in private practice before embarking on a career in public service that had landed him on the circuit court bench. But his daughter Veronica always called him The Judge in a tone of portent and mockery and Dog had picked up the habit, though never to Richmond's face. To The Judge's face, he called him "sir," on those rare occasions he dared croak out any greeting at all.

This was not one of those times. When he saw who was standing at his door, The Judge's eyes hardened. He did not acknowledge Dog with so much as a nod, didn't hold the door for him to come in. Instead, he turned away and bellowed his daughter's name—one sharp bark of command—then disappeared back into the house.

Dog stepped into the foyer beneath the crystal chandelier and waited, cap in hand. After a moment one of the maids came through. She was a short, plump, black woman, and she took his coat and cap without a word. It wasn't just The Judge. The whole house hated him.

Everybody except Ronnie. She came down the spiral staircase now at a trot, smiling in anticipation of him and his heart quickened as it always did at the beauty of her. Flawless skin, high cheekbones, dimples, eyes that danced. Her belly was swollen taut with the life she now carried inside. His baby. His daughter.

He knew why The Judge hated him. Why the maid and the gardener and the houseman who had doted on "Miss Ronnie," ever since she was a child, all hated him too. He was a nothing sitting behind the wheel of a raggedy car that scuttled up their driveway like a bug, a nothing who came to their door trailing two strikes for assault and a juvie beef for dealing drugs. And he had dared to touch her, to soil her, to implant her with his dirty seed.

He knew why they hated him. He didn't blame them. They only tolerated him, only allowed him through the door because of the improbable, the incredible, the astonishing.

She loved him. He couldn't quite believe it himself.

Then she was in his arms, smelling like fresh apples—some stuff she put in her hair—and he couldn't make himself stop grinning. "Hey, baby," he said.

"Ray, honey, you didn't tell me you were coming."

"I was in the neighborhood," he lied.

She kissed him. "'In the neighborhood.' I bet," she said. But she lightened her skepticism with a laugh.

"Okay, then," he said. "I just wanted to see you. How's that?"

Another kiss. "That's fine," she said.

She loved him. How amazing was that?

They had met on the community college campus, he struggling through a math course, she the graduate student from the local university whose job it was to help students like him pull through. They met Wednesday evenings in the library, from six to eight, and at first it had all been business. He knew she was stunning, of course, but he also knew she was so far out of his league that he could be twice the man he was and still not be half good enough for her. He had put out of his mind any thought of stepping to her. She was friendly enough, but as near as he could tell, she never even looked at him close enough to pick him out of a lineup. He was just an obligation to her, just a guy she tutored.

Then, the Wednesday before Thanksgiving, he was running through the parking lot to catch the last bus when he saw her standing two rows over near her car, arms folded, eyes sharp with disgust. He walked over and asked if she was okay. She told him her car had died. The sun was long gone and the campus nearly deserted, people getting an early start on the holiday. The auto-club tow truck could not be there for two hours.

So he waited with her. She told him he didn't have to, but he could tell she was grateful when he insisted. The campus was in a bad neighborhood and she had no business waiting there alone.

They spent the two hours talking. He had never known how powerful just talking could be. But it was just easy to tell her things,

things he never said to anybody, things about his life and the mess he had made of it, about getting in trouble and going to jail and the fact that his mother was disappointed in him and the way he wanted more, even if he wasn't exactly sure what that more was. He couldn't believe the things that were coming out of him, sitting there in the darkness in the front seat of the dead car, couldn't believe what he was saying to this woman he didn't even know.

Dog kept waiting for a sign that she was humoring him, kept looking for the telltale smirk or lift of eyebrow that would say she was laughing at him, poor little hood rat, pouring out his heart to a rich bitch from the right side of town who couldn't care less what he wanted or dreamt. But Dog never saw it. Never saw anything but her listening.

He realized then that he had never had anyone listen to him before, not even his mother. It was a new feeling. A feeling that lifted him above himself.

She told him about her life, too, and he was amazed at the insecurities that lived inside a woman he had thought beyond doubt. She missed her mother. Or more accurately, she missed the idea of a mother, since her mother had died so long ago that Ronnie didn't remember her. And she missed her father, too, though they lived in the same house. But The Judge was a reserved and austere man by nature and he had pulled even further inside himself after his wife's death. Ronnie knew he loved her, but there was no relationship there. No smiles and hugs and secrets passing from father to daughter. "Just once," she said, "I wish he would notice me for something more than how I'm doing in school."

Dog had felt honored that she entrusted him with truths so painful. No one ever had before. He was sorry when the tow truck headlights shone through the cab. The man from the auto club diagnosed the problem quickly: a dead battery. He installed a new one, Ronnie produced a credit card, and that was that. She asked Dog where he was parked. He told her he had no car, but not to worry about it, he would get home fine. She wouldn't hear of it. She gave him a ride home.

They drove down the street past the corner boys standing out there making their illicit deals, past baleful eyes, tiny yards, broken-down cars, and garish light from the place across the street that sold fried catfish. So many times, he had walked down this block without seeing it. It came to his eyes now as if for the first time and he had to fight an urge to sink into the heated leather seat. But if she noticed any of it, she didn't say. Just dropped him off and thanked him and told him Happy Thanksgiving.

People gave him hard looks, seeing him get out of a nice car driven by a woman that fine. He didn't care. They asked him questions. He just waved them off. He and Ronnie became friends after that. And then, they became more.

Until here she was, belly full of his daughter, pressed against him. And now pulling back, nose crumpled in sudden distaste. Dog winced. He had been in such a hurry he had forgotten to get something for his breath.

"You been smoking," she said. Not a question.

"Uh," he said.

"Ray, you promised me you would quit."

"I slipped," he said. It sounded lame even to him.

"Slipped."

"Yeah. Look, I'm sorry."

"No, Ray, *I'm* sorry." Face all business now, no give in it. "We've had this talk before, you and me. You've got to put those things down. I'm not going to have my baby exposed to secondhand smoke. Do you know what's in that stuff? You don't want your child breathing that."

"I know," said Dog. "I'm trying, okay? But it's hard, you know? You don't know what it's like, 'cause you didn't never smoke, but it ain't that easy to quit."

"I know it's not easy, Ray, but I know it can be done. Try the nicotine patch or something. But I'm serious, you've got to stop doing this by the time the baby arrives."

The concern in her eyes made him smile. He placed his left hand on the swell of her stomach, lifted his right, like taking an oath on a Bible. "I swear," he said.

"It's not funny," she insisted.

"I'm not laughing," he told her.

She searched his eyes for mockery. Finally, she just smiled. "I don't mean to be a hard-ass Ray. It's just...this is our baby. I want the best for her."

He caressed her cheek. "Yeah," he said. "I do, too."

Sometimes, Dog thought it couldn't all be real. Sometimes, he was sure this was all just something she was doing to get back at The Judge, to make him wish he had paid attention all those years when she was growing up before his eyes, unseen. But sometimes, he dared to think maybe it had nothing to do with The Judge. Maybe she really did love him.

This was one of those times. She kissed the hand on her cheek. "Come on," she said. "Let's watch some television."

They went into the TV room—she always called it that, not the "den" or the "family room," because this house *had* a den and a family room, and was vast enough to also have a room dedicated solely to watching television—and sank together into the overstuffed leather loveseat. She passed him the remote the way she always did and it made him feel as it always did, like the lord of the castle, loved and lovingly deferred to. For a moment, he allowed himself to pretend it was so, that this was his house and she was his wife curled up next to him, chin on his shoulder, and all was good

But he knew it was just pretend. How did you even get a place like this? What did it cost and how did you go about it? It was like neuroscience to him and after a moment, he stopped torturing himself with wondering, content to click channels in the vague hope that maybe there was something good on ESPN Classic.

"I tried to reach you today," Ronnie was saying.

He made a noncommittal sound. ESPN Classic was showing the Lakers and Celtics, an old Finals game from the 80s. Magic Johnson lobbed the ball in to Kareem Abdul-Jabbar, then cut through the key.

"Spoke to your mother," said Ronnie. "She's not doing well, is she?"

It was the only thing about Ronnie that he didn't like. Sometimes, she wouldn't just be quiet and let him watch television. It was a small thing, he reminded himself.

"No," he said, without looking. "That leg swells up on her something fierce. She shouldn't be on it, tell you the truth."

"Well, when you start working, you'll be able to take some of the load off of her."

A steal. Dennis Johnson going downcourt for an uncontested layup. Underrated player, that guy. Then he realized Ronnie was waiting for an answer. "Yeah," he said. "I've got a line on a couple jobs. I expect to know something by Friday. It looks good, though."

She smiled, leaned against his shoulder, her arm falling loosely across his lap. The maid came through, same maid that had taken Dog's coat, and dusted the bookshelves. She gave him a look that could make water run back into the tap. He didn't care. He felt lordly still. The Celtics were up by six.

"What about your brother?"

He glanced down, surprised. "What do you mean?"

"Is he okay? Do you know when he's getting out?"

This brought a smirk from the maid, confirmation of his worthlessness. Ronnie missed it. "No," he said. "I don't know. They got him on a million-dollar bail. No way we can raise that kind of money."

"It's a damn shame, the way they do black men in this country," said Ronnie.

Now the maid gave a grunt, her contempt audible. "Excuse me," said Dog sharply, "you got a problem or somethin'?"

She speared him with the eyes again. He didn't care. He was tired of being treated like something dirty, even by the hired help, whenever he came to see his woman.

Ronnie caught it this time. Her glanced traveled from Dog to the maid. "Rebecca," said Ronnie in a firm, even voice, "that'll be enough. You can finish this room later." The maid scowled, her scorn so righteous and complete she felt no need to hide it. She tossed the dust rag down and made a show of leaving the room.

"I'm sorry about that," said Ronnie when she was gone. "I don't know what's gotten into her. I'll talk to her about it."

"Don't bother," said Dog. He went back to the game. Magic Johnson leading the break, dishing off to James Worthy. Dog sighed. He wasn't into it anymore. He lowered the volume, looked down and met Ronnie's questioning eyes.

"You shouldn't make people like my brother and me into something we ain't. That's what your maid was sayin'."

She pulled away so she could face him. "I don't understand."

"Well, it's like when you say how bad they treat black men. That's true, but see, it ain't like Fury—I mean, Cedric—ain't did nothing. You don't know my brother. He a stone thug, that boy. They got him for robbery and murder, and you know what? I wouldn't be surprised if he guilty. See, that's what I'm saying. Don't try to make more out of a man than he is. I mean, we are what we are."

One eyebrow lifted. "We?" she said.

He shrugged because he didn't know what else to do. "I'm just sayin'," he said.

But she wouldn't let it go. "What are you saying, Ray?" He tried shrugging again. She wasn't having it. "No, tell me: what *are* you saying?"

"I'm just sayin'…" A pause. Time enough to wonder how a pleasant evening had suddenly gone bad. "We come from a different life than you, that's all. We come from the streets, you come from high society. See, that's what you ain't figured out yet. You can take a nigger out the streets. Ain't so easy taking the streets out the—"

And then his hand was flying to the cheek she had slapped, and his mouth was hanging open. "Bullshit," she said, behind an index finger leveled at his nose. "That's bullshit."

She looked as if she was going to cry. He reached for her. "Baby…"

Ronnie drew herself back from his touch. "You're right," she said. "I don't know your brother. If you'll recall, you never let me meet him. But I do know you, Raiford Willis. You want things in your life. You want to be somebody, somebody decent. That's what you told me, isn't it? You said you want to achieve things. You've got some goodness in your soul. Why do you think I'm with you in the first place? You're not your brother, Ray. You are *not* him."

Feeling flooded him, a sudden tenderness that left him nearly speechless. "Baby…" he said again. He stopped, not knowing how to go on. He reached for her again. This time, her hand intercepted his and guided it gently down to the swell of her stomach.

Her eyes searched him out. "*This* is your baby," she said. "This is your daughter. She's going to need you, Ray. She's going to depend on you to show her how the world works, to teach her what she needs to know. You have to be here for her. Do you understand?"

"Yeah, I do, but…"

She cut him off, eyes still searching him. "You're not your brother, Ray. I know family is family. But I'm your family now, too. And this baby that's growing inside me, that's your family, too. And you have obligations to us. You can't be out there doing all the things your brother does."

"But he's my brother. I have to watch his back."

"Watch his back, yes. But you can't die for your brother. You can't wreck your life for him."

"You don't understand," he said.

"Ray, baby…" She bit her lip. Touched his hand, still molded to the curve of her stomach. "The first time we talked—I mean, really talked—you told me how you wanted a new life. Well, this is it. It's right here inside of me, growing. But sometimes, before you can grab the new life, you've got to let the old one go."

He looked down at her stomach, up at her eyes. Patient, waiting. He felt himself drowning, still buffeted by feelings so new he didn't quite know how to feel them. Then Dog heard himself say, "I'm not sure if I can." He had not known the words were coming till he heard them and it made him curse Fury all over again.

"You're not sure if you can." She said it as if trying to pronounce foreign words.

"Baby," he said, "you got to understand…"

"How can you say that to me, Ray?" she demanded and now there was heat in her eyes. "Do you understand that I went to the wall for you? I went against my own father for you, Ray. Went against him, went against everybody else in my life trying to tell me you weren't good enough. I told them there was more to you than the way you looked and the fact that you'd been in trouble. I told them how you were smart, smarter than they thought, smarter than even you understand. I told them how you make me laugh. And now you tell me this? You're not sure if you can let go of the old life that never brought you anything but trouble?"

He felt small. Felt newborn helpless. "It ain't like that!" he said.

She opened her mouth to reply, closed it. Ronnie regarded him for a moment, her expression turning suspicious. "What have you been up to, Ray? What are you doing out there you have no business doing?"

"Nothin'," he said, wondering how she knew, how she read him so readily.

"Uh-huh," she said. Suspicion hardening to skepticism.

"Baby, I got it all under control," he told her.

"Yeah," she said.

"You don't get it. My brother need me."

"Your daughter needs you, Ray. *I* need you."

"Ronnie, I know…"

He stopped because now she was standing over him, a hand to her temple. "Ray, I don't feel too good. Why don't we call it a night, huh?"

Dog stood, put a hand on her arm. "Ronnie, don't make me—"

"Ray, I just need a little time. Need to do some thinking. Why don't you see yourself out." He teetered there a long moment, unbelieving. She kept her head down, refused to give him her eyes. Finally Dog nodded and went out to the foyer. The maid, Rebecca, was already standing there with his jacket in hand. She held it like it was dirty, kept her face studiously neutral, void of comment. Which was, he knew, a comment all by itself.

He took the coat. And then he couldn't help himself. He looked back toward the TV room. The television was off. Ronnie was gone. Dog felt like Adam, banished from Eden. Rebecca held the door for him. "You must be lovin' this," he whispered as he passed. Still her face said nothing. Dog passed through the door. It closed on his heels. He slipped into the jacket, pulled his hood over his ears, jammed his hands in his pockets, walked toward the Monte Carlo.

A voice said, "It's a shame, isn't it, when a man can't smoke in his own house?"

Dog whipped around. The Judge, huddled up in a parka, was smoking a cigarette in front of the garage. "Don't tell Veronica," he said. "She thinks I've quit. She'd kill me if she found out."

Dog nodded dumbly, his mind unencumbered by words.

The Judge said, "You do speak, don't you?"

Another nod. "But you ain't never spoke to me," said Dog. "Not hardly."

The Judge took a final draw on the cigarette, crushed it against the lid of the garbage can. He lifted the lid and deposited the telltale butt, then came forward, wiping his hands against one another. "I don't like you," he said. "I thought I'd made that clear."

"You made it clear," said Dog.

"Good," said The Judge. He inclined his head toward the car. "You're leaving?"

"Yeah."

"So soon?"

"Yeah. That is, Ronnie wanted to call it a night."

"I see," said The Judge. And then: "So, Willis, how much would it take for you to leave here and not come back?"

It was a punch he never saw coming. "Say what?"

"I didn't stammer, did I? I don't want you around my daughter. Lord knows you've already done enough damage already. I hate to think what else you might do to drag her down."

"I love her," said Dog. "She love me." The words seemed thin like high-altitude air.

The Judge dismissed the protest with a wave. "I'm a wealthy man, Willis. You're not. In fact, as I understand it, you live in some rathole downtown across from a catfish stand. I see niggers like you every day. Come before my bench for car theft and drug dealing, assault, rape, murder. I know what you are and I know what you're about, even if Veronica doesn't. And I don't want you around her anymore. So let's do business. Don't act like you don't know what I'm talking about, don't act like you don't need the money. How much do you want? What would it take for you to go away and leave my daughter alone? Five thousand? Ten thousand? What's your price?"

Dog looked at The Judge. For a moment that seemed as if it would never end, that was all he could do—just look at him. The Judge waited. Gave him those pale gray eyes, the color of clouds with sun behind them. There was something infuriating about the calmness of them, the absolute assurance that they would wait you out if you waited a hundred years. Find your price even if you thought you didn't have one. Dog rehearsed a dozen responses in his mind. He rehearsed indignant cursing. He rehearsed yes. But in the end, he said what he said without conscious thought.

"I love her," he repeated. "She love me." The words sounded stronger now, more sure. That pleased him.

But The Judge just laughed. "Yeah," he said. "So you told me."

Dog pushed past him to the car, not sure he could keep from hitting the old man smack in the middle of that cocky laugh. He opened the door and climbed in.

"We'll talk again," he heard The Judge say, just before the door slammed.

He started the car. Sam and Dave were singing "When Something Is Wrong With My Baby." Dog felt as if he were sinking into a mine, bidding sunlight farewell. Somehow, his life had shriveled itself to a simple choice.

His woman needed him. And she offered a beginning, a chance to be someone he wanted down to the very soul of him to be. But his fool of a brother needed him, too. Needed him for what, he suddenly realized, would surely be a last dark deed. Not a threat, not a beat down, but the darkest of all possible deeds. His brother, his woman. His past, his future.

Dog knew with a sickening certainty that he could not choose both. He would choose one and it would cost him the other.

Sam Moore's voice was dashing itself to pieces on shoals of misery as Dog put the car into gear. And then the Monte Carlo was retreating, the imperious house growing smaller, its master lighting another cigarette and watching him go.

fourteen

Trey took his time, enjoying himself too much to rush. He was up by 12, game point. His father faced him on rubber legs, sweat bubbling on his brow. Trey hadn't noticed before, but his dad was getting old. More gray in his hair, more thickness to his gut. And now a simple game of hoops had his mouth working like a goldfish on a tabletop. Them damn nasty-ass cigarettes had something to do with that, thought Trey.

But there was something else, too, something Trey could not quite frame in his thoughts. His father seemed...not right. Close maybe, but not right. Trey couldn't say how he knew this, but he did.

Then Dad snapped at him. "Come on, boy," he said in a raspy gasp. "Ain't got all day."

The bravado made Trey grin because it was so empty. He started to respond in kind, but didn't. There wasn't any need. Let the old man talk. Talk was all he had left.

So Trey just continued to dribble lazily, the ball pounding a "V" between left hand and right, going between his legs occasionally for show. He was bent almost into a crouch, eyes leveled on his father, making sure the message was getting across.

I'm 'bout to whup your ass and ain't nothin' you can do about it.

He thought he saw the understanding in his father's eyes and it occurred to him that it must be a hell of a thing to know your own child is about to whup you. And to know he knows it, too. He almost felt sympathy. Almost.

Trey watched his father's eyes. Waited. Waited.

Now.

Jab step to the left. His father bit on it like lunch. Trey pulled back in one liquid motion, the dribble crossing over, going to his right, passing his father like a Ferrari passes a mailbox. And there was nothing but air between him and the basket. Trey tensed, preparing to launch himself for the easy lay-in. Then, two arms wrapped themselves around his waist. Yanked off stride, Trey flipped the ball toward the hoop.

"Foul!" he yelled as the ball caromed off the backboard. "That's a foul."

"No...blood. No...foul," gasped his dad.

"Oh, is that how it is?" said Trey, trotting to retrieve the ball. "Okay, let's go, then. Your ball."

Dad lifted his palms in truce. "Let's just...call it a...tie," he pleaded.

"Tie?" Trey didn't bother hiding his scorn. "What tie? I'm winning."

"Yeah, well...if we play it...out...you're going to...have to find...someplace to...plant my ass." Dad dropped onto the grass that ringed the court, swiping at the sweat that swam down his temple.

Getting old, thought Trey. It was a sobering thought. "So you forfeit, then," he said. "I win." He was casually banking in layups.

"Yeah, okay," said Dad.

"You got to say it," said Trey, spinning the ball up through the hoop.

"Say...what?"

"Say, 'I forfeit. Trey wins. Trey is the greatest baller of all times.'"

"Boy, I ain't sayin'... You just got lucky, that's all."

Trey thought about pushing it. He was competitive and hated anything less than clear-cut victory. But somehow, the idea of his father reduced to denying what they both knew to be true was almost as good. "Fine," he said. "Whatever."

He walked over and sat in the grass next to Mo. They were silent together for a moment, still except for the clap of leather against Trey's hands as he tossed the ball into the air and caught it. Finally, Trey lay back, the ball under his head like a pillow and closed his eyes. They were in western Oklahoma. Lunch had been a chain restaurant just off the interstate. The game afterward was Trey's idea. A way to stretch their legs and get a little exercise before getting back on the road.

A breeze brushed Trey's forehead. He took a cleansing breath. The grass smelled freshly mown. Then he heard his father's voice. "Okay," he said, "you win."

Trey's eyes came open. "Say what?"

His father, still sitting, shrugged. "Hey, man, you got the legs. I don't anymore. Wish you could've caught me 20 years ago. I'd have whipped your ass. I was a ball-playin' fool back in the day. Now, I don't know if you're the 'greatest baller of all time'—Kobe and M.J. might want to talk to you about that—but you're better than me. Better than I ever was."

Trey grinned. Then he was suspicious. "Why you admit it?"

"It's the truth," said Dad, simply. "You get to be my age, you like to deny that the young ones are gaining on you, that they're going to pass you up. Maybe you think if you don't admit it, it won't happen. But it happens whether you admit it or not. Nothing stays the same forever, much as you might want it to."

There it was again, thought Trey, that sense of something not quite right. He didn't know how to say this, so he said, "You okay?"

Dad nodded, hand on his chest like he was pledging allegiance. "Just let me catch my breath," he said. Which wasn't what Trey meant, but he didn't know how to say that, either, so he just nodded. His cell phone yelled at him then. "Hey, fool! Pick up the phone!"

Trey flipped open the clamshell. "Who dis?" he said.

"How many times have I told you about answering the phone that way, Trey Johnson?" said his mother.

Trey winced and wished he had thought to check the Caller ID before speaking. "Hey, Mom," he said. He wondered how much of a lecture he was in for.

But she let it go. "Where are you?" she asked.

"Oklahoma," he said. "Some little town. I don't know the name."

"Your father's with you?"

"Yeah, we just come from lunch. We was ballin'."

"Excuse me?"

"Playing basketball," corrected Trey. She knew what he meant. Moms could be such a pain sometimes.

"You guys all right?"

He glanced over at his father, still looking ragged. "We a'ight," he said. And then, before she could correct him, he said, "We're all right."

"English, Trey," she said. "It's the language here in this country. You should try it sometime."

"Oh. You got jokes."

He wanted to ask her if she'd noticed something about Pops, something out of place that she couldn't quite put words to. But his dad was sitting right there and even if he hadn't been, Trey didn't know how to ask without sounding foolish.

"Some guy was looking for you yesterday," she said.

"Who?"

"I didn't know him. He said his name was Raiford."

"I don't know no Raiford."

"He said you all call him Dog."

"Oh. Dog. Why ain't you say so? That's Fury's brother. He say what he want?"

"He said this other boy wanted him to check up on you."

Fury wanting to make sure he kept his mouth shut, didn't turn pussy and start snitching to the cops. Fool didn't know, Trey had no reason to sing. Then he realized Mom didn't know either. He had tried to call her, but she hadn't picked up. "Hey," he said, "guess what?"

It was as if she didn't hear him. "That's how he put it, Trey," she said. "'Check up on you.'"

Had she always been so paranoid? "Ain't nothin', Mom," he said. "Just my boy wantin' to see if I'm okay is all."

"I got a bad feeling from him."

"You get bad feelings from everybody. Now listen, I'm trying to tell you something." Trey caught sight of his father, then, watching him. The expression was unreadable. He turned away. "My lawyer says they ain't got no case against me."

"What do you mean?"

"What I said. He say they offerin' a deal, want me to testify against Fury and DC. But he told me to hold out, because they desperate. He say they gon' have to drop the charges because they ain't got no evidence."

His mother gasped, a loud intake of breath. She was silent so long Trey wondered if she was still there. "Mom?" he said.

"Thank you, Jesus," she whispered, her voice trembling and fervent. "Thank you, Jesus. Thank you, Jesus."

At least his mother knew good news when she heard it. Unlike Dad. Trey grinned. "You need to thank the lawyer, too, Mom."

"You think this is a joke? Boy, do you understand the kind of trouble you were facing? Do you know what the Lord has brought you through?"

"I know, Mom," said Trey.

"No you don't. If you did, you'd be on your knees, thanking Him. If you did, you'd be trying to turn your life around."

Trey sighed. He hadn't meant to bring on a sermon. "Look, Mom," he began. He stopped when he saw the cop. His shoes crunched on the asphalt as he approached. His car was parked in the lot behind the SUV, its lights flashing. "Got to go," said Trey. He closed the clamshell without waiting for a reply.

"Afternoon," the officer said.

"Afternoon," said Dad. Trey did not speak.

"Did you know this was private property?" said the cop.

Trey glanced around. No fence marked the basketball court off from entry. No signs warned against trespassing. There were benches a hundred yards away, ringing a play area with swings, slides and a brightly-painted merry-go-round.

"Didn't look private to me," his father said. "We were just playing basketball, me and my son, here."

Another patrol car was pulling in behind the first. "I'll need to see some IDs," said the officer. He was young, big, with freckles and bristly blond hair. A black name tag on his left breast identified him as Gustaffson. Trey stabbed a hand into his front pocket—the officer flinched, he saw—and came out with his driver's license. The cop took it, studied it for a moment, made no move to return it.

"Mine is in the car," said Mo, nodding toward the SUV.

"Well, let's go get it," said the officer, motioning with his hand like a gate.

Trey felt his fist clench, heard his own breathing like a steam engine in his ear. He followed his father and the cop as they hiked across the grass. Seeing them coming, the two new arrivals stood at their car, waiting.

"We weren't doing anything," Dad was saying. "Just playing ball. I didn't see any signs." Repeating himself like a little kid trying to get out of an ass-whipping.

"Well, I'm sure we can get it straightened out pretty quickly," said the officer in a friendly voice that made Trey hate him all the more.

When they reached the SUV, Dad opened the passenger-side door and reached across the console for his wallet. He extracted the driver's license and handed it to Gustaffson, who studied it, then said, "You're a long way from home, Mr. Johnson."

"Yes, I know. We're driving to California."

"Oh? Business or pleasure?"

"Pleasure," said Trey, cutting in. "We going to Disneyland."

His father shot him a look of reprimand. Trey looked away, still breathing loud. His cell phone shouted at him—his mother, calling back, he knew. Trey turned the phone off.

"You got registration in there?" asked Gustaffson, after giving Trey a hard look. "Why don't you get that for me, too?"

As Dad leaned back into the vehicle, one of the new officers—DeBakey, according to his name tag—said, "This is a pretty nice ride. How much this set you back, Mr. Johnson?"

"Close to $70,000," said Dad as he handed over his registration. Trey knew where they were going with this. Doubtless his father did, too.

"Really?" An appreciative nod for the benefit of the other two cops. "Wish I could afford $70K for a set of wheels. How's it happen that you can afford something like this, Mr. Johnson?"

"He invented the Internet," said Trey.

They turned toward him as one, all pretense of civility momentarily gone from their eyes. They glared at him. Dad squeezed Trey's shoulder, smiled at the cops. "Officers, my son and I would really like to get back on the road. We were just working off a big lunch and we have a long way to go. So if there's nothing else…"

Gustaffson said, "Why don't you two have a seat on the curb for a moment?"

He took their licenses, went to his car, and got on the radio. The other two cops waited by the SUV. Dad sat. After a moment, Trey did, too. It took 20 minutes. Just trying to sweat us, he thought. It didn't take that long to run no fuckin' license plates.

Halfway through the wait, DeBakey said, "So you never did say what business you were in."

"Music," said Dad, staring straight ahead, angry now himself, Trey saw. There was a Dairy Queen across the street. Several teen-agers—white boys sipping on milkshakes—were clustered there, watching. "I'm a singer," Dad added.

"Really?" A theatrical lifting of the eyebrow. "I never heard of you."

"Are you kidding?" demanded Trey. "This is Moses Johnson you got jacked up here. 'My Prophecy?' He won a Grammy Award."

The cop shrugged. "Can't say it rings any bells. 'Course, I mainly just listen to country, myself. You know, Alan Jackson? Randy Travis? You ever meet any of them?"

"Never had the pleasure," said Dad.

A shrug. And then, "You know, I meant it about this car. Really nice. Probably a bitch on gas mileage, though."

"Costs a pretty penny," agreed Dad.

"We search it, we ain't gonna find anything we shouldn't, are we?"

Dad looked a question over at Trey: *You got anything in my car, son?*

Trey turned to the cop, lifted his chin. "Do what you got to do," he said.

"That's well and good, son," said the cop. "But it's not your car."

"He's not your son," said Dad. "And you heard him. Search if you want to."

DeBakey's smile froze. Dad turned back to watching the white boys at the Dairy Queen. There was no search.

Moments later, Gustaffson reappeared, smiling like he'd gotten laid. He reached the driver's licenses and registration back to Dad. "Sorry for the inconvenience, Mr. Johnson," he said. "Everything checks out. You and your son are free to go. Safe trip."

Trey thought he would be perfectly happy to smash the cop right in his face. Right in the middle of all that Officer Friendly bullshit. But Dad just stood up stiffly and accepted the documents. "Thank you," he said. "Good day."

The cops turned to go. Trey couldn't help himself. "Is that it?" he cried. And they all stopped and looked back at him.

"Beg pardon?" said Gustaffson.

Mo squeezed Trey's shoulder again. Trey shoved his hand away. "You haul us over here, make us sit on the curb like we some criminals, 20 minutes, 'cause we playing *basketball*? Why don't you just tell the truth, pig? Y'all seen some niggers you ain't known and you wanted to fuck with 'em, see what they about. Why don't you just say that? Or ain't you racist muh'fuckas man enough?"

DeBakey, scowling, took a step forward. "You got a smart mouth, boy."

"I got your boy," said Trey, grabbing his crotch.

"Somebody needs to teach you some manners," said DeBakey.

"Oh, you think you man enough to teach me, bitch?" Trey was moving toward confrontation, arms wide. "Come on, I'm right here. Or maybe you just pull out your gun and shoot me. Say it was self-defense like all you muh'fuckas do."

DeBakey took another step, lip curled in anticipation. Gustaffson put a hand on his chest, stopping him. Then, his brow creased with a look of concern, he pulled out his notepad and extracted a form. "Young man, I'm going to have to ask you to calm down and stop using abusive language. If you feel you've been treated unfairly, I can give you a form to fill out and the phone number of our citizen liaison, who I can assure you will investigate your concerns."

"Yeah, right," said Trey. "I know 'bout how much good that'll do."

"Are you saying you'd rather pass?"

Trey glared. "Yeah," he finally said. "Whatever."

He thought he saw a smile shadowing Gustaffson's lips as he put the form back into his notepad. He gave a nod and walked back toward his car.

"You need to learn from your dad, kid," called DeBakey. "Have some class."

Trey got back into the SUV. The police cars pulled out. The white boys across the street had gone on their way. Dad got behind the wheel.

Trey's voice was dark. "We wasn't doin' nothin' wrong," he said.

"You don't think I know that?" demanded Dad, both hands on the steering wheel, gripping it like he might break it in two.

"Then why you let 'em treat you like that? Why you just take it from them?"

"You think you're the only one, Trey?"

"What you mean? The only what?"

"You think you're the first? Like nobody before you ever had cops fuck with them when they weren't doing anything? You think nobody else ever hated it, Trey? We've all been there. But sometimes, you got no choice."

"Nah," said Trey, "I don't believe that. See, if it was me—"

His father cut him off. "Childhood's over, boy," said Dad, the engine snarling to life. "You need to grow up."

"What you talking about? I'm 19 years old, I got a kid. What am I if I ain't grown?"

"You may be 19," said Dad, "but you're not grown. You're not even close to being a man."

It was the second time he had said it. The second time in as many days. But hell, it wasn't Trey who had stood grinning like a fool, eager to please three racist white cops. Wasn't Trey who had acted like something out of the old days, back when they had to come bowing and shuffling before the white man. He was more than disappointed in his father. He felt betrayed, felt cut open to the bone.

Trey had always been starstruck by his father. From the time he was little, he had looked for excuses to tell people he was the son of the legend himself, the son of The Prophet. He liked how it made them treat you differently, made them give you second looks, made them want to do you favors. It was an easy way of being great. He wondered what all those people—all the ones who had asked him to get his father's autograph, all the ones who had deferred to him because of who his father was, all the ones who had clustered around asking questions as if he were The Prophet himself—would think if they could see his father right now.

This was the great Moses Johnson? This was the man who wrote the song that people sang as they marched in the streets right up to police barricades, waving their fists and demanding justice? This fat old man, too winded to get through a game of ball, bowing and scraping for the cops?

And now he had the nerve to be questioning Trey's manhood?

Fuck him.

Trey was surprised at how liberating the thought was. So he thought it again.

Fuck him.

It gave him so much satisfaction he almost smiled.

His father droned on. "Yeah, you're a man physically," he said. "You can raise foam in the toilet. Good for you. But to be a man, Trey, you got to know something about how to get along in the world. Take that situation back there, you mouthin' off to that cop. He's got a gun. He's got two other cops and the law behind him. And you think you being a man 'cause you grab your dick and talk shit. That's not a man. That's a fool. A smart man knows when to pick his battles and when to walk away."

"You walk away enough," said Trey, "and you might as well keep walkin'. You can't walk away from everything."

Fuck him.

"Maybe I just ain't scared of cops," added Trey. "Like you are."

To his surprise, that brought a grim smile as his father piloted the truck onto the interstate. "I'd have thought you'd had enough of police to last you awhile," Mo said.

"Man, I told you: you ain't got to worry about that no more. My lawyer said it's about to be straight."

"No, *my* lawyer said he could get you off. And you're acting like that means something, like it proves you were innocent or something. You ain't innocent. They just didn't have what they needed to prove you were guilty."

"What do it matter, long as it come out to the same?"

"Does it?"

Trey snorted in frustration, folded his arms, found something outside his window to be interested in. The big truck ground away a few miles. A road sign said that Texas was 22 miles away.

After a moment Dad said, "The way you behaved back there was stupid, Trey. It doesn't make you a man just because you grab your dick and talk shit. A smart man knows when to fight and when to walk away. You have to pick your battles."

Trey rolled his eyes. "You repeatin' yourself, man."

"What?"

"You repeatin' yourself. Pick your battles, don't grab your dick. You just said that five minutes ago."

Dad looked stricken. "I did?"

"Word for word."

A sorrow came into Mo's eyes then, a deep grief Trey could not place. "Must be getting old," mumbled Dad. "Forgetting things. What I'm trying to say is, you need to grow up. You need to get your shit together."

Trey heard himself say, "You don't think a whole lot of me, do you, Dad?"

His father regarded him now, a long and serious look. "I love you, Trey," he said. "You know that."

"Yeah," said Trey, "I know that." He hadn't failed to notice that his father had not denied it.

You don't think much of me, Trey had said.

And Dad hadn't said, *Don't be silly, Trey.* Hadn't said, *I think the world of you, son. I respect you.*

I love you. That's all he had said. *I love you.* Didn't answer the question. Didn't even try.

Fuck him.

Sorry, tired-ass old used-to-be. Weak, pussy-ass nigger.

He glanced at his father's profile, furious. But the fury would not hold. It softened like a balloon with the air leaking slowly out, deflated itself down to a hard knot of pain.

You don't think much of me, he had said. And his father had not said, Of course I do.

It surprised him how much that hurt.

fifteen

Las Vegas lay wan and languid under the late morning sun. The strip clubs and pawn shops looked tawdry and used-up in the unforgiving light. Flocks of tourists passed beneath the hotel marquees. Mo had always hated Vegas in the daylight. With the sun hanging high in a sky the color of dust, the city seemed bleached out, not quite real. Like a woman you took home the night before, seen now for the first time without makeup or alcohol or pure lust making her beautiful.

Vegas in daylight carried all the cruel revelations of a morning after. It was alive only after twilight, thought Mo. Real only when it was fake. He glanced across at Trey. His son had slept most of the last two hours, lulled to slumber by the numbing monotony of one red mesa after another. But he was certainly awake now, head swiveling like something on a hinge, trying to see it all. Mo smiled quietly as he turned onto Las Vegas Boulevard.

"Whoa," said Trey, as if to himself, "this here is the shit."

"Yeah," said Mo, "I guess it is."

The MGM Grand loomed ahead. A bronze-colored lion taller than a house raised itself on its forepaws in the center of a fountain on the corner of Tropicana. Across the street, the Statue of Liberty, somehow transported from New York Harbor, held her torch high against a backdrop of skyscrapers.

Impulsively, Mo whipped the truck into the parking structure. Trey's head came around. "We're stopping here?"

Mo shrugged. "Why not?"

Trey whispered it again. "This is the serious shit."

He was, thought Mo, so young. He wondered if he had been that young the day he and five other acts rolled in off the desert on a Ransom Records tour bus to perform at the Jack the Rapper black radio convention. That was the first time he'd ever tried cocaine, now that he thought about it. First it made him stupid, then it made him sick. Amazing that he had ever tried it again. And then again after that.

Mo parked the SUV. "We'll spend the night here," he announced. "Get up early and drive the rest of the way."

"How long is it to L.A.?" asked Trey.

"About five hours," said Mo. "But you don't want to try that desert in the middle of the day, if you can help it."

They got their bags out of the back and took an elevator that opened in the heart of the hotel. Mo was almost to the registration desk before he realized that he was alone. He looked back. Trey was walking slowly, head swiveling, mouth open.

Mo had forgotten what a sensory overload it could be. The gambling pits, the clatter of coins, the electronic bleat and beep of the machines, the lights beckoning, the women dressed in barely there, the people moving everywhere at once, the acres of glass and miles of marble, the lights, the shouts, the non-stop. Excitement manufactured fresh daily.

He went back and put a hand on his son's elbow, guiding him gently. "This is the shit," he heard his son say, voice muted by awe.

Mo was in luck. One of the terrace suites was available. A bellman escorted them up, carrying their bags. As Mo was tipping the young man, Trey toured the suite gleefully. There was a big-screen high-def television, a dining room that seated four, a bed sitting on a podium in the center of a master bedroom situated at the top of a spiral staircase, crystal bathroom fixtures, a vast patio, a commanding view of the gambling palaces below, fresh-cut flowers, monogrammed robes.

As the door closed behind the bellman, Trey said, "Now this is a hotel room."

"It is nice," said Mo, folding his wallet into his hip pocket.

"Nice? This is…"

"…the shit," said Mo. "Yeah, I know."

Trey looked at him. It was as if he had never quite seen his father before. "I guess all this is old to you, huh?"

Mo shrugged. "I've stayed in a few hotels over the years, Trey."

"Yeah, well I ain't," said Trey. "Motel 6 don't count. I definitely ain't stayed no place like this."

"I thought you might like it," said Mo.

Mo didn't. All at once, it depressed him, this grotesque display of God bless the child. Had he really come here to give his a son a treat? Or was he just showing off? Just speaking to Trey in the only language—money—left to him, the only one his son's generation seemed to understand? Maybe, he told himself, this was just a way of winning respect he had no other way to win. No other way and no more time.

Mo glanced out on the city, bright and ugly under the sun. He felt heavy-limbed and fatigued. Felt the weight of his own mortality pressing on him like unseen hands.

Trey, frisky as a puppy, didn't see. "Come on," he said. "Let's get out there."

Mo shook his head. "You go," he said. "Think I'll take a nap."

"A nap?" Trey was incredulous.

"I've been here before," said Mo. He pulled his wallet from his pocket, counted out $300 and handed it to Trey, who beamed like birthday and Christmas. "Go have some fun," he told Trey. "Meet me back here by six and we'll get something to eat."

"You sure?" asked Trey.

"Yeah," said Mo, reaching a room key to his son. "Be careful out there, don't be flashing that cash. There's all kind of pickpockets and hustlers out there ready to take it off you."

Trey, already halfway to the door, made a derisive sound. "Hell, I'm from B-Mo. Them fools better be watchin' out for me." The door closed behind him.

Mo shook his head, went up to the master bedroom, and undressed down to his underwear. He drew the legal pad out of his bag, along with a pen. Lit a cigarette, sat there on the edge of the bed smoking, watching the city. He read back the latest version of his suicide note, the latest attempt to try to explain to the world who he was and why he had killed himself. It was lame, like all the rest. Felt dishonest.

And then he decided: Fuck the world. Maybe he didn't owe the world a thing. Maybe the person he owed words to, owed explanations and apologies to, was his son. Mo tore his way down to a blank sheet of paper and began to write. The words poured from him for hours. He worked with hard determination, pausing only to light fresh cigarettes, shake the cramps from his hand, or stare out the window in search of words.

There was something liberating about living in the shadow of your own death, he thought. Something that cut through all the bullshit. Nothing to hide anymore. No ego to stroke, no feelings to protect. His hand moved with sharp, purposeful strokes, determined to tell it all. Finally, tell it all.

When he was done, when he wrote the last words, he wept without sound, tear trails running down to his jaw line, the occasional tear dropping into his lap. He didn't try to make himself stop, didn't dab at his eyes. He just waited it out. When the tears were done, Mo put the pad on the floor beside the bed, then lay on his side, legs drawn up under him, holding his own shoulders tight.

To his surprise, the tears came again. Wrenching, miserable sobs this time. Body shuddering like a junkie in withdrawal. Like cold winds blowing all around. He cried for a long time. Cried for years wasted and opportunities lost and the awful knowledge that there was nothing he could do about it, nothing that would change it, nothing but admit his failures and beg forgiveness. He wondered if that was too much to ask. He wondered if Trey would forgive him after he was gone. Or Tash. Mo closed his eyes. The tears subsided. He drifted.

The band started up the song and Mo ran out onstage in a purple sequined tuxedo, hair gelled into tight, shiny ringlets. A roar went up from the crowd, all but invisible beyond the wall of light, people screaming his name, calling out song titles. He paced the stage with casual authority, walked it the way you walk among guests in your own living room.

He waved to the people down front, his eyes adjusting now so that he could make out a blur of movement and smiles and one nubile young woman in the second row who seemed certain to pop out of her top. He waved to the folks he couldn't see in the cheap seats and got a renewed roar in return. The bass was punching him hard in the gut and he felt that familiar flutter of energy that always met him when he walked out onstage. The band came to his cue, horns punching twice, fast and sharp like a boxer. He opened his mouth. And froze.

He could not remember the words. He couldn't even remember the song. Had he missed a rehearsal? Had somebody changed the set list? He looked his questions over at his music director. His music director gave him back a glare of concern.

The horns punched again, twice, hard and fast. Mo *could not* remember the words. They shimmered at the edge of consciousness like a light half glimpsed. Then the music simply stopped. Like a rider thrown from a horse, Mo fell headlong into a vast and terrible silence. He looked again at his music director, who returned a baleful, accusatory stare.

Mo looked out at the crowd. He could see them now, see them in excruciating detail. They were waiting. Some were pointing at him in confusion. Some were paralyzed in mid-smile, wondering what had happened. And some offered the same hateful stare the bandleader did. Moses could hear his heart, a heavy, liquid thud. He could hear his breathing, a ragged gasp.

Then Tash—a beautiful teenager with those purposeful eyes— was at his elbow, holding up a lyric sheet. Mo had never been so happy to see her. She looked embarrassed for him. He glanced down at the lyric sheet. It was blank. He looked at Tash as if to say, *What is this?* She had an arm around Trey now. Trey was 11 years old and he looked back at his father with yearning eyes, but allowed his mother to lead him away.

Mo's tux was black now. Formal. No sequins or flourishes. And Mo was old. He was fat and gray with yellow eyes, bad teeth, and cheeks slimy with sweat.

Off to his right, he saw the bandleader's baton come down. Mo tried to say, "No," but then the song started again. They played loud now, played with crushing force that made him want to clap his hands over his ears and fall to his knees.

"Too loud!" he yelled to the bandleader.

But it was no use. Mo couldn't even hear himself and the band-leader wasn't paying attention anyway, focused instead on directing his band, baton going up and down and to the side, slashing the air like a rapier. Mo felt the bass thundering in his gut. He looked down. His zipper was undone. His erect penis, big and evil, poked through. People gasped. People laughed.

Mo tugged at the zipper, but it wouldn't budge. "No," he cried, "no! I don't remember!"

But that was no use either. The horns rose, pushed high on a cre-scendo of bass and strings and fuzzbox guitar. They soared, stretching the beat like a rubber band. And then the tension released, the brass section puncturing it with two tart blasts.

"I don't remember!" cried Moses.

He sat upright on the bed, the sweat on his chest chill in the air-conditioned silence. For a moment, it was all he could do to breathe.

Where was he?

Outside the window, the sun was painting a city in amber and shadow. Lights were coming on. All the lights in the world, it seemed. Las Vegas. He was not on a stage. He was in a hotel in Las Vegas.

Memory came back slowly. Mo climbed out of bed on shaky legs. He took a shower and changed his clothes. He fumbled a mo-ment with the buttons of a silk shirt, his fingers thick and uncoor-dinated. He was rattled. Still, he honored the ritual. On went the fancy designer sunglasses. On went the silk shirt. On went the black leather baseball cap with "The Prophet" stitched in glitter across the brow. On went the mask.

Mo faced the bathroom mirror. He fluffed his curls with his hand. He adjusted the cap, turning it just slightly until it sat at a rak-ish angle. As he always did before going out in public, he tested his smile, looking for a sign of any emotions other than confidence and delight, anything that said he was something other than a shining star, happy to meet his adoring public.

You say you have all my records?
Of course you can have an autograph.

A picture? Why yes, I'd be delighted.

The Fan Voice. Play it humble, but play it poised, a mix of flat-tered-at-all-the-attention modesty and deserving-all-the-attention cool. It was a fine line, but Mo had walked it many times. He just couldn't remember when had it become such work.

He let the smile go away. Stood there facing an aging man, thick-ening around the middle, emotions held secret behind a pair of ri-diculous shades. The whole thing was ridiculous, in fact. Maybe it always had been.

Not that it mattered. It was too late to change. Too late even to care. So he smiled again, fingers splayed out before him. Showtime.

From downstairs, he heard the door open and then Trey clomp-ing heavily up the stairs. A moment later, his son poked his head into the bathroom. What he saw pulled a long, low whistle out of him. "Whoa, Pop," he said. "You sharp."

"Why not?" said Mo. "Going on the town with my son. Besides, I've got my fans to think of. You have a good time out there?"

Trey's right foot nudged his left. "Lost a hunnert on the slots," he admitted.

"That's why they call it gambling," said Mo.

"So where we going?"

"Wherever the wind takes us. But first, you've got to get dressed."

Trey glanced down. He was wearing a pair of jeans with the crotch just inches above his knees and a T-shirt that could have been a dress. "What's wrong with what I'm wearing?" he asked.

"That's not for going out on the town in," said Mo. "Maybe good for robbing the town in, but not going out on the town."

"Why you got to be always baggin' on my gear? 'Sides, I ain't got nothin' else to wear."

"Yes, you do," said Mo. "Look in that bag at the foot of the bed."

Trey went away. A moment later, another low and appreciative whistle. "Take a shower," Mo said. "Get dressed."

Twenty minutes later, they stood together in the living room. Trey was wearing brown calfskin shoes, imported from Italy, a tan ribbed mock-T that that emphasized his lean build, dark wool pants, matching sport coat and an expression of deep uncertainty. "Are you sure about this?" he asked.

"Yeah," said Mo.

"I ain't never wore nothin' this fancy," said Trey.

Mo shrugged on his own sport coat, then tugged on the shoulder of his son's to bring it forward a little. "Time you did," he said. "It's fine sometimes to run around looking like one of the boys," he added, brushing at imaginary lint. "But there comes a time when a man's got to look like a man."

He stepped back to appraise his handiwork. After a long moment, he nodded. "Not bad for off the rack," he said.

They rode the elevator down together. On the fifth floor, a handsome, dark-skinned woman deep into her forties got in, saw Mo, and announced his name loudly, as if otherwise, he might not know who he was. "I've got all your records," she added. "I grew up listening to you. I used to love your music!"

Mo smiled as if he had never heard it before, gave her the Fan Voice. "Well thank you, dear. That's very kind."

"You haven't had an album in a long time. You got something new coming out?"

The smile never wavered. "I'm afraid not, darling," said Mo. "You know how it is. All they want to hear these days is that hip-hop stuff. Nobody's interested in real music anymore."

She nodded. "That's true," she said. "I tell my kids, y'all don't know what good music is. Think you know, but you don't."

"Tell mine the same thing," said Mo.

Her sigh was almost mournful. "Those were good days, weren't they?"

"They were the best," said Mo.

Then the elevator door opened, bringing in the noise of the gambling pit. Mo stood aside, allowing the woman to walk out first. Then he touched his hat and nodded.

"Wait a minute," she said, fumbling in her purse, "I got to get a picture. My friends will never believe I met the Prophet."

"A picture?" said Mo, as if flattered and surprised. "Why certainly, darling."

She handed the disposable camera to Trey without looking at him. "Do you mind?" she said. She didn't wait for an answer, curling herself against Mo, like a vine against a trellis; one well-turned leg crooked in front of him like a question mark. Mo draped an arm around her waist and smiled into the flash, feeling not unlike a prop. A wooden cutout would have served just as well, he thought.

How many times had he done this? A hundred? A thousand? More?

The picture taken, the woman uncoiled herself and offered Mo a limp hand. "Maybe I'll see you again," she said and he knew it was an invitation, a door propped open. Was it only a month ago, he'd have gone through that door without thinking? He would have taken her arm and taken her to dinner and taken her to bed as casually as eating a bag of potato chips. Get up the next morning and go on his way and think no more about it. Now it seemed like something another man had done in another lifetime.

So he only said, "Yeah, maybe," careful to keep his voice without inflection.

"Damn," said Trey when she was gone, "she was after your bone, Pop."

"I noticed," said Mo. He was rubbing Purell into his palms.

"You sure you ain't want to hit that? I mean, I would understand."

Mo shook his head. "I want to hang out with you," he said.

They wandered through the gambling pits. Bells and whistles exploded and a man let out a girlish shriek, one fist punching the smoky air. Trey glanced back in awe. Mo watched with a numb detachment. As if what he saw wasn't joy so much as it was a depiction of joy. An artist's conception.

"I guess he hit that jackpot," said Trey at his elbow.

"I guess he did," said Mo.

He led them out the front door, grateful for the cool air that met him there. The semicircle in front of the building was jammed with cars, lollipop-colored metal shining under the lights. The water in the fountain at the lion's feet rushed and gurgled. People pushed in and out of the hotel in an excited babble.

They took a walk, slipping through gaps in the crowd. Trey was still looking about him with dazzled eyes and Mo was content to leave him his silence. At a street corner, another fan recognized Mo. He was a white man, probably in his late fifties—open-collared shirt, bristly white hairs poking through—and he had his arm around a pretty blonde whose blouse was two sizes too small. She couldn't have been much older than Trey.

"You're the Prophet!" the man cried. It was almost an accusation. "Oh shit, man. And me without my camera." He turned to the woman. "You're too young to remember, baby, but this guy here was the baddest motherfucker around back in the '70s. And mind you, I saw 'em all, all the greats. But him—him and maybe Stevie…maybe him, Stevie, and Marvin—they were the ones who weren't afraid to tell it like it was."

Out of nowhere, the man broke into "My Prophecy," which he sang in multiple keys, none of them correct. Then he nudged Mo. "Come on, Prophet, join in here. Give her just a taste."

Mo smiled. It was always hardest with fools. "That's all right," he said. "You don't need me. You're doing just fine."

His eyebrows went up. "Really? I always thought, maybe, I don't know, I could have done it for real. Been a professional singer, I mean. But then the accounting thing took off, and I decided to go with that."

"It's the world's loss," said Mo.

The man looked as if Mo had just volunteered him a kidney. "Really? You think so? That's fuckin' decent of you, Mr. Johnson. You're all right in my book." He touched his fist to Mo's shoulder and added, "Come on, sing with me. Give the kids a thrill."

Mo touched his throat. "I wish I could," he said, "but I've got to save my voice. Got a recording session later. In fact, my manager would kick my ass if he knew I was talking so much."

"Oh. Oh. I dig," said the man. "Well, I can understand that. Got to take care of your instrument, that's for sure."

The woman whined. "Eddie, we're going to miss the show, we don't hurry."

Eddie glanced an embarrassed apology at Mo, then answered sourly. "Look, Ashley, give me a minute, okay? You don't know who this guy is. This guy is important."

He turned back and for a moment, it was as if he didn't know how to proceed. Then he grabbed Mo's hand and pumped five times in quick succession. "I just want to…you know…it was a weird time back then, nobody knew what the fuck the country was coming to and just…you know…thank you for the things you said and the songs you wrote. I just wanted to say, you know, somebody heard you, man."

Eddie held Mo's hand so long Mo wondered if he had forgotten who it belonged to. Then the man let go, made a fist, and pounded his breastbone twice. "Peace, brother," he said. His voice was husky.

Mo nodded. "Peace," he said.

Mo watched them disappear into the crowd. He reached into his breast pocket, found the bottle of Purell and squeezed some into his palm.

"You know, you always do that," said Trey.

Mo was absent. "Do what?"

Trey nodded at his hands. "Always use that stuff on your hands."

Mo shrugged. "I guess I'm just worried about germs," he said. "Don't want to catch what's out there."

"But you only do it with your fans."

Mo had started forward. This stopped him. He looked back. "Say what?"

"I used to notice that even when I was a little kid," said Trey. "You meet somebody and they don't know who you are, and you shake they hands and go on like it's nothin'. But if it's a fan, you always put that stuff on your hands afterward."

"I do?" Crowds swirled around them.

"Yup," said Trey. "Every time."

"Well, I guess…" And then Mo stopped, because he had no idea what to say. Did he really hate it that much, putting on the smile, putting on the voice, being a prop in their pictures? Did he hate them for making him do it? Did he hate himself for doing it? Or maybe the thing he hated was the fact that if he wasn't doing these things, if they didn't ask and he didn't comply, he had no idea who he would be. Or what he would be.

Or *if* he would be.

The thought made him close his eyes for a long moment. He opened them to find his son looking up at him, concern creasing his smooth, young face. "Pop?"

"Come on," said Mo. "Let's get something to eat."

They found a steakhouse off the strip. The lights were low, the walls paneled in dark woods, the tables and chairs heavy and masculine. They gave their orders to a waiter in black slacks and white shirt who called them sir and acted as if their comfort and satisfaction were his reason for drawing breath.

When he was gone, having made sure they were properly supplied with water and bread, Trey leaned back against the wine-red leather. "I could get used to this," he said, his grin expansive.

"Yeah," said Mo, "it is nice."

"Did you see the prices though? Twenty dollars for a hamburger? Forty for a steak? That's crazy."

"You ain't never lived," said Mo.

They glanced around a room full of white men in sport coats and ties and women with necklines that plunged in blouses that glittered. Trey said, "I see why you made me change, though. Sure can't dress like no homie in no joint like this."

"No," said Mo. "Got to step it up."

He regarded his son, his namesake, his only child. Born 19 years before on a night when Mo was floating on white-powder wings and singing idealistic songs to a crowd he couldn't see for the floodlights. Nineteen years. A lifetime. His son's lifetime.

Mo was surprised at the sound of his own voice. "Trey," he said, "I just want to apologize to you. I've never really done that before, never apologized. I just want you to know I'm sorry."

Confusion. "Sorry for what?"

Mo spread his hands. "Everything. From the beginning. For not being there. For not being the father I should have been, the father you deserved. Everything."

Trey grinned. "Dad, you still on that? I told you already, I ain't hung up on that."

"You're not." Mo's inflection was flat. Not a statement, not a question.

"No," said Trey, "I'm not. I know some guys, they get all twisted behind that. 'I didn't have no daddy.' That's what one of my homies says: 'He wasn't nothin' but a sperm donor.' But I ain't with that. What's past is past. You did what you could, man. You sent money, which is more than a lot of my boys can say about they old men. So I ain't mad at you. I ain't walkin' around hurt and holdin' grudges 'cause you wasn't around."

"You came out just fine, me not being there." Still not a statement. Still not a question.

"Yeah," said Trey, "I did."

"It didn't change nothin', me not being there."

"No, man. I'm cool."

"It didn't matter that I wasn't there."

"Man, I—"

Mo's voice turned sharp. "It didn't matter that I wasn't there. Yes or no?"

Trey looked at him now. Stared as if he had not seen his father for a hundred years.

"Because you see, that's not a compliment, you saying it didn't matter. Means I was like a feather on the scale, you know? Add him in, take him away, don't make no difference. It all comes out the same. Is that what you're telling me, Trey? It didn't matter that I wasn't there?"

People were looking. Discreet glances. Hooded eyes. Mo slapped his cap on the table, plowed his fingers through his hair. A moment passed. Finally Trey said, "What you want me to say, Pop?"

"I want you to answer the question, Trey. I want you to answer it and be honest with yourself and with me. It didn't matter that I wasn't there?"

Another moment. Mo saw a group of women pass on the street outside, leaning against one another, weakened by laughter, silent behind the heavy glass.

"It mattered," said Trey after a long silence. "Of course it mattered. But I knew you was busy, man. You was recording and touring, traveling all around the world. I understood that."

"That wasn't it, Trey." Mo's voice was a whisper.

"What you mean, 'that wasn't it'?" said Trey, behind a little laugh. "'Course that was it. You was the Prophet, man. Everybody wanted a piece of you."

"Wasn't it," repeated Mo.

Confusion again. "I don't get it."

"I was busy. Wasn't *that* busy. I could have been there. Maybe not every day or every week, but I could have been there. The truth is, I didn't want to. There were other things that were more important to me. Do you understand? There were other things more important to me than spending time with my son. Girls or friends or just lying in a hotel room doing blow. All of that mattered more to me than you. That's who I am, Trey. That's what your father was about."

He saw the light go out of Trey's eyes. The sun setting behind distant hills.

Mo had time to wonder at the things he heard himself saying. The pain his words imposed. Did it do anybody any good to say these things? Was truth really worth this darkness now settling into Trey's eyes? But the questions didn't matter. He was unable to make himself stop.

"You always forgave me," he said. "That's the hard part. I come by and see you once every year or so when I start feeling guilty or I want to get your mother off my ass. I come by with a new bicycle or a computer or something and you forgive me. Every time. Throw your arms around me like it's just a week since the last time I saw you. You forgive me every time."

Mo felt a tear slip from his eye. "And I hang out with you. I play with you an hour, maybe two. But that's all I can handle, 'cause there's a girl I need to see or some coke I need to score. And I promise you, promise myself, it won't be so long next time. I'll see you real soon. But another year passes before I see you again, and you've gotten taller and bigger and I hardly recognize you and I feel like shit.

But you forgive me again. I don't even have to ask. You have no idea how much that hurt, Trey, how small it made me feel."

Another tear slipped. Mo mashed at it, stared at his son.

"Why you tellin' me all this now?" asked Trey.

He was doing it because something was eating his memory. He was doing it because it needed doing, doing it because if he didn't do it soon, he would forget to do it at all. Trey needed to know all of this. Deserved to know it. But Mo couldn't make himself say it.

So he faced his son and told him part of the truth. "I guess it's on my mind, what with my father dying. I think of what a useless bastard he was. Then I realize I wasn't much better to you. I need to clear the air, I suppose."

"You feel better now?" There was no humor in Trey's eyes.

Mo shook his head. "No," he said. "I don't expect I ever will. But I wanted you to know. You had a right to know."

"A right to know. Is that what this is all about?"

"I just wanted to come clean with you, Trey. Just wanted to be honest for once in my life."

"You just wanted to clear your conscience," said Trey and there was accusation simmering in his voice.

"Yeah," said Mo. "I suppose there was some of that, too."

A woman was at his elbow. She was clutching a notepad. "Excuse me," she said, "but aren't you…"

Mo flicked her with a glance. "This is not a good time," he said.

"Oh," she said, hope wilting.

"No, it's okay," Trey told her. And then to his father: "Go ahead and sign. I don't mind."

Mo stared at him. "Go ahead," said Trey.

Mo's heart felt heavy and dead. He made himself smile. Gave her a dazzling display of carefree and live-for-today that made her clasp her hands under her chin. She looked as if she might cry, just being noticed by him.

"I have all your records," she said.

The Fan Voice had never been so much work. "Why thank you for supporting us, darling. We appreciate it." He took the notepad from her hand, flipped to a blank page, produced a pen from his jacket pocket. "Now," he said, "who should I sign this to?"

He scrawled his name in the pad and sent the woman walking on weak knees back to her table. When she was gone, Mo reached into his coat pocket for the Purell.

He caught himself an instant before Trey said, "Got to wash it off, huh?"

Mo withdrew his hand, empty. "You're angry with me," he said. "I'm glad. Do you know how long I've wanted you to be angry with me?"

Trey shook his head. "I just can't figure you, man."

A shrug. "You always think there's time, Trey. Always think you'll have all the time you need to do what you ought to do or say what you need to say. And then you look up and twenty years has passed and the baby is a boy and the boy is a man. And there is no more time."

Mo met his son's eyes. "I'm sorry, Trey," he said. "That's all I wanted to say. I'm sorry." Trey looked away.

Their meals came. A hamburger and a Coke for Trey. A steak, well done, for Mo. They ate in silence. Ate like strangers at separate tables.

After dinner, they caught a show, Gladys Knight at the Flamingo. She spotted Mo in the audience and called him onstage. They sang a duet of "Best Thing That Ever Happened to Me." Mo got a standing ovation. It was like old times. Mo and Trey returned to the suite shortly after midnight.

"We need to be up early to beat that sun," Mo said. They still weren't speaking.

What did you expect?

Conscience beating him like slave. Whoever said the truth sets you free never told the truth, he thought. They separated without a word in the living room. Trey flopped down on the couch and turned on the big screen. Mo mounted the spiral stairs, paused, looked back. Saw Trey's face from above in sullen profile, switching channels without seeing them. Mo went to his room. He peeled off his sport coat, tossed it over a chair, threw his look-at-me baseball cap to an opposite corner of the room, and fell on his back across the bed.

Mo's eyes closed. He slept without dreams.

Then he awoke, eyes flying open all at once, breathing harsh, panicked without knowing why. The clock said it was 1:47. His heart rattled in his chest. He didn't know where he was.

Mo turned on the light. Found himself fully dressed, lying atop a bed. Alone. Mo sat up. The lights outside the window said Las Vegas. Why was he in Las Vegas? He didn't know.

It was like reaching into a dark closet, trying to identify what you felt by touch alone. Things felt familiar, frustratingly so, but you could not pull them into the light. His memory was dark shapes, no colors, no markers of identification.

Who had brought him here? Why? Then he saw it.

On the nightstand. A set of keys. His wallet. A parking ticket with a row and a space noted on it. Mo silently blessed his luck. He pocketed the items, found a sport coat lying across a chair and shrugged it on. Mo crept out of the room, crept down a staircase that spiraled into a vast living area. He paused a few steps from the bottom. A man was sprawled sleeping on a couch in front of a television that played without sound.

Mo studied the man's face. He looked young, tough. Was this who had brought him here? It took an effort for Mo to make himself move forward again. He had never been so scared. Down the stairs he moved, then behind the couch where the young tough slept. Mo kept waiting for the man to stir, to shift in his sleep like something in a sitcom. But the guy was a sound sleeper. Mo made it across the room without the guard—for that was how he had come to think of him—stirring. He unlocked the door—the sound of the bolt drawing back was unnaturally loud—and eased it open. It did not squeak.

Mo closed the door as gently as he could behind him. He had to fight a temptation to sprint down the hall. As it was, he walked very fast. A woman in the elevator gave him a strange expression and Mo realized he must look a sight. He smiled. She didn't. He put his hand to his brow and it came away wet.

The elevator door opened. Mo skulked across the lobby, teeming with people at two in the morning. He felt like a fugitive. It occurred to him to stop and ask for help, but what could he say? How could he know who was in on it and who wasn't? Best to just get away, as far away as he could, and sort it out later. Later, when he could remember.

He wandered through the garage until he found the spot scrawled on the parking ticket. A black truck was parked there. He had never seen it before. Hesitantly, Mo tried the key he had found. It worked. He got in, backed out, drove to the exit, gave a bored looking attendant his ticket, paid some money. Then the gate came up and Mo rolled through it, took a right. Traffic was light. Mo sailed through it. He was free. *Free.* Now all he had to do was...

What?

And that's when his joy dissolved. Because that's when it hit him. He was free, but free to do what? Free to go where? He didn't know.

Why can't I remember?

The SUV picked up speed. Mo hardly noticed. He hit the steering wheel with his fist. Then he tapped the same fist hard against his forehead.

I'm Moses Johnson, I know that. I'm from L.A. Maybe that's where I should go?

What had they done to him? He pressed the accelerator harder. The SUV leapt forward. Somewhere behind him, a car horn shouted angrily.

I'm a singer. Was I performing here? Is that it?

He glimpsed a woman in his memory. Gladys Knight. Himself singing with her. When had that happened? And the young tough, the guard, he was there in the audience, watching with a baleful stare.

Las Vegas rushed by his window. He didn't see.

Okay, I go to L.A. But L.A.'s huge. Where do I live? Is this my car? Who was that man? Dear Lord, what's happening to me?

His head jerked toward the outraged baritone bleating of the air horn, the sound of tires locked in a careening skid. He didn't make it all the way around.

There was a crash from somewhere far away, metal rending metal. In the same instant, something punched him in his mouth, lightning flashed, he became weightless, the world outside spinning upside down in silence. Bottomless silence. Silence you could wander forever and never find its end.

Sound came back with a suddenness, a sickening shriek of metal tearing itself against asphalt. The car returned to earth, passenger side stove in, tires cocked at angles like broken bones, pebbles of glass flying like hail. It rocked twice and was still.

Silence descended again.

Trey awoke with a start. It was a moment before he knew where he was. The room was dark. He looked up toward his father's room. The door was open, the light was on. "Dad?" he called. It brought back the memory of the night before and that stung. Trey shook it off. "Pop?"

No answer. Trey mounted the stairs, went into the room. Found the bed a mess, the shower empty, his father's luggage there, but—it took a moment to register—his car keys missing. Car keys and wallet. His father was gone. But where? Why?

A needle of anxiety nicked his chest. Where could his father have gotten to after two in the morning? What could he have needed so badly? And even if he did need something, the hotel was practically a city unto itself. You could find anything here, right in walking distance. What could he have gone out for that required him to take the car?

Confused, Trey turned toward the door. Then he saw it, his father's writing pad, on the floor beside the bed. He had been so secretive about that thing, so secretive about a lot of things, now that Trey thought about it. Every time you looked, he was hunched over it, writing something he wouldn't let you see.

Songwriting, he said. *Claimed.*

It was all impulse from there. Trey picked up the legal pad, its pages dense with his father's handwriting. He steeled himself and began to read.

sixteen

Dear Trey,

I guess this a suicide note. By the time you read this, I'll be dead.

The reason won't be any big mystery. I'll have already sat you down and had the worst talk of my entire life with you, told you how this damn disease is killing me piece by piece. What I probably won't tell you is how fucking frustrating it is to watch it happen, to see it take your life from you bit by bit, day by day and know there's nothing you can do to stop it. All you can do is beat it to the punch. That's what I've decided to do, Trey. I refuse to die in pieces. That might be selfish, but that's the way it is.

I have a lot more to apologize for. Mainly that I wasn't around. I wasn't a very good father. I didn't know how to be one because I never really had one. I guess that's the other reason I'm writing this note—so that after I'm gone, maybe you'll know me a little. I'm not asking or expecting you to forgive me. Just know me.

I never knew Jack. He was in jail until I was in my teens. When I was little, it was just me and my mother. Her name was Ruth. I wish you could've known her, Trey. Your grandmother was an angel, sweetest person you ever want to meet. I know everybody says that about their mother, but with her, it wasn't just something to say. It was true.

I remember, she used to work so hard trying to make a life for me. Wasn't easy. We never had any money. We lived in a two-bedroom apartment over an auto parts store. Raggedy little place, but we kept it spotless. Mama used to say, it was okay to live in the ghetto, long as you didn't let the ghetto live in you.

Like I said, Jack was in prison. I guess that's not a big deal now, the way young guys come up these days, but it was back then. It shamed you. It made people pity you.

Jack went away before I was born, but I grew up hearing people talk about him. Before he got locked up, people had had great

191

expectations for my father. They used to say that if he hadn't been a Negro, he could have been a politician. They say he was smart—not book smart, but people smart. They say he had charisma.

What happened to him—what he did—hurt a lot of people. Disappointed them, I guess, made them feel they were wrong to believe in him. They couldn't understand how a man like this could have ended up where he did. They'd had such expectations for him and he just let them down. It was hard, growing up in the shadow of this man I didn't even know.

I think Cooley understood. Arthur Cooley was my father's best friend, still is to this day. A big man but very gentle. Even when he was drunk—and he was always drunk—Cooley was never loud. There was always something dignified about him. And he treated me like his own.

The funny thing is, my mother couldn't stand him. I never knew why. I heard he was mixed up in the robbery my father pulled, but I never could get the straight of it. She wouldn't talk about it. She'd just tell me to be quiet or send me away.

I remember one morning she sent me down to Wong's Liquor for milk. Cooley was in there buying a drink. He put the milk on his tab, bought me a box of Lemonheads, this candy we used to eat. When Mama saw that, she was furious. She beat my behind, then made me march across the street to Cooley's house and give him his money back. She calculated it to the penny.

But bad as she talked about Cooley, she was never above accepting a lift from him once a month to go visit Jack. Those are my earliest memories of my father. Watching him and my mother talk over a plastic partition. It was never about anything important. Mama always wanted to know if he got her last letter and how he'd been and like that. He always asked her how I was doing in school. Then, the guard would come to take Jack away.

The last thing he said before he was led away was always to Cooley: You watch out for my family, Cooley. You take care of 'em for me.

Even though Jack said it all the time, Cooley always jumped a little and looked startled. Then he said, Don't worry, Jack. You know I'll watch over 'em. Watch over 'em like they's my own. You ain't gotta worry about that. Like he was desperate to convince Jack that he was looking out for us.

They were friends, but I always thought Cooley was a little afraid of my father. To see them together, you'd wonder why. Jack was 5'7" and skinny. Cooley was a half-foot taller and a hundred pounds heavier. But the look was deceiving. Jack was like a ton of dynamite packed in a shoe box. If he scared Cooley, well, he scared me too.

I couldn't match that up with the man people kept telling me about. Mama would get in her sentimental moods and talk about how warm and gentle Jack used to be. Sometimes, Old Wong, the guy who ran the liquor store, would ask about Jack. Such a good boy, he would say. You be good boy like you father.

Even at church, they talked about Jack like he was a saint. The reverends or the deacons would see me after service and they would hit me with the questions. How is your father? Do you know yet when he's getting out?

We used to be in church all day on Sundays. You might think I would have hated it, but the truth is, I liked church. Church was where I got to sing. I always knew I wanted to be a singer. I spent hours listening to music, studying it. I'd stand in the mirror pretending I was James Brown, David Ruffin, Sam Cooke, Sam Moore, Ray Charles, Levi Stubbs. Guys you never heard of, I bet.

I was good enough that they put me in the adult choir when I was only nine. It made me feel powerful to make grown people shout. I never forgot that feeling. Only part I hated: when I sang, it made people compare me to my father. Oh, he's just like his daddy. Oh, I swear, it's like Jack all over again.

It was something I heard a lot, how much like Jack I was. It wasn't that he was a singer. Jack couldn't carry a tune in a bucket. But they said I had charisma just like him. Sometimes, it got to me. It was like they weren't even seeing me. They were seeing him. One time, after church, I heard a deacon talking to some visitors about me. He said, If you think he's something you should've seen his father.

Some lady asked was my father dead. The deacon told her he wasn't dead, he was in prison. She said, Oh, that's awful.

The deacon said, Yes, it was a shame, all right. He was the smartest young man you ever saw. A real good boy. It was just terrible, what happened.

What happened. They always called it that. Like maybe he got picked up for driving drunk or stealing a car. But the truth—

and I could never put this together with this good boy people kept
telling me about—was that my father committed armed robbery.
And even though the man gave Jack what he wanted, Jack still
shot him to death.

I was 15 the year he got paroled. That was the summer of
1970. Looking back, that was an amazing time. Nixon was president, we had gone to the moon, we were losing the war in Vietnam. But back then, I didn't pay attention to none of it. If it wasn't
in SOUL magazine or being played on KGFJ radio, I didn't know
about it.

I was going to concerts by then. Saw Stevie Wonder, the
Temptations, Gladys Knight, Aretha. All the great ones. And I was
singing in groups. I had dreams of making it big and those dreams
did not include Jack. I had stopped going to the prison on visiting
days, didn't think too much about him one way or another.

It wasn't that I didn't like him. He just didn't figure in.

Then he got out. I remember Mama and Cooley were so
happy. They threw a party for him, had a bunch of friends over
from the old days. I tried to be happy too, but tell you the truth,
I wasn't. I didn't know what to feel. I didn't know this man. So I
just watched them party and tried to figure out how this was going
to change my life.

Three days later, I found out. That was when he beat up my
mother for the first time. Wish I could say it was for the last, but
that would be a lie. After that, he beat her up regularly.

That first time, I didn't even know what had happened. I had
been out of the house, practicing with one of my groups. Came
back in, found him lying on the couch in his drawers. Wanted to
give me the third degree about where I'd been and what I'd been
doing. Then my mother walks in with some groceries. She's wearing sunglasses and when she takes them off, you see this bruise under her right eye. She was very light-skinned, so the bruise showed
up real good.

I wanted to kill him, Trey. I jumped at him. Next thing I knew,
I was on my ass and my mouth was bleeding. He was too strong for
me and way too fast. I was still ready to give him some scrap, but
my mother got between us. And she was yelling at me. At *me*.

I can't tell you how much that hurt. He hit her, but she's yelling at me, telling me respect your father and all this. Finally, I just
walked out.

That was the pattern for the next four years. Hardly a week went by without him punching her, slapping her. No particular reason. Just because he felt like it. He'd pick a fight about nothing. The soup's not hot enough or the floor needs to be swept. That was all the excuse he needed and he'd jump on her. And every time I tried to defend her, she acted like I was doing something wrong. Finally, I stopped trying. After awhile, I didn't want to have anything to do with either of them. Him especially. He was crazy. I figured that out real quick.

Never got a job, never even talked about getting a job. All he did was lie around the house in his drawers cursing the white man while my mother took the bus to work everyday. Man hated white people more than anybody I ever saw. Once, I saw him take a tire iron to the head of some white boy after they had a fender bender and the white boy called him a nigger. Blood and teeth jumped out the man's mouth. Jack would have killed him if Cooley hadn't stopped him. He was literally foaming at the mouth.

Some nights, I would lie out on my bed and hear him having sex with my mother. Having sex, not making love. Calling her a bitch, making her say it was good. The walls were thin in that old place and I think to this day he wanted me to hear him. It was always quick. That was the one good thing about it.

On one of those nights after the noise in the room had stopped, I heard their door open. My door was open, too. There was a full moon that night and I saw Mama walk out slowly, clutching her robe, cigarette in one hand. She looked frail. There was a red mark on her right cheekbone from a fight a few days before. Her eyes were moist and the hand with the cigarette trembled as she brought it to her lips. I remember thinking that my beautiful mother looked like some pitiful old woman.

Mama must have felt my eyes on her, because she turned around and looked into my room. I closed my eyes and tried to pretend I was asleep, but she knew I wasn't. When I opened my eyes again, she was still watching me with those sad eyes. She looked at me, I looked at her. I wanted to say something, but what do you say at a moment like that? Mama went out and sat on the steps.

I asked her one time why she let him treat her that way. I told her, Sometimes, I think he hates you. She said, real soft, It's not me he hates.

I asked what she meant, but she wouldn't say. Took me years before I figured it out on my own. She meant that he hated himself, because all his charisma had not been enough to change his destiny. His life had passed him by while he was in jail and he would never be anything more than what he was.

And she also meant that he hated me. Because I had talent and charisma like he used to, but I was young enough that my destiny was still out in front of me. I was going to do better than him. We both knew it. And he hated me for it, probably without even knowing.

The thing I never could understand was why, for as much as he hated me and himself, it was my mother he took it out on. I think he beat her for staying with him, reminding him what he had been. And I think he beat her because he knew that more than I loved music, I loved her. It was his way of showing me who was in charge.

Like I say, I hadn't figured all this out back then. All I knew was I was trapped in a life that was strangling me to death. It was your mother that saved me. I saw her for the first time when school started in the fall of '72. Smooth skin, big Afro, those incredible eyes. She was the most beautiful thing I had ever seen. Still is, tell you the truth.

She's always told you that we met in Mr. Vinson's algebra class. Actually that's not true. She tells you that to avoid making me look bad, but the fact is, we met a few weeks before, the day I saw her in the hallway for the first time. I nudged my boys, straightened my collar, and strolled over to her locker, where she was pulling out a notebook. I leaned an arm on the wall to block her escape and said something like, Hey, Miss Lady—we always called girls Miss Lady—you know, thanks to you, I ain't got to go to church no more. 'Cause lookin' at you, I'm already in heaven.

Now, that may not sound like a great line to you, but in my experience, it had never failed. Always made a girl giggle or smile or at the very least, roll her eyes. Something, you know? Something I could work with.

But your mother left me hanging. I might as well have been talking to the water fountain for all the response I got. She just stared at me, Trey, with those big eyes that don't blink. Probably only a few seconds passed, but I swear, I lived through years in those seconds. I broke out in a nervous smile, shifted my feet. Tash made me feel four years old and two feet tall. And all she had done was look at me.

Finally she closed her locker and said, Excuse me, I have to get to class. She ducked under my arm without waiting for me to answer.

It took a moment before I remembered to close my mouth. Then I yelled after her, I'm sorry, Miss. I didn't know you were a dyke. Because my boys were standing across the hall watching, so I had to say something. Your mother didn't turn around, didn't slow down. I wanted to pinch myself to see if I was still real. My boys were laughing at the shot I gave her, but Tash shook me a hell of a lot more than I shook her.

I thought about taking another run at her, but I decided against it after seeing her shoot down half a dozen other guys. I never was the type to rattle easy, always figured I could talk my way in or out of any situation I wanted, but Tash was something I couldn't figure out. I decided to leave her alone.

But I didn't forget about her. I saw those eyes even in my sleep. You know how it is, Trey. Usually with girls, it's physical. You want to get in there, hit it, and quit it. Hell, that's been the story of my whole life. But every once in a long while, there's that other kind of girl. That's what your mother was. You just felt like here was someone you wanted to tell secrets to and she would listen. Like that would be enough. Like you could live just on that.

Of course, I figured I had blown whatever chance I had at her by calling her a dyke, so I tried to ignore what I felt. Then came that day in Vinson's algebra class. We were taking a test and she accused me of copying her. Which was true, but I whispered back, Ain't nobody cheatin' off you, girl.

Tash knew I was lying. She said, If you didn't spend all your time trying to be the next Al Green, maybe you could actually study for a test sometime.

It was a minute before it hit me: How did she know I was trying to be the next Al Green? I waited for her after school. First thing I said was, What you got against Al Green?

I could tell she was startled and that was good, because Tash seemed like the kind who was never taken by surprise. She asked me what I was talking about.

I reminded her what she said in school and asked again, What you got against Al Green? I thought I saw a smile trying to form. But it's like she told that smile it had better not, because it went away and she started walking again. I wasn't about to give up so easy this time. I followed her and I started singing. I sang Love and Happiness, Let's Stay Together, I'm Still in Love With You, practically the whole Al Green songbook.

She ignored me, walking with her head down. Looked like somebody walking uphill in the wind. People on the street were laughing, some pausing to listen. Finally, she couldn't take it anymore. She stopped and said, Would you *please* leave me alone?

I looked her dead in the eye and said, No, I ain't gon' leave you alone. Girl, can't you tell when somebody's trying to be your friend? She said she had all the friends she needed. And I said, You ain't got no friends.

I don't know why I said that. I didn't even know if it was true. But it was. I could tell by the way her eyes got wide at first, then narrow and hard. She didn't speak another word. Just walked away and left me standing there. I knew better than to follow.

No friends. I thought about it all that night and it made sense. None of us knew too much about her, but the one thing we had learned was that she was a military brat, raised all over the world. You hear a lot about how military children become real good at fitting in because they're always on the move, always have to be the new kid in school. It was different for your mom, maybe because she was shy by nature. She had spent her life leaving places. And at some point she just gave up trying to make friends.

Early the next morning, I broke into her locker and left something for her to find. I spent 20 minutes hiding in a doorway down the hall just so I could watch as she pulled it out. That smile that had tried to break free the day before finally made it through when she opened her locker and pulled out a 45 of Al Green's Tired of Being Alone. I wrote an apology on the sleeve.

We became friends after that. And I mean just friends. She told me straight out she wasn't no peanut butter girl. That's what we called a girl who spread real easy. She said she wasn't looking for a man. And she said even if she was, her father would kill her if she came home talking about, This is my boyfriend.

But you know, I was willing to just be her friend if it meant I could spend time with her. We had lunch in the library most days.

Tash fascinated me. She was always showing me things in the paper, then telling me how they connected to other things from the day before. She taught me stuff, made me see the world around me in different ways.

Like I said, I didn't pay a lot of attention to politics or social issues. The things that were going on in the world—the war, civil rights demonstrations, Watergate—all passed right over my head. But Tash was different. She was like one giant raw nerve. Couldn't pass by a story about hungry children or oppressed workers or women demanding equal rights without sighing like it was happening to her. She took it all personally. Empathetic, I think is the word.

She would read to me from books she thought I should know about because she knew I wouldn't have the patience to read them for myself. She read me Native Son, The Fire Next Time, The Autobiography of Malcolm X. After awhile, I started reading those things myself, started looking at the newspaper for more than basketball scores. I started seeing the things she saw. And I realized she was right: the world was fucked up. The question was, would you walk past it and say nothing, or would you take a stand?

She used to tell me if I was really an artist, I didn't have any choice but to take a stand. When she said that, it made me feel small. I was proud she called me an artist, but that word came with a challenge. Like, if you're really an artist and not just some guy out here singing songs, then you have to do something. You have to *say* something. Up till then, I had been singing other people's songs, whatever happened to be on the radio. But your mother made me feel like if I was for real, then I had to find my own voice. Your mother is the whole reason I wrote My Prophecy.

We talked about our fathers a lot. That was something new for me. I never talked about Jack with other people. Most of the time, I pretended he didn't exist. When somebody mentioned coming by my house to hang out, I panicked like when the teacher calls on you and you didn't hear the question. I was scared to death somebody might find out about him.

It was different with your mother. It felt natural to confide in her. I would talk it out with her, and it was like getting rid of something heavy that had been sitting on my chest. The only thing I didn't like was, she was always making excuses for him, telling me I should try to understand him because it's hard out there for a black man. I told her she was wasting her sympathy on the wrong man, but she ignored me.

We talked about her father, too. The Admiral, she always called him. They didn't get along too good, either. You've got to remember, Trey, we're talking about a time when a lot of families were divided. I mean, sons and fathers going at it, people demonstrating in the streets about the war, soldiers coming back home and getting spat on. It was an angry time.

I had ignored the war like I ignored everything else, but Tash didn't have that luxury. Her father was military and that meant the war was in their house all day, every day. She was this power-to-the-people girl, always giving the Black Power sign. And her dad was an officer in the naval reserve. Probably would have been a bigger shock if they hadn't fought.

They argued about the war, race, riots, poverty, everything. The Admiral was a hard guy. He thought black people marching for civil rights should be arrested. He thought the poor needed to get out and find jobs. And he thought everybody who protested the war was a traitor and a Communist.

Tash told me they had to start eating dinner in shifts just so they could get through a meal without having a fight. She and her mom would eat while her dad watched the news. Or else, she would fix a plate and take it back in her room while her parents had dinner at the table. This was how they kept the peace. They made the dinner table a demilitarized zone between the Navy man and his Black Power daughter.

They never managed to make peace. And then, they lost the chance. One day, your mother was getting dressed for school, combing out her hair in the bathroom mirror. The door was open and her father passed by. He told her, You need to cut that mess off. She slammed the door in his face.

Those were their last words.

I guess as you get older, you start thinking how any words could be last words. Makes you want to be careful how you leave it with the people who matter to you. That's why it sat heavy on my heart that day when you asked me what I thought about you. I knew the answer I gave wasn't what you wanted and I kept thinking, What if those were our last words?

But here's my problem: should I lie instead? I hardly know you, Trey, and what little I do know scares me. Hear me on this if you never hear me on anything else: Please don't throw your life away being some petty thug with a gun in your belt. Maybe you think I've got a lot of nerve at this late date trying to give you advice. Maybe I do. But I'm not wrong, Trey. And somewhere down inside, you know it.

What you're reading here, these will be my last words to you. I'm hoping that makes them important in your eyes. I'm hoping you'll hear me when I say the one thing I want here at the end of my life is to see you stand up finally and be a man.

Not like Jack and not like me. Be a man, Trey. Be a father. Teach your boy well. Be there for him. Love him and let him know you do. Love is a powerful tie, son. At the end, it's the thing that pulls us back together when everything else has pulled us apart.

That's what your mom found out that day the Admiral died. She got the news in first period. An administrator pulled her out of class and told her he had suffered a stroke. Tash was running before the woman finished speaking. Woman calling after her to wait, but Tash kept running. Ran through the hall and out the front and down the stairs. Ran across streets and down blocks and across lawns she couldn't even see. Blinded by tears for this man who made her life hell, this man she said she hated. Her father.

On the day her father died, Tash ran like hell to get home.

I went to the funeral, the only person from school as far as I could tell. All that week I had tried to call her, but she wouldn't pick up. I even went to her house, but her mom told me Tash wasn't feeling well.

When I stood across from her at the graveside, I remember she looked so tiny and lost. Two days later, she called. We met at the park. She still looked fragile. Like something that might break if you touched it. I asked her if she was okay. She thanked me for coming to the funeral. I told her we were friends and that's what friends do. I asked her again if she was okay and out of the clear blue, she said, I killed him.

I thought I hadn't heard right. That's when she started crying and said it again, I killed him. She had read how stress causes strokes and she was feeling guilty because they were always arguing and fighting and she had to have the last word.

I held her in my arms and let her cry. Kept telling her everything would be all right. Told her I knew how she felt. Which I didn't. But it wouldn't be long before I learned. You see, one week later, my mother was killed.

She died on a rainy day. I remember what woke me up was the sound of them fighting. By itself that wasn't unusual. But what shocked me when I went out is that my mother had Jack's shotgun and it was pointed at his stomach. She told him it was over. She said, You ain't gon' hit me no more, Jack Johnson.

He said, Bitch, you crazy. Put that gun down. But he didn't try to take it from her.

Then he saw me standing there and he told me to get out. Mama said, He ain't goin' nowhere. You are. And she kind of gestured the gun toward the door.

He asked her what she meant and she said she meant for him to get out of her house. Her house. That's just the way she said it. He said, You don't tell me what to do. I'm the man around this motherfucker.

My mother laughed. It was a frightening sound. She said, I'm the one goes to work every morning to pay the rent. I'm the one buys the groceries. I'm the one pays the bills. You used to be a man, Jack. You ain't no man no more. Hell, I'm more man than you.

He kept saying, Don't you say that. Don't you say that. His voice was down to a whisper.

I wanted her to stop, but she wouldn't let it go. She said, Why not? You can't take the truth? Hell, it ain't no secret. Everybody knows. Cooley knows. Your son sure knows. You ain't no man.

He told her to shut up, but she just laughed that scary laugh again. She said, This my house. What I got to shut up for? You shut up. Bitch.

That's when Jack lunged at her. His fist came down. When he pulled it back, his knuckles were bloody and there was a hole in the wall. He had missed her by just inches. For the first time, she seemed shaken. He saw it. He came forward until the muzzle was pressing his sternum.

They stared at each other. It took a full minute. I was scared to even breathe. Then she sighed and lowered the weapon.

He said, I knew you wouldn't do it.

But she said, Get out my house, Jack.

He was shocked. He said, Say what?

And she repeated it. Get out my house. I don't want you no more. That's when he finally realized she was serious. He started making excuses. Said he knew he hadn't been doing right. Started talking about how he spent 15 years locked in a cage.

She said, You made that choice. Her voice was so cold it didn't even sound like her. To this day, I wonder what she meant.

Jack said, I did the only thing I could.

She went on like he hadn't spoken. She said, We waited for you, Jack. Waited like a child waits on Christmas. And you get out and what happens? You won't work. Act like the world owe you something. You treat me like a dog because you don't like what I remind you of. I used to tell this boy what a great man his father was. He think I'm crazy. Look at him. You got him scared to death. We can't go on like this.

He tried to beg her then, but she cut him off. She said, Don't you understand? Ain't nothin' left in me for you, Jack. I don't love you no more. And I want you out my house. I can do bad all by myself.

There was some more back and forth, but that was it, basically. After a moment, he realized it. He got dressed and threw a few things in a suitcase. All the while, my mother stood there in the hallway with that rifle, waiting. The only thing she said to him was when he was walking out the door. She told him to leave his key.

It was only after the door slammed behind him that she cried.

I was amazed. A little scared, too, to see that side of my mother. But mostly, I was happy to think that from now on, she wouldn't have to be hit and cursed all the time and I wouldn't have to sit there and watch it, wanting to kick his ass but knowing I couldn't and knowing she wouldn't want me to even if I could. It was like I could breathe for the first time in years.

But of course, it didn't last. I was walking my mother home from the bus stop that afternoon when she looked across the street and saw that the lights were on in the apartment. She asked me, Did you leave the lights on? I said, No. We both realized at the same time. I took off running. Sure enough, the lock was broken and he was in there watching television, drinking a beer. Just like he never left.

I lost it then. I started screaming at him. What are you doing here? Why won't you leave us alone?

He looked at me like I was a bug and told me, I live here.

I said, You don't live here no more. Mama said she don't want you here. You got to get out, Jack.

That look in his eyes turned hard. He said, Oh, it's Jack, now, huh?

I was 18 years old. He wasn't pushing me around any more. I said, Yeah, Jack. You got to go, Jack.

He said, There's a bond between me and your mama, boy. Fifteen years couldn't break it, you think an argument can?

That's when my mother came up behind me. She screamed, Then how do you break it? Tell me, Jack. I need to know. How do I make you leave me alone?

He didn't answer. Instead, he started apologizing for the door. But she wasn't having it. She told him to get out.

He said, Ruth, just listen to me, please. I did some thinkin'. Maybe you right. I ain't been much of a man to you and the boy. So you know what I did? I went out today and I looked for a job.

Jack smiled when he told her that. Worst smile you ever saw in your life. She didn't bother to respond. He said, Didn't get hired nowhere. But man at this cafe down on Century say he might need a fry cook. Say call him next week. Got some other people I got to call tomorrow.

Mama said, Jack, that don't change nothin'. It ain't just about a job. It's about you. Didn't you hear me this mornin'? You ain't the same man. You somebody else. I don't know you.

His voice was a whisper. He said, Damn, Ruth. Cut me some slack.

I tried to pull her back, but Mama went right up to him, then, stood right up in his face. She said, How much slack do you need, Jack? You need slack till I'm dead? Till Mo is dead? Or just till we both so crazy we might as well be dead?

You could tell this wasn't going the way Jack had hoped it would. He told her he was trying and that ought to count for something. She told him it was too late for trying. He told her again how he was looking for a job. She said, You just scared of havin' to sleep your narrow ass out in the cold.

Jack slapped her. Her face didn't change. He said, Don't you talk to me like that. It wasn't like it was an order, though. It was like he was begging. He said, You still my woman and I'm still your man. That's the way it's always gonna be.

That's when Mama hawked and spat. A gob hit Jack's cheek and slid down. My mother spoke slowly, looking Jack in the eye, driving the words in like nails. She said, You ain't nobody's man. You ain't shit.

His eyes flashed. I saw crazy there. I screamed, but it was already too late. Jack hit Mama like he'd hit the wall. She flew across the room, landed against the coffee table. Her head hit hard. She didn't move.

I cried out to her. She didn't respond. I knelt by her, touched her face. She still didn't move. I got up then. I was ready to kill that motherfucker, you hear me? He said, Don't make me knock sense into you, too.

Right then I started crying. I couldn't help myself. I said, All you do is hit her. She loved you, she waited on you, and all you ever do is hit her.

He said, One day you'll understand how it is between a woman and a man, boy. One day you'll see.

I told him, I'll never be like you. I'll kill myself first.

He said, Get away from me, boy.

Then I heard my mother moving behind me. It was painful to watch. The side of her face was ruined. Her hair hung down across her eyes. She said, This the last time, Jack. I want you out my life. He planted his feet and said he wasn't goin' nowhere.

All of a sudden Mama laughed. It was this wild, crazy laugh. She said, Fine. You ain't got to go. I'll go. She had been edging toward the door. I called to her.

She laughed again, crying at the same time. She said, You can't stop that, Jack, can you? Big man. Tough man. I'm going away and you can't do shit about it. And then she ran out the door.

I tried to follow her, but Jack knocked me aside, went running down the steps hollering at the top of his lungs, Ruth! Ruth, get back here! Stop this crazy shit!

I climbed back to my feet, ran down the steps after them, turned the corner. Trey, it was like something out of a nightmare, Jack cursing and screaming, Mama, hair flying wildly, all the time looking back over her shoulder laughing at him. Laughing.

It all seemed to happen in slow motion. She ran into the
street, still looking back. A bus and a truck skidded to a stop.
Mama didn't pay them any mind, still looking back, still running.
And then this speeding car came out of nowhere.

I can still hear the crunch. The car hit her like no human being is ever supposed to be hit. My mother became airborne. She
looked like a rag doll as she hung in the air, arms and legs flailing.
Then she came down across the roof of the car, spun off it and
fell into the street. The car never even slowed down. The motherfucker behind the wheel was never identified.

Jack was at the curb when it happened. His legs gave out on
him then. He fell back, landed on his ass, buried his head between
his knees. I raced past him.

In my mind, I said, She can't be. Don't let her be.

I couldn't bring myself to say dead. Not even in my mind.

I ran to her. She was sprawled in a spreading pool of blood.
Her neck was twisted to an impossible angle. Her eyes were open
and she was smiling like she had been laughing even at the end. I
knelt down beside her. I remember, I called to her.

People were coming out of their houses, getting out of their
vehicles, running towards us. Their voices came to me from a distance.

...Lord, have mercy...

...didn't even stop...

...ran right out in the street...

And then everything went white. I couldn't see. I couldn't
hear. I knelt in the street next to my mother and screamed.

I was going to write more, Trey. I was going to tell you about
my life, so you would know. But the rest of it's public record. You
can find it, if you want, in old magazines and newspapers. I never
was much more than what you saw in those articles. Mo Johnson
hanging out with this movie star or that one. Mo Johnson on the
red carpet with a flute of champagne in one hand and some chick
in the other. I thought that was living. I thought that was life.

But this that I've told you here, this is the stuff nobody
knows. Cooley, your mother, me, and now you. That's it. That's
all. Magazine writers would ask me about my life, I'd usually just

make something up. But you deserve the truth, even if I don't have the guts to tell it to you face to face.

I can only imagine how you will feel, reading this, after I die. Forgive me, son. Forgive me for my cowardice, forgive me for my weakness, forgive me for failing. You are the most important thing in my life, making you is the one good thing I ever did, and if I'm late in understanding that, I want you to know that doesn't make me love you any less.

You want to know what I think of you? I think you have the potential for greatness. But I beg you to learn from my mistakes. And from your own.

Be a better man than I was, Trey.

seventeen

Trey let the legal pad slide from his hands. He could not seem to catch his breath.

In that moment, there was a knock at the door. *Dad?* Trey hurtled down the stairs, questions lining up in his head. But when he opened the door, he found two white men in khaki uniforms standing there, sunglasses in their shirt pockets, patches on their shoulders. Not Dad. Cops.

Trey staggered. Actually staggered. *Oh God,* he thought. *Oh, God.* "My father?" he said. And then he couldn't say any more.

The cops looked at each other. Then one said, "I'm sorry to have to tell you this, sir, but there's been an accident."

Twenty minutes later, Trey was trotting down the corridors of a nearby hospital, the patrolmen walking briskly behind him. They pointed him to a set of double doors. Trey shoved through and found himself in the emergency room. Dad lay on a gurney near the nurse's station, guarded by two other cops in khaki. He looked like he'd been in a fight. His left eye was shiny and swollen. There was blood in his hair. His left wrist was in a cast.

Dad looked up at the sound of Trey's arrival. His face opened in a ghastly smile. One of his canine teeth was missing. "You're my son," he said. He said it as though he had just realized it, as though it were the answer to a puzzle he had been working a long time.

"Dad!" Trey said. "They said you were in an accident. Are you okay, man?"

"Banged up," said Dad.

"You going to be all right?"

"Banged up," said Dad. "That's all."

Then Trey noticed that his father's right wrist was handcuffed to the gurney. "Why y'all got him chained like that?" he demanded. "He just had an accident. That's what you said."

One of the cops who had brought him over said, "Well, son, there was something else."

I ain't your son.

But Trey bit that back. "What?" he demanded.

"We're waiting on a drug test."

"Drugs?"

"Yeah. We have reason to suspect drug use may have played a part in this."

"My dad don't use drugs. Well, he did. Long time ago. But he don't use drugs now."

"Maybe there's been a relapse?" said the cop.

"He don't use drugs," repeated Trey.

"Don't worry about it," said Dad. "The test will come back fine."

Trey glanced at his father, then back up at the cop. "There. You see? You wasting your time."

"Maybe we are," said the cop. "But Mr. Johnson, your father drove through a red light into the path of an 18-wheeler. When I rolled up, both vehicles were smashed so bad I expected to find the drivers dead. But the trucker didn't have a scratch and your father, well, as you can see, he wasn't hurt near as bad as he could have been. Except, well…he didn't seem right."

"What you mean?"

"He asked me if this was Las Vegas."

"Well, what you expect?" asked Trey. "He just been in an accident. Probably hit his head."

The cop was patient. "Yes, sir, but then he told me he'd been kidnapped."

"Kidnapped?" Trey looked back at his father, whose gaze flickered, then turned away. *"Kidnapped?"*

"Said he had escaped and was trying to get away when the accident happened. Said he was being held at the MGM Grand. I almost believed him."

Trey addressed his father. "Dad, what he talking about?"

"There's one thing more," said the cop. "He told me he was a singer."

"He is," said Trey.

"I know," said the cop. "My mom has all his records. But the thing is, he told me he had a concert last night at the Zephyr Hotel. Mr. Johnson, the Zephyr closed down 18 years ago."

Now Trey stared at his father, feeling and fear colliding hard inside him. There was awful knowledge coming. Suddenly Trey knew it as surely as he knew his own hand. That long suicide note, that persistent tickle of something wrong that had chased him all the way from Baltimore and now this. He swallowed a throat full of dust, tried to ready himself. But it was difficult and he couldn't help wishing his mother was there.

"It's not drugs," said Dad.

"I know," said Trey. And he did.

Dad looked up at the four cops. "Is there any way we could have a little privacy here?"

The cop who had spoken to Trey shook his head. "I'm afraid not, Mr. Johnson."

A sigh leaked out of Mo. "This isn't the way I wanted you to find out," he said.

Something hot scalded Trey's chest. "Find out what?"

Dad spoke in a whisper. "You always think there's going to be more time," he said.

"Time for what?" insisted Trey.

Dad looked up. Overnight, age seemed to have settled more firmly into the creases of the familiar face. The swollen lips tugged themselves into a sad, tight smile. The single visible eye shone. And then he said, "I have Alzheimer's."

"What?"

"I have Alzheimer's disease, Trey."

"Alzheimer's?" He laughed. "You can't have no Alzheimer's. That's that disease where you forget stuff. You too young for that. That's something old people get."

"There's another kind," said Dad. "They call it early onset Alzheimer's. You don't get it from getting old. It's genetic."

Trey laughed again, more determinedly this time. A short, sharp bark of denial. "You ain't got no Alzheimer's. Come on, now." He was distantly aware of the cops passing glances over his head.

Dad nodded. "That's what I've got, Trey."

"When they tell you this?"

"Few weeks ago."

"And you ain't said nothin' to nobody? Did you get a second opinion? 'Cause you know, Mom's a nurse, and she says you should always—"

"I got a second opinion," said Dad. His calm was infuriating. "I got a third opinion, too. I didn't want to believe, either."

"Okay, so you got it. But they can give you some medicine or something, right?"

"Not really."

"What do you mean, 'not really?'" Trey was surprised at his own anger. "You can take some medicine," he insisted. "They can treat it."

"There's nothing that cures it," said Dad.

"Nothing that cures it? So what happens? You just keep forgetting stuff until…"

It hung there. Finally, Dad plucked it down. "Until I die," he said. "I keep forgetting until I die."

"But that don't make no sense. How can forgetting stuff kill you?"

"It's not just about forgetting. The disease destroys your mind. It makes you helpless. And one day you just stop breathing."

"Why you so calm?" The question jumped out. Trey hadn't even known it was there.

Dad shrugged. "I didn't expect any of this to happen," he said, gesturing with his free hand. "I thought there was more time."

"Why you didn't tell me?" To his surprise, Trey shouted it.

Dad regarded him with the same pacific expression. "I was going to," he said. "I was just waiting for the right time."

"So you gon' die? Is that what you saying? You gon' die?" He didn't know why he was furious, but he was.

Dad nodded. "I am. I'm dying, son. I'm sorry. I'm so sorry." Apologizing. For dying.

Trey couldn't take it. He turned his back, pushed it all away with a swipe of his hand.

He heard his father say, "There's something else."

But Trey didn't stop. He couldn't. He took off down the hall, back through the double doors, nearly blind from sudden tears. Through the watery gray haze, he saw eyes following him, little kids staring with the open fascination of the very young and never hurt. Then automatic doors whisked open and he was in the emergency room parking lot, sitting on the sidewalk near a police cruiser, arms wrapped around his knees, tears dripping off his chin. It wasn't fair. It wasn't right.

The night air was brisk. The full moon shone unfeeling light. The parking lot was quiet. Trey cried. It was too much. Too much, too fast. The suicide note, the accident, Alzheimer's.

There's something else, Trey.

What else? Wasn't this enough? What else could he need to know? How could it get worse?

It all made sense now. All the silences, all the cryptic words and glances of reflection. The whole trip, in fact. This father-son thing, this big drive across the country to watch his own father die. All made sense. Trying to get stuff straight right at the end when you never cared all through your life. Trying to get into heaven on the affirmative action plan. It brought a bitter laugh. And then more tears.

He had to stop crying like some little girl. Trey mashed the heels of his palms against his eyes. Enough tears.

He heard the door whisper open behind him, the jingle of keys and cuffs as two of the patrolmen walked past him. One said, "Tough break, kid. Keep your head up, okay?" Trey nodded. He didn't trust himself to do more.

Car doors slammed. An engine came to life. Tires hissed on asphalt. Then the cops were gone.

Trey remembered his father's cell phone. He had thought to grab it when the police came for him. Now he pulled it from his jacket pocket, punched in the number at home. He had to call his mother. She would know what to do.

The phone rang. Voice mail picked up. Trey shut the clamshell, glanced at his watch. It was 3:55. That made it…what, 6:55 at home?

Why wasn't she answering? Fresh fear knifed through Trey's chest. He keyed in the number to Tash's cell.

———————————

Al Green was singing "Call Me." The sound from the cell phone was tinny and small. It brought Tash's head up from the pillow with a start. It was a moment before she located the clock in the unfamiliar room. When she did, she was alarmed. 6:57. Who could be calling her at 6:57 in the morning?

Wide awake, Tash plucked her phone off the nightstand and flipped it open. The Caller ID showed Mo's number. "Moses? What's wrong?"

"It's me, Mom." Trey. A bad connection, but Trey. Sounding wrung out, beaten.

"Trey, it's 7:00 in the morning. What's wrong? Where are you?"

"Las Vegas. I'm at the hospital. There was an accident."

"An accident?"

At the sound of the word, Philip's head came up off the pillow to her right. "They had an accident?" he said. "Are they all right?"

Tash held up a hand to quiet him, spoke into the phone. "Were you hurt? Was your father hurt?"

"I wasn't in the car," said Trey. "Dad, he busted up some. Broke his wrist, I think. Face all swole up. But I think he gon' be okay."

Relief. "Thank God," said Tash. She told Philip, "There was some sort of wreck, but they're okay. Well, Mo broke his wrist, apparently, but other than that..."

Trey spoke sharply. "Who you talking to?"

Tash was embarrassed. Then she reminded herself that she was a grown woman and did not answer to children. "I'm with Philip," she said. She said it firmly, daring him to respond.

She could hear the smirk. "Oh. That guy. That's why you didn't answer the phone at home."

"I'm not at home," she said.

A silence followed. Finally Tash said, "So your father's going to be all right?"

Another silence. And then: "Yeah, I guess."

"You guess?"

"He's fine," said Trey. "I just wanted to let you know. Sorry I woke y'all up."

Tash called his name, but the connection was already broken. She stared at the phone, finger hovering over the call button. Something was not right.

"Everything okay?" Philip, a shadow in the dark, a weight on the other side of the bed.

Tash closed the phone. "I don't know," she said.

"What do you mean? You said it was just a broken wrist, right?"

"Yeah," she said, "but I got the feeling there was something else."

"Like what?"

"I have no idea. He was going to tell me, I think."

Philip finished the thought. "Then he realized you and I were together and he clammed up."

Tash lay the phone on the night table and sank back into the pillow. "Something like that," she said.

She felt his hand circling her waist, pulling her toward him. The night before returned. The pickup at the hospital. The flowers on the seat. The car without little girls chattering in the back seat or Christian songs on the radio. The dinner at the nice restaurant. The reservations in the hotel, yet another surprise. And the biggest surprise of all. The proposal. His ring on her finger, a modest diamond taking the place of the costume jewelry she had worn there for years. It felt strange. Wonderful and strange.

She felt Philip smile in the darkness. "Well," he said, "he's going to have to get used to that, isn't he?" And he kissed her, his lips lingering warm and hungry against hers, his breath filling her mouth.

There's something else. Something's not right.

Tash's last thought before she surrendered. It felt distant and disconnected, urging her in directions she was not willing to go. She ignored it, refused to hear it, wrapped her man in her arms and pushed her body against him as his kisses trailed down her neck.

Trey went back inside. He found his father's gurney empty, the remaining two cops just standing there. One of them answered his questioning look with a nod toward a curtained-off exam area. "He's getting dressed," the cop said.

"You lettin' him go?"

A nod. "The drug test came back. It was clean."

"Like he said."

"Yeah, like he said."

The cop—his name tag said his name was Stans—regarded Trey for a long, speculative moment. Then he asked, "How old are you, Mr. Johnson?"

"Nineteen. Why?"

"You drive? You got a license?"

"Yeah. Why?"

The patrolman came closer. "Look, we've cited him for reckless driving, but he's not going to jail. He'll have to call his insurance company, of course. But as a legal matter, there's no reason he can't rent a car or, for that matter, buy a car, and drive away from here. Still, I think you and I both know he doesn't belong behind the wheel. He's a danger to himself and to those around him."

It took a moment. Trey looking for the trap in the cop's words. Finally, he nodded.

"If you're smart, you'll take his keys. Make him let you drive."

"That ain't gon' be easy," said Trey.

"No, it's not. It represents a loss of independence. He may resent you for it."

Trey studied the cop. He was a young man maybe five years older than Trey with brush-cut hair and earnest blue eyes. "Sound like you been through this," said Trey.

The cop nodded. "Lost my grandmother to this disease last year. You're in for a rough ride, sir. I hope you have some help."

"My mom," said Trey. And then wished he could take the words back. Mom would be too busy, wouldn't she?

"That's good," said Stans. "With my gram, we needed all the help we could get."

"What you mean?"

"It doesn't just make them forget, Mr. Johnson. It changes them. It diminishes them. At the end, we had to do everything for Gram.

Everything. Feed her, change her like a baby. And sometimes, the disease just makes them plain mean. They lash out, particularly at the people they love. They try to hit you sometimes. Or bite you. They don't mean it. They're not in their right minds. My gram was convinced we were stealing from her. Or she would hallucinate my grandfather was in the room. He died in '79. One time, I made the mistake of telling her that. She clocked me upside the head with those bony little fists of hers." His smile was rueful and fond.

Trey swallowed hard. "That's what's gon' happen to my dad?" he asked.

Stans shrugged. "I don't know what's going to happen to your dad," he said. "I'm just telling you it's not going to be easy. I'm just telling you to be ready."

He held Trey's eyes a moment longer, then called over his shoulder to his partner. "Hey, Mel, you ready to get back out there?"

The other officer said yes. Stans wished Trey good luck and they headed for the door. "Hey," called Trey. The cops turned. Trey said, "Thanks. You know, for everything."

Stans nodded. Trey watched them go, then took a breath, and stepped through the curtain. Dad glanced around. His shirt was open and his fly was undone. "Oh, good," he said. "This is hard to do with…" And he held up the broken wrist.

Trey set about helping his father dress. "So," he said, his voice airy, "you said there was something else I need to know. What was that all about?"

No answer. Trey pulled back. "Dad?"

His father would not meet his eyes. "You may have it, too," he said.

"What? What you mean?"

"It's like I told you, son: this kind of Alzheimer's is genetic. I got it from someone in my family tree. And I can pass it down the same."

"But I feel fine."

"Yeah, I know. Still, the doctor says that once you get 30 years old, you're going to need regular screenings." He paused. Then he added, "Same for your son."

"DeVante?" asked Trey, stupidly.

"Yeah," said Dad. "All my blood descendants."

"But I feel fine," insisted Trey.

"Yeah, I know," said Dad. "I did, too."

Trey finished dressing his father in silence. The weight of this new knowledge seemed to crush the air out of him. His father was dying. Maybe he was dying, too. Maybe even his son. It was unfair. So monstrously unfair Trey wanted to scream. At somebody, something. But he didn't have the energy. He felt sluggish, slow. Like he was moving underwater, and watching himself from somewhere high above. It didn't feel real. Dad seemed to understand. He kept silent.

They had to wait 45 minutes for the doctor to sign the release papers. Another 30 minutes after that for a cab. It took them to the hotel. They napped for a few hours, then checked out. Midmorning found them at an auto mall. Dad picked out a black SUV identical to the one he had totaled. He drew a credit card from his wallet and paid for it on the spot. After the papers were signed, the salesperson shook Dad's hand and thanked him for his business and handed him the keys.

As they stepped out of the showroom, Trey nudged his father. "You need to let me drive," he said. And how many times had they joked about Trey's lust to get his hands on the big, glamorous truck? But now it wasn't a joke. Now it was an acknowledgement that something had changed between them. Something irrevocable.

There was a moment. Finally Mo said, "I guess you're right. I guess I'm just a passenger from now on." He passed the keys over and without another word, climbed into the passenger seat.

eighteen

In silence, they circled the mountains. Earth and rock towered majestically above them on both sides of the highway. The wind rushed down from an unforgiving blue sky to toy with them, shoving the car hard every now and then as if to remind them that they were but puny things.

Mo was distantly aware that Trey was scared. Scared of getting what his father had, but more immediately, scared of piloting this gleaming black behemoth with the smell of new on it, scared of the winds that came out of nowhere and nudged the truck just for spite. Trey was hunched over, both hands on the wheel, barely doing the speed limit. Other cars were whizzing around them in great gusts of impatience.

Mo knew he should encourage his son. Tell him he was doing fine. Tell him it would be okay. Something. After all, Trey had just absorbed a hell of a blow. He was dazed, shocked. He needed a good word. That's what a father would do.

But Mo couldn't. Wouldn't. Instead he sank gratefully into silence, wrapped himself in it like a blanket against the cold. Selfish, he knew, but it was hardly the first time, was it? That was the whole point, wasn't it?

Besides, didn't he deserve to spend some time in his own thoughts? He wouldn't be able to much longer, would he? Or maybe he had it backwards. Maybe, as the disease progressed, he would spend time *only* in his thoughts, except that they would be thoughts with no basis in reality, fantasies from which he would create his own reality in which to live. Never knowing the difference. Never knowing it was not real.

A tear slipped from his right eye. He knocked it away, leaned his head against the window.

"Are you okay?" asked Trey, sparing a glance.

Okay. What a stupid word it was. Stupid question. He wasn't okay. He'd never been okay. And he never would be okay.

Trey touched his elbow. "Dad?"

"Just drive," said Mo. His mouth felt thick. He didn't recognize his own voice.

It occurred to him to be thankful for the small favor of being in the car where it was unlikely anyone would give him a smile of recognition, require him to put on the Fan Voice yet again, fake the easy confidence he had faked so many times before.

Glad to see you.

Thank you for buying my records.

Oh, that's so nice of you.

He knew he couldn't pull it off. He was vaguely astonished that he ever had. Or that doing so had ever seemed important. Even as recently as last night. The night he had finally made his son see him for the fraud he was. And, perhaps not coincidentally, the night his Alzheimer's made itself more than theoretical. The night he broke with reality for the first time.

This wasn't forgetting the way to a nightclub, forgetting the words to a song. This was forgetting his son. And his own self. Mo thought he had resigned himself to the cruelties of the disease. He had thought himself prepared. Now he realized he wasn't.

He wished he had his gun. He would end it all here, now. Sure as hell he would.

Trey cleared his throat.

Don't.

"I wanted to tell you..." his son began.

"Just drive," Moses said. Pleaded.

Silence. The sound of the wheels murmuring on asphalt. Shadow of a hawk drifting between sun and earth.

Trey spoke again, deliberately. "I just wanted to tell you," he said, "that I found what you wrote on that pad."

Mo closed his eyes. After a moment he said, "It doesn't matter."

"It does to me," said Trey. "I don't want you to do...what you're thinking about."

"Why?"

"Why?" Trey's head came around in surprise. "Because you're my father, that's why." He said it was though it answered something, explained something.

"I'm tired," said Mo, eyes still closed, leaning against the head-rest, exhausted.

"I don't want you to kill yourself," said Trey.

"I'm not about to kill myself here," said Mo. "Do you know how much I just paid for this car?"

"It ain't funny!" Trey shouted it.

Mo opened his eyes, managed a smile. He said, "No, I guess it's not."

He closed his eyes again. Trey said, "Dad." Mo didn't answer. "Dad." More insistent.

"Yeah?"

"That stuff you wrote. About your life, I mean. I didn't know."

"That's why I wrote it. So you could know."

"Your mom, she sound like she was a great person."

"She was."

"I'm sorry what happened to her."

"Yeah, me too. Every day."

"And your father, man, I don't know."

"I don't either."

"I can see why you ain't talked to him all those years."

"Can you see why I'm going back now?" Mo asked it in the darkness of eyes still closed, threw it down as a gauntlet. The sun felt good on his face.

Trey seemed to think about it for a moment. Then he said, "No, I can't."

"Me neither," said Mo. "I mean, I don't forgive him. I *can't* forgive him. He killed her, sure as if he shot her with a gun. I'll always hate him for that. *Always*. But still, at the same time..." He let the words trail away.

"At the same time, he's your father," said Trey.

"Yeah," said Mo. "I guess that's it. The son of a bitch is my father. Now he's dying and I'm dying and it just seemed like it was important for me to see him one last time, before...you know, before it happens. I don't know why. Maybe to say something. Maybe to do something. Maybe just so we can lay eyes on each other one last time."

"Are you nervous?" asked Trey.

Mo thought about it, shook his head. "No."

"Then how you feel?"

"I don't feel," said Mo. "That's just it."

His cell phone went off then. Mo's eyes came open. He thought about ignoring the sound, leaving the phone for Trey to answer. But his son was still driving with two hands, hugging himself to the wheel. The last thing the boy needed was to try to answer a telephone, too. Mo reached across his body with his good hand and picked the cell up from the center console. He flipped open the clamshell and said, "Yeah."

"Moses, it's me," said Tash.

"Hey, girl," he said. It was the title of an old Temptations song she used to like. He had often greeted her that way back in '74.

"Hey yourself," she said. "Trey said you were in an accident."

"Trey tell you anything else?" he asked. And immediately wished he had not.

"No," she said suspiciously. "What else is there to tell?"

"I just meant, did he tell you I totaled the car?"

"I'm sorry to hear that. I know how much you loved that car."

"It's not a problem," said Mo. "I went out and bought a new one."

"You're incorrigible," she said. She said it fondly.

"Yeah, I think I've been told that once or twice." Keeping it light. Mo was thankful Trey hadn't told his mother more. And then he wondered why.

"So, are you all right?" asked Tash.

"Broken wrist, black eye, lost a tooth," he said.

"Oh, my God," she said.

"I'm fine," said Mo, touched, despite himself.

"So how did the accident happen anyway?"

"My fault," said Mo. "I didn't see a truck. Ran out in front of it."

"Mo, how you miss a truck?"

"I guess my mind was somewhere else," said Mo and his own cleverness, the opaque truth of what he had said, disgusted him. He made a self-promise that he would tell her everything as soon as he got back to Maryland. No sense saying it now, with 3,000 miles between them; she would only worry needlessly. But as soon as he got back.

"Well," she said, "I'm glad you're all right. Where are you any-way?"

"San Bernardino County," said Mo. "A couple hours away."

"Mo, are you sure you're okay?"

He smiled. "Fine as wine," he said.

"Well okay," she said, but he could tell she was not convinced.

They said their goodbyes and Mo flipped the clamshell shut. "You didn't tell her," he said.

Trey shrugged.

"Why?"

"I figure, you'd tell her when you was ready."

"That's nice. Now what's the real reason?"

"That is the real reason," snapped Trey, too quickly.

"You're angry with her."

A moment, then Trey nodded, eyes fixed on the road. "She was with that guy, man. They spent the night together."

In spite of himself, Mo almost smiled. "So?"

"'So?' What you mean, 'so?' Why she got to be spendin' time with that fool?"

Mo said, "Trey..." And then he thought better of it. "James," he said. At the sound of his real name, Trey's head came around in surprise. Mo sighed. "Everybody needs somebody, son. Your mother is 48 years old. Do you really think she should have to spend the rest of her life alone because you're waiting for her and me to get together?"

"I ain't waitin' for that."

"Yes, you are," said Mo quietly. "And yeah, I should have asked your mother to marry me a long time ago. But there's nothing either of us can do about that now. Now, Philip, you may not think much of him, but he makes your mother happy. And she deserves to be happy. So I want you to promise me you're going to quit giving the guy crap, quit coming between him and your mother."

"Dad," Trey began.

"Promise," said Mo. "It's important to me."

A sigh. "I promise," he said.

"Thank you," said Mo. He leaned his seat back, folded his arms and closed his eyes. After a moment, Mo slept.

He awakened to Trey tapping him urgently on the shoulder. Ahead the freeway was splitting and splitting yet again, a tangle of interchanges and bridges and bypasses and overpasses, overseen by a confusion of signs. They were coming into downtown Los Angeles.

Without a word, Mo pointed Trey to the proper asphalt artery. It was late afternoon. Traffic going into the city was moving at about 30 miles an hour. Traffic going out was not moving at all, white lights snaking toward them to infinity. The air was a sickly color, a haze of yellow and brown. Trey, a little more at ease behind the wheel now, was gazing up and around in awe.

"Welcome to the big city," said Mo.

They turned south on the Harbor Freeway. The canyons of downtown slid past the window, followed shortly by the campus of the University of Southern California. And now Mo felt the nervousness he had not acknowledged before, a tense anticipation that crept over him with the stealth of shadows. He tried to imagine the meeting, to steel himself for the sight of his father. For the first time in 30 years, he would confront Jack Johnson not as a memory, not as an object of hate, not as an abstract of every wrong and regrettable thing, but as a real and actual presence, taking up space and breathing air.

What would he look like? There were the years to take into account. There was the cancer, too. Would he know his father? Would his father know him? What would it be like, standing there before him again? Would Mo feel 15 years old again? Would all the old emotion come rushing back, just as raw and unresolved as ever?

"Are you ready for this?" asked Trey, as if sensing his father's unease.

Mo shook his head. "Not even a little bit."

"Well, ain't no turnin' back," said Trey.

"I know," said Mo.

"Maybe it won't be that bad."

"Yeah, it will," said Mo. He pointed to an exit ramp. "Get off here."

Down the ramp they went. They paused at a stoplight. Mo studied his son's profile for a moment. "Been some kind of day, hasn't it?" he said.

"Yeah," said Trey. "But it'll be a'ight."

"All right?" Mo was incredulous. "How will it be all right?"

"Got to have faith," said Trey. "That's what the preacher say."

"I never knew you to listen to anything a preacher said," Mo told him.

A shrug. "Lot of things you don't know," said Trey. He smiled to soften it.

They drove through the intersection and turned left on a street Mo had once known like his favorite song. It was strange to him now and he wondered if that was because of the disease or just the natural effect of change itself, the tendency of things to move around on you, to shift when you weren't looking. So that you could get back and be a stranger in your own places.

The record store was gone. The barber shop too. Pasted on a section of chain link fence circling a vacant lot were flyers for rap CDs, parties, and a radio station he'd never heard of. Many of the signs on the stores were in Spanish. Where Wong's had been was a store whose sign promised Mariscos y Pescados. Mo racked his high school Spanish vocabulary and after a moment, came up with Seafood and Fish. Everything must change, the song said. But change is hard. That's what the song didn't say.

"Turn here," said Mo. A few seconds later, he said it again. "Turn here. Park right there."

And there it was. It had been a weathered yellow last time he saw it. Now it was powder blue. The tree in the yard next door was fuller, almost obscuring the stairwell up to the front door. The auto parts store downstairs was shuttered. Looked as if it had been for a long time.

Mo stared across his son at the building on the other side of the street. Home. Indecision pinned him to his seat. After so many years of only memory, the realness of it, the thereness of it, was overwhelming. Then Mo noticed that they were drawing attention. Hands that had been polishing an old Cadillac paused in their rhythm. Two women chatting over a length of fence hesitated in their gossip. Eyes looked toward them. Faces hardened in suspicion.

Mexican faces, but that was the only difference. Even when he had been a child, you didn't just let somebody drive up on your street without checking them out, without tensing while you waited to see what they were about. It was a matter of survival.

Mo nudged Trey. "Come on," he said. "Let's go."

They crossed the street without looking left or right. Halfway across, when it was clear their trajectory would take them to the stairs, when it was clear they had a purpose there, life came back to the street. Mo had forgotten what it was like to live this way.

He mounted the stairs, Trey coming up behind him. Stood a moment before the door, then knocked sharply. It opened and Cooley was there. "Yes?" he said. Mo would have known him anywhere. He hadn't changed so much. Maybe a few more wrinkles pinching the corners of his eyes, a little more gray in the fringe of hair that ringed his smooth scalp. But he was still big, still had that elegant bearing. Still drunk, too, Mo saw as he looked into the glassy eyes. He said nothing, waited for recognition. It came after a moment.

"Mosey? Is that you?"

"Hey, old man," said Mo. And then Cooley had him wrapped in a crushing hug. Mo could smell alcohol in his sweat.

He waited for the hug to be over and when Cooley showed no signs of letting go, he gently worked his way loose. "This is my son," he said, nodding toward Trey.

Cooley didn't even look. "I'm sorry, Mosey," he said. "I'm really sorry. He tried as hard as he could. That's a fact."

Mo was confused. "What are you talking about?" he said.

A big hand landed on Mo's shoulder.

"Jack. He died this morning."

nineteen

The room was wreathed in shadow. It smelled of bourbon and body rot. And it was smaller than Mo remembered. Stepping inside, he had an unmistakable sense that he had entered a waking dream, walked into something not quite real. It felt more like the set of a stage play than a home where he once had lived.

At one wall stood a hospital bed with gleaming metal railings, angled toward a television and a boom box on the floor in the far corner. "He wouldn't let me put it in the bedroom," said Cooley, following Mo's gaze. "Didn't want to move the bed out of there because that's where your mother slept. He kept the whole place the way it was when you and her lived here. You should see your room."

"In a minute," said Mo. He was still trying to take in *this* room.

The furniture was the same cheap, overpriced easy-credit-store kindling he remembered. Same couch, same chairs, same lamps, same coffee table and end tables. Except for the television, the hospital bed, and the boom box, the only thing in the room that was new was a metal stand next to the television. Framed photographs crowded its top shelves. Eight by ten glossies of Moses Johnson in beaded jumpsuits, black tuxedoes, wide lapels, and wider hair. Later pictures with the hair gelled and shining, plastered to his forehead in stiff ringlets. And pictures showing Mo, face fuller and older, staring meaningfully into the camera. The Prophet.

Below the pictures was a shelf of albums, 45s, CDs, a couple of boxed set compilations. They were all of Moses Johnson. Even rarities and one-shots and things that had been released only in England or Japan. As near as Mo could tell, everything was there. Everything he'd ever done. On the bottom shelf were a dozen scrapbooks. Kneeling, Mo picked one up and opened it. Old interviews. Press releases and bios. Clippings of concert and album reviews. Everything. Every damn thing. He put the book back on the shelf, stood.

"He followed your career," said Cooley.

"So I see," said Mo.

"He loved you, Mosey. It was in his own way and it was strange, I'll grant. But he loved you."

Mo didn't answer. An unseen finger tickled the nape of his neck. A shiver worked its way through him. It unsettled him to think he had been so closely watched by this particular fan. This fan of all fans. Then he saw the bourbon bottle open on the coffee table. "Shot glasses still in the same place?" he asked.

Mo didn't wait for an answer. He crossed to the kitchen, went unerringly to the right cabinet and plucked a shot glass off the shelf. He blew into it as he returned to the front room, then poured himself a healthy dose. "You want to drink to Jack?" asked Cooley, reaching for the bottle as Mo put it down. Mo shook his head briskly. Drained the glass in one shot. It hurt going down, but the hurt was clarifying. Mo fell into a chair. Cooley sat down companionably across from him.

Trey said, "Nice 'fro, Dad." Mo craned toward the voice. Trey was staring at a high school graduation picture on the wall. Mo, his Afro mashed in a semicircle beneath a powder blue mortarboard, clutching a diploma in his hand and gazing dreamily, soulfully, toward the future.

Mo didn't recognize the picture. At first he thought it was because of Alzheimer's. Then he realized: he had never seen it. He had posed for his senior picture two weeks before his mother died. The portrait had been in transit the day he left this place for the last time. It occurred to Mo that he didn't have any pictures of himself as a boy. Every photo he owned, every memento of his life, was from after. It was as if he had been born the day he left. He had gone out from here and invented himself.

"Yeah, thanks," said Mo, reaching for the bottle again.

Cooley took a sip, indicated Mo's face with one of the fingers that held the glass. "So, you gon' tell me what happened to you?" he said.

Mo touched his swollen cheek. He had forgotten. "Had a lit-tle car accident this morning," he said. "We would have been here sooner."

"Too bad," said Cooley. "He held out as long as he could. I thought he was gon' make it, too. You know how stubborn Jack could be."

"Probably for the best," Mo said. "It would have been awkward. I have no idea what I would have said to him."

Cooley shrugged. "You start with hello. See where it goes from there."

"Easy for you to say," replied Mo, taking a drink. "So, what fu-neral home did they take him to?"

They spoke for a few minutes about the funeral, made basic deci-sions. The body would be ready for viewing late the following day. They would have the funeral two days after that, Mo said. Cooley asked if they shouldn't wait a little longer, give people coming from out of town a chance to get there. But Mo was definite. He wanted it over, wanted to get back to Baltimore as soon as he could.

"Well, he's your father," said Cooley with a shrug. "It's your deci-sion. So, you want to see your old room?"

Mo pursed his lips, nodded. Cooley hauled his bulk out of the chair. "Come on," he said and led them down the short hall. Mo wondered briefly why the big man thought he needed to play tour guide in the place where Mo grew up. Then, he went through the door behind Cooley and he understood: Cooley had wanted to see Mo's face at this particular moment.

He stood at the foot of the bed turning slowly, taking it in. Boxes of comic books. Writing pads filled with his scribbling. Albums, cas-settes, and a couple of eight tracks stacked neatly on a rack beneath an all-in-one turntable with cassette player and radio built in. Clothes in the closet. The Temptations, sleek and young, dancing weightlessly on a poster on the far wall. Most of them were dead now.

Everything in the room was yellowed, peeling, and tattered, but it was all there, exactly the same as it had been that awful day. Mo might have been gone 30 minutes instead of 30 years. It was as if time had stopped in this room, as if the clock paused and forgot to go forward again. Another shiver jagged through Mo. He dropped to the bed.

Cooley nodded knowingly. "It's something else, ain't it?"

Mo's face was slack. "Why, Cooley?" He whispered, because whispering seemed appropriate.

Cooley shrugged. "You'd have to ask Jack. And you know how that could be. Worse cussing out I ever got was a few years ago when I said maybe it was time to box this stuff up. Clean out the room. It was a little weird coming over here sometimes, tell you the truth. I kept half expecting you to come around the corner, or your mother to walk out the kitchen and give me a dirty look. She never did like me much, you know." This was said with a wistful smile.

Mo was surprised. "I didn't think you knew," he said.

Another shrug. "I knew," said Cooley. "But she had her reasons. You know, he didn't change their room, either. At least, that's what he told me. I never saw it myself. I mean, he might let me sleep in your room sometimes when it was late and I was drunk. But that room, he kept it locked up, like a secret." A conspiratorial grin. "You want to go in there?"

Mo hesitated. Remembered the night he had seen his mother come through that door, wraithlike, her face still bearing the print of his palm. "Yeah," he said.

Cooley led them across the hall, where he produced a key that went into the doorknob. He gave it a turn, opened the door, then stood aside so Mo could go in first. It was dark, the blinds closed against the fading light. There was the loud chemical odor of moth-balls and, beneath that, a deeper mustiness, a settled odor of things unmoved, untouched, unstirred for weeks unto months unto years. There was almost a weight to the smell, almost a physical presence. Mo took a deep breath, then reached behind him to the light switch on the wall and flipped it.

His hand remained on the switch. He couldn't even gasp. Filling the doorway behind him, Cooley breathed a soft cry. "Jesus," he said.

Mo's mother was there.

She was everywhere. Every space on the wall, every horizontal surface, the back of the door, the curtains, the glass panes of the windows, the ceiling. Pictures in ornate frames, pictures held to the wall by Scotch tape. Hundreds of pictures. Maybe more. Some images repeated two and three times. Formal portraits. Snapshots. Ruth at the beach. Ruth and Jack at a nightclub back in the day. Ruth making faces for the camera. Ruth caught pensive, looking away. Ruth in her wedding gown. Sepia-toned pictures of a fat toddler—Ruth—in the arms of her mother, circa 1934. Colors fading, photo paper curling and going brown. Ruth Desireé Johnson, dead now for 30 years, lived in this room.

Mo let his hand drop, forced himself past the door jamb. He sat on the bed, the only thing in the room not covered with her. It was neatly made with a threadbare old cover, but his weight made dust rise. Cooley followed Mo in. "I didn't know it was like this," he said. And then he beseeched his dead friend. "Jack, why you do this?"

"To torture himself," said Mo. "He couldn't say he was sorry. Had nobody to say it to. This was his way of saying it. Forcing himself to sleep in here every night with her staring down on him. Reminding him, like a conscience."

Her perfume bottles, long empty, were arranged on a mirror atop an old wooden vanity. Framed photographs stood sentry. One showed her in her wedding gown. Her smile was beatific. The closet stood open. Her dresses and blouses were arrayed on hangers. Mo knew that if he opened the bureau, he would find her underwear, folded neatly. She was a presence here. Everything but alive.

"My father was crazy as a betsy bug," said Mo. "One crazy son of a bitch."

"He was tortured," said Cooley, easing his bulk down onto the bed.

"Same thing, ain't it?" said Mo.

"So, what you gon' do with all this stuff?" asked Trey.

Mo hunched his shoulders. "Throw it away, I guess."

"Throw it away?" Trey was scandalized.

"If you want to keep a few pictures of your grandmother so you'll know what she looked like, go ahead. But the rest of this stuff, these

dresses, and all that shit piled up in my room, and all those scrapbooks and things, ain't no reason to keep it. Throw it out."

A movie scene came to him. *Cooley High*, 1975. Glynn Turman
standing at Lawrence-Hilton Jacobs's grave. G.C. Cameron on the
soundtrack singing "It's So Hard to Say Goodbye to Yesterday."

Bullshit. Sometimes, yesterday says goodbye to you.

"But Mosey," said Cooley, "don't you want to keep some of this
stuff? You know, to remember them by?"

"I'm not going to remember, Cooley. If I drag every bit of this
shit home, I won't remember."

"I don't understand."

"I'm dying, too, Cooley. That's what I didn't tell you. I'm dying
just like Jack."

Cooley's eyes widened. "What? What are you talking about?"

"I've got Alzheimer's disease."

"But you're not—"

Mo cut him off with a curt wave of his hand. "Yeah, I know. But
see, sometimes, this disease doesn't care how old you are. Sometimes,
it doesn't matter."

The big face went slack. "Mosey, I'm so sorry."

"It's all right," said Mo. "Really, it is."

"Damn, that's…that really hurts me to hear, Mosey. You have no
idea. Isn't there anything they can do?"

"Not a thing," said Mo.

"Did they tell you how long?"

"Not really. I did some reading, though. Book says I could linger
with this for years. Look at Reagan. Took him ten years to die."

Cooley brightened. "So you could live for awhile yet."

"Yeah," said Mo, "you want to call that living."

Mo lifted himself from the bed, went to the closet. He took the
sleeve of a flowered blouse between thumb and forefinger and rubbed
it absently. She had worn this to church. The material was coarse.
"So tomorrow," he said, "we get rid of all this stuff." He walked out
without waiting for an answer, went to the front room, got himself
another bourbon, lit a cigarette. It was awkward with just the one
hand.

"So," he said, squinting through the smoke with his one good eye as Cooley and Trey came down the hall, "I guess we'll go get a bite, find a place to bed down for the night. Then we'll come over here tomorrow and help you clean the place out."

"Are you sure you don't want to sleep in your old bed?" asked Cooley.

"You must be kidding," said Mo.

"Just thought I'd ask," Cooley said.

Mo motioned to his son. "Come on, Trey. I know a place downtown you'll like. Assuming they haven't shut it down. City's changed so much."

"Yeah," said Cooley, "everything has."

They said their goodbyes then. Trey drove the SUV and Mo directed him to a gleaming glass tower of a hotel downtown. They got a room, ordered room service, watched television, turned in early. The day had been long and awful.

It was shortly before noon when they returned to the house in South Central. Cooley had already gathered boxes and was packing dishes. Trey knelt to help him. Mo did too, but he lasted only a few minutes. Then he took the bourbon bottle, sat on the couch in the living room for what he said was a rest, and did not get up again. He called for Trey to bring him the old turntable out of his bedroom and spent the afternoon smoking, drinking, and playing his old records and CDs. Providing a soundtrack.

Trey and Cooley worked—sweeping, bagging, boxing, and hauling things out. And the Temptations sang "Ball of Confusion." Earth, Wind & Fire sang "Keep Your Head to the Sky." The Stylistics sang "Betcha by Golly Wow." And Mo Johnson sang "Rhythm in the Night," "Deep Inside You," and the signature song, "My Prophecy." Mo sang along with it all. He hit high notes alongside Philip Bailey of Earth, Wind & Fire, growled alongside Dennis Edwards of the Temptations, and harmonized with himself.

His voice had lost a bit, he conceded sadly. He hated to admit it, but he was too much a professional not to. No longer could he command the silken purity of his youth. Too much alcohol. Too many cigarettes. Too long ago. But he could remember the lyrics and surely that counted for something. He would have his music for awhile, at least. Mo was aware of the worried glances passing between Cooley and Trey. Occasionally, he would allow himself to wonder what they might be saying about him as they huddled together, filling up bags. Then the horns would stab the melody or the harmonies would rise or the strings would sweep him away and it didn't matter. Nothing else mattered. Music had always had that effect.

And so the afternoon passed. At some point, the medical supply company came for the hospital bed. Trey and Cooley worked until there was nothing on the walls, nothing on the shelves, nothing in the apartment except bare furniture and the stereo where Mo sat drinking and listening and singing. He was in a pleasant haze but, by his own estimation, far from drunk, when Cooley came over and said, "We need to get down to the funeral home. They said the body would be ready about now and you need to give your approval before they can put it out for viewing."

"Sure," said Mo. He tried to get up, but doing so was harder than he'd expected. He braced himself a couple of times and pushed up, but without effect. Finally, with a sigh, Trey extended his hand. Mo took it and allowed himself to be pulled upright.

"Guess I need to knock off the bourbon for awhile," he said jauntily.

For his effort at good humor he received in return only a pious frown. "I guess you do," Trey said.

They piled into the car. Mo took the back seat. His car, he thought, but there he was in the back seat. Cooley drove. It took 20 minutes. Darkness had begun to creep into the sky when they pulled into the parking lot on the side of the Franklin Brothers Mortuary. Mo remembered their advertisements on the church fans of his childhood: *Your friends in time of need.* He repeated the slogan out loud. One of those looks passed between Trey and Cooley. Then Cooley explained. "That's the motto for the funeral home. They been in business around here for years."

"I could have told him that," said Mo. Who did Cooley think he was?

There was another look. Cooley and Trey got out of the car. Mo was having difficulty with the lock; for some reason, it refused to respond to his fingers. Trey opened the door, staring at him with another of those church-deacon frowns, and extended his hand. Mo slapped it away. He climbed down from the seat heavily, cocking his index finger at his son. "I done had about enough of you disrespecting me," he said.

Trey had the nerve to look surprised and then to turn to Cooley for help. As though Mo had been speaking a foreign language. "Fuck both of y'all," said Mo, turning to go inside.

Cooley put a hand against his chest. His voice was gentle, but there was no give in it. "Mosey," he said, "don't be that way. There's no call for that. You need to have some respect, now. We're here to pay honor to your father. You might not think he was much, and I know you got your reasons, but still, he was your father."

Mo was stung. Felt 13 years old all over again. Cooley was right, of course. "I'm sorry," he said. "I'm sorry." And he was. He was ashamed. He felt like weeping.

A horseshoe driveway fronted the building, which was the color of eggshells. The portico was two stories high, supported by Doric columns. The double doors were of a dark, reddish wood with brass handles. As they reached it, the accent lights came on and the building seemed momentarily a mansion of heaven. Mo stopped to look.

"I always liked this place," he said. "When I was a child, I mean."

"Yeah," said Cooley. "It's a nice building." He held the door for Mo and Trey.

Inside, they were met by a short fat man, unctuous in that way of people who make their living dealing with the bereaved. He took their names and asked them to wait in the spacious front hall. There were plush, dark red leather seats below a painting from which the four Franklin brothers themselves stared out with stern compassion. Mo considered taking a seat, but it occurred to him he might not be able to get up again. Maybe he was a little tipsy after all.

After a few minutes, the fat man came for them. He led them past viewing rooms where the lights were subdued, the coffin lids were raised, and dead clay husks that once had been people stared up into eternity. All at once, Mo's legs felt watery. He didn't know if he could do this. Without meaning to, he reached for Trey's hand. He gripped it hard. Trey spoke softly. "It's gon' be all right, Pop," he said.

They were led into a bare room. The floor was concrete. The walls were unadorned. The lights were bright. At the far end of the room was the only thing in it. A casket with an open lid. His father's dead profile was visible, barely. Mo faltered. Trey caught him. Cooley braced him with an arm across his back. Mo wondered briefly where this tidal wave of feeling had come from. Where, after 30 years? Suddenly the pleasant haze was gone. In its place, a pitiless clarity too hard and bright for hiding.

"Let me go," he said.

Trey was unsure. "Pop, are you—"

Mo repeated it. "Let me go. I've got to do this by myself."

The hands that held him hesitated. Then they released him. Mo stood straight, tugged at his shirt. He went to see his father. The walk was long. His steps echoed. Then he was standing there, looking down on a stranger in a black pinstriped suit. Jack was small, made smaller by cancer. It seemed to have drawn him in on himself. The contours of the old man's skull were nearly visible, the skin darker than Mo remembered. Jack's face was deeply lined and his expression was sour, as though something in the afterlife displeased him greatly.

Probably the heat, thought Mo. And then he had to stifle a nervous giggle. He touched the skin. It was cool, smooth, dead. Jack's hair was nearly gone. What was left was gray. This was the man who had authored his frightened days and wakeful nights. This was the man on whom he had lavished years of extravagant hate. This matchstick of a man. This nothing. It didn't seem possible. It didn't seem real.

Mo heard Cooley arrive on his left. "He looks just like himself," he said. "Cancer really ate him up, though." He touched the thin hair fondly. "Hey, buddy."

Trey appeared on Mo's right. He didn't speak.

Mo said, "I forgot he was so small. Used to seem so big."

"Yeah," said Cooley, "but you weren't nothing but a kid."

"I was taller than he was even then. Bigger than he was. I don't know why I was so scared."

"Jack had that way about him," said Cooley. "I ever tell you about the first time we met?"

Mo shook his head. "He kicked my ass," said Cooley. Mo turned to him, surprised, and the big man laughed. "We were in high school. I was the school bully, he was the new kid. I seen him coming, this little runt. I figured I could make him pay the toll to use the hallway same as I made all the other kids. How hard could it be? Well, he kicked my ass, Mosey. Big as I am, he kicked my natural ass."

"Wow," said Trey appreciatively. "He had some scrap in him, huh?"

"More scrap than any man I ever knew. That was always important to Jack. Don't back down, no matter what the odds. Always stand up for yourself."

"Be a man," said Mo. "That was his thing. Every time you turn around, be a man, be a man." Remembering a tire iron crashing against a white man's head on a long ago day.

"Yeah, he was worse after he got out," said Cooley. "You know why that was, don't you, Mosey?"

Mo pondered for a moment, shook his head. "Think about it," insisted Cooley.

Mo gave it another moment, then hunched his shoulders. Cooley's gaze was steady. "They took his manhood in that place."

Mo's grip on the coffin hardened. "What do you mean?"

"You know what I mean," said Cooley from behind that unwavering gaze. "He never wanted you to know—never wanted *anybody* to know—but that's what happened."

"How..." began Mo, but left the sentence unfinished, hanging in midair.

"You know what happens in prison," said Cooley, evenly. "Especially when you small and young like Jack was. They came one at a time at first. Nobody liked Jack no way, 'cause he kept to himself. In prison, you get by from your alliances. But that wasn't Jack. He wasn't with nobody but Jack. He went his own way, didn't bother nobody, didn't join nobody. They hated that. So they came for him. First one, Jack sends him to the hospital. Warden puts Jack in solitary. He defending himself, but *he* the one end up on lockdown. 'Cause see, the guards and the warden, they don't like him no better. Don't nobody like a man they can't figure.

"So anyway," continued Cooley, "a few nights after Jack gets out, the second one tries him. He end up in the hospital, too. More solitary. They finally got him the third time. Set him up. Six of them in the prison laundry. Guards were in on it. Had to be, 'cause they weren't nowhere around. And them six, they weren't in no hurry. They took turns. They took their time. They used a mop handle on him. When the guards found him, they had stuffed it in his mouth."

Cooley's eyes glittered. Trey said, "Damn." Mo felt the world reeling.

"Jack like to died that day. What they did, it tore him up inside. Cut him up bad. He was in the hospital for weeks. Prison wrote your mother that he had got hurt, that he was in the infirmary and couldn't have no visitors. He didn't tell me the truth till years later, after Ruth died. We drinkin'. Sloppy drunk like when you start putting your arms around each other and singing old songs and talking about all the shit you regret in your life. And it comes out of him all at once, out of nowhere. He's crying as he tells me, and that's the worst sight I ever seen in my life, Jack Johnson crying. The next day when he got sober, he couldn't look at me all day. Finally, he come up to me and says, 'That thing I told you yesterday. I'll kill you if you ever tell it to anybody, Cooley.' I must have looked shocked, 'cause he said, 'I'm not joking. I mean it.'"

Cooley's smile was tight. He touched the gray hair again. "And you know, even now, standing here, I think he might jump up out this box for me telling you. But see, I think you need to know."

A moment passed. Then Mo said, "So what you're telling me..."

"I'm telling you Jack became a different man that day. Those six, they killed Jack, the Jack I knew, sure as if they put a gun to his head. When they was done, that man was gone. Wasn't nobody left but this mean little customer you see right here, this man who didn't let nothing pass."

"What happened to the six men?" asked Trey.

This brought another tight smile. "What you think? Jack killed them. Took him ten years. He wanted them to forget what had happened so they wouldn't tie none of it to him. He wanted the killings to look like just part of the everyday of life in the prison yard. But one by one over the years, he got them all. He shivved them, he beat them, and the last one, the ringleader, he got him with a garrote and left him hanging in his cell. And each time, the guards came and swept things up and did their paperwork and nobody ever made the connection that these was the six who had hurt Jack Johnson."

Trey gave a low whistle. "Wow," he said. "My gramps was a bad man."

Mo said, "Why you telling me this, Cooley?"

Cooley pressed his lips together for a moment in thought. Then he said, "Maybe so you'll understand a little bit better why he couldn't be the father you needed him to be. Maybe so you'll forgive him."

Mo gave it a moment. He pondered the figure below him. The room was so quiet he could hear the susurration of the air conditioning unit in the ceiling far above. Mo said, "It doesn't really matter though, does it?"

"Beg pardon?"

"Why he wasn't there. Why he couldn't be the father he was supposed to be. The reasons aren't important."

"Of course they are," protested Cooley.

"No, they're not," said Mo. "When you're a kid, you don't know about none of that stuff. All you know is that you want your dad and he's not there. All the reasons in the world, all the excuses in the world, don't change that."

Cooley's voice was soft. "But you're not a kid no more, Mosey."

Mo meant to laugh at that, to lighten the mood with some little joke. But he glanced over at his son, his serious, concerned son he didn't even know, and the laughing came out as tears. And the tears wouldn't stop. He sobbed, helplessly, then cried out in a raw inarticulate voice. No words, just hoarse bellows and moans that echoed off the stark walls.

Cooley patted his back. "That's okay," he said. "Just let it all out. It's going to be all right."

And in some detached part of his mind, watching all of this from somewhere far above, Mo marveled that his friend could misunderstand so fundamentally. Could get it so wrong. There was not sorrow in these cries. This was rage. This was lacerating fury. At God. At the universe. At the dead thing that once had been Jack Johnson.

There were things that needed saying here, things that needed hearing. Things without names, but things so important they had brought him all the way across the continent. Irresolution had come 3,000 miles in search of resolve, and one more time, Jack had escaped. One more time, Jack had not been there. It did not matter why.

Mo heard himself whisper, "I'm sorry, Trey. I'm sorry."

He looked around and realized that somehow, he had ended up on the floor. Cooley and Trey helped him to his feet and got him out of the room. They passed the unctuous man in the hall and told him the body looked fine. Then Mo was sitting in the front passenger seat of the SUV, head against the headrest, window open, cool breezes brushing his brow. His sobs were arrested, his tears slowed to a trickle.

"I'm sorry," he said.

"That's all right," said Trey, from the back seat.

The driver's side door opened and Cooley hauled himself in. He started the car, but didn't put it in gear. For a moment he just sat there. The radio was playing jazz lite. Mo looked at him. Cooley lowered the volume.

"Mosey," he said, "there's one other thing you need to know."

twenty

The SUV rolled to a stop in front of a Jack in the Box restaurant on Central Avenue. "You're hungry?" said Mo.

Cooley's smile was thin. "How much do you know," he asked, "about what your daddy went to jail for?"

For no reason he could name, the question made Mo's heart kick hard. He sat up, the last of the pleasant, drunken haze trickling away. "I know enough," he said.

Still that thin, patient smile. "Really? What do you know?"

"I know he robbed some white guy," said Mo. He hardened his voice. "Robbed him, then shot him to death."

"Yeah, that's what he told your mama to tell you, ain't it?"

Mo didn't know how to answer. He could sense Cooley shading toward some unpleasant truth and he was impatient for him to hurry up and spit it out already. But he could also sense that the big man would not be hurried. This truth would come in its own time.

"I don't get over here much anymore," said Cooley. "Really no reason to. But, Mosey, you should have seen Central back in the day. It was something else. Night clubs and movie theaters and all kinds of colored business. This street used to jump back then. Now…"

He let a nod toward the fast food restaurant finish the sentence for him. It was painted in unsubtle reds and whites. The drive-through was doing brisk business. A young mother, a toddler in her arms, two squalling kids walking on either side, was making her way doggedly across the parking lot.

Mo shrugged. "World changes, Cooley. I don't see what—"

Cooley ignored him. "This used to be your father's club," he said. "Right here on this spot." He held up a hand to frame the words, breathed them as if they were perfumed. "Le Desireé," he said. "Named it after your mama."

"Ruth Desireé LaChance," said Mo.

The big man's smile finally opened. "Fancy name, wasn't it? You know how them Creoles is. High toned. But on her, it fit. Didn't hardly seem like puttin' on airs at all. Your mama was special, Mosey. Everybody uses that word, but with her it was true. Jack was special, too. I know you won't believe that, but it's also true."

"Yeah," said Mo, "well, I guess I never got to see that side of him."

"I know you didn't," said Cooley, "and I'm sorry about that, because you really missed something." A laugh. "I used to call him the mayor of Central Avenue. 'Cause he knew everybody and everything and they all turned to him when they needed help. Need some reefer? Jack's the man to see. Want tickets to see Ella? Ask Jack. Done got your girl in a family way? Talk to Jack. I asked him one time how any business ever got done before Jack Johnson got there. He just laughed. Your daddy, he had that thing you got. Charisma. Could talk to anybody about anything. People believed in him. They liked him and didn't even stop to wonder why."

"I still don't understand what any of this has to do with him robbing some store," said Mo.

The big man sighed. "Mosey, you got to let me tell this the way I got to tell it, okay?" His eyes were imploring. Mo didn't reply.

"So my grandfather owned a club right here?" asked Trey, leaning across the seat.

"Yeah," said Cooley. "Brought me out here from Mississippi to be a bartender for him. Well, that, and to be best man at his wedding. That was when I met Ruth."

"How he get the money to open a club?" asked Trey.

"He had a partner. White boy named Tommy Knight."

The words had to squeeze through clenched teeth. "You ain't liked this guy too much," said Trey.

"Jack introduced me to him my first night here, standing in that empty club. Said he wanted us to be friends. Skinny boy in a white stingy brim with a red feather. Dressed like colored, talked jive like colored. 'Hey, Cool, slide me some skin.' I'm just off the bus from

Buford, Mississippi. What I know about 'slide me some skin?' Him and Jack laughed at that. Said I was square as a box."

"But you didn't like him," insisted Mo.

"I liked him fine at first," said Cooley, "while him and me and Jack and Ruth was paintin' the walls and installing the bar and putting in the decorations. Liked him just fine then. I didn't know no better."

He pulled back out into traffic, driving slowly. Central Avenue was hamburger stands and thrift shops and the Department of Water and Power. On the sidewalk, a group of teenagers shrieked with overloud laughter.

Out of nowhere, Cooley said, "Your mother was beautiful."

"I know," said Mo.

"Inside and outside, I mean."

"I know that, too."

"She was the type of person see the same bum begging for money on the same corner day in and day out, stop and give him a coin every time, ask him how he doing, tell him she praying for him. That's how she was. She cared about people."

A sudden realization made Mo sit up straight. "You were in love with her," he said.

For a moment, Cooley didn't speak. His jaw was like granite and he stared straight ahead. Reflected light climbed the windshield and disappeared. Finally the big man said, "We all loved Ruth. Me, your daddy, Tommy. Difference was, I loved her enough, and loved him enough, to leave it alone. Tommy was another story."

"Are you saying this guy tried to make a move on my mother?"

This brought a bitter chuckle. "'Make a move.' No. That wasn't the kind of thing Tommy did. You have to understand this guy. Rich man's son. Full of himself. Free, white, and over 21, like they used to say. Jack liked him fine, but after awhile, I didn't so much. Didn't trust him. Always talkin' that hepcat jive. Never serious about nothin'. Seem to me like he spent so much time listening to black music and screwing black women and hanging out in black neighborhoods that sometimes he forgot he wasn't black."

"They still got that kind," said Trey.

Cooley glanced at him. "Yeah, but this was different," he said. "Fifty years ago, didn't no ofay and no nigger just hang around together, casual like they do today. It was a big deal then. I remember one time, one of Tommy's white friends from the hills came down to see the club. Ended up gettin' into it with one of the regulars. White boy must have forgot he was on Central Avenue, 'cause he called my man a nigger. But before anybody could do anything, Tommy had his friend by the scruff of the neck, shoved him through the door, kicked him in the ass for good measure. Everybody stood up and applauded, 'cause that was something you didn't see every day."

"Sounds like he was okay," asked Mo.

"Yeah, that's what I thought," said Cooley. "Week later, him and your daddy almost come to blows. You know why?"

"No."

"They got to arguin' over an act Jack wanted to book for the club and Tommy called him a nigger."

"*What?*"

A grim nod. "Jack was 'bout to put a foot in his ass, but Ruthie stopped him. She said, 'Look at his eyes.' We did. They were shiny like glass."

"Cocaine?" said Mo.

"Yeah. First time I ever saw anybody high on that shit. Turned out he was a fiend for it." He turned off Central, traveling west on Slauson. The traffic was heavy.

"What did Jack do about it?" asked Mo.

"Nothin'. Tommy apologized when he got straight and Jack didn't press it. See, it was about money. Tommy's old man, it turned out, fronted the money for the club. Jack couldn't afford to mess that up. Besides, he figured he could handle Tommy. Then I found out Tommy was stealing from the till. Actually, wasn't me who caught him. That was Sis."

"Sis?"

A nod. "That's what I used to call your mother. 'Cause me and Jack was like brothers."

"I never heard you call her that."

"She wouldn't let me, afterward. After everything happened, she made me stop."

"Why?"

Cooley regarded him for a long moment. Then he said, "I hurt her. I broke a promise to her."

"What promise? You ain't making sense, old man."

Cooley grinned. "You'll get old some day. Just keep livin'." Then he remembered, and the grin went away. "Oh, Mosey, I'm sorry."

Mo put his hand up. "Just go on," he said. "Help me understand."

Cooley nodded. "Well," he said, "the club did good right from the first day. Your daddy, he was a genius about knowing what people want. I mean, I had thought we was going to throw some tables in there, get a jukebox, and call it a day. But he had other ideas. We did the room up in pink trimmed in a red like the color of wine. And we put all these fancy fixtures on the walls. Art Deco, your father called it. Something he read about in some book.

"I didn't like it," continued Cooley. "Thought it was kind of fruity, you want to know the truth. But Jack explained that what he had in mind wasn't just a bar. It was a club. A sophisticated place where you would get dressed up and take your best girl to have drinks and hear some jazz. He wanted something that felt uptown. Special. As usual, Jack knew what he was doing. The place was packed from the first night. Stayed that way. We was making big money.

"And this guy Tommy was stealing it.

"Well, like I say, I didn't know that at first. Sis kept the books, you see. And one night a few months later after we were closed for the night, she excused herself and said she was going in the office to do some bookkeeping. A minute later, Tommy yawned and said he was about done in. Said he wanted to get some breakfast. He asked if me or Jack wanted to join him at Patsy's, this diner we always went to. We said no."

Cooley brought the car to a stop at a light. His eyes were distant. "Some time passed," he said. "Jack stacking chairs, me counting out the register. After he got the chairs stacked, Jack sat on a barstool. A moment later, he put his head down on the bar and fell asleep. And that's when something told me to go in the back and check on Sis. I tried to ignore it, but the feeling was strong. So I went back there and I opened the door without knocking.

"Tommy was back there with Sis. He had doubled back and come in from the parking lot. Now Ruthie was sitting at the desk and he was leaned over her. They had been talking and their faces was close together."

"What were they talking about?" asked Mo.

"That's what I wanted to know," said Cooley. "I asked them, 'What y'all conspiring about in here?' Trying to keep it light, but I was serious. Tommy, he straightened up and gave me this grin, said he just came back to get his hat and Miss J.—that's what he always called your mother—had some questions about one of the bookings. He says, 'I think we got it all cleared up now, though.'"

And Sis said, 'Yeah, I think we got it straight.' Her voice was almost like she was scared. Tommy brushed by me, then stopped to look back at her. He said, 'That Jackie's one lucky son of a gun, ain't he?' And he dropped the hat on his head and walked out. I asked Sis what was going on. She said it was nothing. I told her it didn't look like nothing to me. She told me to stop being an old woman.

"And right there I knew something was wrong, because Sis didn't talk to people like that. She got a look on her face like she was reading my mind, but before I could say anything else, she went to wake up Jack so they could leave."

Cooley made a left that brought them into the parking lot on the side of a dark hulk of a building that took up the entire block. All the signs were in Spanish. There were no lights and the building was boarded up tight. The Escalade came to a stop before a wall so heavily tagged with gang graffiti that its original color was no longer discernible. On the opposite side of Slauson, a freight train rumbled down the railroad tracks that ran parallel with the street.

"What is this place?" asked Mo.

Cooley ignored him. Both hands on the wheel, staring straight head. "I thought about talking to Jack, but I didn't know what to say. The two of them huddled up like that, you could take it any number of ways. In fact, it could have been completely innocent. Didn't feel innocent, though. It wasn't until months later that Sis finally told me what was going on. Took me aside one night and told me how money had been coming up missing and she had confronted Tommy about it. He had promised to put it back, but he hadn't done it yet. That's what they was talkin' about that night in the office."

"Why she wait to long to tell you?" asked Trey.

"She wouldn't have told me even then," said Cooley, "except she knew I was going to take over doing the books for awhile because she wasn't going to be able to work. She was pregnant with your father."

There was silence again. Mo repeated himself. "Cooley, what is this place?"

Cooley spoke from far away. "She told me Tommy was using the club's money to buy that white powder. And all of a sudden, I understood. I said, 'That night when I walked in on you, was he threatening you?' She didn't answer and of course, that was an answer all by itself. I was ready to kick his natural ass. She begged me not to. She said he was high when he did it, said he apologized the next day and promised to get the money back. And she asked me not to say nothing to Jack. Please don't tell Jack, that's what she said. She didn't want them falling out because if they did, Tommy would pull his daddy's money out of the club."

Mo said, "Cooley, why won't you tell me what this place is?"

Cooley glanced up at the brick wall as if he had forgotten it was there. "I don't know what it is now," he said. "Some Mexican place. But this is where it happened."

"Where what happened?"

Cooley held him with just the force of his gaze, repeated himself. "Mosey, this is where it happened."

"You mean the robbery. Where my father shot the guy."

There was pity in the big man's smile. "You know better than that," he said softly. "Wasn't no robbery. And it wasn't no 'guy.' This is where Tommy was killed."

"Because he threatened my mother? I don't get it."

Cooley said, "Tommy, his father used to own this place. Back then, it was a furniture store. He got rich selling couches and dinette sets to black people on easy credit. Arnie Knight was always frontin' his son in one deal or another. Boy never worked an honest day in his life, and why should he? Wasn't nothin' his daddy wouldn't do for him. Boy thought the world was his box of Cracker Jack. Thought the Dez was his private piggy bank.

"But Sis swore she could handle him. She said, 'Cooley, things going real good right now. It keep working out like this, Jack's gon' be a rich man someday. I don't want to mess that up over some foolishness. So we got to keep this between you and me, okay?' I didn't answer right away. She took my hand and asked me again to keep a secret from my best friend. My sister asking me to betray my brother. Finally, I agreed. I said I wouldn't say nothing to Jack."

"But you did."

Cooley shook his head. "No, I didn't say nothing to your father. It's the other promise I broke. I talked to Tommy. We went down to Patsy's that night when the club closed and I laid into him. Told him I knew what he had done and if he tried it again, I would break his neck. He tried to laugh it off and I slapped him. Hard enough, it left the print of my hand clear on his cheek. Everybody looking at us and you could tell I had embarrassed him. That's just what I wanted. I grabbed me a piece of his collar and told him if he ever stepped out of line with Ruthie again, I would kill him. I wasn't just saying it. I meant it. And he knew it."

Mo could hardly breathe. "Oh, my God. It was you."

"Mosey, I—"

"It was you. You let my father take the rap. You let me think… But all the time, it was you?"

All at once, Mo felt the SUV pressing in on him. He shoved the door open, stepped out into the freight train roar, one hand to his temple, pacing in front of the idling vehicle. He felt…upended. The past, closed book, finished story, solid ground, had betrayed him, changed, become something else. Something he could never have envisioned. And if your past wasn't what you thought it was, then how could you be who you thought you were? How could you trust anything you thought you knew?

Trey had climbed out after him, and now laid a tentative hand on his shoulder. Mo shrugged it off angrily. "Not now, Trey!" His hands were fists.

Cooley climbed out of the car. "Mosey," he cried, yelling to be heard above the train.

"Don't," yelled Mo. "Don't you 'Mosey' me, old man. All this time, all these years, you let me think my father was...but all the time, it was you...you dirty motherfucker!"

"Moses," he cried, "let me finish. You see, your mother, she..."

At that moment, the last car of the train rushed by. The silence was thunderous. Cooley sighed, repeated himself in a softer voice. "Your mother, she came to work three days later, and she was sick. Moving slow, skin pale as paper. After about an hour, her legs buckled and she fell into a chair. I yelled for Jack and ran to her. Sis was out of it, didn't even know who I was or who she was. Then all at once her eyes jumped into focus and she saw me. 'You get away from me,' she said. Just like that. 'You get away.'"

He leaned his bulk against the graffiti wall. He spoke to the ground. "We got her an ambulance. Last thing I saw before they covered her up was a splotch of red on the front of her dress. Bright red. Jack rode in the ambulance. It took me awhile to get a ride. I left a sign on the door saying we was closed 'cause of an emergency. Actually, the Dez never opened again."

A sigh, as if the telling caused physical pain. "When I got down to County General, I found Jack sitting in the waiting room. The look on Jack's face scared me worse than anything. It was like he wasn't even seeing the world around him. I saw that face and I thought the worst. I said, 'Jack, how is Sis? Is she...?'

"I couldn't bring myself to even say the word 'okay' because that was like admitting there was a chance she wouldn't be okay. A chance she might even be dead. I kept thinking of that blood on her dress. Jack looked at me like I was a stranger. His voice was so soft I had to lean in to hear what he was saying. He said, 'The doctor say she bleeding bad, Cooley. He say she might lose the baby.'

"I tried to tell Jack that Tommy did it. I told him how Sis found out he was stealing and how I got in his face. Jack didn't say nothing for awhile. He had his eyes closed. Finally, he said, 'Would you just shut up, Cooley? Shut up and let me pray.'"

Now Cooley lifted his head. His eyes were pools of black, impenetrable. "Mosey," he said, "I wasn't for no praying. I was for finding that little son of a bitch who hurt Ruthie because of me. All I could think about was killing that muh'fucka."

Mo stood next to Cooley. After a moment, he leaned against the wall, folded his arms across his chest.

"I understand why you wanted to kill him," he said softly. "What I can't understand is how you let my father take the rap for it."

"Mosey, you don't know how it was."

"*Make* me understand, Cooley! Make me understand how it was."

twenty-one

Cooley left Jack at the hospital and went hunting Tommy Knight. His first stop was the Desireé, where he went behind the bar for the big chrome .45 Jack kept in case of trouble. He tucked it in his waistband, covered it with a windbreaker, and hit the streets.

Any remaining doubts Cooley had that it was Tommy who had hurt Ruth Johnson disappeared in the next hours. Because Tommy, who ordinarily haunted Central like a ghost, who was known on sight in its pool halls and Chinese restaurants and liquor stores and you-buy-we-fry fish markets, was not to be found. It was as if he had disappeared. As if he had never been anything more than a rumor.

Everywhere he went, Cooley got the same answer. Nobody had seen Tommy all day. Nobody knew where he was.

It was a Friday night. The street was busy, cars moving slowly up and back. Soldier boys with the stubs of freshly cashed paychecks in their breast pockets walking like they owned the street, slapping each other's backs and laughing a little too loud. Girls with their hair pressed and curled and bouncing on their shoulders, clinging to the soldiers' arms, a little too charmed. Dealers and hustlers and numbers men loitering on barstools, waiting on the evening trade. Music blasting from every other doorway, paperboys calling out the headlines, lights blinking and flashing.

Cooley had always enjoyed watching as the street stirred itself to life for another night. But tonight, all he saw was Ruth slumped in a chair, her skin an unnatural white, blood staining the front of her dress. Guilt gnawed him like rats. Anger scalded him like water. She had asked him not to. But he had known better. Had made a promise and then broken it a few hours later. Worse, he wasn't the one paying for his faithlessness. She was.

He wanted Tommy Knight like water or sex. It was that primal.

But after two hours of wandering up and down the avenue, poking around all the side streets, Arthur Cooley had come up empty. He slumped onto a bus bench, exhausted. Thought about calling the hospital, but was scared it would be bad news. Bad news could wait. Cooley knew he wasn't thinking straight. He was forgetting something. Some obvious thing that nagged at the rim of consciousness. But he could not give it a name.

After a few minutes, a police car rolled up. The passenger side window came down and Sgt. Mick O'Reilly, a big Irish cop well known on the avenue, beckoned. Cooley went to him with a sigh. He didn't have the time for this. Or the patience. "Cooley," said O'Reilly, "is it true what I hear about Ruthie? She had to go to the hospital?" Because even the cops loved Jack and Ruth.

Cooley nodded. "Yeah. That's what I heard, too."

"Jesus," he said. "Well what happened? Did she take sick?"

And how to answer that? How to say there was this rich man's son with a coke habit and he had been stealing from the till and Cooley had threatened him for it and he had hurt Sis in response? How to say that? Cooley could not. Tommy was white and the cops were white and it was 1955. The cops might like Jack and Ruth, but they didn't like them enough to change that. So Cooley swallowed hard and said she just took sick without warning. O'Reilly nodded gravely and said, "Well, you tell her to get better real quick, now." The window went back up and the black and white rolled back into traffic, gliding like a shark through the sea.

And that's when Cooley knew what he was missing. It hit him out of nowhere and he leapt to his feet, looking down the street for a bus. Didn't see one, so he took off walking. Got five blocks before he looked over his shoulder and saw it finally coming. He made it to the next stop just ahead of the bus.

Fifteen minutes later, it brought him to the place he should have thought of first. The main showroom of Knight's Quality Furniture. Atop the building was a ridiculous cartoon of Tommy's father wearing a foil crown. Arnie Knight, The Furniture King. It was late and the store was closed, accordion gates stretched across the display windows. Cooley walked around the building. He could feel Tommy in there. Where else could he go? Central Avenue wouldn't be safe for him once word got out what he had done. And somehow, Cooley knew he had not gone home to his father's house. No, he was in here. Cooley could smell him.

He circled the building three times, trying to find a way inside. Considered cutting the chain on the gate and throwing something through the window. But if he did that, the alarm would ring and the cops would come. He didn't care, except that would mean he'd have to rush. He didn't want to rush. He wanted to take his time with Mr. Tommy Knight.

So Cooley sat down in the parking lot on the side of the building and waited. Tommy couldn't stay in there forever. He had to eat. Or if he didn't care about eating, sooner or later, he would have to score. When he came out to do either one of those things, he would find Cooley waiting.

The hours took their time passing, but Cooley didn't mind. If he had learned nothing else in the Army, he had learned how to wait. So he sat there in the parking lot in a shadowed corner where he could see the door without being seen himself.

And Cooley waited.

An hour dragged by. Then two. Then four.

And Cooley waited.

He never doubted Tommy was in there. It was something he knew as surely as he knew which horizon births the sun. So he wasn't surprised in the least when, about five in the morning, he heard the lock. The door opened slowly and Tommy's head peeked around. His hair needed combing. His tie was untied. His eyes were like an animal's.

Cooley was on his feet without even thinking about it, the gun in hand. He circled around the edge of the lot, keeping to the shadows, moving as quietly as he could. Tommy took another step forward, his hand still on the door. Just another second. That was all Cooley needed.

But just then, his shoes scuffed against the asphalt. It was a loud sound in the silence. Cooley cursed himself, thinking he might have lost his chance. And he might have, except that instead of doing the smart thing and ducking back inside, Tommy did the instinctive thing and looked toward the sound. It gave Cooley just enough time. He crossed the last couple of steps, then raised the big gun about an inch from the bridge of Tommy's nose. He had both hands on the grip, arms locked against the recoil.

Tommy's eyes went wide. The front of his pants darkened with urine. But he managed to keep his voice steady. "Hey, Cool," he said.

Cooley gestured with the gun. "Get back inside." Tommy retreated through the door, hands high. Glancing around to make sure he wasn't being watched, Cooley followed, the gun barrel pressed against the back of the white boy's head.

Streaks of light from the street lamps outside cut themselves on the accordion gate and made a latticework of shadows on the furniture nearest the front windows. Otherwise, the showroom was dark, a maze of couches and armoires and dining room tables. A maze, thought Cooley, that Tommy doubtless knew like the rat he was. Cooley pointed to a couch and told Tommy to sit down. Instead, Tommy turned around to face him. "Look, Cool…" he began.

That was as far as he got. With his gun hand, Cooley chopped down against the bridge of Tommy's nose, hard. He felt the cartilage crumple. Tommy gave a shout and fell to the couch, his hands covering his nose. He started weeping.

It made Cooley sick. "Shut the fuck up," he yelled, "before I hit you again!"

It took Tommy a moment. Finally, he sniffled and got himself under control, took his hands off his face. There was blood everywhere, all over his teeth, dripping off his chin. The whole lower half of his face was red. He said, "I'm a mess, huh?"

Cooley sat on a barstool with the gun resting against his thigh, pointing at Tommy's forehead. He said, "I told you what would happen, didn't I, Tommy? I warned you, right?" Cooley felt oddly calm, considering what he was here to do. It surprised him.

"Come on, Cooley," said Tommy.

"Why you hurt her, Tommy? Why you have to hurt her?"

"I don't know what you're talking about, Cooley."

Cooley hit him again. A backhand this time that knocked him into a corner of the couch. Tommy started crying all over again. Cooley stood above him, yelling down. "You couldn't leave it alone, could you? Couldn't just let it go. No, you had to put your hands on her. You had to hurt her. And why? Because she caught you stealing. Because she told you to find another way to feed your dope habit. For that, you beat her up."

Tommy looked up, his face slick with blood, tears and snot. "I didn't beat her up," he said.

The lie was so bald-faced, Cooley drew back his hand for another blow. Tommy flinched. "I didn't mean to hurt her, Cooley," he said. "For God's sake, I love her, too."

Too.

It made Cooley's vision blur red. He had known Tommy had a crush on Ruth. Every man who knew her had one. But that one word was as if he was trying to say he and Cooley were somehow the same. As if this was a secret they had in common. The next thing he knew, Cooley had picked the white boy up by the collar and thrown him away like garbage. Tommy crashed against a grandfather clock and it fell and shattered. Glass flew everywhere. The noise seemed as if it would never end.

For a moment, Tommy Knight laid still as dawn. Then he started laughing. Chuckling at first, and then louder, giggling like he could hardly contain himself. It made Cooley furious all over again. "What the fuck is so funny?" he demanded.

Tommy sat up painfully. His face was a mess. Slashes of red criss-crossed purple bruises. Glass glittered in his hair. He said, "I was wondering if the insurance covers this. Because if it doesn't, my old man is going to plotz."

It wasn't until that moment that Cooley realized Tommy was high. He seemed to get himself under control, but then he looked up at Cooley and whatever he saw in the angry face made him start laughing all over again, clapping his hands and whooping and acting for all the world, thought Cooley, like a monkey.

He waited Tommy out. It took a few minutes. Every time it seemed he had it under control, it would seize him again and he would start giggling that maniac giggle all over again. Cooley didn't want to feel sorry for him, but he almost did. Tommy Knight was the most pathetic thing he had ever seen. All at once, killing him seemed a waste of energy. Cooley let the gun drop.

Finally, Tommy calmed down. Cooley spoke as you would to a not-particularly-bright child. "Tommy," he said, "I just want you to tell me why. Why you hurt her?"

Tommy looked up, his eyes pale blue in the shadows of that empty store. And he said in a soft voice, "She forgave me."

Confusion creased Cooley's brow. "She forgave you. What do you mean, she forgave you?"

He yelled it this time. "She forgave me! That night, back there in the office, she forgave me. Can you believe that? Can you beat that shit?"

Cooley had a feeling of moving in slow motion trying to grab for something just out of reach. He said, "So, what you telling me? You're mad that she forgave you for what you done and then she went and told me? Is that what it is?"

He shook his head. Cooley was surprised to see tears on his cheeks. Tommy hammered his chest and yelled again, "She forgave me. She said it was all right. Who the *fuck* is she to forgive me? For a fuckin' 900 dollars? Do you know how much money my father makes? More than God, that's how much. That joint wouldn't even be in business if it wasn't for me and my old man. And she *forgives* me? What a nerve. What a fucking load of jive."

Cooley watched him for a long, disbelieving moment. Then he turned away. There was no point in killing Tommy. It would be like killing some dumb animal.

But if Cooley was done, Tommy wouldn't let it go. He started laughing again and said, "Now here you come with your great big old pistol ready to take revenge? Big country nigger fresh off the farm. You're going to shoot me, is that it?"

He flung his arms open, still sitting there on the floor and said, "Well shoot my ass, then, if that's what you feel like you've got to do,

Cool. But me, I got no regrets. Because I'll tell you this much. It was worth it. She was *good*."

It seemed to Cooley as if it took all night for those three words to register. *She was good.* And it hit him. When he had seen Sis at the Desireé, her face was unmarked. Cooley had assumed Tommy beat her, because of the way she was staggering around. But Tommy had just said he didn't touch her. And now that Cooley thought about it: *not a single mark on her face.* No mark anywhere, except for the blood on the front of her dress. And now Tommy saying she was good.

Because Tommy Knight had not hit her. He had raped her.

In the instant that realization hit Arthur Cooley, the white boy started laughing. Like Cooley suddenly seeing the truth was the funniest thing in the whole world.

The gun came up without thought. The boom echoed forever.

And then silence. Cooley was surprised. Surely the whole world had heard. He half expected sirens and lights. He had just shot a man in cold blood. It didn't seem possible the world could still be the same, could still go on as if nothing had happened.

But there were no lights or sirens. The world didn't stop. The store was dark and quiet and Tommy was on his back, a pool of blood spreading across his chest. His eyes were open and he had a silly grin on his face. He was dead. That's when Jack spoke up. "That wasn't your place," he said.

Cooley spun so fast he almost fell. Jack's clothes looked as if he had slept in them. His eyes were red. His hair was lumpy. Cooley asked the question that had been topmost in his mind all night. "Is Ruthie okay?"

Jack ignored him, nodding to Tommy's corpse. "It was my place to do that," he said. "My responsibility."

Cooley yelled it. "Is Ruthie okay!"

Jack stared at him a moment. Then he said, "Doctor say she'll be fine."

"What about the baby?"

He nodded slowly. "The baby gon' be okay, too." Cooley's legs weakened with relief. Jack gave him a hard, appraising look. He said, "You got feelings for my wife, Arthur Cooley?"

Cooley gave him an answer that wasn't an answer. "You know I would never betray you, Jack."

He waited for Jack to press it. The small man watched with eyes that seemed as if they could see every thought and secret. Cooley stared back. Finally Jack said, "Yeah, I guess you wouldn't." He looked again at Tommy, still grinning on the floor of his father's showroom, his shirt black with blood. The room smelled like shooting. Jack said, "Come on, let's go."

They left through the side door, walked east on Slauson. Neither man spoke for two blocks. Finally Cooley said, "She told you what he did?"

Jack nodded. "Raped her," he said. Two words. Hanging there like a bad smell.

"My fault," Cooley said.

Jack's step didn't slacken. He didn't look up. "How you figure?" he said.

"She told me he had his hand in the till. Told me not to tell you and not to say nothing to him about it. I kept the first promise, but the second, I ignored. I went to Tommy and told him what I knew. Told him I would kick his ass if he didn't straighten up and fly right. That's why he…" Cooley couldn't force the words from his mouth. He said, "That's why he did what he did."

It was quiet, but for an occasional car passing by. Jack said, "It wasn't your fault. It was mine. I trusted that little cracker too much. Trusted him so much my wife didn't think she could hip me to the truth. Didn't figure I'd listen. She's probably right."

Cooley glanced at him. "He was your friend."

Jacks smile was bitter. He said, "Yeah, so I thought. That was my first mistake."

They walked another mile in the darkness without speaking. It was beginning to dawn on Cooley what he had done. He didn't regret it. As far as he was concerned, Tommy Knight needed killing. You couldn't do what he had done without paying the price. And yet, right or wrong, deserved it or not, Cooley had taken a man's life. Taken him away from everything and everything away from him. And no matter what he did from that moment on, the act would always be a part of him. A stain that would never erase. All at once, he wanted nothing so much as to get to the club and pour himself a drink.

Jack spoke up out of the silence, repeating himself. "It wasn't your place to do what you did. It was my place. She's my wife. You should have left it for me."

Cooley said, "Yeah, Jack, I know, but…"

Jack ignored him. "Of course, you had a right to wonder if I would do what needed to be done. I mean, I was so blind to how the guy really was, you had a right to think that way."

"Jack, that wasn't it."

Jack went right on. Cooley had a sense that he was thinking out loud and didn't even know his friend was there. He said, "Still, it was my place to do it. I should have been the one."

They walked the rest of the way in silence. Cooley was dying for a drink. He had never been much of a drinker. But he needed it that morning. Had needed it ever since. The sun was hanging low in the sky as Jack opened the padlock and then the deadbolt on the front door of the club. It was dark inside. They left it that way. Cooley poured himself a bourbon. Drank it like water. Poured another. Caught Jack looking.

"You all right?" Jack said.

Cooley said, "So now what?"

"Now we wait," said Jack.

Cooley drank down the second bourbon, put the glass down hard, opened the bottle to pour another. Jack said, "Liquid courage." There was no reproach in his voice. He spoke softly, as if doing nothing more than stating a fact.

Cooley thought he had a slender hope of getting away with what he'd done. It wasn't like Tommy had a shortage of enemies. Between all the hustlers and drug dealers he did business with, maybe the cops would say it could have been anybody. He knew it was a silly thought, especially after he had spent so many hours the night before telling everybody he could that he was looking for Tommy. But he couldn't help clinging to it, silly or not. The thought of sitting in the electric chair made him want to vomit.

Jack said, "Give me the gun." Cooley gave it to him and he took out a handkerchief and wiped it carefully. Then he placed it on the bar and dropped into a chair.

Cooley kept drinking, but he couldn't get drunk. No matter how many he tossed back, the room stayed in focus. As did the memory of Tommy flopping back, still grinning that stupid, stupid grin He and Jack sat together for hours, speaking little. One drinking, both thinking, the sun up now, the street coming to life with day people, school teachers and school children and deliverymen and milkmen and janitors, rushing to get where they had to be, do what they had to do.

Somebody looking in from outside might have thought they were statues, except for Cooley's elbow bending from time to time. Finally Jack said, "So tell me, Cooley: you think there's ever going to be a Negro president?"

Cooley recognized it as a question Jack had once asked him when they were still in school. He had asked it then as he asked it now. Out of the blue. Cooley thought about it two seconds, then gave the same answer he had given before: No. White folks would never stand still for it.

When Cooley had told him that years before, Jack had nodded and said that while he might not be president, he was going to be something big someday. Cooley had always remembered that. It impressed him because back then, you just didn't hear colored people saying such things.

But this time, Jack just nodded and said, "Yeah. Honkies go crazy, some nigger ever get *close* to being president of this muh'fucka." He lit a cigarette, blew out the smoke and waited. Cooley poured himself another drink.

Twenty minutes later, the door came slamming in and the room filled with police. Cooley came out from behind the bar. A big cop in plainclothes, with wide eyes and a Marine crew cut, looked from one to the other and said, "Which one of you niggers is Cooley?"

Cooley heard himself say, "I'm Cooley."

The words were hardly out of his mouth when the big cop hit him. Then they were on him, pinning his arms while the big one hit

him in the gut, in the face. They took him down to the floor, scatter-
ing tables and chairs, hitting and kicking and even stomping as if he
was a snake they were trying to kill.

And as bad as it was, Cooley knew it was just the beginning.
They were only softening him up for the real beating downtown. So
he curled himself up tight as their fists and feet fell down on him like
rain. He heard his jaw crack. He gagged on blood. He vomited on
the floor. He thought he was going to black out and hoped he would.
Which was when he heard the sweetest sound he had ever heard.
Jack, saying in a calm, matter-of-fact voice, "I did it."

The fists and the feet froze. Cooley got his eyes open and twisted
his head around until he saw Jack, arms pinned behind him by two
officers. The whole room stared at him. The whole room was quiet
as death.

Jack said it again, "I did it. I killed Tommy Knight."

Cooley wanted to cry out, no. *No!* He wanted to tell them he
was lying. Jack had a wife and a baby on the way. He couldn't do this.
Cooley could not let him do this.

He wanted to speak up. But it felt so good not be kicked. Felt so
good just to be able to spit the blood out of his broken mouth, to lie
there and breathe. He wanted to say, "I did it." But he was silent.

The big cop went over to Jack then, sweating from his exertions.
He used his thumb to push his hat back on his forehead, put his
hands on his hips. He said, "What do you mean? I got a dozen witnesses say this nigger here was looking all over town for the dead guy
last night."

Jack lied with a straight face. He said, "He was looking for Tommy because Tommy hadn't showed up at the club. He was worried
about him. But I'm the one killed him. Shot him through the heart
with that .45." He nodded toward the counter and the cop's big eyes
grew bigger at the weapon lying in plain sight that they had missed
in their eagerness to beat Cooley like an animal. He nodded to one of
the uniformed officers, who lifted the weapon by the trigger guard.

The big cop turned back to Jack. He said, "This one help you?"
Nodding down at Cooley.

Jack said, "He didn't know nothing about it till you just come in here."

The cop said, "Why you do it?"

Jack said, "The muh'fucka raped my wife. She five months pregnant and he raped her. She in the hospital right now. You check it out if you don't believe me."

The cop said, "Why didn't you call the police?"

It was a stupid question and Jack didn't dignify it with an answer. Just looked at the cop for a long time. Gave him a hard look, right in the eyes, like Negroes didn't do in 1955. Finally he said, "I did what I had to do."

The cop nodded and said, "Uh huh."

Jack said, "So, you gon' beat me up?"

The cop said, "You willing to sign a statement?"

Jack shrugged. He said, "Yeah, sure. Why not?"

The cops melted off Cooley then, left him lying on the floor. They cuffed Jack, spun him around roughly and headed him toward the door. And finally Cooley found his voice. "Jack," he called. His voice was thick, his teeth seemed to be in the way of his tongue. He wanted to say the truth. He wanted to say they had the wrong man.

But the words wouldn't come. And at the sound of his name, Jack gave Cooley a look that warned him to be silent. The words Jack had spoken echoed in Cooley's mind. *It wasn't your place.*

Cooley climbed to his feet. It took a long time. Jack lifted his chin. He said, "You take care of 'em, Cooley. My wife, my baby. You look after 'em for me, you hear?"

There was a catch in his voice. And a threat, too. Cooley said, "Yeah, Jack, I will."

He said, "Give me your word?"

"You got my word."

And then the police hustled him out. Cooley watched through the window. A crowd had gathered, drawn by the flashing lights of a dozen cop cars. Many of them were people Jack knew. They watched in horror as Jack Johnson, this smart, quick, good-looking colored man everyone said was going places sure as Dizzy Gillespie blows like nobody's business and Ella has perfect pitch, was marched out and stuffed into the back of the police car like any nigger anywhere. People's jaws dropped open. Like this couldn't be happening. Like it couldn't be true. A woman dabbed her eyes. A man turned away, muttering to nobody.

Jack didn't look at them. He didn't look at Cooley. He looked straight ahead.

Two months later, he was convicted of murdering Tommy Knight.

twenty-two

Morning sounds reached Dog in his sleep. Feet knocking on the stairs. Mama yelling at the girls to hurry up. The beep and whistle of cartoons.

Dog sighed heavily as he tossed covers aside and rolled over on the pullout in the living room. When he opened his eyes his mother was standing over him, wrapped in a white terrycloth robe so old the fabric was smooth. She nodded tartly when she saw that he was awake. "I was just coming for you," she said.

"I'm up," he mumbled, the words cumbersome in his mouth. He drew a forearm across his eyes. The sun was searing its way through the thin curtains.

"Good," she said. And then she hobbled toward the kitchen. The swelling was bad this morning, he saw. If you didn't know better, you'd think she didn't have a foot.

The smell of eggs and sausage filled the room. He heard plates going onto the table. The rising pitch of glasses being filled with juice. Mama didn't have much use for cold cereal. She thought corn flakes and raisin bran were child abuse.

Dog rolled himself to a sitting position, scratching idly at his armpit. The girls came clattering down the stairs then, feet punishing the floorboards, arguing over which had stolen a poster belonging to the other. Fourteen and twelve. They argued a lot lately.

"It's too early for that noise," Dog called after them as they disappeared into the kitchen. They didn't bother to answer. Badass little girls. Thought they were grown. Dog wished he had a cigarette. His mother didn't allow smoking in the house. She was as bad as Ronnie.

Mama lumbered back into the room, a spatula in her hand. "You have class this morning?" she asked.

Dog nodded. "Yeah. At ten."

"You be back here this afternoon?"

"I probably go see Ronnie."

Her lips knotted with distaste, her hand went automatically to her hip. "You spend a lot of time with that girl," she said.

"We gon' be together, Mama," he said, his response smooth and practiced after months of going with a girl his mother couldn't stand. "You need to get used to that. She carrying my baby. Your grandchild."

"Yeah," said Mama, "so she say. All you know, that's some other man's bastard she carrying and you just the fool she done hooked to carry the weight. Miss Thang don't fool me none."

"It ain't like that, Mama," he said. There had been a time his mother's words would have stung him into a hotter response, but these days, Dog didn't bother. He had come to realize his mother's anger toward his girl, whom she had never met face to face, was primal and reflexive, a force of nature impervious to reason.

"You going to see your brother today?" Mama asked, and Dog was grateful for the change of subject.

"Yeah," he said.

"How he doing?"

Dog thought of Fury behind that yellow plastic barrier, itching with the need to be out. And with the belief that he was being betrayed. "He all right," he said. "Wish he was out."

"He keep his ass out of trouble, he wouldn't have these problems."

"I told him that."

"Armed robbery," she said in a whisper of disgust. "Murder, too. Lord Jesus, what they got my boy mixed up in?" A sigh. "You tell him I'm gon' try to get there to see him. It's just hard, my leg and everything. And I got to work."

"He understand," said Dog, the lie smooth and guiltless.

She nodded. "Your breakfast be ready in a minute."

"Let me get dressed," he said, coming up off the couch. "I take you to work."

He took her whenever he could. The times he couldn't, he was bruised by guilt, knowing she was out there on that leg, waiting for the bus. She tried to hide the pain, tried to keep them from knowing how much it hurt, but Dog knew. Maybe Fury didn't. Maybe the girls didn't know or even care, the way you don't care about too much of anything when you're twelve and fourteen. But Dog knew.

He would graduate in June. And the school's placement counselor had all but guaranteed him a job when he got out. He would make Mama sit down, then. Quit her job and get off that leg. He would take care of her.

Dog went upstairs, got clothes and fresh drawers from the footlocker he kept in his mother's room. He closed the bathroom door behind him, ran the shower hot, let the water run over his body, burying his face in it, letting it rinse away insecurities and doubts. He took a deep breath of steam and felt cleansed.

Moments later, he came down the stairs at a trot, his long coat over his arm, gloves in the pocket. He was in a good mood. Thinking about the things he would do, the way he would change things, always did that for him, always lifted the shadows that seemed to hover above him like gremlins.

The girls, Shani and Monique, were dressed for school and walking out the front door, still bickering. He wondered if he had been like that not so many years ago, cocooned in the busyness of his own life, blind to the struggles and anxieties playing out right in front of him. The thought brought a secretive smile. Of course he'd been that way. Fury still was. But that, too, would change.

Dog ate fast and was ready to go when Mama came slowly down the stairs, dressed for work in the mannish denim jeans and shirts she always wore, a name tag—"Willis," it said—affixed to her left breast pocket. He held the door to the Monte Carlo for her as she lowered herself, slowly and painfully, into the passenger seat. When he started the car, James Brown screamed. "I feel good!" he cried, the horns shimmying in a tight lockstep behind him. Dog reached to turn down the radio. Mama smiled. "You always was an old soul," she said.

Seeing her smile made him smile. It didn't happen that often, her smiling. "Aw, Mama, you know I like that old stuff," he said, putting the car in gear and pulling out.

"You was born too late," she told him.

"I think the same thing sometime," he said.

"The world crazy these days," she said. "Maybe it always was. But back then"—she nodded at the radio—"at least you knew you could count on people. Your friends, your family." She shook her head. "Can't count on nobody these days."

"Yeah," he said. "But what you going to do?"

She shifted painfully in her seat, turning to look at him. "You know, we ain't got nothing but each other in this world, Raiford. You, me, your brother and the girls. All we got is each other."

"Yes, ma'am."

"Got to take care of each other."

"Yes, ma'am. But…"

Her eyes turned knife sharp. "But what?"

"I got Ronnie, too. Ronnie and the baby, too, soon enough. I got to take care of them, too."

She made a sound of disgust, fell silent. After a moment, she spoke. "You treat that girl like a queen," she said.

"She is a queen," said Dog. "She my queen."

This brought another sound of disgust. Mama folded her arms.

"You should meet her," Dog said.

"We'll see," said Mama. Which was what she always said. They drove in silence for a moment. Dog stopped at a traffic light. A flock of schoolchildren in identical uniforms went by. Catholic school.

"I used to wish I had the money to send Cedric to Catholic school," said Mama. "Maybe he wouldn't be in trouble now."

"It ain't your fault, Mama."

"They got my baby locked up in a cage like he some kind of animal."

"They say he killed somebody."

"'They say.'" Sarcasm dripped off her voice.

"Mama," he said gently, "Cedric ain't no angel."

She surprised him by yelling at him. "He ain't no animal, neither!"

"He be okay," said Dog.

"I hope so," she said in a voice that was not hopeful at all.

"He will," said Dog, more forcefully.

She looked at him. "I want to believe that, Ray. And Lord know, if you can come through all right, then anybody can, much trouble as you was in. But see, your brother different from you. Your brother ain't strong like you. "

Dog glanced over. Her eyes were moist and fragile. "Cedric okay," he said, and it sounded weak even to him.

An emphatic shake of the head. "No, he not," she said.

The brutality of her candor shook him. And even though he had often said the same things in the privacy of his mind, Dog found himself denying them now. "He ain't that bad, Mama. He just doing some stupid stuff right now, same as I did. But he'll straighten up, you'll see. I did it and he will, too."

Aretha Franklin was playing piano. "Looking out on the morning rain," she sang, "I used to feel so uninspired." Background singers cascading gentle "a-whoop" sounds behind her. Mama said, "A mother knows her children, Ray."

That was all she said. It was enough. Dog felt seen through. Felt transparent. And he wondered why she was telling him this, why she had drawn him into this awful intimacy with her. Behind him a car honked. Dog realized he was sitting at a green light. He accelerated through the intersection. Dog said, "Mama, why you talking like this?"

"I'm sorry," she said.

"I don't know what you want me to do."

"Just look out for your brother. That's all I'm asking, Ray. He weak. I think he gon' always be weak. And he gon' need you to look after him."

"Mama…" he said and then stammered into a silence because he didn't know what else to say. Did she know what she was asking? Did she have any idea what kind of fool that boy was?

"Just promise me you'll look out for him," his mother was saying. "Just promise me that."

Dog thought of his brother, small and nasty in the little cubicle behind the yellow plastic. The boy was like some ferret, constantly sniffing the air for threats. Convinced against all reason that his homeboys were snitching him out. Paranoid and panicky and mean. Mean just for the sake of being mean. But still his brother, for all that.

Damn. Still his brother. "Yeah," he said. "I'll look out for him. I promise."

She nodded, patted his hand. "You a good son, Ray. You a good son." He let her out five minutes later in the parking lot of the high school, watched her walk in a swarm of teenagers, them quick and chattering, rushing past her as they would a stone post, her grim and determined and slow on that monstrous chunk of a leg. As always, the sight of it made him impatient to do well.

He would be a mechanic somewhere. Ronnie had shown him on a website one time where a master technician could expect to make as much as $100,000 a year. That was damn good money. So he would finish these last months of school, get himself a job and work his ass off, first one there in the morning, last one out at night. He might even own his own shop after a few years. Make some real money. Get his life together. In his mind, he had it all worked out.

When the door closed behind his mother, Dog drove away. Half an hour later, he pulled into student parking at Baltimore Community College and climbed out into the crushing cold. Dog muttered a curse as he brought his hood up. He tightened his coat, pulled on his gloves, remembering as he did that snow was in the forecast for that afternoon. It was ten years till spring.

Grabbing his backpack off the seat, Dog closed the car and quick-stepped toward the building, eager for the embrace of heat. He had to hurry. Class started in five minutes and Mr. Nobleski, the teacher, got real pissy if you were late. Then James Jamerson played the pulsing opening bass notes to "My Girl." It was a special ringtone he had assigned to calls coming from Ronnie's cell. Smiling, Dog plucked his phone from his coat pocket and flipped it open without breaking stride.

"Hey, girl," he said. "You know I got class in a minute."

He got a babble in response. People talking over one another. Dog stopped. "Hey, Ronnie! You there?"

A man's voice said, "Hello?"

"Who this?" demanded Dog.

The voice said, "Is this Willis?"

"Who is this?"

"Willis, this is Veronica's father, Charles Richmond."

The voice was distracted, bereft of its usual certainty and contempt. Something hot bubbled in the bottom of Dog's stomach. "Where is she? What's going on?"

The Judge seemed not to hear. "Veronica asked me to call you," he said. "She gave me her cell phone. She's in labor."

Dog said, "Put her on. Let me talk to her."

"You can't..." And here the Judge paused and sighed, as if gathering himself. "You can't talk to her," he finally said. "Not right now."

"What's wrong with her?" demanded Dog.

"It's the baby," said the Judge. "There's some kind of problem with the baby. We're at the hospital. You should get over here."

"What kind of problem with the baby?"

"I don't know for sure. Just get over here," said the Judge.

"What's wrong with her?" cried Dog. "What's wrong with the baby?" But the phone was dead. The Judge had hung up on him.

For a long moment, Dog stared at the cell fixedly, dazedly. Then he was running, hurtling back across the parking lot, the heavy backpack flopping hard against him with every step. He didn't feel it. All he felt was panic riding him hard, bent low across his back, whispering terrors at the nape of his neck. The baby wasn't even due for nine weeks. They had been keeping track of it on a calendar she got from her obstetrician. This was supposed to be a late April baby. How was Ronnie going into labor in February?

The car started with a roar, and the radio came up loud. Dog snapped it off and threw the old Monte Carlo hard into reverse. A little Toyota coming down the aisle looking for a parking spot had to slam on its brakes. The driver hammered the horn. Dog ignored her. He stomped the gas and the car leapt forward in a squirt of blue smoke and an outcry of rubber.

It was still rush hour. Traffic was ponderous. Dog leaned on the horn. If anything, that made the traffic slower. Apprehension sat heavily in his chest. Dog tried calling Ronnie's cell again. The call went straight into her voice mail. Five times, straight to voice mail. He pictured the Judge, seeing his name come up on the screen, refusing to answer. Laughing at Dog's fear.

He knew the Judge was Ronnie's father, but swear to God, Dog would strangle that old man. He surely would. A space opened up in the lane next to him. Dog spun the wheel hard, lurched into it, stopped just short of the car in front of him. Horns blew.

Dog's cell phone jangled some New Age jazz theme. He glanced at the Caller ID. It came up "Nikki." Fury's girl. One of them, anyway. Only one reason for her to be calling. His brother was trying to reach him. From the jailhouse, you could only call collect, but since cell phones can't accept collect calls, Cedric had asked Nikki to link them up on a three-way from her house phone. Dog pictured his brother standing at the payphone, having waited an hour in line. He didn't answer. He couldn't deal with Cedric now.

Dog tried to pray. He didn't know how. He tried anyway. "Hey, God," he said aloud, "if you up there, man..." He stopped. It made him feel foolish, talking to the roof of his car. Then he shrugged. "Look out for my girl, man. That's all."

It took a long time to get there. Finally, Dog pulled into the lot. Took precious moments to find a parking space. Left the car at a sprint. He stopped when he saw the Judge standing in the ambulance bay to the right of the sliding door smoking a cigarette.

"How is she?" demanded Dog. "Where is she?"

The Judge looked up. "Willis," he said, as though to remind himself who Dog was. "They took her in."

He dropped the cigarette, mashed it under his shoe. Produced a pack from his coat pocket, shook another loose, and lit it mechanically. Dog rushed up to him. "What you mean, 'They took her in?' Took her in where? Why?"

"Surgery," said the Judge, his breath leaking out in a fog. "They said something about fetal distress. Said the baby was in trouble. They had to deliver by caesarean."

"But she's going to be okay, right? They both going to be okay."

The Judge looked at him but did not reply. Dog felt a chill. There was a bench next to where the Judge stood. Dog collapsed onto it. After a moment, the Judge sat next to him. They didn't speak for a few minutes. Then the Judge said, "It was never personal, you know."

Dog looked at him, confused. "What?" he said.

"About you, I mean. It was never personal. Never about you. It's just…she's my daughter. And you…"

"And I'm a thug," said Dog.

The Judge said, "Yeah."

"But she changed me," said Dog. "That's the thing you ain't never understood. I ain't like that no more. Ronnie, she the best thing ever happened to me."

The Judge shook his head sadly. "People like you don't change, Willis," he said. He chased it with a soft sigh, as though it hurt him to have to say this, but there was no getting around it.

Dog said, *"What?"* Then felt stupid that he couldn't muster anything stronger.

The Judge repeated it. "People like you don't change."

"People like me?"

A nod. "Thugs," said the Judge.

"Man, how you gon' say that to me?" said Dog. "I'm in school, I'm doing good, I ain't been in no trouble in two years. How you say something like that to me?" The saying of it stoked his anger. He repeated the question sharply. "How you *say* something like that to me?"

The Judge turned to him. To his surprise, the man's eyes were filmy and sad. "Do you know how many like you I've seen, Willis? All those years on the bench, do you know how many I've seen who were just like you? Hundreds. *Thousands.* Same faces over and over again until after awhile I didn't even see faces anymore. They all looked the same to me, all of them with cornrows and jailhouse eyes and needing a shave. And all of them saying the same thing to me, 'You give me a chance, Judge. I'll get my life together. I'll do better. I'll change.' And then I see them in my court again six months later saying the same thing. They never changed. Your type never does."

"But I'm different!" cried Dog.

"They all say that," said the Judge.

"Fuck you," said Dog.

The Judge smiled. "They say that, too."

Dog bolted from the bench. Suddenly, he could not be close to the man. He was scared he would bust him right in the mouth. He stepped across the concrete walkway and stood at the edge of the parking lot. An ambulance was coming in, lights flashing without sound. The doors slammed open almost before the vehicle had stopped and the paramedics rolled out and went to the back.

"You ain't got to believe me," said Dog, wheeling around at the Judge. "Ronnie believe me. That's all that count."

The back of the rig opened and out came a gurney bearing a little girl. She was wincing in pain. Her head was heavily bandaged. Her right cheek looked as if it had been chewed. A crying woman came out of the back behind the gurney. The paramedics rushed toward the sliding doors. Then one of them went back and closed the ambulance. He was looking at Dog as he did it.

The Judge chuckled as the paramedics rushed the little girl inside. There was no humor in the sound. "You know why he closed that door, right? You see the look he gave you? He knows, just like I do."

"Man, what you want from me, huh?"

The Judge shrugged. "I want you never to have met my daughter. I want you never to have touched her, never to have made her pregnant."

"Yeah, well that's impossible, ain't it?"

The Judge's eyes flickered. "Yeah," he said. "It is."

Dog turned his back on the old man, preferring to study the parking lot rather than look at him. After a moment, he sat on the curb. Time passed. He said, "They say how long it was gon' be 'fore they knew something?"

"No, they didn't," said the Judge. "Just said they had to get her in there fast."

More time passed. Dog's cell phone went off. He checked the Caller ID. "Nikki" again. He pressed ignore. Dog was beginning to get hungry. He wondered how it was that you could be hungry and scared at the same time. Then the door whisked open to let a doctor in scrubs out, his hands pinned under his arms for warmth. "Judge Richmond," he said.

Dog was on his feet at once. "How is she? How the baby?"

The surgeon glanced a question at the Judge. "This is...the baby's father," said the Judge, the hesitation in his voice microscopic, but there. "His name is Mr. Willis."

The doctor took him in at a glance and nodded, but didn't extend his hand. Dog said, "How is Ronnie?"

"Ms. Richmond is in recovery. She's going to be fine. You can go back and see her soon. And congratulations, Mr. Willis. You have a little girl."

The fear went out of him in a great rush that left him staggered. His fist churned the air. He shouted, "Yes! That's what I'm talkin' 'bout!" And then he stopped at the realization that the Judge had said nothing. Instead, he was staring in expectation at the doctor, his eyes hard and discerning.

"There's something more you haven't told us," he said. "What is it?"

The doctor, an Asian man with a receding hairline, nodded. "We had to deliver by caesarean, as you know. We had to give her medicine to stop the contractions. Every time the uterus contracted, our monitors were reading fetal distress. We found that there was compression of the umbilical cord. It was wrapped around the fetus's neck and each contraction drew it tighter."

The Judge's eyes went out of focus. Dog looked from one man to the other. "What that mean?" he asked.

They didn't look at him. The Judge had a hand to his mouth. "So what's her..." He coughed, started again. "What's her prognosis? The...the baby, I mean."

"It's hard to say," said the doctor. "We should know more in a few hours. Of course, it'll be years before we know for sure."

"And Veronica?"

"She'll be fine. She'll be off her feet for a little while, but she'll be just fine."

"What are you talking about?" demanded Dog. "What's wrong?"

LEONARD PITTS, JR.

They looked over at him. Dog had the distinct impression they had forgotten he was even there. The doctor opened his mouth, but the Judge lifted his hand. "Willis," he said, "the baby had the umbilical cord wrapped around her neck. It tightened every time Veronica contracted. The umbilical carries nutrients to the fetus. It also carries oxygen."

Dog glanced from one to the other, uncomprehending. He felt like when he was back in high school and it always seemed like the teacher was speaking another language. He'd try to understand, but how can you understand another language? It made him impatient. Like they were making fun of him.

He said, "So? What the hell do that mean?"

The Judge sighed, then spoke with exaggerated patience. "Living tissue requires oxygen, Willis. Things die without oxygen."

"But the baby is alive. She's alive, right?"

The Judge said, "The brain, Willis. Without oxygen, brain cells begin to die."

"You're saying, she could be, like, retarded?"

"I'm saying there could be a slight potential for brain damage," said the physician. "Whether there is or not or how severe it might be, it's too early to say."

"Can you give me an idea of the probabilities we're talking about?" asked the Judge.

The doctor smiled as if grateful for the question. "She'll probably be just fine. There's certainly no cause for alarm at this point. We've done reflex tests on her and she checked out okay. You have to remember, on the plus side, we got Ms. Richmond here very quickly and we took her right into surgery. So all of that's to the good. The other stuff, that's more like the worst-case scenario, something to keep in the back of your mind. But if I had to bet, I'd say there's nothing to worry about."

"Can I see her?" asked Dog.

The doctor said, "Ms. Richmond is in recovery. She's out of it right now. Give it about an hour, then you can see her. But you can go in and meet your daughter."

The doctor gave him directions and he went without another word, eager to get away from them and their smug condescension. It hit him as he padded down the long, bright corridors: He was a father now. A father. Had himself a little girl. He had never felt so unprepared.

Dog stopped when he came to a sign that read "Neo-Natal Intensive Care." Through the window, he could see them, three rows of plastic incubators, tiny babies snugged tight in blankets, surrounded by machines flashing mysterious numbers and lines. Nurses, their faces and hair masked, bustled down the aisles of incubators, adjusting machines, writing on charts. One of them looked up then, saw Dog frozen there, and motioned him in.

He pushed the door open. Someone handed him a mask and a covering for his head. He accepted them dazedly, put them on dumbly, eyes never leaving the rows of babies. Tiny babies. Someone said, "You're the father?"

He nodded.

"Mother's name?"

"Ronnie," he said.

"Beg pardon?"

"Veronica," he managed. "Veronica Richmond."

The woman consulted a clipboard, then told him, "Your daughter is in the sixth incubator. First row on the end." He nodded, went where they told him, and looked down into the plastic box that contained his daughter.

She broke his heart. So tiny he could have covered her from head to heels with just the palm of his hand. He could have smuggled her out of the hospital in a child's shoebox. Pale skin with reddish blotches, a head full of dark hair. Adhesive pads from monitoring devices attached to her chest, machines tracking her body works. Sleeping with eyes squeezed tight, as though troubled by unwelcome dreams.

"She so little," he heard himself say.

"Yes, she is," said a voice. Dog glanced up. He hadn't realized the Judge was there, standing across from him. Their eyes met over their masks. Dog touched an index finger to her cheek. The skin was warm and dry. The finger was massive.

"I can't believe how little she is."

"She's two months early," the Judge reminded him.

Dog ignored him, the huge finger still tracing her tiny cheek. "How you doing, Little Mama?" he asked. "What up, girl?"

"'Little Mama,'" said the Judge, disapproving.

Dog said, "Yeah. You got a problem with that?" And he chased the question with a hard stare.

The Judge said, "Call her what you wish. She's your daughter."

"Damn right," said Dog.

He touched her hand. It was no bigger than his thumbnail. Yet it was complete. Tiny little nails. Tiny little wrinkles at the joints. Tiny little lines across the palm. Everything there. "Man," he breathed, "she so little."

"You already said that," said the Judge.

"What?"

"You keep saying it. 'She so little, she so little.' Of *course* she's little. She's premature. She's two months early."

It was enough. "Man, what's your fuckin' problem?" demanded Dog. It made one of the nurses look up sharply. Dog raised his palm to save her the trouble of a reprimand. When her head went back down, he whispered to the Judge, "Why you ridin' me, man?"

"Because you don't get it," the Judge said evenly. "This is not a doll here, Willis. This is a life. This is your child. You have responsibilities here."

"You think I don't know that? Why you think I bust my ass in that school every day? You think I don't know I got responsibilities?"

"I don't know what you know," said the Judge. "Especially about being a father. Do you have a father, Willis?"

The question blindsided him. He hesitated. The Judge jumped on the uncertainty. "That's what I thought," he said. "You don't. So what happened to him? Was he a stickup man? Crackhead? Is he on lockdown somewhere for killing some other fool?" The Judge shook his head. "Doesn't matter though, does it? However it happened, he wasn't there. Didn't teach you a damn thing about what it takes to get along in this world. So how the hell are you supposed to teach that to this little girl?"

"I'll be fine," insisted Dog. "I'll be a good father."

"Yeah, right," said the Judge.

"I will."

The Judge shook his head. "Willis, you don't even know what a father is." He sighed. Then he pointed down. "What do you see when you look at her?"

Dog said, "What?"

The Judge said, "Do you see 3 a.m. feedings, and boxes of diapers, and pushing on the swing at the playground, and parent-teacher conferences? Do you see her with fevers and skinned knees and smoking cigarettes under the bleachers at school? Do you see how scared you get when she's out of your sight, out there in the world and you don't know where she is and who she's with?"

"I see my daughter," said Dog.

"And what does that mean?" shot the Judge.

Dog repeated it. "I see my daughter."

"Do you love her?"

Dog sputtered confusion. "What?"

"Do you love her?"

"Of course I do. What kind of question is that?" He laughed to show how crazy the question was. The laugh felt hollow.

For a long moment, the Judge just looked at him. Finally he said, "You don't even know how. You don't even know what the word means."

Dog felt as if someone had hit him. "You crazy," he said, throwing up his hands. "I stay around you, we gon' fight."

He left the room. Found a spot in the hallway, a little alcove where a payphone was mounted. His breath pushed from his nostrils in angry gusts. His fists clenched and unclenched. Dog wanted to hurt that old man so bad. Wanted to strangle him. Wanted to punch him right in his smug, judgmental face. Who was he to say things like that? Who did he think he was?

And was it all true?

That was the worst thing about it: this needle the Judge had pricked him with, this burrowing worm of irresolution he had deposited way down deep in the soil of conscience. This terrible question.

Was it true?

Dog's cell phone rang. "Nikki" again. This time, he was glad for the distraction. "Yeah," he said, putting the phone to his ear.

"Where you been, nigger?" Fury was seething.

"I'm at the hospital. Ronnie just had the baby."

"Been trying to reach you all day."

"I'm at the hospital," said Dog again.

"Listen: you need to do what you said you was gon' do."

"What?"

"Don't play the fool, nigger. You know what's up."

"But…"

"I just heard they dropping charges on Profit. You know what that means."

"That ain't necessarily true," said Dog. It sounded weak, even to him.

"You know what that means, muh'fucka!" He yelled it so loud Dog had to jerk the phone away from his ear.

"Maybe they droppin' the charges on all three of you," he said. "Have you talked to your public defender?"

"Talk to him? I ain't even met the muh'fucka yet! Ain't nobody been here to see me."

"Well, you don't know—"

"I *do* know!" cried Fury. Dog leaned the cell away from his ear again. "Bitch-ass nigger been talking! Sold me out to keep his ass out of lockdown."

"I just had a baby," Dog said. "She might have brain damage." His voice was a whisper.

"What you mumbling about, muh'fucka?" demanded Fury. "What *I'm* talkin' about is serious. It's time for you to do what you said you would. Step up, put yo' rep up. You got to handle business."

Dog looked down the hall to the sign that said Neo-Natal Intensive Care. Thought of how enormous his finger had been against his daughter's cheek. (His *daughter!*) Remembered how warm she felt.

"I can't do this no more," he whispered.

"What? Don't you bitch out on me, muh'fucka. I'm your brother, case you forgot."

"I ain't forgot," Dog said.

"You promised me," said Fury.

"Yeah, I know that."

"Then handle your fuckin' business," said Fury.

Dog sighed. He felt trapped. Back against the wall, nowhere to go. Caught between his brother and his child. And that was no choice at all, was it?

"No," he said. "I ain't doing it." He flipped the phone shut on his brother's angry screams.

twenty-three

A police car was parked at the curb. Two uniformed officers were at the door. They both turned as Philip's minivan pulled up to the curb. One of them, a blonde woman Tash thought too impossibly petite to be a real cop, had her hand up as if to knock. The hand fell when she saw them.

Fear jabbed Tash hard. Her first thought was that they were somehow there about Trey. Philip said, "What are the police doing at your door?"

"I have no idea," said Tash.

Philip turned so he could look into the back seat. "You girls stay put," he said. Ashanti and Kadijah, eyes and mouths matching ovals, nodded vigorously.

The police officers met them on the curb. A light snow was falling, small flakes tracing curlicues in the air on their way to the concrete. The blonde's partner was a beefy man with nicotine-stained teeth. He pushed his hat up from his forehead, identified himself as Officer Pulaski, his partner as Officer Chavez. He read Tash's name off a notepad and she nodded. "Yes, that's me," she said. "What's going on? Is something wrong?"

Chavez said, "Ma'am, do you know a Michaela Watkins?"

"Not well," said Tash. "Her daughter and my son have a child together."

"That would be DeVante Watkins?" asked Pulaski. He read the name from his notepad, pronounced it with long "e's." Dee-Vantee.

The sound of her grandson's name coming, mangled, from this policeman's mouth, panicked her. "Has something happened to him? Is he okay?"

"He's fine," Officer Chavez assured her. "In fact," she said, inclining her head, "he's in the car there." Tash craned her neck to see.

"What's this all about?" asked Philip.

Pulaski faced Philip. "And you are?"

Philip's chin came up. "My name is Philip Reed," he said.

"He's my fiancé," Tash snapped. "Now would you tell me what's going on?"

"There was an altercation, ma'am," said Chavez.

"An altercation."

"Miss Watkins and her daughter got into it. Apparently, this wasn't the first time. But this time, police had to be called."

"You took them to jail?" asked Tash.

A look she didn't understand passed between the two cops. Then Pulaski corrected her. "Well, we took *one* of them to jail," he said.

"What do you mean?" asked Tash. Philip put an arm around her.

"The younger one"—Pulaski checked his notebook—"LaShonda Watkins, she's in the hospital. Multiple stab wounds."

"No." Tash reeled. Philip's grip tightened. "Is she going to be okay?"

"Paramedics couldn't say," said Pulaski. "Her mother cut her pretty bad."

"But why?" asked Tash. "Why would she...?"

"We don't know," said Chavez. "All we know is that they were arguing."

Michaela sipping her beer. "I'm tired," she said softly. "Don't know how much more of this I can take." Two days ago. Two days.

Tash blinked her eyes against the image. "So you brought my grandson here," she said.

Pulaski shrugged. "It was either that or Children's Services."

"We try to keep them out of the system if we can, ma'am," said Chavez, gently. "Is it going to be a problem for you to take him?"

Tash shook her head, feeling as if she were trapped in a nightmare, unable to wake up. "No, of course not," she said.

It hit her then. "Was he there? Did he see?"

Pulaski hesitated for the briefest instant, then said, "Yeah. He saw."

"Can I see him?"

Pulaski nodded. They went to the car. Pulaski opened the door. Tash knelt and there was her grandson, small in the vast backseat of the police cruiser. He looked up at her, his eyes alight, his face breaking open in a smile. "Nana Tash," he said. "I got to ride in a police car."

"I know, baby." Tash's eyes were moist.

"Nana Tash," he said, "Nana Mike hurt my mom."

"I know," said Tash. She spread her arms. "Come here." Tash buried her grandchild in her embrace and wept into the crook of his neck.

The police left moments later. Philip freed the girls from the van and they followed Tash and DeVante inside. The two adults debated whether to ask DeVante what had happened in his house, why his grandmother attacked his mom. In the end, they decided against it. No telling what the child was going through. Might be the worst thing in the world to make him relive it. He was going to need counseling, they thought. Lots of counseling. And prayer. Lots of that, too.

Tash sent Philip out for dinner—takeout chicken. They ate noisily around the kitchen table. Afterward, the three children sat watching cartoons on the television in Trey's room. Tash and Philip sat together on the couch in the living room, his left arm around her, neither speaking, just listening to the children's giggles. Tash looked up at him.

"I'm sorry," she said.

"Sorry for what?"

"All of this," she said. "I guess you think I come with a lot of baggage."

"You do," he told her. A smile. "And I do, too. Anybody that's lived long enough comes with baggage."

"Still," she said, "you sure couldn't have known you were signing up for all this. If you want to take your ring back, I'll understand." She said it lightly, a cover for her anxiety.

Philip kissed her forehead. "Hush," he said.

Tash laid her head on his chest. It rose and fell gently beneath her, a comforting rhythm. "I should have seen this coming," she said.

"What?"

"This, with Michaela. You remember I went to talk to her just the other day? She told me she was tired of children's foolishness. You know, LaShonda was pregnant again. *Is* pregnant again."

"You hadn't told me that. Is it Trey's?"

"Some other boy," said Tash. "Girl came over here at two-some-thing in the morning because her mother had kicked her out when she learned. I tried to talk to her, but she was convinced this boy loved her."

"So you went to see her mother."

"Just to talk to her," said Tash. "That was all. You know, we're grownups, we're supposed to be Christians, and she and I had never really talked. Too busy being angry. She was mad at me, I was mad at her. Least, that's what we both thought. But the more I think about it, the more I think what we're mad at is our children. She kept asking how LaShonda could do that again, come up pregnant again. Girl sees the trouble her mother is having, she sees how Trey treats her, but she goes anyway and does it again."

"The definition of crazy," said Philip, "is to keep doing the same thing but expecting a different result."

"I suppose," said Tash.

He looked down at her again. "You got a better explanation?"

Tash shrugged. "I think that girl just wants somebody to love her," she said.

"You're reading too much into it," said Philip. "You're rationalizing it."

"Maybe," said Tash. "You know what her mother told me?"

"Hmm?"

"Said she couldn't take any more. That's exactly what she said."

"You could not have known this was going to happen," Philip said.

Tash nodded, but his words were small comfort. After a moment she said, "So what are we going to do now?"

"What do you mean?" he asked.

"About DeVante," she said. "If, God forbid, something happens to his mother."

He thought about it for a moment. Then he said, "Seems to me that's not our problem."

"How do you figure?"

"The child has a father," said Philip.

And he did, of course. Tash wondered how she could have forgotten, even just for a moment. Then she was annoyed at Philip for reminding her. "Yeah," she said. "Well, technically, I suppose that's true."

"No," said Philip. His voice was firm. "Not 'technically.' The child has a father, period. A living, breathing, flesh-and-blood father."

"Fine," said Tash. "But you know as well as I do there's no way Trey is ready to take care of a child. He's still a child himself, Philip. He's a father in name only. I'm going to have to step in and do it."

"Okay, Wonder Woman," said Philip. "Do what you got to do."

She lifted her head and stared at him. "What's that supposed to mean?"

"Nothing," he said and turned away.

She raised her hand to his cheek and brought his eyes back around. "What is that supposed to mean, Philip?"

"Wonder Woman," he said. "Strong as an ox. Bear any load. Nothing's too much. Nothing's ever too heavy. Wonder Woman."

"I'm not—"

He cut her off. "Yeah, you are."

"I'm not Wonder Woman, Philip. I'm only woman, period."

"Then *act* like it," he said. "For goodness sake, Tash, let yourself be human. Let yourself be tired sometimes. Maybe sometimes, when something needs to be done you don't have to automatically take it all on your shoulders. Maybe if you required Trey to step up and be a father to this child, he might actually do it. He might just surprise you."

"That's a big risk to take," said Tash.

"Yeah. Maybe. But you know something? People have this way of getting away with exactly what you let them get away with. They have this way of doing just enough to get by. So maybe the biggest favor you could do your son would be to demand that he step up to the plate. He's a grown man. He's got responsibilities. Maybe you should tell him that. *Show* him that."

She looked at him for a long moment. Then she lowered her head back to his chest. "This is silly," she said. "There's no point in having this discussion. That girl is going to be fine."

"Let's pray on it," said Philip.

And they did. The prayer centered her like prayer always did. It steeled her, reminded her that even the worst trials had this way of working themselves out if left in the hands of God. When Philip said amen, she felt her surety, her faith, rising in her.

Tash went to see LaShonda the next morning at work. Her faith wilted in the face of what she saw. The girl's face was swathed in gauze, her eyes and mouth barely visible. Most of the cuts were superficial, Tash knew, but they spoke to the fury with which Michaela had attacked. The worst of it, though, was not in the face. According to her chart, LaShonda had sustained damage to her left ventricle. She was scheduled for cardiac surgery that afternoon.

Tash replaced the chart and went to the head of the bed. She touched the child's forehead, closed her eyes, and lifted a silent prayer. LaShonda was heavily sedated. Once in awhile, she moaned softly. Otherwise, the only sound in the darkened room was the hiss and beep of the machines.

After a moment, Tash stepped into the hall. She pulled out her cell phone and punched up Trey's number. The call went straight to voicemail. "Trey," she said, "this is Mom. Look, give me a call. There's some bad news here. LaShonda is in the hospital. She was... she's been hurt. DeVante is fine; he's with me, but LaShonda...just give me a call, okay?"

Tash closed the phone, returned to the darkened room. She was surprised to see that a man had entered. He stood over the bed, LaShonda's right hand closed in both of his. The stranger looked up when he heard Tash enter. "Are you Shonda's nurse?" he asked.

"No," said Tash. "I'm...well, she's my grandson's mother. I'm Trey's mom."

"Oh," he said, his eyes dropping back to the girl on the bed. "I'm Shonda's father."

"Daryl," said Tash.

"That's right. How did you know?"

"Michaela told me."

"Michaela. Of course."

Tash moved closer. "Do you know how this happened?"

He shook his head. "If you mean the details, no. But those two never really needed a reason. Do you know Michaela?"

"Not well," said Tash. "Just enough to say hi when we're dropping off DeVante."

"That's your grandson?"

"Yours too," said Tash.

For just a beat, his eyes went out of focus. "Yeah, I guess he is, isn't he? You know, I never met him. Me and Michaela, we weren't close after the divorce. And Shonda, she knew her mother wasn't happy and she blamed me for that, so she never wanted me to come around."

"And yet, here you are," said Tash.

He looked down on his daughter. "Here I am," he said.

"You should meet your grandson," Tash told him.

He didn't answer. Tash came forward until she faced him across LaShonda's bed. Daryl Watkins was not tall, maybe 5'7" or 5'8", but he was solidly built, with a square jaw, salt-and-pepper hair, and sad eyes that were, just now, rimmed with tears yet to be cried. "You probably think I'm a terrible man," he said after a moment. There was no apology in his tone. If anything, thought Tash, there was a note of defiance.

"It's not my business to think anything," she said. "I don't know you."

"I love my daughter," he told her. "Even love Michaela, in a way. At least I did, before she went and did this."

"This wasn't her," said Tash. "She wasn't in her right mind when she did this. She couldn't have been."

"I don't care what was going on with her," said Daryl. "She didn't have to do this. She didn't have to cut up our baby. There's no excuse for that."

"I'm sure she didn't mean it," said Tash, wondering even as she said it why she was defending Michaela Watkins. The woman had tried to kill her own child. Nothing you could say could make that right. Tash was grateful when Daryl didn't reply.

He lay LaShonda's hand gently atop the covers. "I haven't seen her in years," he said. "I wouldn't have recognized her."

"Michaela said you had a family up in New York?"

"Yeah. Wife, two daughters."

Tash's cell phone rang. She excused herself and stepped into the hall to open the clamshell. "Hello?"

"Mom, what's wrong with Shonda?"

Tash told him what she knew. He kept saying, "Oh, man. Oh, man." At the end, he asked her, "How's my little man? Is he a'ight?"

"He's as all right as he can be, considering what he saw," said Tash, lowering her voice as a doctor went by trailing a covey of med students. "He was okay last night, so long as Philip and the girls were over. But he wouldn't sleep in your room alone. He slept with me. And he wet the bed."

"Little kids always wet the bed," said Trey.

"Bed wetting can be a sign of emotional distress, Trey," she said.

He smacked his lips dismissively. "Ah, I think you makin' too much out of it. My boy a soldier. He be a'ight."

"He is *not* a soldier!" she said, and then realized from the upturned eyes at the nurse's station down the hall that she had yelled it. She lowered her voice and repeated it in a hiss. "He is not a soldier. He is a little boy."

"Well, I'm just sayin…"

"Stop, Trey. Just don't."

A silence ensued. Tash did not rush to fill it. Finally, Trey said, "Well, I got somethin' to tell you, too. I think you need to come out here. Dad sick."

"What do you mean, he's sick? What's wrong with him?"

"He got that disease old people get when they forget everything. Only the kind he got, you get when you're young."

"Early onset Alzheimer's?" Tash breathed the words in disbelief.

"That's the one," said Trey.

"Oh my God," said Tash. "How do you know? How does *he* know?"

"He been to the doctor for it. Told me he took the tests and everything. It's for real. That's why he had that accident. He woke up and didn't know where he was, didn't know who I was, didn't know nothing. He got scared and drove through a red light trying to get away."

"Oh, God," said Tash. She fell back against the wall, lowered her head, feeling as if she was being hit, over and over again, one disaster after another, a series of blows so constant and so relentless that it drove all the breath out of her. The devil was busy here. Trey, LaShonda, Michaela, DeVante. Now this. She gasped.

Trey went on, heedless. "And guess what? He said, if he got it, that mean I might get it. Even DeVante might get it. It's in the blood."

"Hereditary," said Tash. Another hit. Her faith of just the day before was autumn leaves, fallen down, crushed beneath uncaring feet, blowing away.

"Yeah, that's the word he used. So you going to come out here?"

"What?" It was as if the conversation had accelerated into another language and she could not keep up.

"To help me get him home," said Trey. "I mean, he a'ight most of the time. But what if he blank out again? Especially if he do it while he behind the wheel. Cops say he shouldn't be driving. And I don't know if I can do it by myself. I need your help."

She tried to envision Trey bringing his father back home. Trey, who thought his son was "a little man" and "a soldier" who could see his grandmother stab his mother and be all right. No—"a'ight." It would be hard to find somebody to cover for her on such short notice. Weariness escaped Tash in a long sigh.

"Okay," she heard herself saying. "I'll get a flight."

"That's what's up," he said. "Thanks, Mom." He sounded relieved.

Tash said goodbye and closed the clamshell. Not knowing what else to do, she wandered back into the room. She was numb. Sleepwalking. Daryl Watkins had pulled a chair up next to his daughter's bed. He sat there, facing the window. He was crying.

Tash waited. After a moment he noticed her, swiped impatiently at his cheek. "You were trying to defend her," he said, his voice raw.

"What?"

"Michaela. Even though she did this, you were trying to defend her."

Tash said, "I didn't mean—"

He cut her off. "It's always the same, isn't it? The man's always wrong. No matter what he does, the man's always wrong."

"I'm sorry," said Tash.

"I did my best," he said. "Do you understand? It may not have been perfect, but I did the best I could. And I don't deserve to have you coming in here trying to defend this woman who cut up her own daughter, this woman who…who…"

The anger that had propped him upright failed him then. He crumbled, composure shattering, tears washing down his face, wails of grief tearing out of him. Tash went to him, knelt in front of him, put her arms around him. He tried to push her away. She held him fast and in the end, even that bit of resistance failed him. He caved in on himself, crying and wailing and clinging to her like a child to a blanket.

She was numb.

She was numb.

She was numb.

Too many feelings, too much pain. She walled it all off, secluded it away from her, so she could function. So she could breathe. She put all her concentration into the man in her arms, the faint scent of his cologne and sweat, the heaving of his shoulders, the gasps and moans of his grieving. She held this stranger until he cried himself out, until the room was silent again except for the whispers of the machines. And when he stopped crying and pushed away from her, embarrassed, she let him go without a word. Got to her feet and left the room, walked down hallways she didn't see, past conversations she didn't hear.

She was numb.

Tash was distantly aware that something was wrong with her, that something had finally broken inside. Automatically, she tried to breathe a prayer, but the words were not there. She couldn't pray and that was the most frightening realization of all. The devil was busy this day. That was all her mind would say. The devil was busy.

And then she saw him.

The sight jolted her back into her body and she stopped short. For a moment she was disoriented, didn't know where she was or even why she had stopped. Then, the world swam back into focus. She was in the NICU and he was there, the tall, rail-thin man who had come to her door after Trey and his father left for California. She almost didn't recognize him. Seeing him here, in this unfamiliar context, in this place where she had always been safe, jarred her. But it was him, all right. The one who called himself Dog. The one who scared her. He was sitting on a bench in the hallway as if he had been waiting for her.

The sight of him made her want to get away. But her legs made another decision. They carried her right up to him as if she had no say in the matter. "What are you doing here?" she heard herself demanding.

He looked up. There was no recognition in his eyes.

"What?" he said.

She jabbed at him with her finger. "Are you going to hurt my son? Is that why you're following me around?"

His face showed only surprise. Then recognition crept slowly into his eyes. They were red, she noticed for the first time. "I ain't following you," he said. His voice was low, his throat seemed coated with gravel. "I had a baby. I mean, my girl had a baby. But she sick. They think she might have brain damage."

More pain. Too much pain. Tash refused to let it in. It sat on the surface of her, like rainwater pooling atop saturated soil. Yes, Lord, the devil was busy. "Things are tough all over," she said. For the second time in as many minutes, he looked surprised by her. Tash aimed her index finger at him like a gun. Her voice was pinched and hard. "You stay away from me," she said. "You stay away from my son."

She didn't wait for an answer. Her shoes clicked furiously on the tiles as she walked away.

Tash left work early that afternoon. She called Philip and told him she would not need a ride. Then she took a cab—a horrible expense, but she didn't care—to the women's correctional center.

She gave them her name and ID, she filled out the paper, she waited, she heard her name called, she went through the metal detector, she surrendered her heavy coat, she listened to directions, she walked down the long and featureless halls. And still she did not feel. LaShonda was stabbed and Michaela was in jail and Trey was in trouble and Moses, her first love, was dying. Better not to feel.

Because the only thing feeling brought you was pain. Yet even at this late date, she could not stop herself from wanting to know…why?

She sat in the room on the one side of the yellowed plastic. She looked into the empty room on the other side. She waited. Then the door on the other side opened and Michaela walked in. At the sight of Tash, she scowled. "I don't get but two visits a week," she said, turning away. "Rather save that for family, you don't mind."

"Michaela, wait."

She paused. Tash said, "Please. I want to talk to you. I need to."

Michaela snorted. *"You need,"* she said. But she sat down. Her gaze was steady. Her hair was in braids. She was dressed in a red jumpsuit. "What do you want?" she said.

"I want to know why," said Tash.

"You want to know why." Michaela's voice was a monotone.

"I want to know what happened."

She shrugged. "We got in an argument about the baby. She called me a bitch. I'm taking care of one of her little bastards and she got another on the way and she got the nerve to call me a selfish bitch because I told her I didn't intend to spend my old age taking care of her babies. I don't remember nothing after that. They told me I stabbed her. I might have."

"Oh, Michaela. I'm so sorry."

She shook her head impatiently. "How the baby?"

"He's with me. He saw it all. He won't stop talking about it."

"Probably good for him. Help him get it out. Least, that's what my psych professor back in college always said." The hesitation was infinitesimal. Then she said, "What about that dumbass daughter of mine? Is she dead?"

Tash shook her head. "She's bad, though. They've got her in heart surgery. Trying to see if they can save her and the baby."

"She's alive?" Michaela's voice climbed toward hope.

Tash said, "Yeah, she's alive. Your ex-husband is with her."

"He hate me, I know."

"He's very upset."

She pursed her lips. "I don't blame him. She ain't had no call talking to me that way, but I shouldn't have done what I did. I didn't mean to. Still hard for me to believe it happened."

"'I'm tired. Don't know how much more of this I can take.'"

"What you mean?" asked Michaela.

"That's what you said to me, last time I saw you. 'I'm tired. Don't know how much more of this I can take.' I keep wondering if maybe I had paid more attention to what you told me, maybe I could have said something or done something..."

"Is that what this is all about?" Michaela's flinty eyes softened. "Girl, stop. This ain't your fault. Ain't nobody's but mine."

"Yeah, but maybe I could have helped you or..."

Tash paused when she saw Michaela smile. It was a sad smile filled with regret. "Ain't nothing you could have done," she said. "This is just life, Tash. You know, my daddy, when we kids were cuttin' up and he'd had enough of it, he'd start hollerin' at us. 'I'm tired,' he used to say. 'Even iron give out, goddamn it.'"

She chuckled at the memory, then fell silent for so long, Tash thought she had forgotten Tash was there. But all at once, Michaela looked up at her. "See, it was the same thing with me," she said. "I thought I was iron, but I give out."

Another laugh. Then laughing became tears. Michaela's hand came to her mouth. Water glistened on her eyelashes, tumbled onto her cheek.

"Michaela," said Tash.

No answer. Tash called her name again. Michaela looked up, her hand still on her mouth. "I'm going to be here for you," said Tash. "I promise you that."

"Thank you," said Michaela. Her voice was fragile. "Thank you."

They made small talk until the guard came and took Michaela away. Tash watched her go, waving once as she was led away. Then she left the room. She walked back down the featureless halls, she reclaimed her heavy coat and her ID, she walked out of the waiting room, through a vestibule, stood at the edge of the parking lot. Philip was in the car waiting. She could see him, though he couldn't see her. The dome light was on, the girls were eating takeout chicken and laughing at some joke. His eyes were closed, his head was on the headrest and he was singing.

How had he known? But then she decided it didn't matter how he had known. It was enough that he had. Wonder Woman, he had called her. What a day Wonder Woman had had. Tash pulled out her cellphone and keyed in a number. After a moment, Trey picked up. "Hey, Mom, what's up?"

"Nothing," she said. "How are you and your dad?" Her breath was visible in the twilight air and she retreated to the warmth of the vestibule.

"I'm good. I don't know about him. He been kind of quiet."

"You have to expect that, Trey. His father is dead. They might not have talked for 30 years, but that's still his father."

"Yeah, I know. Funeral tomorrow."

"Listen, the reason I'm calling: I changed my mind, Trey. I'm not coming out there."

"Oh, man. What happened? You couldn't get time off?"

She didn't even consider lying. "No," she said, "that's not it. I just didn't want to."

"What you mean?"

"I mean that you're a grown man, Trey. You're a licensed driver. And that's your dad."

"I know all that, but…"

"Unless you're telling me he's completely lost his memory to the point he can't help you read a map…"

"No, no, it ain't nothing like that yet."

"Good, then. You and he should have no problem getting home."

She heard the anger in his voice. "Mom, why you doing this? Why you won't help me?"

"I've already helped you, Trey. I've helped you for 19 years. Probably helped you too much, you want to know the truth. You need to do this and you need to do it on your own."

"You ain't worried?"

"Petrified," she said. "But I'm not going to be here to rescue you always and I don't feel like I should have to be. Even iron wears out, Trey."

"What that mean?"

"You'll figure it out," she said. "I've got to go."

When she closed the clamshell, her hand was shaking and there was a knot in her stomach. Los Angeles, her mind screamed at her, was 3,000 miles away. Three thousand miles. A scared teenager who didn't drive well and a man whose memory was failing him. Lord, what had she done?

She wanted to open the phone so badly, take it all back, tell him Mama was coming. Instead, she made herself shove the phone into a deep pocket of her coat. She heaved a sigh—resignation or resolution, she wasn't sure—then pushed open the door and stepped out into the cold.

twenty-four

The chapel in the mortuary was punishing hot. The funeral director came to them, hands pressed together as if in supplication, and apologized for the heat; the air conditioning was not working, he said. Fans twirled languidly in the ceiling high above without disturbing the air much at all. One of them needed oil, its periodic squeak a plaintive counterpoint to the disinterested meandering of the lady on the piano. "Amazing Grace" becomes "Precious Lord" becomes "Blessed Assurance" becomes "How Great Thou Art," flowing in a river of seamless sameness.

It was just the three of them, Mo, Trey, and Cooley. At the end, thought Mo, this was what Jack's 74 years on the planet came down to. Nobody to mourn. Nobody to say goodbye. Nobody to send you off down the last mile.

His own funeral would be different. Obituaries in all the papers, a few minutes of tribute on cable news, a church packed with other singers, former sidemen. And Fans, of course. Maybe they'd get Mario Gaines to play piano. Maybe somebody would sing "My Prophecy" in his honor. It would be a good funeral.

He sat in the front row of the chapel, Trey and Cooley right next to him, his father's casket five feet ahead. The lid was open and you could make out the profile of Jack's head, resting on a white satin pillow. The black pinstripe suit swallowed him like a guppy, folds of fabric pooling on his arms and chest. Once, he had seemed so huge. Bigger than Cooley. Bigger than anyone Mo ever knew.

They were watching him, he knew. He caught Trey and Cooley glancing worriedly every few moments. Mo wore sunglasses to keep his blackened eye private. It was a perk of celebrity he had always enjoyed, the ability to wear shades indoors and have nobody call you on it.

There had been a moment he thought of just avoiding the funeral altogether, just getting back in the Escalade and going east. He
had come here for last words and Jack had cheated him out of that
like he cheated him out of so many other things, had died, taking last
words with him. So what was the point of staying for a funeral? But
Cooley and Trey had talked him out of leaving. He had come this far,
they said. Might as well see it all the way through. And reluctantly,
Mo had allowed himself to be persuaded.

Now he sat here, sweat tracing the contours of his cheek, his tie
too tight, his jacket too heavy on his shoulders, the cast on his wrist
itching, his son and Cooley watching him closely and maybe whispering about him like he wasn't there.

Mo look okay to you?

You think he crying?

Yeah. Like he wasn't there. Soon enough, he wouldn't be. Just a
body without a mind. Unless he took matters into his own hands.
And he would. The very day he got home, he would. Drop Trey off
at his mother's in Baltimore, drive down to Bowie, let himself in to
the rot and stench of his house, go straight up the stairs, pick up the
gun, press it against the roof of his mouth, exert a little pressure on
the trigger.

Bang.

All gone. All done.

"Mr. Johnson?" The voice at his ear made Mo start. He turned
and found himself facing an older black man, dark skin, scalp as bald
and round as an egg. His smile showed his teeth to be crooked and
coffee stained. "I'm sorry," he said. "Didn't mean to startle you. I just
wanted to introduce myself, tell you how sorry I am about your dad."
He extended his hand. "My name is Lou Rogers. I own a little diner
down on Century. Jack worked for me a lot of years. Started out as a
fry cook, took over as night manager about 15 years ago."

Desperate words from 30 years back echoed in Mo's ear. *"...man
at this café down on Century say he might need a fry cook. Say call him
next week..."*

Jack pleading for another chance. Right before he drove his wife
out of the apartment at a run. Right before he drove her into traffic,

where a car hit her and never slowed down and she hung on the air for a bright, brittle moment before she came down with a sickening bounce.

Lou was still talking. "Never missed a day of work, your father. Can you believe that? Didn't even have a car, the first few years he was there. Used to walk or ride the bus. But he was always there. Sick as a dog, once. Coughing so bad I had to get him away from the food, put him back in the office and let him count receipts. But he never missed a day. Hardest working man I ever knew, and that's a fact."

"I didn't know," said Mo. He was aware of Cooley and Trey watching him. "Me and him, we weren't real close."

Lou's eyes flickered. "I know," he said. "He told me about it one day. You know how Jack was. Play everything close to the vest, don't confide nothing to nobody. We had known each other about seven or eight years by then. One of your records was on the radio and he was back there putting burgers on the grill and singing along with it. You know Jack: he wasn't the singing-along type. So I teased him about it. I said, 'Hey, Jack, what's got you in such a good mood all of a sudden? You get laid last night?'" Lou seemed to remember where he was right then. He gave a sheepish nod to the cross on the wall. "Sorry," he said, and Mo wasn't sure if the apology was meant for him or for the cross.

"But anyway, that's what I said. And he points the spatula at the radio and says, 'No, man, that's my son, Mo. His new record just come out.'"

"I told him he was full of sh…" Another sheepish glance, a rueful smile. "I told him I didn't believe him. And what I want to say that for? He drops the spatula without a word, goes out to his locker, and comes back a few minutes later with this picture of a kid in a cap and gown. And it's you. I recognized it right away. I said, 'Wow, Jack. I'm sorry, I didn't know. So that *is* your son?' He goes, 'Yup. My only child.' And he picked up the spatula like, yeah, I really showed you something."

Lou shook his head, still smiling. "He was proud of you. I know he might not never have said it, but he was. I thought you'd like to know that."

"Thank you," said Mo.

Lou nodded, returned to his seat. Cooley nudged Mo. "You all right there, Mosey?" he asked. "Lookin' a little green around the gills."

"I'm fine," said Mo. "Just hot."

Cooley looked dubious, but didn't challenge him. "Be over before too long," he said.

Mo studied the program in his hands. It was cheap looking, thrown together quickly to accommodate his demand for a quick service. Looking at it, he wished he had given them a few more days. The front piece showed some picture of Jack that Mo had never seen—young and smiling, eyes penetrating and lively, mouth gaping in laughter.

"He was so young," said Mo.

Cooley glanced over his shoulder. "Took that not long after he first come out here."

Mo only nodded, because "young," now that he thought of it, wasn't what he had really meant. The man in the picture looked so free of care, so free of fear and doubt. He looked…happy. Pleased with the world and his prospects in it. Mo had never known Jack to look that way. Had never known he could.

He felt the air shift in the room and glanced behind him. Two tiny older women, wearing knee-length black dresses and extravagant black hats, had entered. They walked, tottering a little, to the casket in front, trailing a perfume that made Mo think of being locked in a closet full of flowers. After a moment, he heard one of them say, "He looks peaceful." Through the narrow space between them, he saw one of them reach down and touch Jack's brow with the back of her fingers. "You sleep now," she said.

Cooley was on his feet. He tapped Mo hard on the shoulder and Mo stood, too. After a moment, the women turned. Their faces opened, first with wonder and then delight. "Arthur?" asked one. "Arthur, is that you?"

She had light skin and was a little on the plump side. Her eyes danced and Mo thought she must have been pretty in her youth. Cooley grinned. "Yeah, Connie, I'm afraid it is." And he enveloped her in a hug.

"Lord, have mercy," said the other woman. "I'd have known you anywhere." She was darker, thinner, and held herself with more reserve.

Cooley took her hand, lowered his head slightly. "Miss Sadie," he said, solemnly. They regarded one another soberly for a moment. Then, as if on cue, they both smiled. She allowed herself to be hugged.

"It's been a long time," breathed the first woman, Connie. "A long time." Then she noticed Mo and tapped Cooley on the shoulder. "Is this Jimmy's son?" she asked.

"This is him," Cooley said. "A little banged up, though. He was in a car accident coming out here. Mo, these here your aunties. This your Aunt Connie and your Aunt Sadie. These Jack's sisters."

Aunt Connie smiled her pretty smile and opened her arms. Mo took off his sunglasses, gave her a hug. After a moment, she pulled back, regarded his injuries with concern, touched his battered face lightly. "You look like you got the worst of it," she said.

"I'm fine," Mo assured her. He turned toward the other woman. She held her hands crossed at the wrist in front of her and regarded him with pinched lips and narrowed eyes. "You the one said we had to have the funeral in just two days," she said. "You the one made me have to get on an airplane. I'm scared of airplanes, you know."

"I'm sorry," said Mo. "I don't like 'em much either."

"You could have waited. Give people time enough to get here on Greyhound."

"Yes, ma'am," said Mo, vaguely amused to be chastised by this stranger.

The eyes softened. "But I guess you had your reasons," she said in a voice he had to lean forward to hear. "I know my brother could be difficult. I know things wasn't always easy for you."

"No, ma'am, they weren't."

Connie touched his sleeve. "See, son, we never knew that side of him. We only heard about it, after. He was our big brother, you see. So we only knew him for taking care of us. Getting us up in the morning and getting us off to school, cooking dinner in the evenings.

Mother was always on the way to work when we got up in the morning and she didn't get home till after dinner and our father was...well,
he wasn't no good."

Sadie frowned her reproach. Connie drew herself up defensively.
"Well, it's the truth," she said. "And Jimmy, he taken care of us like a
parent would. He weren't but five years older than Sadie here, seven
years older than me. But he took care of us just the same. So see,
that's how we know him. We know him as the brother who looked
after us."

She glanced behind her at the figure in the casket and sighed.
"That's funny, isn't it, how you can know him one way and we can
know him some way completely different. Funny how a person can
contradict their own self."

Mo didn't answer. He didn't know how. After a moment, Connie
seemed to sense this. She pointed to Trey and said, "And who is this
handsome young man?"

Mo made the introductions and Trey stood and dutifully em-
braced the two small women as they made a fuss over how tall and
handsome he was. They made small talk for a few minutes. Then the
piano stopped playing. The funeral director coughed. It was time for
the service to begin. Connie and Sadie took seats at the end of the
bench.

The family section, thought Moe ruefully, was five people. And
that was counting Arthur Cooley, who wasn't blood. He'd known
in some vague sense that his father still had relatives somewhere in
Mississippi, but he'd never cared enough to find out who they were.
Or maybe he'd known at one time and then forgot. He could never
be sure anymore.

Mo glanced around the room. Three or four more strangers had
come in while he and his aunts were being introduced. The room was
far from filled, but at least it wasn't just him, Cooley, and Trey sitting
in here alone. His father had had some kind of life. For some reason,
that felt good to know.

Cooley tugged at Mo's jacket and he realized he was still standing and the funeral director was waiting for him. With a nod of
apology, Mo slipped into his seat. The funeral director stepped to

the podium, opened his Bible with white gloved hands and practiced ease, and the ceremony began.

A woman sang "Precious Lord." The funeral director read the obituary in the program, a stiff and spare recitation of milestone dates. When he was done, he slipped it inside his Bible, interlaced his fingers, and offered a few words worn smooth and meaningless from years of repetition. Earth has no sorrow that heaven cannot heal, he said. Weeping may endure for a night, but joy cometh in the morning, he said. We'll understand it better, by and by, he said. It was, Mo saw, a performance. One he had given dozens of times. Generic funeral words. None of which had anything to do with Jack Johnson.

Mo lurched to his feet and that surprised him because he hadn't known he was going to do it. The funeral director went silent. Mo felt their eyes on him, the touch of a dozen gazes all waiting, expectant. Mo heard himself breathing. The funeral man said, "Did you want to speak?" He stood aside from his lectern. Mo nodded and went there as if magnetized.

He looked out over the room. A couple more people had walked in. The funeral was that much less an embarrassment. Somewhere in the tangled jumble of his thoughts, it occurred to him that he had sung for presidents and princes and been less apprehensive than he was now, facing less than 20 people at a funeral home in South Central. He cleared his throat.

"Everybody called him Jack," he said. "Even the funeral program says Jack. But that wasn't really his name. His name, his real name, was James Johnson. James Moses Johnson, same as mine. But he called himself Jack Johnson after the boxer. Some of you may know about him. Jack Johnson, he was the first black heavyweight champion. He was a hell of a man, Jack Johnson, man who did whatever he wanted to do, whenever he wanted to, and didn't care much what people thought about it. He married white women and drove fast cars and lived the high life. This was back in the early 1900s, when they were killing black men for stuff like that. But Jack Johnson was the kind of man who didn't let nobody else tell him what to do, a man who made up his own rules. I think that's what my father liked about him."

Mo gripped both sides of the lectern hard. He looked down into the casket, down on the wizened little man staring stonily into death. "I'm not going to stand up here and pretend he was something he wasn't," said Mo. "The fact is, my father was a hard man. Very hard man. Hard to live with, too. Some of you probably know my mother was running to get away from him when she was killed."

A murmur ran like electric current though the audience. Mo shrugged. His ruined mouth framed a sad smile. "It's true," he said. "That was just about the last day he and I ever spoke. Thirty years ago this year. Except that now he's dead and so I come back out here, because that's what you're supposed to do when your father dies. I don't care who you are, I don't care what goes on between you. You're supposed to come back out and be with him because that's your father."

From the corner of his eye, Mo saw the funeral man moving toward him. He held up a hand to stop him. "But you know what?" he said. "I'm dying. Hell, we're all dying. All of us, everyday. And maybe, you know, it's not such a bad thing that we know that, that we keep it in mind. Maybe that would help us to love the people we're supposed to love, tell 'em the things we're supposed to tell 'em. Or at least, you know, get things out in the open so that when you die, there's nothing there but death. I mean, no words you forgot to say, no thing you forgot to do. Nothing that hangs on after you. So it's just death. It's only death. 'Cause Lord knows, death is enough. Death is a bitch."

He tried to go on, but suddenly, there was something in his throat. His voice came out of him an unrecognizable croak. To his surprise, he was crying. Through the gray and watery haze of his own tears, Mo saw Cooley get to his feet. The big man moved with a solemn dignity as he came around to the lectern. Mo moved aside to make room for him. Cooley rested a hand lightly on his shoulder. He faced the audience silently, in no hurry, allowing his thoughts to gather.

"You know," he said, through a rumbling chuckle, "at funerals, they always try to make the deceased sound like he was a saint. Well, let me tell you something. Jack Johnson was my friend. He was my best friend. Me and him more like brothers than friends, tell you the truth. I known him since we was both nothing more than boys. So believe me when I say, he wasn't no saint.'"

In the back of the room, somebody laughed. "That's right," said Cooley, smiling. "Y'all can pretend if you want 'cause it's his funeral and we all dressed up in Sunday clothes, but you know I ain't lying. Jack definitely had his ways and he wasn't always easy to be around. Take it from me. He had a mean streak, especially right after he got out of jail. If I had a dollar for every time he said he was gon' kick my ass, I'd be a millionaire. He was a hard man, but see, he had a hard life. He got through it as best he could, same as all of us do. He was loyal and he was honest. Hell of a lot more than I can say for some. And he might love you, but he didn't always know how to show it. I guess he just expected you to know. But you got to say something sometimes, because people don't always know. I used to tell him that a lot. So yeah, Jack made some mistakes. Made a lot of mistakes. But I still miss him." Pause. Cooley looked over at Mo. "I think a lot of us gon' miss him," he said.

A few people in the audience said, "Amen." Cooley whispered to Mo, "Let's go." And they left the podium and sat back in the audience. It went quickly after that. Someone read sympathy cards. The woman sang "His Eye Is on the Sparrow." The funeral director gave a short homily whose point was that Jack Johnson was merely sleeping but would awaken on the "great getting-up day."

Mo barely heard any of it. Cooley had to nudge him to stand for the recessional. The casket was closed now. The attendants wheeled it toward the door. Mo, Cooley, Trey, Connie, and Sadie followed. Jack's sisters were dabbing at their eyes. Cooley and Trey donned the white gloves and helped four other men bear the casket into the hearse. Connie and Sadie got into the funeral home limousine. The three men piled in after.

It took a moment to get the procession organized. Six cars stringing out behind the limousine. That was it. A bare handful of people who cared that Jack Johnson was dead. The hearse pulled away from the curb. The limousine followed. The silence inside was stifling. Then Connie said, "He liked to dance. Did you know that?"

Mo looked up. She was talking to him. "No, ma'am," he said. "I didn't know that."

She chuckled as she shifted in her seat. "Yes, Lord. We used to have these barn dances after harvest time. I wasn't nothing but a little kid and he was a teenager, but I always remember him getting ready to go. Practicing his steps out on the dirt in front of the house, pretending like he holding a girl in his arms, humming the songs to himself. We ain't had no radio. Ain't had much of nothing, tell you the truth." She chuckled again, smoothed away imaginary wrinkles in her dress. "Yes, he really loved to dance."

"He was a good big brother," said Sadie. She was not smiling. "We lost touch with him after everything that happened. Mama and Papa died and he couldn't even come to the funerals because he was, you know…" She frowned, waving dismissively at the word she couldn't speak. *Prison.*

"Like to broke both their hearts," said Connie. "It hurt them so bad. They wouldn't even allow us to call his name." She was gazing out the window with solemn eyes.

"After your mother died, we kind of lost touch," said Sadie. "You know, Jack never was one for Christmas cards or writing letters. Until one day out of the blue, I get this call from him and he told me about the cancer." She dabbed at her eyes. "I wish we had stayed in touch."

Connie patted her sister's hand. "He was a great dancer," she said. Her smile was vague. After a moment, she turned back to the window.

It took 15 minutes to reach the cemetery in Inglewood. The casket was borne to a spot on a low rise, seated carefully on the straps that would lower it into the dark rectangle of earth below. Two men stood next to a backhoe parked at a respectful distance, smoking cigarettes and waiting.

The small group of mourners assembled on chairs beneath a canvas tent. The funeral director opened his Bible and read from Psalms. He lifted a prayer. Then he pronounced the service done and said that if any of them faced bereavement in the future, he hoped they would remember Franklin Brothers. His voice was sonorous and cool.

Mo stood. His legs felt uncertain. Someone thrust a hand in front of him and he shook it, barely hearing the consoling words. Someone else gave him a hug. He barely saw her face. People were plucking flowers off the casket for keepsakes. Mo only gave the sleek gray capsule a last look, then walked off. He saw Cooley and Trey watching him carefully. He didn't go far. Five steps, in fact. And he knelt at her headstone. Ruth Desireé Johnson. You could barely read her name. Thirty years of weather had all but scoured it away.

He made a mental note to order a new headstone. Then he realized what a foolish thing that was, him making mental notes. Might as well write a note in beach sand. Mo was thankful when he heard footsteps on grass and looked over to see Trey's shoes. He turned back to the headstone. "I want you to remember something for me," he said.

"What's that?"

"I want to order a new headstone for my mother."

"This where she buried?"

Mo looked at him. "I'm serious," he said. "You need to remember it for me, because I might not. I want her to have a new headstone. Look at this. You can barely read her name."

"I'll remember, Pop," said Trey.

Satisfied, Mo fingered the dry grass atop the grave. It was strange to think that his mother, so distant in time and memory, was yet so close. Just six feet down through soil and clay. And yet, not close at all. Irretrievably gone. Mo felt sorrow pushing up from his gut like something molten. He swallowed.

"Last time I ever saw him was right here on this spot," said Mo.

"Yeah?"

"Yeah," said Mo. He swallowed again. The molten fist inside him would not budge.

"Tell me what happened," said Trey.

Mo said, "It was two days after the funeral." That was as far as he got. And then he was crying. Great, serrated sobs ripped up out of him, filled with as much anger as remorse. He hit the ground with his fist—frustration—then sagged into the grass. Surrender. From somewhere far away, he heard people coming toward him, words of consolation already forming on their lips and he tried to wave them off, tried to scream, *Get away from me!* Because he knew what they would think, that these were tears for Jack. And that thought infuriated him, because really, they were tears for everything.

It was still raining three days later. Three days after his mother's funeral.

Cooley had gone to work and at first, Mo had thought he might walk to Hollywood. He felt drawn there like metal filings to a magnet. Whatever was to happen in his life, whatever he was to be, it was there. He knew that now, more strongly than he ever had before.

But then he chanced to look out Cooley's kitchen window. It faced the place across the street that had once been home. A man walked in to the auto parts store below, carrying an alternator in a grimy fist. Above the man's head, Mama's curtains fluttered in the kitchen window. They were the color of roses. Her favorite.

Mo started as the door opened and Jack came walking down the stairs. It was the first time he had seen him since...it happened. Jack had sunflowers in his fist, a spray of yellow etching sharp contrast with the darkness of his fist and the gray of the day. Jack walked with a hesitance toward the corner. He moved, thought Mo, watching, as if his feet ached. As if his very existence ached. Then he was out of sight.

Mo knew the sunflowers meant one thing. Jack was going to the cemetery. Going to the grave. The thought of it filled him with a choking fury. What right did he have to go to the graveyard like a mourner?

Jack had not attended the funeral, a compromise with Mama's family brokered by Cooley. They had wanted to take her back to New Orleans to be buried in the family plot and Jack had refused. But he had agreed to stay away from the funeral. What would it look like, they said, if the man who chased her to her death was among the mourners?

Mo had heard Cooley explaining it on the phone, his voice gentle, but also hard. Accusing. And Mo had heard, too, the sigh of relief from Cooley that meant his father had given in. So the funeral had been held and the church had been filled and Mo had sagged across the casket and cried until they had to carry him away, and Jack had not been there. He had given them, at least, the solace of his absence.

Now, there he went off down the street pretty as you please with flowers in his fist, going to the cemetery, going to sit by the edge of the grave. It wasn't right. *(Stay away from her!)* It just wasn't right.

Cooley had a pistol, an old revolver he kept on his bedroom nightstand under a stack of bills and letters and girlie magazines. Mo had seen it in there one day when Cooley sent him in to fetch a blanket for the bed in the guestroom. Now he retrieved it, shoved it into his waistband. He shrugged on his coat and went walking.

It took an hour to reach the cemetery. Mo walked through the gates without pausing, his stride long and purposeful as it carried him up the grassy slope in a mean, misting rain. And there he was, sitting on the grass next to the depression in the ground, the sunflowers lying next to him. James Moses Johnson, Sr. Nasty little drunk with hard fists and a cruel mouth. Father.

Jack heard him coming. He looked up. The last days had stitched themselves indelibly in the lines of his face. His skin was ashen. His eyes were those of a wounded thing. Mo pulled the gun, leveled it. His finger was on the trigger. His hand did not shake.

Jack's eyes noted the gun, but that was all. They did not show surprise. He did not flinch.

"You killed her," said Mo.

Jack did not respond.

"You killed her!" he cried.

Jack said, "I know."

Mo said, "I need to kill you, too."

He waited. He waited. Finger firm on the trigger. Swallowing, trying to push sudden hesitation down. This was the man who had killed his mother, after all. Killed her sure as if he had put a gun to her head. And yet...killing him was harder than Mo had thought it would be. He waited, but he didn't know what for. And then, almost imperceptibly, Jack shrugged.

The explosion filled the space between them. The bullet dug a hole in the grass, six inches from Jack's right leg. Mo said, "I never want to see you again. Forget you ever had a son." He lowered the weapon, put it back in his waistband. He regarded Jack for a long moment. Jack lowered his head. Mo spun around and walked away.

"I could have done it," he said. "I came that close," he added, holding thumb and forefinger so near one another that light barely inched through. His hand dropped. "I came that close," he said again.

They were sitting in the back of the limousine, Trey and Cooley, Connie and Sadie.

"My God," said Sadie. "I never knew that."

"I never told anyone," said Mo. "That was the last time I ever saw him."

"You didn't want your father's blood on your hands," said Connie.

"Yes, I did," said Mo.

"Pop…" began Trey.

"Yes, I did," insisted Mo.

"Then why are you here?" demanded Sadie. "Why would you come all the way across the country to be at his deathbed?" Her voice was sharp.

Mo looked at her, this aunt he had never known. He thought of all the years. He thought of all the cursing, all the fights, and of his mother, standing in the moonlight's glow that one night long ago, watching him watching her. He thought of the weight of the gun in his hands, the rain misting down, the skeletal eyes looking up at him, waiting.

Mo hunched his shoulders. "He was my father," he said.

twenty-five

Mary Willis knew the routine almost as well as her son Ray did. She held her arms out and did the Christ-on-the-cross pose and the cop ran the wand over her. She put her keys and cell phone on the conveyor through the X-ray machine before they could ask her. Then she surrendered her purse to the cop, who placed it in a cubby behind his chair and gave her a tattered little strip of white cardboard with a number written on it in orange marker in exchange. She tucked it into her shirt pocket.

She never spoke to the cop, never even looked at him. Mama hated cops, thought Dog with a private smile as he held his arms out to begin the same procedure. As far as she was concerned, they were always picking on her boys for no reason. Dog glanced at her, waiting there for him with arms folded across her massive chest, sour patience on her face as the cop did his pat down, pressing his hands into the folds of Dog's hoodie. He wondered if Mama believed all that or if it was just something to say so she didn't have to face the fact that her boys were no good.

The thought jolted him and he had to remind himself that he, at least, had changed, that he had a new life. Ronnie, and now the baby. A whole new life.

When the cop was finished, he waved Dog through the metal detectors, gave them directions neither one needed. The moment he was done, Mama gave a curt nod, then set off at that painful gait through the security doors, Dog following close behind. They went down a covered walkway. Off to the left was a field ringed by a high chain link fence topped with razor wire. "I hate this place," Mama said. She seemed to be speaking more to herself than to him and Dog didn't reply.

At the end of the covered walk, a double glass door took them inside the detention building. A cop at a desk glanced up when they

310 LEONARD PITTS, JR.

opened the door, sized them up, then returned to his newspaper and coffee. It was a large room, empty except for the desk. At the far end was a flight of stairs. Mama sighed. She crossed the room, grabbed the railing, and began to pull herself up. It was painful to watch. At the sound of her first grunt, the cop lifted his head again. Dog couldn't read his face. Just as well, he thought.

On the landing, Mama leaned her bulk against the railing. A young woman with a teenage daughter in tow came up the stairs at a trot and went around them without pausing. She had a nice ass, Dog saw. Her daughter looked just like her.

"You okay, Mama?" he asked.

"I seen you looking at the woman," she said in response. "You can't do that no more. You a married man now. Family man."

She liked to poke at him sometimes, just to see if she could get a rise. He didn't know why. "I can look all I want," he said. "Just can't touch."

She seemed disappointed at the mild response. After a moment, she said, "They should have an elevator in here."

Dog nodded. "Yeah," he said. "Elevator be good in here."

She took another moment. He heard her breathing. "Come on," she said finally, "let's go." She put the swollen leg gamely up on the next step. Dog saw her wince.

He knew she had no business being out on that leg. It had flared up so bad last night she had slept on the couch downstairs rather than climb up to her bedroom. It was a Saturday morning and she needed to be resting up from the week behind, getting her strength up for the week ahead. But she had not seen Fury since his arrest. Might as well try to keep the ocean from coming in to the shore as to keep her from coming to see her baby boy after so long. He knew this, so when she asked him to bring her down here, he hadn't even bothered to complain. Even though he knew she wouldn't get any rest tomorrow, either, what with spending most of the day in that church of hers, listening to that jackleg preacher grunt and strut and beg for money.

But the one good thing, thought Dog, since she was already out, she could come by the hospital and see his baby, his little girl. They had not given her a name yet—the Judge had pleaded with him not to give her what he called "one of those made-up ghetto-princess names like La'Neshia or RayQuanda." But Dog had no intention of naming her that. He had taken to thinking of her as his precious little girl and he liked the sound of it. Precious. It struck him as a nice name and he wanted to ask Ronnie what she thought.

It hurt him a little that his mother had not seemed in any special hurry to meet her first grandchild. But he knew she was preoccupied, what with her leg and Fury being locked up and all. Plus, there was her lingering dislike for Ronnie, her sense that this little rich girl was somehow pulling a fast one on him.

But since they were going to be out anyway, he had casually mentioned that they might go by the hospital on the way home and she had not protested. Dog hoped that meant she was coming to terms with the fact that Ronnie was the most important part of his life now. He tried to imagine what her first meeting with the Judge would be like and that almost made him smile. If the Judge was smart, he would keep his cutting remarks to himself while Mama was around. Dog didn't imagine that even Charles Richmond could keep up with Mary Willis if she got going.

They walked the featureless halls until they came to the door the cop had indicated. Dog pulled it open for her. She sat gratefully in the chair. Dog stood behind her, arms folded. They were silent for a moment. Then she said, "This baby, she look like you?"

Dog was surprised. "Yeah, I guess," he said.

"You guess?" She didn't bother hiding her scorn.

"Everybody say she look like me. I don't see it yet."

"'Everybody say.' You mean this girl and her daddy."

"Yeah," said Dog miserably, not liking the turn this conversation was taking.

"You thought about having the baby tested?"

"What?"

"DNA or something. Just to be sure."

"Mama, it's my baby."

"Don't hurt to find out for sure. All you know, this girl trying to set you up. Have you taking care of some other man's baby."

The anger caught Dog by surprise. "Set me up? Mama, don't you get it? Ronnie *rich*. Her daddy, he some kind of judge and he got all kind of money. What I got, Mama? Huh? What I got?"

Mama didn't answer. "Yeah," said Dog, "that's what I thought. See, she don't need me to take care of no baby. She need me because I'm the baby's father."

"I'm just saying," said Mama.

"Well don't. I'm lucky to have this girl. I'm lucky to be with her."

Mama just grunted. She didn't agree, but she wouldn't push the argument. They were silent for five minutes and Dog welcomed the solitude. He let his thoughts wander and as they inevitably did these days when he gave them rein, they turned to his girl and his daughter. Yesterday, for the first time, he had seen his baby nursing at her mother's breast. They were alone in the room, the dawn sun slanting in through the blinds. He had not known until that moment that your heart can break with love, that it can fill with such inexpressible tenderness till you just about can't stand it anymore. And he had heard himself say something he had not known he was going to say.

"We got to get married, you know." When he heard the words, he was shocked. And in the next moment he wasn't, because it just felt right.

Her head came up sharply and she stared at him. Then she smiled mischievously. "Your mother won't like it," she said. "My father will have a heart attack."

"That's their problem," he said.

She looked down at the baby tugging peacefully on the nipple, eyes squeezed tight. The smile turned secretive and mysterious. She brought her eyes back up to his. "Okay," she said, "let's get married."

They would do it as soon as she was out of the hospital. Just the thought made Dog giddy.

The door opened and Fury came through scowling. He stopped short when he saw his mother sitting there. For a moment, he seemed confused. The scowl wavered as if looking for somewhere to go. Then it melted and he looked like a little boy. "Mama?" he said. He sat down and stared at her like an apparition. "Mama?"

Dog hated to let the memory of Ronnie's face go. He liked him-self when he was thinking of her. He liked his life. But he let it go anyway. Mama had her face close to the window. "How you doing, Cedric? They treatin' you okay in here?"

Fury shook his head emphatically. "Hell no, Mama," he said. "They treat you like a dog in here. I'm ready to go home." Dog turned away so his anger wouldn't show. Why tell her something like that? There was nothing she could do. It would only make her feel worse.

She sighed her pain. "I know, baby," she said. "Mama know. But there ain't nothing we can do. That damn judge done set the bail so high couldn't nobody raise it. You just gon' have to tough it out in here till the trial come. You can do that, can't you?"

Petulance barged into his eyes then and Dog braced himself. But Fury remembered himself in time. "Yeah," he said, "whatever."

Mama brightened. "So, have your lawyer been in to see you yet?"

"Some fool come through here last night, but he ain't even had the right files. Had a file for some other nigger. Said he might try to get back through here Monday."

The news slumped her shoulders. "That's it? That's all? He couldn't tell you nothing about your case?"

"He ain't had the right file, Mama."

Fury's tone of voice called her an idiot. She seemed not to no-tice. "Lord, when these people gon' stop messin' with my boys," she exhaled. Her eyes were shining. Fury regarded her with disinterested eyes. Dog knew why: His mother wasn't useful to him. He felt a hate opening up within him, a black maw swallowing all the good times they'd ever had, all the memories they'd made in common. Swallow-ing their very brotherhood itself.

Cedric looked at him. "So, what about you, nigger?"

"What about me?" answered Dog evenly.

"Look, I know you got the baby now, you and that girl all lovey-dovey and shit, but I know you ain't meant what you said on the phone the other day."

Dog was aware of his mother's eyes swinging from him to Fury now, curious. He heard himself say, "My baby, she might have brain damage."

"What?"

"That's what I told you on the phone. Did you hear me say that?"

"Baby might not even be his," said Mama. "He just going by what that girl say."

He wanted to tell her to shut up. But she was his mother, so he only ignored her, boring in on his brother instead, watching the news digest, the hard eyes going cloudy. "Did you hear me say that?" he repeated.

"Naw," said Fury finally. "Ain't heard that. That's...that's messed up."

"Yeah, it is," said Dog.

"But it ain't got nothing to do with you handling this business for me."

"Yeah, it do. I told you on the phone: I can't do this."

"Oh, it's like that?" No clouds in his eyes now. Gone like they were never there.

"Yeah," said Dog. "It's like that."

"Then I guess you and me, we ain't got nothing else to say."

"That's your call, baby boy. It ain't mine."

"What's going on?" demanded Mama, her eyes still going back and forth. "What are you two talking about?"

Fury didn't look at her. "Ask your son," he said.

"What you mean?"

He didn't answer, yelling over his shoulder instead. "Guard! Guard!" He hammered his fist on the door. "Let me out of here!"

"Cedric, don't go," she pleaded. "We only had a couple minutes to talk."

"Got to, Mama. Can't deal with this no more." The door opened and he stood.

"What's wrong with you?" demanded Mama. She was crying.

He glanced at her. "I told you, woman: ask your bitch-ass son."

Then he was gone and they were staring into an empty room. Dog sucked his teeth angrily. Mama struggled to her feet. He held the door open for her.

They didn't speak. Not as they walked the long corridors, not as she struggled down the stairs, not as they retrieved their things from the cop at the metal detector, not as they made their way back out into the cold sunlight, not as he opened the car door for her. Dog was fascinated by her restraint, at the fact that she knew better than to ask him anything in a building filled with cops. Being the mother of two thugs—and the old lady of two more, he reminded himself—had apparently taught her a few things. He didn't quite know how that made him feel.

"Why can't you do what your brother asked you to do?" she demanded finally as he started the car and put it into gear. He glanced at her, then looked to make sure no cars were coming and took off so sharply his tires squeaked.

"You heard me," she said.

"Yeah, I heard you," he said. "I'm taking you to meet your granddaughter."

"Why can't you do what your brother asked?"

Twice now. She had not yet asked him just what it was his brother wanted him to do. Just, why hadn't he done it. If she had any idea what that boy was asking, she would have been shocked. Hell, how would he tell her? It would break her heart.

"I'm taking you to meet your granddaughter," he said. "We'll talk about anything else you want to talk about later."

She sank back into the seat, arms folded across her chest. Stared pointedly out the window. Dog reached automatically to turn up the radio, then changed his mind. Leave it off. If she could take the silence, he could, too. He accelerated through traffic, speeding and not caring. Dog was surprised by his own anger. Fury was her favorite; he had known that for years and it never really bothered him. Dog had spent so many of his teen years on lockdown, away from her all the time, and she had been home with Cedric, who was small and needy, sickly a lot of the time, ear infections every other week. It only made sense that she loved him most. He had needed her more.

Still, Dog was her son too, wasn't he? And shouldn't that count for something? Did she really expect him to go around always getting that boy's dumb ass out of trouble? Didn't Dog have the right to his own life, his own desires? He could not be Cedric's keeper forever. The boy had to grow up sometime. And she had to understand that he was not some poor, misunderstood little lamb. He was a punk-ass thug who shot a man for no good reason. Not for business, not for necessity, but just to shoot a man.

"He not strong like you are, Ray."

Mama's voice startled him. It was as if she had been reading his thoughts. He glanced over at her. "What do you mean?"

"A mother know her children, that's all. And I know that one, he ain't strong. Maybe I babied him too much, I don't know. But he ain't got your heart. He want to be hard, but he ain't. And he know he ain't." She touched his neck and he looked over. "Why you think I ask you look out for him all the time? It ain't just because he younger. Mostly, it's because he weaker. I mean in his heart, where it count. He need somebody to help him sometime, show him the right thing to do, tell him it gon' be okay."

"Mama, I got my own problems to take care of," he said. She let her hand fall away. He knew he was only making her angry all over again, but he couldn't help himself. "That nigger a grown man," he said. "He need to learn to stand on his own feet."

She didn't answer. After a moment, she turned away again. Dog punched the button on the radio. The car filled with Profit's pops singing that song from back in the day, "My Prophecy." Like even Dog's radio was against him.

Mama said, "Turn that down. I got a headache." Dog turned the radio off. They did not speak again until they were alone on the elevator going up to the maternity ward. She said, "Y'all chose a name for this baby yet?"

"No," said Dog. "We still deciding."

"You been to visit this girl every day since the baby come," she said.

"Yeah," said Dog, wondering where the observation was leading.

She sniffed. "Couldn't pay Big Ray enough to come to no hospital to see my ass," she said. Big Ray was Dog's father. "Nigger hated hospitals. He come by once, the day you's born, and I think that's 'cause his mama made him. Drunk as a skunk." She laughed. "So drunk I was scared to let him hold you. I said, 'Don't you drop my baby, fool.'" Another laugh.

"Yeah," said Dog, "well, that ain't me. I'm here every day." He wondered what the point of the story was. Certainly it wasn't news to him that Big Ray was an asshole.

He was grateful the elevator stopped right then and the door opened. He led the way to the nursery first, eager to show off the baby, but she wasn't there, which meant she was in the room with Ronnie. The room was dark when they got there, the blinds closed, the television playing soundlessly, the baby sleeping in the incubator next to Ronnie's bed. Ronnie had been dozing, but at the sound of the door, her eyes opened. When she saw him, she gave a tired smile.

"Hey, baby," she said.

"Hey yourself," he said, leaning over to kiss her mouth. "I brought somebody." He pointed toward the doorway, where his mother stood as if waiting for an invitation. "Ronnie, this is my mother. Moms, this here is my girl."

For months, he had dreaded and dreamt this moment, but now that it was here, it went off without a hitch. His mother did not say some nasty thing or ask if the baby was his. She only came forward in that lumbering gait of hers, both her large hands extended to catch Ronnie's small one.

Ronnie smiled. "Mrs. Willis," she said, "we finally get to meet. I just wish it could've been sooner."

Mama waved the words away. "Shush, girl. That's my fault. Between working and taking care of my girls and then this bad leg I got, I don't get out too much."

The lie was so smooth Dog almost believed it. This was the same woman who had told him she didn't have any interest in going to tea with some snooty niggers on the hill. He watched, fascinated, as Ronnie said, "Well, it's good to finally make your acquaintance, Mrs. Willis." And if he hadn't known better he'd have thought she didn't know his mother considered her a spoiled rich girl slumming with a thug from the 'hood. But of course she knew, because he had told her. The whole thing, then, was a polite and elaborate lie. It occurred to him that nobody lies quite like women do.

"Call me Mama," his mother said. "Everybody do."

"Okay, then," said Ronnie, through a sweet and earnest smile. "And you please call me Ronnie."

It was like watching a tennis match, a volley of shameless lies, one after the other. He didn't know what he had expected, but he had not expected this.

Mama clasped her hands. "And is this my granddaughter?" she said, moving toward the incubator.

"That's her with her greedy self," said Ronnie.

Mama looked down on the sleeping infant. "Hmpf," she said. "Ray, she don't look nothing like you. Ronnie, she must take after your side of the family."

Ronnie's smile kicked up a notch. "Really? I think she has her father's eyes, actually. Of course, you can't tell with her being asleep."

"Maybe you're right," said Mama. "Hard to tell while she's sleeping. Pretty little thing, though."

Ronnie said, "Ray, why don't you get your mother a chair so she can sit down?"

Dog pulled the chair to where his mother was. She sat down with difficulty.

"Your leg is bothering you?" asked Ronnie, concerned.

"My leg always bothering me," said Mama.

"You know," said Ronnie thoughtfully, "my father has a friend who's on staff here. Specialist in circulatory problems. I'm sure he'd be happy to take a look at you."

A look. Mama said, "Thank you just the same, but I go to County Hospital. I can't afford some fancy specialist."

"Oh, I'm sure he wouldn't charge you anything," said Ronnie. "Dr. Horton is an old friend of our family. I'm sure he'd be happy to do it just as a favor to my father."

"Well, like I said, I thank you, but I don't think so. I don't believe in taking favors I ain't in no position to pay back. You know, my children and me, we may be po', but we proud."

"I didn't mean to offend you," said Ronnie.

"Oh, honey, don't worry about that none," said Mama. "You couldn't offend me if you tried."

Dog sensed a sharpness there he could not quite put his finger on. This was not going as well as he had thought. He couldn't say how or why he knew it was going wrong, exactly, but that it was going wrong, he had no doubt.

"Well," said Ronnie, "that's good to know." Her smile was fixed.

Mama said, "So, 'Ronnie,' why don't you tell me about yourself?"

For the next few minutes, Ronnie talked about how she wanted to finish her master's degree, then go on to law school. She wanted to be a lawyer like her father, except that she didn't want to be a judge and she didn't want to go into private practice. She wanted to be a public defender because so many poor people, and so many of them black, got railroaded every year by a legal system where money, not truth, too often determined who went free and who did not. Mama listened attentively and Dog knew she was thinking about Fury. But when Ronnie was done, Mama only said, "My goodness. All them plans and all you got going for you, what in the world you want with my Ray?"

"Excuse me?"

Mama smiled. "Oh, don't get me wrong. Ray my son and I love him to death, but let's face it: You and him, y'all come from different worlds. You a rich girl and you got this fancy career planned out and all this education going for you. And poor Ray here, he had to take the GED to get out of high school and now he going to community college trying to be some kind of mechanic. It's just hard to see what the two of y'all could possibly have in common."

A voice behind Dog said, "Am I interrupting?" Startled, he whipped around and found himself facing the Judge. Dog wondered how long he had been standing there. Then he saw the righteous satisfaction in the man's smile and he knew: long enough. Dog marveled that he had thought it might be a good idea to bring his mother here.

Ronnie said, "Hi, Daddy," and there was resignation in it. She saw what lay behind his smile, too.

"Daughter," he said. And then he entered the room, crossing in front of Dog in one long stride, like he was a table or a vase. The Judge extended his hand to Mama. "Charles Richmond," he said. "You must be Mrs. Willis. I'm pleased to meet you."

"Likewise," said Mama, taking his hand.

"I have to admit," said the Judge, "I was glad to overhear what you were telling Veronica just now. I've been saying the same thing to both of them for months now, but it's been falling on deaf ears. No offense to your son. He seems a nice boy. Very capable, in his way. But you're right: He and Veronica come from entirely different worlds. I'm at a loss to understand what they could possibly have in common."

"We got this baby for one thing," snapped Dog.

"We've got more than that," said Ronnie. She reached for him. He came to her side and she grabbed his hand, held it fiercely, lifted it so they both could see. "We've got this, too," she said. "I love him. He loves me. We want to be together. Why can't you get that through your heads?"

"Love," said the Judge, as though she had said something inexcusably childish.

Mama chuckled. "How many bills love gon' pay? Love ever paid a bill for you, Charles?"

"Not one," said the Judge. "But you know, it's more than just money. Veronica at least will have a good income and combining that with whatever Willis here—'Ray'—is able to scrounge up, I'm sure they'll never starve even if they never prosper. But the thing I wonder is, whatever will they talk about with one another after this...infatuation has settled down? They have absolutely nothing in common."

"How dare you?" Ronnie's voice was filled with a lacerating anger. "How dare you talk about us like we're not here? We're not children, Daddy. And this is not your courtroom. We don't need your permission to be together. Yours either, Mrs. Willis. We would like your blessing, but we don't need that, either."

In the silence that followed, the baby began to fret softly in her sleep. After a moment, Ronnie reached across and stroked her gently, like a cat. "Hush, Miss Greedy," she said. "You go on back to sleep." After a moment, the baby fell quiet again.

Dog swallowed hard. "She right, Mama," he said and just saying it made him feel oddly weightless and unmoored. "I love you, you know that. But hell, I'm a grown man. Be thirty this year. I don't need neither one of you telling me what I can and can't do. This my business, not yours and not his. Ronnie my woman and that's my baby and I love them both and we gon' be together and that's just the way it is."

His mother only looked at him, her eyes somber. And maybe, he thought, a little unsure. No one spoke, so he went on.

"I know I ain't no genius. I know I done some bad things in my life. But I'm trying to change all that so I can be the kind of man Ronnie and my baby can look up to. I know she come from money. I know she got education and I'm just a thug with a GED. Best I'm ever gon' be is a mechanic. I know all that. But I love her and she love me and yeah, far as I'm concerned, that's all that matters."

He fell silent. Ronnie took his hand again and gave it an affectionate squeeze. Mama's eyes were still on him. He could not read them. The Judge coughed. "Well, Willis," he said, and his voice was gravelly, "I guess you got us told. And maybe you're right, son. Maybe so. But see, here's the thing I don't get and maybe you can help me with it. Okay, you say you love each other. You love her and she loves you. But why?"

Dog laughed. "Are you crazy? Man, she beautiful and she sweet, she care about people, she always got my back, and she smart, too. Before I met her, I never cared about too much of nothing. Never thought about too much of nothing 'cept what's for dinner tonight. Sure as hell never thought about the future. But Ronnie, she make me want to be better, you know? Better than I am."

The Judge shook his head. "No," he said, "I'm afraid you don't understand. I know what you see in her. The question I'm asking is: What does she see in you?"

The Judge was looking past him now, looking at Ronnie. Almost against his will, Dog turned, too. Because the question struck him deep, right at the heart of irresolution held so close and hidden so deep that it was a secret even from himself. Now the Judge had laid his finger on it, stabbed right into the fundamental mystery—what was a girl like her doing with a guy like him?—and Dog couldn't help himself. Like her father, like his mother, he turned to Ronnie and waited for her answer.

She took her time surveying their expectant looks and for an awful moment that made his stomach drop, Dog was afraid she would not answer. That she could not answer. Then she spoke, and her voice was calm like waters. She said, "There are many things, actually. I know Ray will do anything for me. He would die to protect me. He would sacrifice anything he had for me. He respects me. And he makes me laugh."

She sat up on the bed, wincing a little with the effort, waving Dog away when he reached toward her in concern. Her eyes never left her father and his mother. "But see, here's the thing," she said. "I get tired of people telling me my man isn't smart. I mean, you do it right in front of his face, like he has no feelings. Like he's not even there. Bad enough you do it, Daddy. But you, Mrs. Willis, you're supposed to be his mother. So you should know better than anybody that Ray is smart. Oh, it isn't the kind of smart that shows up on tests, I'll grant you that. But there's different kinds of smart. Ray knows people. And he knows situations. He understands things about life that they don't teach you in school."

"You're talking about street smarts," said the Judge through a smirk of distaste.

"I'm talking about survival," she said. "See, you don't know anything about that, Daddy, because you've never had to fight for survival. You had the right parents and you grew up in the right house and you went to the right school and you had the right career."

"You think it was easy for me?"

"I think it was *easier*, yes. And I think you go through your life looking down on everybody who's not you."

"So is that what this is all about, then?" said the Judge. "He's not me? My, God, Veronica, do you hate me that much?"

Dog held up his hand to forestall an answer. "Look," he said, "y'all need to cut it out before it's too late. One of you is gon' say something you can't take back."

The Judge looked as if he had not realized Dog was in the room. "It's already too late," he said. "If you'll excuse me." A nod at Mama, a last hard look at Ronnie. And then he was gone.

Dog said, "I can go after him if you want."

She said, "No, don't bother."

"But y'all shouldn't be fightin' like this."

Her eyebrow went up. "No? Then how should we be fighting?"

"Beg pardon?"

"I'm sorry," she said. "I'm not in a very good mood right now. And I'm tired. I think I'm going to take a nap."

Dog felt…dismissed. She had never made him feel that way before. "Okay," he said, brightly—too brightly—"well, I guess we'll go. I'll be back tonight."

She nodded and pulled the covers up under chin. It made her look five years old. "I'll see you then," she said. "Love you."

He kissed her on the lips. When he pulled back. Mama was already on her feet. She nodded at Ronnie. "Goodbye, Mrs. Willis," Ronnie said. "Nice to meet you."

The elevator was crowded and Mama didn't speak, but he could sense the words building inside her, gaining force as the floors ticked down. Finally, the doors slipped open on the hospital lobby. They walked past the reception desk, past the gift shop, past the giant caduceus on the wall. As soon as they were in the parking lot, she turned. "That girl don't care nothing about you."

And even though he was braced for it, the vehemence of it took him by surprise. "What the hell you mean, she don't care about me?"

"Ain't you got ears, fool? She using you to get back at her daddy. That's all this about."

"Yeah, I got ears, Mama. I heard her say she love me. I heard her say she want to be with me. Why you hate her so bad, Mama? I thought you be happy for me. I thought you be proud. I got me a nice girl, got a baby. Going to school, trying to make something out myself, ain't getting in trouble no more. I thought you be proud of me."

"Proud?" she said. "I be proud you don't forget where you come from."

"Forget? You think I forget? I ain't forgot a damn thing."

"Oh yeah? Is that why you treat your brother like a stranger?"

"What the hell you talkin' about?"

"Today in the jail. He ask you to do something—been asking for a long time, sound like to me—and you act like you don't know him no more. Is that how it's gon' be, Ray? You an' Miss Thang off living high and to hell with the rest of us niggers down here?"

Dog was stricken. "Mama, don't talk like that. That's my girl. She's gon' be my wife. I want you to be happy for me. I got a family now."

"What about us, Ray? Ain't we your family? We your blood kin. Don't that count for something?"

"Of course it do. I ain't never said it don't."

"Then why you make your brother beg you to do something for him?"

"Mama, you don't understand. What he want me to do, it's a bad thing. A *real* bad thing."

He had expected that to shake her. But to his surprise, the eyes that bored into his were steady. "Sometime," she said, "we do things we don't want to do for people we love. That's what family is all about." She watched him a second, then walked off toward the car, leaving him standing there with his mouth agape.

Did she understand what she was asking? Did she really know?

But that was a foolish question, wasn't it? Of course she knew. Of course she did. And the realization froze him, left his stomach a bowl of ice sitting heavily in the middle of him. He looked at his mother waiting by the car, settling gingerly into her seat once he beeped it open, the vehicle sinking a little under the weight of her. For the first time in his life, the very first time in his life, he hated her.

Or he tried to, at least. Tried mightily. But it is a hell of a thing to hate your own mother, to hate where you came from, to hate what succored you and nourished you when you could not do it for yourself. A hell of a thing to hate that, even when it hates you, even when it calls you a nothing, calls you garbage and tells you to throw yourself away. Because even then, she is still your mother.

And now she looked back at him, expectantly.

What are you waiting for? Let's go.

But Dog didn't move. Instead, he looked back toward the hospital, his eyes traveling up to the sixth-floor corner window where his woman and his daughter slept. He thought again of that morning when dawn came in through the blinds and he watched his daughter nurse and his entire world narrowed down to that room and it just felt right.

But the world seldom felt right, did it? Less often stayed that way.

So he supposed he should not be surprised that his mother and the Judge had come into that same room where he had felt this... holiness, and twisted everything until it felt dirty and soiled. That's how life works, isn't it?

Life gives and life takes away. And life makes you make decisions.

That was something he had not realized back when he was like Fury, out there ripping and running, acting a fool and not thinking too much about consequences. Life is thinking about those consequences, even when you're not. Life says, you can do this, or you can do that. You take this, but it will cost you that.

Now, choose.

Now. *Choose.*

Life makes you make decisions.

And Dog breathed a curse as he moved toward the car. Because he had made his.

twenty-six

The California Highway Patrol car pulled abreast of them on a desert road ten miles from the Arizona border. The cop in the passenger seat gave Trey a good, long look. In response, Trey nudged his father, who was sleeping. "We about to get pulled over," he said.

As he said it, the squad car dropped back. By the time the red and blue lights came on, Trey was already pulling over to the side of the road. He lowered the windows on both sides, put his hands at 10 and 2, waited. "Why are they stopping you?" asked Mo. He was groggy.

"Why do they ever?" said Trey.

In his sideview mirror, he saw the officer speaking into a radio on his shoulder. He wore a drill sergeant's hat and sunglasses. His uniform was khaki and crisp. He was white, not quite six feet, broad across the shoulders. Trey sighed, bracing himself.

"Take it easy," his father said.

"Yeah," said Trey, still watching his mirror.

"I'm serious," said Dad. "Take it easy, else I'll have to drive and if that happens, you may wake up and find yourself in Mexico."

Trey looked at his father, surprised to hear him making fun of his own sickness. Trey obliged him by chuckling. "I'm okay," he said.

"License and registration." The cop was at the window, cop face on, giving nothing away. A second cop showed up in the window next to Mo, peering around in the car. He was black, young, so muscular the fabric on his sleeves was taut. Mo ignored him.

Trey pulled his wallet from his hip pocket, fished out his license, and handed it over. "The papers are in the glove box," he said. The cop nodded. Trey reached over and opened the door on the glove compartment. The only thing inside was the packet of papers from the car dealership. He handed it to the cop.

"You want to tell us what this is all about?" said Mo.

The white cop—his name was Randall, Trey saw—said, "You've got an obstruction on your windshield."

"What are you talking about?" said Dad. "There's no obstruction on this windshield."

The cop nodded toward the rearview mirror. A cardboard air freshener in the shape of a Christmas tree dangled there. Trey had picked it up when they topped off the tank that morning after leaving Cooley's. "What do you call that?" said the cop.

Mo held the cardboard so he could read it. "I call it Pine Forest Dawn," he said.

The cop smirked. "Yeah, well, I call it an obstruction of the windshield," he said. And then, to Trey: "This your car, son?"

"It's his," said Trey, nodding toward his father. "Just bought it a few days ago in Vegas."

"Nice vehicle," said Randall.

"There a problem with that?" asked Dad.

Trey put a hand on his father's shoulder. "Thank you," said Trey. "My dad, he likes the best."

"Must have cost a pretty penny."

"My dad is—"

"It's none of his business what I am," snapped Mo, cutting him off. Trey glanced over in surprise, but his father had turned and was addressing the black cop. "And who you s'pose to be, bruh? The spook who sat by the door?"

The black cop's face tightened. Trey hissed at his father. "Dad, cut it out."

Officer Randall said, "Sir, there's no need for—"

Dad shouted him down. "Why don't you get to the point, man? Why don't you do what you came here to do?"

"And what would that be?" asked Randall.

"You want to search the car, right? You and Tom here saw a black kid driving an Escalade and you said he had to be up to no good and you didn't have a real reason to pull him over, so you come up with this bullshit about the 'obstructed windshield.' I mean, how many white boys you figure drove by you today with air fresheners on their mirrors? So why don't you just be a man and do what you came here for?"

Before Randall could answer, a second police cruiser approached from the opposite direction, lights flashing without sound. The driver executed a U-turn and pulled in front of the SUV. As the doors on either side of the squad car opened, Randall said, "Sir, I'm going to have to ask you to step out of the vehicle."

Mo said, "Finally." He opened the passenger side door so sharply the black cop had to jump out of the way.

Trey shook his head slowly from side to side. "Yeah," he said. "Whatever." And he opened the door.

He sat with his father in the dry grass by the side of the road. They watched as the doors of the SUV were pulled open. A woman officer fumbled with the latch on the back window. "You be careful with that," Dad yelled. "If that's busted, I'm filing a complaint."

Trey said, "Man, what's wrong with you?"

"What do you mean, what's wrong with me?"

"Why you actin' like this?"

"I get tired of cops thinking they can do whatever they want with you just because you're black and they're cops."

"That's what I said last week and you told me to be cool."

"What are you talking about?"

"'There's a time to fight.' 'Pick your battles.' All that stuff you were preaching to me last week when them cops started messin' with us."

"What the hell are you talking about?" snapped Mo. "No cops stopped us last week." He didn't wait for an answer, yelling to the woman cop, "Be careful with that suitcase, damn it! It cost more than you earn in a week!"

She said, "Sir, you need to quiet down and let us do our jobs."

It might as well have been happening on television. Trey was barely aware. A coldness knifed through him so hard he actually shivered. Sitting there in the middle of the Mojave Desert, his body shook.

He had thought he understood what was happening to his father. He realized now that he had not. The disease had not been quite real before, not even when his father had taken the old Escalade and smashed it. But this, him sitting there and angrily, peevishly denying a thing that had just happened a few days ago, a thing that was factual and concrete and fixed in Trey's own memory, this made it something Trey could not deny or ignore. His father was losing his memory. Losing his mind. And it was happening right there in front of him.

"My dad sick," he heard himself say.

The woman cop turned. "What?"

Dad started yelling at him. "Don't you tell them that! Don't you tell them that!"

Trey put a hand on his father's shoulder, sought out his eyes. They were livid. "It's okay, Dad," he said. "It's okay." And then, to the woman officer: "My father sick. That's why he yelling at you. He don't mean no harm."

Her only response was a dubious scowl, as if she was sure she was being conned and could not figure out how. Then she turned back to the luggage. Dad crossed his arms over his chest and stared into the middle distance. Trey watched him for a long moment, then lowered his head.

It was real. And the fact that it was real meant that Trey had to contend with a whole raft of concerns that had not even entered his mind until this moment. Maybe he had not allowed them to. But now, all of a sudden, he had no choice. His father was dying. But Trey would lose him long before he died. He probably couldn't take care of himself, definitely couldn't be left alone in that big house of his. Trey would have to move in with him. Or Dad would have to come live with Trey and Mom. But how long could even that last? As the disease progressed, would they need to put his father in some sort of place where they cared for people like him?

He thought of that other cop, that Officer Stans in Las Vegas whose grandmother died from the disease. "It doesn't just make them forget, Mr. Johnson," he had said, standing there in the emergency room. "It changes them. It diminishes them. At the end, we had to do everything for Gram. Everything. Feed her. Change her. Like she was a baby. And sometimes, the disease just makes them plain mean."

Would he have to diaper his own father? Feed him? Fight him? So many hard questions without knowable answers. And the not-knowing depressed him, sat heavily on top of him, smothering him so that he could barely breathe.

Trey felt dumb and dull and slow that he had not thought of all these things before. The moment he found out Dad was sick, he should have gotten a book, looked on the Internet, done something so that he would understand what his father was dealing with and have a better idea of what he himself should do.

It wasn't too late. That was good, at least. But the moments be-tween now and the time it was too late were dwindling, ticking down fast, and Trey was seized with a need to hold on to them, to make them slow down, to treasure them. And at the same time, he was seized with a knowledge that he could not. The pain was profound.

"I said, let's go."

He looked up. His father was standing over him. The police were headed back to their cars. Dad smiled down on him. "Had to call you three times," he said, cheerfully. "You were a million miles away."

"Sorry," said Trey, climbing to his feet. "I guess I was."

His father was walking toward the driver's side of the vehicle. Trey said, "Dad, I'm driving, remember?"

Mo stopped with his hand on the door. His eyes filmed over for a moment. Then he said. "Oh yeah, that's right." And he went to the passenger side of the car and got in.

Trey dusted off his backside and climbed into the driver's seat. He was quiet the rest of the day. That afternoon, they arrived in Flag-staff and took a room at a hotel. The desk clerk was a black woman who looked to be in her forties. She gave them a disinterested, pro-fessional smile as she took Mo's credit card and driver's license and began tapping her computer keyboard. But after only a few strokes, her fingers stopped and she looked up, smiling. It was a real smile this time.

"You're the singer," she said. "From the '70s?"

Moses smiled a sad smile and shook his head. "No," he said, "but I get that a lot. I don't see the resemblance, myself."

She looked at him closely. "Are you sure?" she said, and then laughed at herself for how it sounded.

"Yeah, I'm sure."

"That's too bad," she said. "I used to love that guy's singing. You remember who I'm talking about, right? They used to call him 'The Prophet of Love.' He had some good songs back in the day."

"Yeah, I remember," said Mo. "But you know, that was a long time ago."

They had dinner, watched television, slept well. In the morning, Trey took the wheel again and found Interstate 40, which took them east toward New Mexico. Mo turned on the radio and a woman's voice, smoky and full of passion, came up singing about a lover who was leaving her on a midnight train bound for Georgia.

Trey grinned. "Gladys Knight," he said.

"And the Pips," said Dad.

"That was her background singers, right?"

"Yeah. Two cousins and a brother. One of them's dead. A lot of those old singers from the '60s and '70s, they're starting to pass away now."

Trey surprised himself. "Tell me what it was like back then," he said. "The music, I mean."

"Back then," said Mo, "we sang about love and the things we went through just as men and women trying to get along. Wasn't no need for a whole lot of cussing and violence. We knew how to get our point across without all that."

Gladys Knight faded out and a guitar came in, winding straight into the voice of a man stretched to the very end of his endurance. He moaned, "I've been really trying, baby, trying to hold back this feeling for so long." The guitar percolating like coffee behind him.

"Is that Al Green?" asked Trey.

"Marvin Gaye," said Dad. "'Let's Get It On.' Now, that song scandalized people when it came out, because it's about straight-up, let's have sex. Let's make love. Folks thought that was pretty raw back then. But see, if you guys made it, it would be called 'Let's Fuck.'"

Trey barked out a surprised and mortified laugh. "Dad!" he complained.

"I'm sorry, but it's the truth, ain't it? Back in the day, we believed you had to have some class about yourself. You had to have some dignity."

After a moment, Marvin Gaye went off. The disc jockey played a station ID. And then, "My Prophecy" came on.

"Now this guy," said Trey, "I heard he was pretty good."

"He was all right," said Mo. "Maybe a little naïve, but he was all right. The world falling down around him, and there he was talking about how he could foresee a better world. He was a dreamer, that boy. But you know, back then, you were allowed to be."

It was nothing his father had not told him many times before. But Trey discovered that he had never really heard before, never really allowed himself to think too much or care too much about the world his father described. Mostly, Trey had simply listened for a convenient pause so that he could change the subject, or put in a good word for hip-hop. But suddenly it was important to listen just because this was his father and he would not have the chance to do so for long.

So Trey was silent as his father told his stories of being backstage with the Commodores and opening for the O'Jays and what it was like to hear Cher read his name among a list of nominees for R&B Song of the Year at the Grammy Awards and what it was like to hear his name again as the winner of the award and to float onstage as if in a daydream and see the whole Shrine Auditorium, the whole music world, rising to applaud him.

And his dad told him about the cocaine, too. About the money he spent and the friends he alienated and the shows he missed and how his records stopped selling and the work stopped coming in and the right people stopped inviting him to the right parties and he just stayed inside his mansion for a year and drank and used.

"I was high the night you were born," he said. "I think that's part of the reason I didn't come around too much. I was ashamed of myself. I was ashamed for you to see me like that. But that wasn't the whole reason, I guess, because even after I got clean, even after I went and did the whole Betty Ford routine, I still didn't come around much. I guess by then not coming around was a habit.

"But your mother, God bless her, she never spoke bad about me to you. And that made me feel all the worse. I tried to give her money. You know, extra money so she could buy nice things for herself. She would never take it. She would never let me buy my conscience clean."

Mo paused, lighting a cigarette. He lowered the window as he exhaled and the rushing desert air took the smoke and whirled it away. "You know," he said, "when I die, it all goes to you. The house, the cars, the royalties. I mean, I left a nice sum of money for your mom, too, but most of it goes to you. You get it after you're 25, and until then, she handles it for you."

For the first time, Trey interrupted. "Dad, we don't have to talk about this now."

"Yes, we do," said Dad. "We have to do it while we still can. Now, one of the things you'll get is my song. I mean, you'll get all my songs, but 'My Prophecy' is the most valuable one and it's certainly the one that matters the most. It'll be up to you to determine who gets to use it and how."

"Dad, I won't let nobody disrespect your song. And I won't use it in no rap, if that's what you worried about."

His father shook his head. "That's not my point," he said and he waited until Trey had turned to face him. "I'm telling you to make your own judgment. I don't want you going around the rest of your life trying to figure out, 'What would Dad do?' You use the song however you see fit, whatever seems right to you. It's just a song, Trey. It's just a song."

He sucked deeply off the cigarette, let the smoke leak into the wind. "There's a whole lot of things more important than that," he said.

They had the highway to themselves, but Trey kept his speed down to give the police less of an excuse to mess with him. They roared east against the sun and didn't talk much about music the rest of the day. They talked about basketball and women and politics and the future. Then Mo said, "So, what do you want to do with your life, Trey. Really?"

That one arch word—really—seemed to sweep aside all his half-considered answers, to demand a seriousness he had never given before. Trey shrugged helplessly and his answer was as much a confession to himself as it was to his father. "I don't know," he said.

His father regarded him. There was fondness in the gaze. And, too, a little regret. "Think about it," he said. "Find what you love. Because I'll tell you something: Life is too short to do anything else."

They talked some more, the give and take easier and freer than Trey could ever remember. They laughed a lot. It made Trey sad. They could have talked like this a long time ago, he realized. They could have laughed like this all along.

The sun passed them overhead, beginning its long, slow fall toward night. They rolled into Albuquerque, found a Mexican restaurant not too far off the highway, and had lunch. Mo flirted with the waitress in stilted Spanish. He was feeling good. Trey could tell.

When they had finished their tacos and camarones del fuego and had pushed back from the table feeling pleasantly sated, Mo said, "I want to drive for awhile."

Trey was alarmed. "You shouldn't—"

"Maybe I shouldn't, but I want to." Trey hesitated. "Come on, I promise I won't take us to Mexico. You can stay awake and keep an eye on me, just to make sure."

Trey said, "Dad, are you sure?"

His father shook his head. "I'm only sure of one thing. I'm going to die. And I want to live a little more before I do. I want to grab every chance I can." He reached his hand out, waggled the fingers. "Come on, son, give me the keys. Just an hour or two and I'll give 'em back to you. I promise."

Trey dug in his pocket, pulled out the key. His father waggled his fingers again. Wondering if he would live to regret it, Trey handed the keys over. Mo's hand closed decisively. "Come on," he said, "let's roll." They climbed into the SUV, Mo snapped on his seatbelt, put his key in the ignition, then paused and looked up at Trey, eyes round with confusion. "The one on the right is the accelerator, right?"

Trey's heart jumped. His father laughed heartily, clapping his hands and doubling over. Trey deflated into his seat. "Don't play like that," he said, crossly.

It was lost in the throaty roar of the SUV firing to life. Mo threw the truck into gear and took off. Moments later, a freeway onramp lifted them into a magnificent vista. A sky so painfully blue and cloudless it broke your heart framing mountains that stared down in silent indifference upon the comings and goings of sons and their fathers. And a road that twisted and turned and rose to meet it all. On the radio, the Spinners sang "Mighty Love" and Mo sang along, word for word, even through the tricky ad-lib at the end. Nailed every grunt, every hiccup and moan. Remembered it all.

Trey heard himself laughing. He knew he would remember this day for the rest of his life.

twenty-seven

Shortly after 11:00 that morning, Trey wheeled the big Cadillac onto his street and pulled up before the powder blue row house with the bedraggled flower box on the porch. He had never thought he could be so happy to be home. Fatigue soaked him like water in a sponge and he was sure he could live happily the rest of his life if he never saw another interstate, another rest stop, another highway patrolman sidling up to the car saying "license and registration."

Mo had been dozing, but he came awake as the car glided to a stop. Trey had learned to fear these naps because you never knew how Mo would be when he awoke. It was increasingly the case that he would be petulant and confused. As they passed through Oklahoma, he had spent half an hour accusing Trey of stealing his cigarettes. It turned out the pack had fallen between the passenger seat and the door, but when he found it, Mo offered no apology. Just stopped cursing midsentence and said, "Oh, here they are." He lit one up and enjoyed it in silence. In Kentucky, he got into an argument with a waitress, calling her names because she brought him what he had forgotten he ordered. She went away crying and Trey was so mortified that when the check came—$25.98—he grabbed his father's wallet from his hands, extracted a $50, and slapped it down on the table. Dad protested, but Trey cut him off. "That's enough," he said. "Now, let's go."

These last couple of days, Trey had come to feel like a father traveling across country with a very large, very unruly toddler. He hated that feeling, thought it was a betrayal of his father—his real father, not this stranger who sometimes took over Mo's body. But Trey couldn't help the way he felt, any more than he could help bracing himself as he put the car in park and his father yawned. But Mo just said, "We made it. God, I'm tired."

At the hotel in Kentucky the same night Mo cursed the waitress, Trey had waited until his father was sleeping. Then he grabbed his cell phone and crept out of the room into the hallway where he sat on the floor, called his mother, and told her there was no way Mo could live alone any more. They would have to get him some help. He kept glancing at the door as he spoke, unable to shake a sense that he was stabbing his father in the back.

Tash had seemed surprised. "I'm sure you're exaggerating," she said. It made him angry at first and then he realized that what had once been true of him was still true of her. Mo's illness had not yet become real for her. She knew he was dying, but the knowledge was theoretical, intellectual. Not real. Only staring into the aquamarine eyes of a stranger she had known and loved since she was a girl could make it real. So the anger lifted off him like a winter coat removed on a sweltering day and he just said, "Mom, trust me: I'm not exaggerating."

And something in his voice must have convinced her because she didn't speak for a moment and when she did, her voice was a surrender. She said, "Okay. We'll get him some help." They decided that Mo would stay with them—he would sleep in Trey's room—until Tash could hire a nurse to live in his house down in Bowie. They had not bothered to consult with Mo. Now that Trey thought about it, he realized his father still didn't know.

"Hey, Dad," he said, "I meant to tell you: me and Mom thought you could spend a couple days here with us. We gon' work on getting you some help."

Suspicion narrowed Mo's eyes. "Help with what?" he demanded.

The hostility of it rocked Trey. "Well, because you sick, we were gon' get you a nurse. You know, to live at the house and help you."

"I don't need any help."

Trey tried to jolly him. "Come on, Dad, it's just somebody to stay at your house to keep an eye on you, help you do things."

This time, he shouted it. "I don't *need* any help!"

To his own surprise, Trey heard himself yelling back. "Don't need no help? The hell you don't! You already forgettin' things, man. You cussed out that poor waitress because you forgot what you ordered!"

Mo's index finger came up like a gun. "She did *not* bring me what I ordered and you will *not* talk to me this way. I'm still your father."

"Yeah, you forgot that, too, in Vegas."

The moment the words were out of him, he wanted them back, wanted them unsaid. Unheard. "Dad, I'm sorry."

Fury melted to simple regret in the gaze his father now lifted to him. "I don't want to live like this, Trey. Can't you understand that?"

Trey said, "What are you talking about?" But his father was already out of the car, walking toward Tash's front step. Trey hurried after him, breathless with adrenaline, not wanting to have heard what he had heard. "I said, 'What are you talking about?'" he cried. Mo turned.

Bang.

The first bullet took Trey in the chest, high and on the right. The force of it spun him against the hood of the Cadillac. It burned. He had time to look down in shock and see blood spurting out of him.

Bang.

The second bullet took him in the stomach. Reality turned sideways. His mind could not process. It kept screaming at him in outraged fury. *What? What? What?* But he had no answers. He was lying on the sidewalk. His hand was on his stomach. Warm blood trickled beneath his fingers. The clouds moved in broken pieces across the sky. It was cold.

Shoes moved toward him. Beat up set of Tims walking sideways. He followed the shoes to legs, followed the legs to a torso, followed the torso to an arm, outstretched, a pistol in its hands, finger on the trigger. And at the top of the torso, a face, contorted, snarling at him. It was—it took him a moment, his mind maddeningly slow—it was Fury's brother. Dog, they called him. His voice came to Trey as if through tin cans tied with string, boomy and thin, but clear for all of that. Trey heard every word.

"Why you couldn't just keep your fuckin' mouth shut? Pussy ass muh'fucka. Fucked up everything!"

And then four things happened simultaneously. The hand with the gun moved. There was an explosion. Someone said, "No." Cried it, really, in a voice torn with fear and rage. And something landed on Trey, something so heavy it drove the air out of him with a groan. He recognized the smell of Kool cigarettes and Paco Rabanne cologne. His father's smell. His father had dived on top of him. His father had taken the last bullet.

Above the curve of Mo's shoulder, he saw Dog. And Dog saw him. Dog's eyes were watery and sad. The hand with the pistol trembled violently. And then it came down. Dog shook his head slowly as if in great disgust or regret. His free hand came across his braided scalp, kneading it. He seemed tired. One more glance he gave. And then he walked—did not run, but walked—slowly away.

After that, darkness closed in on Trey from all sides.

It had been a moment of piercing, sudden clarity.

His son was in danger. He had to get between danger and his son. Realization and action were simultaneous. He had launched himself.

Now he pushed himself up on wobbly arms, saw the sleeping face beneath him—pecan-colored skin, a noble nose, high cheekbones, a wisp of goatee—and did not know it. It was a good face, but he didn't know it.

He asked himself: *Who...?*

Then his strength was gone and he fell heavily across the son he no longer knew. After a moment, he closed his eyes.

twenty-eight

Their funerals were held on consecutive days.

The death of the Prophet of Love was front-page news. It merited inset pictures on the covers of *Time, Newsweek, Entertainment Weekly*. There were retrospective pieces on CNN, FOX News, *Today*, and *Entertainment Tonight*. Old photos of Mo with his big Afro. Old footage of Nixon, of the Black Panthers, of Vietnam, of the world as it was when the Prophet sang his famous song. The White House issued a statement. The *New York Times* called him "The conscience of a generation."

Sitting there before his casket, Tash couldn't help but think how much Mo would have loved all the attention. He had been an A-list star for just a few years, before changes in music and his own deepening dependence on drugs had driven him from the top to make room for something new. She knew that behind the expensive shades and the shiny grin and the façade of never worried and always cool, he had wondered how he would be remembered. Those kinds of things were important to Mo. And somewhere, she thought, his spirit was surely gratified at the answer.

Thousands of people, black and white, had come to view Mo's body, waiting up to two hours in the cold for the chance to see him, to touch his face, to say goodbye. The funeral was at a megachurch with seating for 10,000. And still, hundreds were turned away. Stevie Wonder was there, as were Patti LaBelle, Al Green, Bobbie Smith and Henry Fambrough of the Spinners, Otis Williams of the Temptations—Mo's peers, thought Tash, looking around, that dwindling union of women and men whose music she had danced to, gone to school to, raised a child to, lived to.

"Let's Stay Together."

"Superstition."

"You Are My Friend."

"My Girl."

"Love Don't Love Nobody."

Tash smiled watching them, grayer and balder and heavier than they had been in the days when they wore sequinned jumpsuits and loud plaid jackets and appeared on *Soul Train* and spoke in *SOUL* magazine and sang songs you memorized without half trying and still knew word for word 30 years later, and seemed so large and looming as to be untouchable. And if you didn't know who they were and what they were, well, looking at them now, in their fifties and sixties, you never would. But Tash knew. And she knew the proudest achievement of Mo's life was that he had made himself one of them.

Philip, sitting next to her on the front row, knew, too. He kept looking around and whispering, "Isn't that…?" And usually, it was. She knew it made him feel…outclassed. Tonight, she would have to tell him yet again, and in such a way that he would have to believe her, that he did not have to compete with Mo. Mo was her past and she would always love him. But Philip Reed was her future. And he needed to understand that, once and for all. For now, she just took his hand and held it, and when he looked down at her she said simply, "I love you." And he smiled, surprised.

Lionel Richie gave the eulogy, most of it taken up by a warm and funny story of the time the Commodores and Mo Johnson performed in Africa and Mo, dizzy with the flu, nearly got them all kicked out of Senegal when he threw up on the shoes of the health inspection officer at the airport. After Richie was done, Mario Gaines came to the stage and he and Richie sat across from one another at black and white baby grand pianos and did a duet of "My Prophecy."

Tash caught Cooley's eye. He nodded distractedly. Jack Johnson's old friend seemed heavier than his weight, older than his years. The building was full—SRO, as Mo would have said, standing room only—but it saddened her that she and Cooley were essentially the only family Mo had. For all the people he had touched, for all the people who loved him, there was a hole in Mo's life, an emptiness that never was filled. He had made millions of people happy, but had never managed to do the same for himself.

Two days after he died, she had let herself into his house, looking for a burial suit. As soon as the door opened, the smell of the place, rolling out on warm, heavy air, knocked her back a step and she had to put a handkerchief over her nose before she could proceed. It smelled like bad meat and sour milk. Tash entered cautiously, half expecting to encounter someone's dead and moldering corpse.

The house was ghastly, dishes piled in the sink, food rotting in the refrigerator, garbage overflowing the can. Upstairs, she found the disheveled bed, the cigarette burns in the dark, reddish wood, and then the gun. The sight of it made her flinch as if she had been struck. She crept toward it as though any sudden move might cause it to leap into the air and start shooting. Tash could not bring herself to touch the thing, but she knew instinctively what it was for and the realization hammered her so hard in the chest that she dropped onto Mo's bed and wept. He had given her the old smile, the old song and dance, right up until the end. It had never occurred to her that Mo was in so much pain.

When the funeral was over, the announcer—and how many funerals had an announcer?—told the audience the interment would be private and asked people to remain seated so that the "family and personal friends of our departed brother, Moses Johnson" could leave the building first. The casket lid was down. Attendants were gathering flowers. Pallbearers were pulling on their white cotton gloves.

An usher touched Tash's elbow and indicated that she was to follow him. He led her and Philip through a maze of concrete tunnels extending back from the pulpit, past offices and dressing rooms and expanses of wall covered with drawings from children in the church school. They emerged in an open concrete space behind the building where limousines were lined up behind a hearse. They were at the bottom of an incline; at the top, fans—for that was how Tash instinctively thought of them—were lined up on either side behind yellow tape, screaming and laughing and yelling for Stevie Wonder and Patti LaBelle and taking pictures with disposable cameras.

Tash took a deep breath and the air was like a knife, it was so cold. The day before, there had been an ice storm and the barren winter trees were encased in it. The whole world seemed made from glass and therefore, not quite real. Beautiful, yes—unspeakably so—but it also gave you the sense that life itself was just a show and all the people and all the pain, just props.

The hearse slammed shut on Mo's casket. "Are you okay?" asked Philip.

Al Green walked by at that moment, dressed dramatically all in black, his eyes hidden behind sunglasses, smiling and waving at the cluster of mostly women who stood at the top of the ramp. They squealed like the girls they had once been. A diamond-encrusted cross big as a lug wrench hung against his stomach which, she saw, was thicker than it was back when he first sang "I'm So Tired of Being Alone." She smiled, remembering the day Mo Johnson accosted her on the way home from school, singing Al Green songs. He would have loved this.

Tash said, "I'm fine, Philip." And to her surprise, she was. She climbed into the limousine for the drive to the cemetery.

The next day's funeral was harder in a lot of ways. The crowd was smaller and younger, reflecting a life less celebrated—indeed, a life barely begun before it ended. The children, these gangly, lanky teenagers, still learning to walk in their brand-new bodies, would go to the coffin wearing their street faces, their can't-be-touched faces. And their faces would break and they would cry bitterly, cry with the righteous fury of the betrayed. Tash had seen it many times before, when young people died in the emergency room and their friends responded not just with grief, but with a sense of having been cheated, played unfair by life itself, because teenagers aren't supposed to die.

LaShonda Watkins lay in a pink coffin, her hair pressed and held in place with ribbons, her expression serene. She looked like she was 12 years old.

Tash sat in the second row. Philip was not with her. LaShonda's father sat just in front of her, flanked by his wife and children and a dozen other relatives Tash didn't know. The poor man was inconsolable, weeping loudly into his wife's neck, an older son pinching his shoulder blade lightly from the other side, looking ahead, saying nothing. TV news cameras recorded it all. This was a big story, after all. Just last night, the district attorney had announced he would seek the death penalty.

The minister struggled for words to comprehend the tragedy, a girl and her unborn child murdered by the girl's own mother. He invoked the story of Job, a good man who saw his life shattered by unearned suffering. He reminded Daryl that God himself knew what it was like to have a child murdered. He exhorted the family to hold on and be strong. He told them earth has no sorrows that heaven cannot heal. He screamed at them in Baptist cadences handed down from olden days, that joy comes in the morning.

Then he sat down, mopping at his brow, his entire countenance shining with the sweat of his exertions. Tash pitied him. A thankless task, she thought. How do you make the death—the *murder*—of a child okay? How do you even make it make sense? She looked at the heaving shoulders in the pew ahead of her, the shameless grief of a man forever broken, and that provided her answer.

You don't. It's never okay. It never makes sense. You just learn to live with it if you can. Tash did not know if she could, did not know if she had that much strength, that much faith. She prayed a silent prayer that she would never have to learn.

The service ended and she lowered her head in prayer as the coffin was wheeled past her, down the aisle and out the front. The broken man and his family followed. His wife and his oldest son both had hold of him, as if without their help, he might crumple to the floor like something thrown away. Their countenances were ashen, their steps measured and slow. The woman on the piano played "Precious Lord."

Tash felt her eyes welling. Enough, she thought. Enough. No more death for awhile. She recognized it as a useless protest—what made her think death would listen to her?—but she couldn't help herself. Bad enough to see Mo shot to death trying to save their son, then to see this girl die after being hacked up by her mother.

And then there was Trey.

Tash shuffled from the quiet church in the crowd of mourners, older people weeping and teenagers with shining eyes and gazes slightly bewildered at the abrupt realization that loss comes to children, too. She made a decision then. She had thought to go to the cemetery for the interment, but…

Enough. She could not take anymore.

Tash went out into the stabbing cold. She hugged Daryl Watkins and told him she was praying for him. She squeezed his wife's shoulder and said to tell her if there was anything she could do. Then she went to the parking lot and climbed into the sleek black SUV she had been driving since Mo's death, thinking as she always did that it was too much, that it was a look-at-me car. And that always made her think of Mo, her look-at-me-man, vain and proud, but wounded, too, in a place he kept hidden so nobody else could see.

She turned the radio on. The deejay said, "All this week, we're celebrating the life and legacy of the Prophet." One of Mo's lesser hits was playing behind him. She clicked the radio off, drove in silence.

The hospital was not far. Tash entered through the front door rather than the ambulance bay. When she returned to the ER next week, she would have to endure work friends gathering around, wanting to know if she was okay, if her son was okay, if there was anything they could do. Tash was an intensely private woman and the thought of it, even though she knew it was well-intentioned, filled her with dread. Today, at least, she could avoid it and she did.

She walked past the caduceus on the marble wall in the lobby, stepped into the elevator with an older couple. At the third floor, they got off. Neo-Natal ICU. The day after Moses and Trey were shot, Tash had gone there looking for that person, that…Dog. There had been no witnesses to the shooting, but she knew it was him. She *knew* it was him. He hadn't been there then, wasn't there now. The unit was quiet and almost empty.

The police had been looking for Dog, too. They had interviewed his family, his girlfriend, his teachers at the community college. They couldn't find him. The local news media had joined the search for him and a camera crew showed up at his front door. They did a live interview with his mother, whose name was Mary. Tash happened to see it. "I ain't seen Ray in a few days," the woman told the redheaded white girl who thrust a microphone in her face. "I don't think he done what they say he done, but if he did, he must have did that on his own. Ain't nobody told him to do it. He done it 'cause he love his brother. And while y'all out looking for Ray, you need to be investigating about what these people doing to his brother. They got my baby locked up on a million-dollar bail, say he shot some guy. How I'm suppose to raise a million-dollar bail? That just ain't right, what they doing to him. You think y'all can look into that for me?"

The reporter responded with scowl of disgust, then remembered she was on live television and substituted a more neutral expression, knitting her brow and looking appropriately concerned. But Tash carried the memory of the reporter's first response, her human response, with her down the sixth-floor corridor to Trey's room. Seeing the little white girl's unmistakable revulsion had made her feel a little better, verified her belief that the people who had done this to her boy were human garbage, nothing more.

Trey's room was dark and Tash made a sound of disgust. How many times had she asked his nurse not to leave him lying in shadows like a coat forgotten in the back of the closet? He was a living, human, being. He needed light. She went to the blinds and pulled them open. The winter sun was pallid, filtered by clouds. It couldn't banish the shadows. It only turned them a lighter shade of gray.

Tash settled herself into the seat next to Trey's bed. Her hands traced the curve of his brow as carefully as if she were blind. The short dreadlocks were gone, his head shaven close. She liked the look. It brought out his cheekbones. His wispy goatee was getting long. She made a mental note to cut it for him.

"Trey," she said, and her voice seemed unnaturally loud in the stillness of the room. She cleared her throat. "I just came from the funeral. Oh, honey, it was so sad. That poor girl. And her father, he was just…torn up. Poor man could barely walk. I'm almost ashamed to tell you what I felt, looking at him, Trey. I mean, I felt sorry for him, but I also felt glad it wasn't me. So glad it wasn't me. I don't know if I could take it. I mean, it was bad enough burying Mo. I've known that man since I was a girl. But to bury your own child, that's unthinkable, Trey. It's unspeakable."

The heart monitor beeped. Outside, an elderly man walked slowly, a little girl's hand nestled in his. He pushed an IV pole with his free hand. Tash leaned close to her son. "Don't you die on me, Trey Johnson. I'll never forgive you if you die on me."

———————

Trey opened his eyes nine days later, startling a nurse who had come in to check his catheter and replace his fluids bag. "Where's my dad?" he asked. His throat felt coated with crust. It was just after 2:00 in the morning, 15 days after he was shot. It was the first day of spring.

The nurse leaned out the door to call for a doctor, and the doctor rushed into the room. He took Trey's vital signs, checked his vision, asked if he knew who he was and where he was. Trey said, "Where's my dad?"

The nurse touched his shoulder. "We've called your family," she said.

The first thing Tash did when she came through the door half an hour later and saw his eyes seeing her was to clasp her hands together and say, "Thank you, Jesus."

The doctor had to step nimbly out of the way as Tash rushed to her son. She could not rightly hug him—too many tubes and still too much pain—but she gathered his head in an awkward embrace and hugged that. Tash held Trey so tightly he thought she might smother him. Trey waited her out, her tears falling heavily on his freshly shorn head. Finally, she pulled back, still holding his face in her hands, regarding him with naked affection.

Trey said, "Mom, where's Dad?"

He saw the light change in her face, the look of affection turning wistful and melancholy. "You don't know," she said. It was not a question, but a realization, stated.

Trey shivered. He turned inward, trying to recall his last memory of his dad. It was an argument. The two of them leaving a restaurant in Kentucky, Mo accusing him of stealing $50 from his wallet to give to an incompetent waitress. When had that happened? How long ago? "I don't know what?" he said.

She drew back from him and was silent. Trey said, "Mom, what is it I don't know?" His tone was insistent. Foreboding iced his chest.

"Honey, you were shot. It happened when you and Moses pulled up in front of the house. It had to be the brother of that boy you got in trouble with. You had just gotten out of the car and he walked up and shot you twice. You were on the ground, losing blood. He was going to shoot you again, but your father..."

She stopped, breathed. Wept silently. The doctor had his head down, studying his charts intently. Trey waited. He knew now what was coming. But for some reason, he needed to hear it spoken. After a moment, Tash wiped the last of her tears with the heel of her palm. "The police say your father jumped on top of you and he took the last bullet. It went through his heart. He died right there on the street."

Trey sat up. It hurt, but he didn't notice. "Dad's dead?" The words seemed to need speaking.

Tash nodded. "He died saving your life," she said.

"Dad is dead." Words seemed to have lost meaning, to have become a random collection of sounds. He needed to say it to make himself understand it. The man who had made him, the man who had loomed over his life like trees and mountains over valleys and plains, the man whose infrequent visits he had anticipated more than Christmas, birthdays, and summer vacations, the man who had shone his way through his days, an impersonal smile beamed from behind designer shades, the man Trey had argued with and cursed at and measured himself against, the man he had never really known until maybe, just a little, right before the end, was gone, was shot to death like some common nobody? Over something *Trey* had done?

"My dad is dead?" He looked to her confirmation that the words had meaning after all.

She nodded. "I'm sorry, Trey," she said.

He broke slowly, his face crumpling like used-up paper. Mourning tore out of him in ugly sobs. He brought his hands to his face and wept as he had not wept since he was a child, wept bitterly and unreservedly, unable to control it, unable to even try. His body shook with the force of his grieving. Tash wrapped her arms around him and hugged him tightly. He did not feel it.

His father was dead.

Trey left the hospital a week later. A nurse wheeled him out the front door. His son walked beside them, voluble and eager, his hand tight in Trey's. DeVante had lost so much, thought Trey. Lost his mother, lost a grandmother, lost a grandfather, and almost lost his father. Not hard to understand why he held on so tightly. He didn't want to lose anyone else.

The sky was clear, temperature in the 60s. It felt good to be outside. He had not been outside in a month. Tash pulled up in his father's SUV. Her SUV now. Mo had left everything he had to them: the house, the cars, all his recording equipment and effects, all the rights to his music, though Trey would not come into his share for six years. She had already said he could have the house when he was ready; she couldn't expect Philip to live in what had been another man's house. He had too much pride for that.

His mom was busy these days. Planning for a wedding, still working long shifts. He had asked her why she didn't quit. Tash could afford to now; she could live quite handsomely on her share of Mo's publishing rights. She had just shrugged and said she might quit someday, but not now. What would she do with herself if she quit working? Just sit around all day? She couldn't do that. She needed to feel useful.

Tash came around and opened the door. Then she and the nurse each took one of his arms and braced him as he lifted himself from the chair. It hurt. Trey could not remember what it felt like to move without pain. DeVante still held Trey's big hand with his small one. It took a long time to get into the car.

Mom wanted to take him straight home. Trey prevailed upon her to make a stop first. She was reluctant, but she agreed. Fifteen minutes later, the SUV rolled slowly uphill on a winding lane amid barren trees and stone monuments and then Tash stopped the car. "There," she said, pointing.

By the time Trey got his seatbelt unbuckled, she was already at his door, opening it and extending her hand. It was maddening to him that he moved so slowly. Trey accepted her help to climb down from his seat, but he waved her back when she tried to walk with him, supporting one arm. "Let me do this myself, Mom," he said softly.

She nodded. "Okay."

It took him a moment. He tottered slowly across dry, yellow grass that crunched under his feet. Somewhere, high in the skeletal branches, small birds chirped. He could just barely hear the hiss of traffic from the highway far below. Two trees stood sentinel above a massive stone monument at the top of a hill. It was jet black, made of polished marble and almost as tall as Trey. It bore his father's name— James Moses Johnson Jr.—and below that, in quote marks: "Mo." Further down were the dates of his birth and death and finally, at the bottom, were words Trey knew well:

"I see a world that never was."

It was the refrain from "My Prophecy," though Mo had told him once it was adapted from something he had heard attributed to a man named Bobby Kennedy: "Some men see things as they are and ask why. I dream things that never were and ask why not." Trey reached out to touch the glassy black surface. His fingers lingered on his father's name. How angry Mo had been, leaving that restaurant in Kentucky. "You had no right!" he had cried. "You had no right!"

It wasn't just money that had been taken from him. Trey realized that only now. It was dignity. It was self. And that was the last memory he had of his father. Trey wished he could remember the shooting. He wished he could remember his father, saving his life.

"You a fan too?"

The man's voice surprised him. Trey wheeled to his right, and paid for it with a sudden bolt of pain. A white guy had come abreast of him unheard, silver hair tucked under a Chicago Cubs cap. "Beg pardon?" said Trey.

The man nodded at the monument. "I asked if you were a fan, too. Because, you know, you seem kind of young."

Trey turned back, looked at his father's name. "Yeah," he said. "I was a big fan."

The man shook his head. "Hell of a thing to happen," said the man.

"Yeah," said Trey. "Hell of a thing."

"He was one of the greatest," said the man.

"Yeah," said Trey, "you got that right."

He turned and hobbled painfully back across the dry grass to where his mother stood waiting.

Two weeks later, in Richmond, Virginia, the manager of a motel near the interstate used his pass key to investigate complaints of a foul odor emanating from room 6C. He opened the door and found a body swinging from the light fixture. Police were called and the dead man was identified as Raiford Leroy Willis, age 29. The coroner said the cause of death was suicide.

───────────

The trees were just beginning to dress up for spring when Trey received the call from Axel Cordero's assistant. Just a courtesy, the assistant said. There would be a hearing next week, but it was only a formality and Trey didn't need to appear. The district attorney's office would officially drop all charges for lack of evidence. The gun that had been used to kill Nasrallah Patel had never been found. The ski masks had never been found. The money had never been found. Fury and DC had never talked.

It was over.

Trey hung up the phone. Emotions were in collision inside him. He knew how he should feel. Elated. Relieved. Jubilant. But what he actually felt was something else entirely. He felt sad. He felt let down.

"Daddy?" DeVante's voice, tentative. At the sound, Trey realized that he hadn't moved for a full minute.

"Yeah?" he said.

352 LEONARD PITTS, JR.

They were sitting on his mother's couch, watching cartoons. Tash was at work. DeVante's eyes were guileless and round. "Are you all right?" he asked.

"Yeah," said Trey, and because his son seemed to need a smile, he tried to give him one. It didn't feel convincing and after a moment, he stopped trying. Something about the moment, something about all of it, just felt wrong. "I'm fine," he said. "Just watch your cartoons."

The boy lowered his eyes and Trey was instantly sorry. Trey nudged him. "Hey, man," he said. DeVante gazed up. "I just got some things on my mind, that's all."

"That's okay, Daddy," said the boy.

He turned back to the television for a moment. Some cartoon elf's eyes had distended themselves about a foot from his body in shock, accompanied by a discordant bleat of horns. DeVante said, without looking at him, "Me and Mama used to watch this show."

He talked about his mother a lot. Obsessively, said Tash. And about "Nana Mike," too.

Nana Mike had a dress that color.

Mama used to like that song.

I went there with Nana Mike one time.

Mama liked to eat chocolate.

He never talked any more about what had happened. Only about things he had done with Michaela or his mother, stories the one had read him, things the other had bought him. Tash said he needed counseling. Trey was inclined to leave well enough alone, but his mother was insistent.

"He's only four," Trey had told her.

"All the more reason," said Tash. "He needs somebody to help him process what he's seen. It would be hard enough for you and me. I can't imagine what it's like for a baby his age. We've got to get him some help, or this is going to be something we end up dealing with later. And I guarantee you, it'll be a whole lot harder then." She had already begun asking for references from friends at the hospital.

Trey looked down at his son. DeVante was intent on the misadventures of the cartoon elf, his legs swinging idly off the edge of the couch. Tash was probably right.

He cupped the little boy's close-cropped head in his hand. What had LaShonda and Michaela—and he himself—done to this child? The question squeezed from him an unintended sigh and DeVante looked up. "It's okay," said Trey, before his son could ask. But it wasn't. Trey could see himself too easily ending up like Mo, struggling on the eve of demise to make things right. And as much as he loved his father, as fiercely as he admired him, Trey knew there was something pathetic about that.

He went to the hearing anyway, taking DeVante along because his mother had to work. When Trey walked into the room, Cordero was at the defense table. His eyebrows lifted when he glanced around and saw Trey sitting in the last row. The detectives, Bradley and Stump, were also in the courtroom, sitting on a bench in the front of the room reserved for police officers who had been called to testify.

Bradley was whispering animatedly to a highway patrolman and both were grinning when Stump jabbed his partner with an elbow and pointed. When Bradley glanced up and saw where his partner was directing his eyes, his smile went away and his eyes went dark and cold. Stump half rose from his seat as if going to confront Trey. Bradley put a hand on his shoulder and pulled him down.

The courtroom was far from filled. There were a few court watchers, a few mothers and girlfriends come to support their men. On a bench in the front row, directly behind the assistant district attorney, sat an Indian woman, flanked by two girls. They could have all been the same person, captured at different points in the same life. Their hair was identical—long, straight, and glossy black. Their faces—what Trey could see of them from where he sat—were also similar, same strong chins and expressions of wounded dignity. Most of all, their posture was the same. They held themselves stiff and straight-backed, their gazes never leaving the judge's bench.

The hearing went much as Cordero's assistant had told him it would. The case was called, and the assistant DA rose to say his office would drop the charges for lack of evidence. The Indian woman's head went down for a moment as she heard the failure pronounced. Then it came back up again, resolute. The judge ordered the two defendants still incarcerated to be freed. And the hearing was gaveled to a close.

Bradley snatched his hat up angrily and left the courtroom with long strides, looking neither right nor left. Stump followed, glaring baleful threats at Trey. Trey did not turn away, but watched him until he was out of the courtroom. The Indian woman went to the bar separating the spectators from the lawyer's tables and conferred briefly with the assistant DA. He seemed to be consoling her.

"Is it over?" asked DeVante.

"Yeah," said Trey distractedly. "I guess it is." He was still staring at the Indian woman. At one point, she turned to say something to one of her daughters and he finally saw her face full on. Her expression was drawn. Her eyes brimmed with a sad beauty.

"Did you get away with it?" asked DeVante.

At first, Trey wasn't sure he had heard him. "What did you say?" he asked.

DeVante repeated himself through a four-year-old's sinless smile. "You were innocent. You got away with it."

They were, of course, two different things, being innocent and getting away with it. But you couldn't expect a four-year-old to understand that, could you? "No," Trey heard himself say, "I wasn't innocent."

His son's smile shrank into a frown of confusion. "I don't understand," he said.

Trey opened his mouth—to say what, he did not know. Then he froze, because the Indian woman was coming toward him. She did not look his way. Her head was high and her glittering eyes did not so much as notice him.

It seemed impossible. How could she not know that one of the men who killed her husband was standing here, right in front of her? Wasn't the guilt written in his face? Weren't they connected by it as if by tiny cables, unseen wires, tethering him to her wherever they went, wherever they should go, from now to eternity, forever and ever, amen? She drew abreast of him, and then passed him by. Trey half expected to be tugged along in her wake.

He had been there. Sweating and itching beneath a ski mask, heart banging against his rib cage, he had been there and he had watched as his friend killed her husband. How could she not know?

Trey felt as if he was losing his mind. Cordero was at his elbow. "Didn't you get the message?" he asked. "I told Shelley to call and say you didn't need to be here."

A distant voice, barely heard.

A little girl leaned over her mother, screeching at him with hot, accusing eyes. Hating him with every fiber of her five years. A husband and father clutched at his throat, blood pouring over his fingers like milk pours from a pitcher. Falling heavily.

Trey reached out. Touched the sleeve of the man passing him by. The assistant district attorney. Short, balding, white, turning with an impatient air. Trey said, "Do this mean they gon' get away with it?"

"Beg pardon?"

"Fury and DC." He caught himself. "Cedric Gamble and Carter Clark."

"And you are?"

"Trey Johnson. James M. Johnson."

Cordero said, "Trey, this isn't helping."

Trey ignored him. Understanding crept slowly into the ADA's eyes. "You're one of the defendants," he said. "The one who made bail."

"Yeah, man," said Trey, making a hurry-up motion with his hand. "So answer the question. Do this mean they ain't gon' do no time?"

Cordero said, "Trey, let's go. *Now.*"

The assistant district attorney might as well have been looking at a stain on his favorite suit. "Listen to your lawyer, kid. Let him answer your questions for you."

He walked away. Trey yelled at his back. "What if somebody was willing to testify?"

The ADA stopped, took his time turning around. "You?" he said.

Trey nodded. "Yeah," he said.

Cordero grabbed his arm so hard it hurt. "Not another word," he said. "Come with me."

Trey wrenched his arm loose. "Well?" he said.

The ADA said, "I repeat: you should listen to your attorney. There's not even a deal on the table. I'm not even sure what I could offer you. I'd have to talk to my boss."

"I didn't ask you about a deal," said Trey. "I asked you what would happen if somebody testified. Somebody who knows? Would that help?"

"Do you understand what you're saying here?"

"Would that help?"

The ADA pondered for a moment. "Does this somebody know where the gun is?"

"Let's say he do," said Trey. "Let's say he know where the money is, too."

"Let's talk in my office. Your attorney should be there, too." He turned to walk off, then turned back. "One question, Johnson: Why?"

Trey didn't answer. He knelt and picked up his son instead, braced him on his hip and touched his chest with his index finger. "Nobody gets away with nothing," he said. "Somehow or another, it always comes back on you. And if nobody else knows what you did, you'll always know. Remember that."

DeVante's nod was somber. "I will," he said.

The case went to trial that summer. Trey testified against Fury and DC. Told the jury how the three of them planned the robbery, how there wasn't supposed to be any shooting and nobody was supposed to be hurt, how Fury flipped out, pistol-whipping the woman and shooting the store owner. He told the court what Fury said afterward: "Nigger shouldn't of made me wait."

On cross-examination, the defense attorney asked if it weren't true that Trey was actually the mastermind of the robbery, and was seeking now to shift the blame. Trey said no. The defense attorney asked if his testimony wasn't part of some plan to get revenge on the man he blamed for his father's murder. Trey said no.

"So you are asking this court to believe," said the lawyer, his voice larded with sarcasm, "that you are giving this testimony out of some sense of civic duty, Mr. Johnson?"

Trey's smile was distant. "The day I got the call from my lawyer that they was gon' drop the charges, me and my dad was driving in

Kansas and we got in this argument. He told me I wasn't a man, said I ain't had no honor. And I guess it was true, even though I didn't think so at the time, 'cause I ain't cared about nothing but myself. When the call came and I was celebratin' 'cause I wouldn't have to go to jail, my father got real quiet and he had this funny look on his face, like he wasn't happy. I always wondered about that. They sayin' they ain't gon' to send me to jail and he over there frowning like that's bad news or something. Then when we went to court and the DA dropped the charges, my son—he four years old—he looked up at me and said, 'You innocent. You got away with it.' He just a kid, I know, but I swear, it was almost like my father talking to me through him."

A sour smirk. "What's your point, Mr. Johnson?"

Trey shrugged. "My point? I guess there ain't one. I guess I just didn't like my father thinkin' I ain't had no honor. And I don't want my son to grow up thinking the same thing. I don't like him having the idea you can get away with doing bad things. 'Cause you don't, you know? That's something I've learned. You may think you do, but you really don't." His gaze fell on his mother. She was sitting in the first row, next to Philip. She was crying.

The trial took a week. The jury deliberated for two days before returning a verdict: guilty on all charges.

The sentencing hearing was three weeks later.

Fury was sentenced to death. DC got 25 to life. Trey Johnson, having previously pleaded guilty and testifying for the prosecution, was sentenced to 5 to 15 years.

twenty-nine

For eight months, Tash refused to visit her son in prison. Eventually, Philip stopped asking. He had never seen her so embittered. "He didn't have to do it," she said one night as they lay in bed. "He didn't have to throw his life away." Her eyes were piercing in the moon-bathed darkness.

"Apparently, he felt otherwise," Philip had said. She didn't reply. Just turned her back to him and drew up the covers. The temperature in the room plunged by 30 degrees.

That was the last time Philip suggested driving to the prison to see Trey. He also stopped handing her his letters out of the day's mail, only to see them days later lying on the kitchen table unopened, gathering dust. He stopped passing her the phone when the machine voice at the other end said she had a call from an inmate at a Maryland correctional facility. He stopped mentioning his wife's son altogether.

Talking about Trey put too much stress on their young marriage. So he was surprised one night in February when she said, almost casually, just before turning over to go to sleep, that this weekend she'd like to visit her son.

He sensed her waiting in the dark for him to reply. He didn't know what to say. He knew she felt Trey had ruined his life—willfully, foolishly, selfishly. "Why couldn't he leave well enough alone?" she had moaned to Philip as the bailiffs led her son away in handcuffs. "Why did he have to be so damn stupid?"

But Philip, on the other hand, hadn't seen stupidity in what Trey did. He had seen conscience. A level of morality higher than he would have expected from someone he had grown used to thinking of as a callow and thoughtless boy.

This was something he had repeatedly tried to tell her, until he learned that it was best and safest to say nothing. Still, as he had watched his wife's son being led away to begin his sentence, he had felt a newfound respect for this boy—this young man. And even when Tash wouldn't take Trey's calls or answer his letters, Philip did both.

He told Trey how his son was progressing and sent him pictures. He put money in Trey's prison account so that he could buy snacks for himself. He sent a Bible and other books he thought Trey might like. He even provided a small television for his cell. And when Trey became distraught one night on the phone and asked why his mother hated him so much that she wouldn't even speak to him, Philip consoled him. "She doesn't hate you," he said. "This is just hard for her. Give her time." He asked Trey if they could pray together. Trey said yes. Philip marked that as yet another surprise.

Over these last months, they had built a relationship of sorts. Philip found that gratifying. And mildly amazing. Now Tash wanted to go see her son and wanted to know what Philip felt about it. He swallowed. "I think that's a very good idea," he said.

They drove down to the prison that very weekend. The visit went bad from the start. Trey's eyes, happy to see them at first, became confused when he realized they had come alone. "You didn't bring DeVante?" he said.

Philip shot a look at Tash. They had argued about that very thing this very morning. Tash said, "I didn't want him to see you like this."

They sat at a circular table in a large, cold room ringed about with guards. Most of the other tables were full—hard men in prison jumpsuits talking to girlfriends and mothers, holding their children. Occasionally, a child shrieked in laughter. The radio in the corner was playing oldies. Al Wilson was singing "Show and Tell." Philip felt sorry for his stepson.

"He need to see me," said Trey. "I need to see him."

"Not like this," said Tash, glancing about the room, her hands pinned beneath her arms. "Not here."

"Yeah, Mama. *Just* like this. Right here. However I am and wherever I am, he need to see me. He need to know who I am. He need to know I love him."

"He's not wanting for love. He knows I love him. And Philip, he's a very good grandfather to him."

Trey slapped the table with an open palm. "You're not his father," he hissed. "Neither one of you! He needs his father. Take it from me, I know." His voice tapered to a whisper on the last words.

"If he needs his father so much," said Tash, coldly, tremulously, "then why did you leave him? Why did you come here? You know you didn't have to. So why, Trey? Why?"

"I did it for him," said Trey.

She made a disgusted sound and turned away, eyes rolling toward the ceiling.

"I did," said Trey. "I tried to tell you before: we standing in that courtroom and I'm free to go and he smiles and says, 'You got away with it.' And it hit me: that's not what I want my son thinking. Because you *don't* get away with it. You *never* get away with it. What I did, it'll be with me the rest of my life. Whatever else I ever do, that's always going to be there. I wanted him to know that."

She regarded him for a long moment without speaking. "Words," she said finally. "You're very good with words. Just like your father was. I swear, words fell out of that man like snow. How he was going to do this, and fix that and change the other. And God help you if you made the mistake of believing him because in the end, all his words always came down to nothing at all. You're just like him," she said, and it made her face ugly. "I can't take it any more."

"Mama, please," said Trey. "It's not just words."

But she was already in flight, hands to her face. A guard opened the door for her with practiced timing. They had seen this scene many times before. Automatically, Philip half rose from the metal bench to follow her. Then he changed his mind and sat down.

"She thinks your father ruined your life," he said. "But you don't, do you?"

Trey shook his head. "My father ain't ruined my life. He saved it."

"You're not talking about him taking that bullet."

"No." Trey's gaze turned inward. He kneaded his lip with his thumb and forefinger. Philip waited. Finally, Trey nodded toward a table where a massive slab of a man—dark skin and a bald, bullet-shaped head—sat in sober conversation with a young woman. "That's

Smoke. Beat some dude up in a bar over whose turn it was to use the pool table. Other guy lost an eye. This is his second strike. Told me once he ain't seen his father but three times in life."

Another nod. This one to a nervous-looking young man Trey's age, his hair braided in an elaborate design, tattoos climbing his neck, smiling desperate smiles at bashful twin boys while their mother watched balefully. "Drug dealer," said Trey. "His daddy say to this day that he ain't his son. They had the DNA tests and everything, but his daddy say they must have made a mistake because he know he pulled out the woman in time."

Trey's gaze fell on a third man, his face baggy with frown lines, his eyes glowing with sadness. He seemed to be pleading his case to the woman across from him. Her arms were folded, her legs crossed, her eyes averted. "That's Red," said Trey. "Robbed a gas station 20 years ago. Guy gets killed. Cops come to the house. They search the place and find the money. As the cops are hauling him away, Red's father is cursing him out because he left the cash where the police could find it. He a crackhead, right? Not a word about the man Red shot. Not a word about Red getting arrested. He just pissed because Red ain't hid the money good enough."

At this, Trey paused as if surveying the room had fatigued him. Finally, he sighed and leveled his eyes right at Phil. "My father wasn't the best," he said. "I know that. Hell, he knew it, too. But the one thing I can say for him is this: he finally saw what he did wrong and tried to fix it. That's more than a lot of men will do."

He stared at Philip defiantly, as if waiting for an argument. Philip had no argument in him. "You're right," he said.

A nod. A silence, eyes scanning the room. Trey shook his head. "What the hell was I doing out there with those guys, man? I ask myself that a thousand times a day and I can't come up with an answer. Make me so mad I could kick my own ass sometimes. Because it ain't had to be this way. My mama, she worked hard, she gave me a good home, she taught me right from wrong. Yet there I am with those two raggedy-ass muh'fuckas—excuse my language—robbing some guy out of money he done worked for and earned. And he get killed because of me."

Trey gave him the level gaze again. "And see, that could have been the end of it right there, the end of *me*, you know what I'm saying? 'Cause DC and Fury, they sure as hell ain't gave a damn about what we done. This man lying on that floor choking on his own blood and they act like it's something on TV. Because they *dead* inside, you see? And who knows? Maybe I could have been dead inside, too. Maybe I could have learned that from them. Tell you the truth, it would have made my life easier in a lot of ways. But my father, he wouldn't let me."

A memory curled Trey's lips into a smile. "He come get me and drag me clear across the country so he could make me face it. Wouldn't let me run from it or make peace with it. We driving 3,000 miles across the country, listening to all that old-school stuff and him hammering at me. 'You got to be a man. You got to be a man.' And I keep thinking: What the hell am I if I ain't a man already? But see, I come to understand: He talking to me, but he also talking to himself. He saying, own up to your responsibilities. Stand up for what you done. Carry yourself in a righteous way so you can look any man straight in the eye and ain't never got to apologize. I didn't get that till after he died, but that's what he was telling me. That's what he was telling himself."

Philip said, "Have you thought about what you're going to do with your life once you get out of here?"

The smile surprised him. "Ain't thought about nothing else," said Trey. "They give me 5 to 15, but my lawyer say if I keep on like I'm doing, stay out of trouble, keep my nose clean, it'll probably be closer to 5. He say even the assistant district attorney say he might write a letter on my behalf to the parole board if I keep doing good. So I could get out of here, be 24, 25 years old, just coming into the money my dad left me."

"You're looking forward to having a good time with all that loot, huh?" Philip was smiling but he felt a vague disappointment.

Trey said, "That'll be fun, but that ain't the main thing I'm talking about."

"Oh?"

"No, man. I'm taking business classes in here. I want to take some more when I get out. I want to manage my dad's music. You know, he left hundreds of demos in the studio at his house. He was always working on stuff, but he never had no way to release it. But see, I figure if Tupac can release ten albums and he been dead since '96, maybe somebody be interested in what the Prophet had to say. I been thinking maybe I could put it out online."

"That's a good idea."

"I'll tell you something else," said Trey.

"What's that?"

"Whenever I do get out of here, I ain't never coming back. I guarantee you that. You'll never see me in this place again."

It moved Philip. He sat back, crossed his arms and appraised his wife's son without speaking. Trey said, "Is something wrong?"

Philip shook his head, smiling. "You've changed," he said. "That's all."

"This place will change you," said Trey.

"What I mean is, I'm proud of you, Trey. I want you to know that. And I can't imagine there's anything I can do to help you, but if there is, I want you know I'll be here for you. All you have to do is ask."

Trey said, "Thank you, man. I appreciate that. But you know..."

Philip got there first. "Your mother," he said.

"I wish I could make her understand."

"It's going to take time," said Philip. "I'm sure she'll come around eventually. But you have to understand how much this hurt her."

"I know she hurt," said Trey. "But I told her I'm sorry. I told her I've changed."

"Words," said Philip.

"What you mean?"

"Isn't that what she said about your father just a moment ago? 'Words fell out of that man like snow?' How many words do you think she heard from your father? How many promises to change? And he never kept a one. That's what makes it hard for her to believe, Trey. Tell you the truth, that's what makes it hard for a lot of our women to believe. We men, we lie the faith right out of them."

Trey's face puddled into sadness. "You saying she ain't never gon' believe in me again?"

"I'm saying it's hard. I'm saying you've got to give her time. And maybe—"

He stopped when he saw Trey's expression lift. Trey was looking at something over Philip's shoulder. Philip turned. Tash had come back into the room and was standing by the door. Her hands were clasped in front of her and she seemed almost to perch on tiptoe. It was a pose of uncertainty, a pose that made it impossible to say if she was about to come forward or, just as likely, turn again and run back out the door.

Trey stood and a guard flinched. The prisoners were prohibited from leaving the tables. But he didn't move. He waited. His mother looked at him. She shook her head slowly, as if warring with herself. Her eyes were red. Then she closed the distance between herself and her son and opened her arms to him. They both cried.

Trey said, "Please don't stop believing in me."

She said, "Shush."

He said, "I need you to believe in me."

She said, "I believe in you."

He said, "I know it's hard. I know I ain't gave you no reason."

She said, "I know. I believe in you anyway."

And that, thought Philip, listening, was a miracle in itself. Then he became aware of what was playing on the radio and it made him smile. Unheard by his son and by the woman he had loved, but not well enough, the Prophet was singing, his voice high and startling in its purity.

"I see a world that never was," he sang. "And I believe. I surely do believe."

acknowledgments

Thank you to: Janell, for persistence and faith; Mikey, for a great suggestion; Judi, for sweating the small stuff.

Leonard Pitts, Jr. won the 2004 Pulitzer Prize for commentary for his syndicated column, which appears in more than 200 newspapers, and has won numerous other journalism awards. Born and raised in Southern California, he now lives in suburban Washington, DC, with his wife and children. He is the author of the nonfiction books *Becoming Dad* (Agate, 2006) and *Forward from This Moment*, which will be published by Agate later in 2009. This is his first novel.